Clint Folsom

Mysteries

Compendium

Volume One

www.barbarianspy.com

This book is copyright © habu
Published by BarbarianSpy in 2012
Cover design © S Bush 2012
Cover images: © Les3photo8 | Dreamstime.com
ISBN: 978-1-922187-00-0
All rights reserved

BarbarianSpy
Jindalee St
Toronto, NSW 2283
Australia

Clint Folsom Mysteries Compendium

Volume One

habu

BarbarianSpy

Table of Contents

Introduction

In this first volume of the *Clint Folsom Mysteries Compendium*, which includes a previously unpublished Clint Folsom adventure, *Death in Manhattan*, the initial development of Clint Folsom, the promiscuous NYPD homicide detective, into a life as a satyriasis and adventure-ridden police investigator is traced chronologically. This four-book set takes Clint from his upbringing in the Hollywood homes of movie stars, surrounded by the influences of hedonism and sexual want and preference for men, through his training for a career in law enforcement, and beyond, to the tragic loss of his first serious lover, and to his steeling as a detective in a special NYPD homicide squad.

Clint Folsom was no stranger to murder even before he lost his innocence to other men. The distinction of the NYPD homicide detective is his celebratory gay male promiscuity, which the police department frequently finds helps it close certain cases and thus makes Folsom a valuable investigative asset. The first segment in this compendium, *Death to Innocence*, is a precursor to the Clint Folsom mystery series. This book illuminates the elements of the slow, but relentless, death of young Folsom's adolescent innocence under highly unusual circumstances in narcissistic and hedonist Hollywood. The events that not only developed and sharpened Folsom's sexual proclivities are revealed, but the book also illustrates why men gravitate to him like bees to honey. The murder mystery that is folded into the plot of a young man's journey to manhood illustrates why Folsom is haunted by his past and driven by his subsequent chosen profession.

The previously unpublished *Death in Manhattan* traces the path of Clint's first attempt at a committed relationship. Memories of his relationship with Brad feature prominently in all of the following books. This first volume of the Clint Folsom Compendium series moves on to *Death on the Rhine* and *Death in Eden*. The *Clint Folsom Mysteries Compendium* series will continue and conclude with the forthcoming second volume. This volume, which will extend Folsom's adventures to Key West, Florida; the Rocky Mountains; and even back to his roots in Hollywood, also includes—and concludes with—a previously unpublished book, *Death to the Past*.

I enjoyed writing this series. My premise when starting it was a no-holds-barred treatment of an unabashedly promiscuous, laid-back, "good-guy" homicide cop with movie-star looks and extraordinary sex appeal to other men—and to do so in the context of a mainstream-worthy murder mystery plot. I hope you will agree that this is what I have given you in the detective, Clint Folsom.

Death to Innocence

Chapter One: No Surprise

"Now, don't go barging in there, Clint," Robert said as we drove under the bar of the Moreno Valley ranch and were approaching the main house. "In fact, I probably should go in first."

But I was young and hadn't seen my parents in more than a week, and, more than that, I was excited about the brush fire that had driven us away from the Malibu house three days before I was to come back to the ranch. So, as soon as Robert stopped the car in front of the house, I was out and racing for the door.

"Wait, Clint," my tutor—and primary companion and guardian—called out as I took the front steps two at a time. "They have visitors."

And, indeed, I could see that they did. There were two automobiles in the drive, both sleek sports cars—and I remember at the time being surprised to see two of those unusual gull-winged sports coupes together like that, a silver Mercedes, which wasn't familiar to me, and the sand-brown Bricklin I knew that costume designer who was here so much drove.

So, what happened then was in no way Robert's fault. He was blamed for so much after that—and of much more serious failings—but this one was wholly on me. He'd had little choice but to bring me to the ranch early. We'd been everything but hauled out of the Malibu house on short notice—without even any time to telephone ahead to the Moreno Valley ranch—because of the encroaching fire. They didn't think it would get to our house—we were in a line of beachfront houses that the L.A. fire chief would probably have called out the National Guard to save because of who owned them—but there was every reason to believe that the Pacific Highway would be breached by the fire in both directions, and this would have cut us off from civilization. It was quite natural that we would have come straight back to the ranch.

And Robert had tried to stop me—to warn me off—probably knowing all too well what the two automobiles in front of the ranch house meant. If there had been more cars, he probably wouldn't have worried.

My parents entertained pretty much nonstop when they were back in Hollywood. It was more or less expected of them. The presence of many cars would have been safer—but probably not much. Because, regardless of what Robert might have thought, I wasn't wholly oblivious to how my parent lived, what they did—indeed what the whole, narcissistic, hedonist world of Hollywood in the late 80s—or any other decade, for that matter—was like.

I was already half way up the stairs to the second level of the house before Robert had gotten the Chrysler wagon out of gear, so there was little he could have done. And he wasn't the last line of defense. Efenia, our housekeeper, met me on the stairs and put out a restraining hand.

"No, Master Clint. Do not come up here. I have something for you in the kitchen. Come tell me why you are home early while I find you something to eat and drink. It must have been a long, slow ride through the city traffic."

All of the time she had her hands on my arms and was trying to coax me back downstairs, she also was shushing me, imploring me to be silent. But she, herself, was speaking loudly—as if she wanted to be heard on the level above.

And of all that, the only thing I took in and heeded was the admonishment to be quiet. This I understood. My parents could be boisterous and have raucous friends, but I was always to be quiet and withdrawn—usually someplace else. It wasn't that they weren't loving parents—not that I'd have any idea what loving parents were, of course. They were just so busy and hands-on with their work and their paying fans that parenting wasn't something that came easily to their minds or figured centrally in their priorities unless there was a family magazine article in the offing.

Thus, my mother didn't even know I was there when I entered her room and found her in her bed with Magda, the costume designer who seemed always to be around my parents somewhere. Nor did my dad notice I was there when I stumbled upon him and that young actor, Gordon Fields, in the room at the back of the hall that he used as a study and to memorize his movie scripts. My first thought was that he and Mr. Fields were practicing for a motion picture, but as I got a clearer picture of what they were doing—and at age seventeen, very nearly eighteen, I was not a backward child by any means in what one person would do with another in the heat of passion—I saw less of a possibility that they were practicing for the sort of motion pictures my parents starred in.

My parents were stars—both of them. Glittering stars at the moment in Hollywood's firmament. They often worked together in a duet that was an automatic box office draw, though, more often of late, they also worked apart from each other. My dad, the swashbuckling romantic lead, Scott Sloan, holding down leading men roles into his mature years by moving into the more suave roles. And my mother, the mysterious and gorgeous Laura Lake, who was one of the most celebrated dramatic actresses of the decade—and indeed of the decade before that as well.

Scott Sloan and Laura Lake. And, the meaningfulness of it increasingly occurring to me in later years, me, their son—probably a surprise to them both when I arrived and somehow had to be fitted into their filming and carousing schedule. My name was Clint Folsom. I can appreciate the irony of the three different names now—clearly delineating the largely separate lives of the three. And me being the only down-to-earth one, the one going by a legal birth name, while my parents, the ones who were supposed to be the adults, both living a separate fantasy—as separate from me as they were from each other.

And today, which marked the start of the death to my innocence, my mother was living her fantasy with a female costumer hanger-on ten years her junior while my dad was living his with the foremost heartthrob supporting actor of the day who was twenty years his junior. Not much older than I was.

I wasn't completely surprised. There had been hints and signals earlier—and there had been open sex aplenty at my parents' almost continuous pool parties at the ranch. And the private separation of my parents in contrast to their public "can't get enough of each other" pretense was something I fully understood.

I can't say I was shocked by it at all. Mine had been an unusual upbringing in an unusual circumstance. Nothing that I had experienced in life instilled the sort of moral foundation that would see hedonist sex as shocking. But this was the day—my day rather than my parents' because I tip-toed away from both trysts unseen and unheard and never mentioned my early homecoming to either of them ever—all self-denial was at an end. And this was what I marked as the beginning of death to my innocence.

Robert was standing in the foyer, running his hand over the brim of his hat and looking hangdog and devastated when I came down the stairs.

"I should not be here. I wasn't expected," was all I said through tight lips. I could not say more, because I was perplexed. When I had seen them, in their separate rooms and their separate embraces, something had stirred inside me—especially in the tableau in my dad's study. I'm ashamed to note, now that I look back on it, that it wasn't repulsive, just perplexing. What it had stirred inside me was an arousal, a sense of want.

"Yes," Robert said in a low, said voice. "Perhaps we should—"

"Back into L.A., maybe. We can maybe stay in a hotel or something until we were expected."

"Yes, right. Back in the car, I guess."

Robert was a brick about the whole thing. We drove back toward the city, and he stopped at a motel that looked slightly on the seedy side to me.

"I thought the Belvedere," I said as he pulled into the forecourt of the motel, which consisted of a series of early-50s style cottages in a semicircle around a small, empty concrete swimming pool in the center of a nearly grass-less square.

"I don't think that would be a good idea," he said tightly. "A man and a boy—here in L.A. And we wouldn't want any place where you might be recognized and where there might be press."

For the first time, the "big bad world" was beginning to descend on me, and I was becoming aware of the problem this was for Robert and the possible risks he was taking.

My mind started to work lickety-split, maturing and becoming more worldly wise by the second. That people "did it" was something I'd grown up with and had often seen the preliminaries for—and sometimes the act itself—as I quietly walked the perimeter of my parents' lives. I had taken it as natural and for granted. Only now was I beginning to see how complicated and problematical it was—and how desperately I wanted to do it too.

I could see the implications of what Robert was taking responsibility for in the eyes of the desk clerk at the motel, as I sat in the car while Robert registered for a room and the clerk cast furtive, "knowing" glances through the plate glass window at me sitting in the Chrysler.

And hours later, as I watched Robert preparing for bed, having carefully gone through a ritual of making me choose one of the two lumpy-mattress twin beds and quite deliberately placing his small suitcase on the other bed, my quickened education in what was what in the world of people relating intimately with other people caught up to me. I had reached the point where I realized I was in love with my tutor, Robert Sinclair—and probably had been for years. Or at least I thought of it as love at the time, only then beginning to open up to the existence of lust.

17

He had come into our lives when I was twelve and it had dawned on my parents that I was more than an occasional hanger-on in their entourages and that I was getting only the minimal amount of education—and thus wouldn't be half as entertaining for their friends as I might be with better preparation.. During my early years, my parents were establishing themselves as a "couple" in the cinema, churning out drama after comedy of "dashing him and clever her" movies that the public delighted in—and tucking me away somewhere in the entourage they traveled the movie studios and sets of the world with.

Apparently someone clued them into the fact that, as practical as my exposure was to their world, it didn't provide the basics in an education that would lead to college or being celebrated as their offspring in mansion lounges. In response, they had hired Robert to be my live-in tutor.

Over nearly six years, he had become so much more than my tutor. My parents were always around somewhere, no matter how vaguely their presence was to me, so Robert wasn't, in my awareness, a parent figure for me. But he most certainly was my most constant companion, someone who had been there—focused on me as my parents weren't—for almost as long as I could remember.

So, ultimately, it was natural for me to form an attachment to Robert and even, nothing about my life being conventional, to become emotionally attached to him to the point of infatuation.

What I lacked was a compass, a sense of social barriers and limitations. I had grown up with the running joke that everyone in Hollywood was a Jew and/or queer—and there was no one in my life to suggest that there was anything questionable or wrong or limiting about that. Which, of course, there isn't. I had seen men showing affection for men and women for women. And now, within the last few hours, I had seen how deeply that had seeped into my own family unit.

There was nothing in my upbringing that established any barriers or even second thoughts in this regard. When I saw my parents earlier in the day, I wasn't shocked that they were having same-gender sex. What was new and shocking to me was the obvious separation—and the obvious mutual-consent separation—that existed between them.

I had no defenses to the realization—or belief, genuine or mistaken—that I loved, or, more precisely, lusted for my tutor. And there were no barriers to believing that if it was OK with my dad, there was no reason why it shouldn't be OK with me.

Nothing happened that night. Robert shrank from me and carefully kept his distance. It was weeks before he could acknowledge that the attraction was mutual. And even then nothing sexually intimate—other than an exploratory kiss—happened between us—at least from his side—because, although I soon was looking for the same satisfaction my dad did and Robert also sought that satisfaction, we both were looking for the same experience. We didn't fit each other.

Chapter Two: Origins of a Slut

My tutor, Robert Sinclair, told me that the summer before I was to travel east to go to college would be one I'd never forget and that would leave an indelible mark on me. That proved to be prophetic. Hardly surprising. I imagine that the period in which any young man turns eighteen and begins a new life journey is a notable one. But I'm sure few experienced as momentous a turning point in their life as I did that summer. Some of that was because of what happened with Robert. What happened with Robert just steeled my decision to become what I have become.

Robert warned me that there were dangerous shoals ahead as I approached my eighteenth birthday, but I didn't give what he was saying its full value. For one thing I thought he was too emotionally involved—and that I, in turn, was being overemotional myself.

For Robert and me the end of a life was quickly approaching—and just at the time that we were awakening to each other. It all began to unravel after those three nights I spent with Robert in the motel rather than disappoint my parents' plans by returning to the ranch early from Malibu.

The proximity of Robert to me in those three nights and the inevitability of seeing his body in the close confines of the motel room as I never had seen him before—on top of the shock of seeing both of my parents in flagrante delicto with same-sex partners and within moaning distance of each other—had opened the floodgates of feelings and desires that I had being keeping tucked inside my unconsciousness for years.

I had always known that I was attracted to men—to men, not to other boys my age. And there were no mechanisms in the social makeup of my family or my greater experience—there not having been much greater experience because of the sheltered, yet "few values" life I'd led—to call me off from that direction.

But there also had been no flame, nothing to unleash what I, in my loose upbringing, hadn't seen as any more passionate a desire than my love for chocolate chip ice cream or Lord Titan. Lord Titan was the horse my parents had bought me the year they'd bought Heaven Ranch, the Moreno Valley ranch that had been developed into a showplace by a famous and now-moldering director of early talkies—and later near porn. Such a desire not having been instilled in me as a shameful taboo, it's power of titillation hadn't been built up in me either.

And, more important, perhaps, there had never been an opportunity to develop such an arousal.

My parents had kept me almost completely isolated, with only Robert as a man in my life.

But that was all going to change—drastically—in the eighteenth summer of my life. And the change started to come, like the breaching of a dam, during that three-night exile with Robert following having seen my parents "in the act."

Robert had been sublimating his feelings and desires for me for so long that he wasn't, I'm sure, purposely trying to arouse me and move our relationship to a different, more dangerous level when he was stripped down to his sleeping pants and I first saw him leaning over the basin in the motel room's bathroom and brushing his teeth.

There had been male skin magazines lying about our houses for years. Not having any moral compass available for such things, I had never even thought about whose they were and why they weren't under lock and key. I suppose at the

22

time, I subconsciously assumed they were my mother's. Now, of course, I assume they were my dad's.

But Hollywood is the center of narcissism and exhibitionism. Both of my parents were self-consciously beautiful people—with beautiful bodies—and they surrounded themselves with beautiful, narcissistic people. I'd seen both of them in various stages of undress on the silver screen and thought nothing of it.

I admired the photos in the magazines, and I worked to be like them, which I was able to do with the help of Robert, who was very much into body sculpting himself.

So, I'd even seen Robert stripped down to almost no covering in the six years he was with us. We had a pool at the ranch, and the pool is the center of life in southern California. And at the other house, we had the beach and an ocean. We rarely had more than a bathing suit on—any of us. The flame of sexuality and sensuality was only applied to that and personalized in my response to Robert himself, though, when I saw him move fluidly and in the context of a bedroom situation there in the motel—and then only because it conjured up what I had just seen my dad and the younger actor, Gordon Fields, doing with their naked bodies in my dad's study.

I had encountered them in the throes of a passionate and deep kiss. Both of them naked. Both of their bodies well worked and well cut. My dad had been on his back on the surface of his desk, his mature-bodied, well-muscled legs spread, his toes pointed at the doorway where I stood, mesmerized and in shock from the unexpectedness of what I was seeing. Fields was standing between his legs. My dad had just raised his torso off the surface of desk and he was breast to breast with Fields. My dad had an arm flung around Fields's neck, and they were kissing. All was in suspended animation except for the two forms of motion that focused my attention and burned themselves into my brain: the movement of Fields's plump butt cheeks—a rhythmic forward and backward movement accompanied by a contraction and release of the muscles of his cheeks—and the curling and uncurling of my dad's toes in rhythm with the undulation of Fields's buttocks.

The second night in the motel, when Robert came out of the bathroom, I was waiting there on my bed—naked. He couldn't take his eyes off me, and I could see from the tenting of his pajama bottoms that he was aroused by me. I posed for him in a manner I'd seen in those magazines of my dad's and I tried to give him bedroom eyes, dredging up all of the love scenes I could remember from the movies I'd been permitted to watch.

"Clint—"

"Please, Robert. I know you want—"

"Clint, no, not now. Not like this. I shouldn't have—"

And then he was in his bed, the covers pulled up to his neck and facing away from me.

"Robert. I didn't realize. I didn't know. I know you—"

"Turn out your light, Clint. This can't be. Maybe in a couple of weeks, but not—"

"In a couple of weeks? Do you mean after I've turned eighteen, we could—?"

"Let's not discuss this now, Clint. I should have done something else, thought of some sort of other arrangement. It shouldn't have been like this. Turn out your light."

I lay there, brooding, for a couple of hours. By the irregularity of his breathing, I could tell that he wasn't asleep either. And the raggedness of his breathing told me that he was thinking of me and that he wanted what I wanted.

In the dark of the night, I moved to his bed, pulled the sheets up, slipped under them, and stretched my body full length along his, cupping myself into his back. He shuddered and turned, and we went into a frenzy of kissing and groping and running our hands over each other and mingling our moans of want and need.

"Oh, god, Robert. Make love to me. Fuck me. I want to feel you inside me," I cried out.

And then, as quickly as the frenzy had started, it was over, and Robert had pulled away from me and was sitting on the side of the bed away from me, wrapped tightly in the sheets he'd pulled away from our writhing bodies. He flipped the light next to the bed on and turned and scowled at me.

"Fuck you?" he said with a voice that stabbed. "That ain't a gonna happen."

"Why? Because I'm not eighteen yet? Because I'm two weeks shy of that?" I answered with a snort.

"Partially that, yes. But also partly because you have no defenses, Clint—and now I've seen the magnitude of your proclivities. You are a walking disaster. I've failed you as a teacher—not a teacher of math and history, but as a teacher of life. God knows your parents have been hopeless in that vein. But I should have done something. I should have given you more protection. And now it may be too late. And, worse, now I can see what you want—and the intensity with which you want it."

"I don't understand."

"Precisely. You don't understand. And now, oh my god, I've seen where you are headed, the capacities you have for a life of unfettered debauchery. I mourn your innocence, the beautiful child on the edge of the abyss of loss."

"You've lost me. I want you to make love to me. I didn't realize until we came here what I wanted—and who I wanted it from. Is that bad?"

"Not normally, no," Robert answered. "But that's the crux of the problem. You have no sense of 'bad' or inappropriate or what you risk in your innocence and lack of ingrained limitations and sense of self-protection. And you aren't going to get what you want from me."

"Why? Just because I'm two weeks shy of legal age. Because if it's that, I can wait two—"

"No, dammit. Not just that. Because . . . what is it we were just doing, Clint?"

"Making love? Preparing to fuck? I don't know, Robert. You tell me. I'm the inexperienced one here."

"We were fighting for who was going to do the fucking, Clint." And then, having said it, Robert laughed a bitter laugh. After a pause, he continued. "Age be damned—you had me so hot; you've had me so hot for months—that I

25

would have done it. And taken the consequences, if they unfolded. But, Clint, you don't realize that we were fighting for who was going to fuck and who was going to be fucked."

"I still don't understand," I answered dumbly.

"We both wanted to be fucked, Clint. You even said it—you wanted me inside you. That's the moment I realized we weren't going to work out—at least in terms of going the whole way. And anything short of that can certainly wait until it's safe. Then there are things we can do, if you still want—although you are so superhot I'm not sure I can hold you no matter how much I ache for you or that you profess to love me. But, ironies of ironies—considering how long I've dreamed of being with you that way—we don't fit. We both want exactly the same thing. And unless we are more versatile in what turns us on—which I'm not, and I now fully suspect you aren't either—neither one of us, to put it crudely, is going to put a dick inside the other one. And that means neither one of us can be fully satisfied."

"Oh."

"Yes, oh. It's part of the uniqueness of your situation, Clint. You were raised developing no boundaries and yet you are reaching the age of consent with no protections."

"Oh, and that's bad?"

"Not in or of itself, but what you have revealed to me tonight explodes the dangers to come."

"How so?"

"How so? Let me tick them off for you, Clint. You are achingly young and handsome and desirable, you come from celebrity—and a hedonistic celebrity at that—which means you are in a predatory environment, you have no internal checks and balances, and you intensely are open to having a man making love to you. This is walking time bomb fodder. We have little time, but when your parents disperse this summer, I suggest you run for the nearest exit—that you go straight to Pennsylvania, to Penn State, and not look back and get into a more normal, less sexually charged environment."

"So, you're sending me away."

"God, Clint. I'm trying to save you. It's against all of my instincts, all of my wants and desires. And I wouldn't be this selfless if I thought there was a chance you were versatile—that you could love me the way I need to be loved. But I sense you're not, and I can't live with that. And I don't want you to be taken and ruined by all of those predators milling about in your parents' circle of friends. I love you that much."

"I could try. This is all new to me. Maybe I would enjoy—"

"Oh, God, Clint. Oh, god. Give me strength."

And then he was out of the bed, still wrapped in the sheet and reaching for his clothes. He went into the bathroom and closed the door. I heard the lock being shot home.

When he came out he was fully dressed. And for the rest of that night and all of the third night, he sat in a chair, across the room from my bed, while I fitfully slept and pouted.

When we arrived at the ranch on the day we were expected, my parents had no idea I had come home early and then left again. And they didn't even show any curiosity about my reports of the brush fires around the Malibu house. My mother babbled on about the movie shoot she was about to leave for in Norway, and my dad spoke of my eighteenth birthday and how he was inviting a clutch of friends—their friends, my not having any friends beyond Robert—over for a pool party to help me celebrate my ascendance to adulthood.

Chapter Three: Setting Up

My dad had a party for me—but it wasn't an eighteenth-birthday party. He jumped the gun on that. And although I was partying on my eighteenth birthday, it wasn't at the ranch, and my dad wasn't there. But, in hindsight, I think he would have wanted to be.

Dad started the party early because my mother took off in early June for her photo shoot on an art film in Norway and my dad too was scheduled to start filming in the timber area of northern California soon thereafter.

As chance would have it, I also was gone from the ranch—not back East much to Robert's chagrin—by early July. That left two weeks for my dad to host a rolling pool party at the ranch. And, with my mother gone—although I'd come to realize that her presence probably didn't dampen anything my dad wanted to do—we partied my dad's way.

He used me as bait. I didn't realize that for some years later. I did, however, fully appreciate already that he was setting out bait. The day my mother left, my dad went "shopping" down in L.A. What he came home with was a Hispanic youth barely older than I was named Emilio Munoz.

"Meet Emilio," my dad told me when they pulled up in front of the ranch house in my dad's silver Bentley convertible. "He's the new pool boy."

We already had a pool boy—actually a pool man, but it didn't take much for me to catch on what a pool boy did rather than a pool man—and it wasn't clean pools. Emilio was quite young looking, but he was strongly built and had a face that some would call beautiful rather than handsome. Big brown cow eyes and eye lashes that looked like he had to comb them. His black curly hair was a plus, especially the one unruly lock that kept curling down across an eyebrow. I'm sure he wanted to be a movie star—and thought my father could make him one. He wasn't stupid. It was a well-worn path to stardom in Hollywood.

"Had lunch yet?" my dad asked me as the two of them exited the Bentley. Emilio wasn't wearing a shirt, although there was one on the backseat of the car, and he had a dreamy-eyed look on his face and my dad had an agitated look on his that indicated there'd been a stop along the route somewhere on the way up the canyon road from L.A. into the Moreno Valley. "Why don't you go in and have Efenia fix you a sandwich while I show Emilio the ropes with the pool equipment?"

I must have finished my lunch sooner than my dad thought I would, because I was out at the pool in time to see that "showing" Emilio the ropes entailed Emilio being on his back on a lounge in the pool house, his wrists tied together, and with my dad's pelvis between his legs.

The sight of my dad fucking Emilio brought back what Robert had been trying to tell me back in the motel. I'd seen my dad being fucked by Gordon Fields in the house, but now he was the one poking the Hispanic youth. So, my dad was one of those versatile men Robert had talked about—and had suggested that neither he nor I was. While I watched them fuck, which I did find arousing, I tried to imagine myself in my dad's position. But I just couldn't do it. My eyes kept going back to the contracting and releasing of my dad's buttocks muscles, and I couldn't get past having my arousal centered on what a man could do inside my body rather than me doing it to anyone else.

Score one for Robert—another one for Robert; I found he rarely was wrong about anything. That undoubtedly was why he'd been hired to tutor me. He had read me right. I only wanted to be made love to, apparently. And the interesting thing was that I felt no reason not to want it from my dad, just as Emilio was getting it. It struck me that this was another thing Robert had been right about. My understanding was that I should have some internal barrier against an incestuous act. I didn't. I didn't even know what incest meant until months later—when it did me no good anymore. My instincts were that I wanted a man. And maybe not just one; and I wasn't too choosy about who it was. That was another tendency Robert had said he was afraid I had.

Two days later the rolling pool party started. And for the first time in my life, my dad made no effort to put me in the background. Indeed, he fronted and centered me—and I saw that Emilio was ever there as well, decked out in a skimpy Speedo and, more frequently than not, walking away toward the parkland around our pool with one of my dad's guests, the guest's hand either on Emilio's back or his buttocks.

And all of my dad's guests those two weeks were men.

Most of the men were from the film industry, and they tended to separate into two groups: the rich and powerful—and pretty old—in one group and the young hunks in the other. I was told that some of the hunks came from a gym down near the movie studio. It was where hunks went who wanted to break into film, because sometimes it happened at that gym. I'm sure all the guys who had come to this party thought they were auditioning. And maybe they were.

During that two weeks I saw my dad walking away with a hunk almost as much as I saw Emilio walking away with a rich and powerful man—and mostly I sat by the pool with the rich and powerful—and pretty old—men buzzing around me as well.

Most of the time I tried to be somewhere close to Theo Kline, the big-name producer, who had been a close family friend for as long as I could remember. I had always thought of Theo as family, and I sometimes stayed with him when my parents were on location. Theo had an apartment overlooking a yacht basin near Venice Beach, and during the periods I was foisted off on him, I often went out on the ocean with him in his old fan-tail yacht, the *Final Curtain*. He produced many of the films my parents were in, and he spent about as much time at our ranch as anywhere else. He was a mountain of a man—more big boned muscle-meaty than fat. He wasn't much more than in his mid forties at that time, but already was balding on top. He had a voice that boomed out over the landscape and immediately caught everyone's attention and respect.

I looked to Theo as something stable, someone familiar to cling to as my world revolved and moved in directions that were both apprehensive and tantalizing.

In those two weeks I had no difficulty sensing both that the men my dad was inviting to this rolling party were attracted to me and that as long as I stayed close to Theo Kline and Robert, who also bravely glued himself to my side, I was on safe ground—although safe from predators or from my own inclinations, I could not have said.

Principal among the guests who buzzed around me were Charles Tilton, the relatively young movie director, many of whose films no one seemed to fully understand but—possibly for that very reason—enjoyed critical acclaim. Tilton sometimes slums and directed films that moviegoers actually wanted to see to keep his bank account flush. These were the Tilton films my parents appeared in. One of the hunks from the gym, named Gene, also spent time in our little circle under umbrellas between the house and the pool. He, more often than not, sat off to the side by Robert, Robert looking on silently with a wary look on his face, and Gene being equally silent but with a look more of lust in his eyes.

I would have liked Gene to be my first—and I spent those two weeks shopping for my preferred "first," anxious to move on to that level. He had a great body and an "oh my gosh" helpful-neighbor manner about him. He was blond and smooth skinned and had a square-cut jaw that made me think he had a shot at taking up the reins of Number One Heartthrob when Gordon Fields passed on the baton.

But Charles Tilton was always there too. He'd stand behind me and put his hands on my shoulder and give me a soothing rub—losing interest only when some fine piece of male tail walked by and gave him the eye, begging for an audition.

"Watch out for him," Robert had whispered in my ear the first day my dad put me on display—and putting me on display I now have to acknowledge was his ploy to get the right men to the party—"He's running along the edge of indictment for his interest in underage boys."

"But I'll only be underage for two more weeks," I whispered back.

To this, Robert winced and looked up to heaven and muttered, "God, give me the strength to get this one on a plane east unscathed."

This Charles Tilton looked pretty good to me—and was high on my "first" shopping list. He wasn't young or old—and I already was developing an eye for the older, more experienced men. And he was in good shape. And by this time, I craved experience. I wonder whether my dad would have set me out as a honey pot to attract men for himself this summer if he had known how ripe and wanting it I was. Probably yes, I must admit.

"My, my, my. Where has Scott been keeping you?" Tilton had asked when we were first introduced. He had my hand in his and he wasn't going to give it back. One of his fingers was stroking my wrist where the vein went down into the hand, and it was having an arousing effect on me. Naïve as I was, all I could think about was wondering if he realized that what he was doing with that one finger was arousing me.

"He's not legal," Theo said in a low but cutting voice from beside me, "And that's exactly what you can't afford right now."

But when Tilton spoke next, it was directly to me, as if he hadn't heard Theo at all—didn't even know he was there. "I knew you were up here, my lad," he spoke to me in a silken-smooth voice. "I could smell the honey from down at Hollywood and Vine."

Theo had interceded more forcefully then, and turned me to meet the other man who followed me around like a puppy dog for two weeks—the television game show host Andrew Dix. He was always there in the background in our little group too except for the times he was off in the pool house with a hopeful hunk having his cock polished. He seemed to be satisfied with the blow jobs.

So, for two weeks I was courted closely by a famous movie director, a wholesome blond hunk, and a well-known television game show host—all under the watchful eyes of a major movie producer, and, from just outside the golden aura created by these men by my nervous tutor, Robert Sinclair.

The attention went right to my head. I had been closely sheltered up to just two weeks previously. And now I was sought and pursued and wanted.

If I had any thought that my dad was worried about what was unfolding, that was dispelled one night after all of the rest had left or been bedded down in the various guesthouses on the ranch, invariably in pairs or greater number combinations, and I was preparing to go up to my room as well. Robert had already gone ahead—to set out some school work he wanted me to do in the morning before the party started rolling again.

I was passing through the lounge when I encountered my dad and Gordon Fields, sitting in oversized, leather-covered wing chairs in the lounge and smoking cigars and drinking Scotch.

"Come sit with us for a few minutes, son," my dad said as I was passing, and almost in shock at the unexpected invitation, I sat on the edge of a coffee table and eyed the Scotch bottle—with absolutely no success.

"He's a fine boy, wouldn't you say, Gordon?" my dad said. I glowed at the pride I could hear in his voice. "He'll be a real heartbreaker, don't you think?"

"Yes, he's a fine boy; and I'm sure you know he's already a real heartbreaker," I heard the young actor say—himself the major heartbreaker of the screen of the moment.

And the low, throaty-voiced way Fields said it made me look into his eyes, where, even at my age and in my naiveté I could read raw lust. The image of him fucking my dad in my dad's study upstairs came immediately to mind, and I lowered my eyes and blushed.

"Have you thought of what you want to do when you've finished college?" my dad suddenly asked.

This sent me in a tailspin. I couldn't remember when my dad had ever asked such a question of me—indeed had shown he was giving any thought to my future at all—let alone my present. Even all of the college application process had been goaded and managed by Robert, not by either of my parents.

"Uh, yes. Maybe a lawyer or a doctor. Or maybe a vet. I like working with the horses." What I really wanted to be was a police detective. But I couldn't say that. I'd told my dad that once and he had laughed derisively at the notion.

"You know you could be a movie star, don't you, Clint?" My dad cut in. "He could be a guaranteed hit in the movies, don't you think, Gordon?"

"Yes, guaranteed. His parentage and looks. He'd knock them dead. the auditions will be a 'gimme.'"

"It's a good profession, son. Lots of money and most anything you want."

"Ummm. Sounds possible," I stammered out. "Something to think about."

"You know you have a golden opportunity here, Clint," my dad continued. "The men I see you with at the pool—Tilton and Klein, even Dix—these are men who could grease the wheels for you, could make it easy for you to get established. You understand that, don't you, Clint?"

"Umm, yes, I understand," I almost whispered. But did I understand, or was I reading something wrong in this? Was my dad actually green-lighting my pent up emotions and frustrations? Was he telling me it was OK to let these men manhandle me—all for what they could do for me? Was that how he got to where he was? I knew the answer to those questions would be a "yes," though, so I didn't dwell on the thought.

And before I could think further on that, Robert was standing at the top of the stairs and calling out softly, "If I'm going to show you what you need to go over in the math book in the morning before we both have to go off to bed, you'd best come up, Clint."

As I stood, I looked into Fields's face. The lust there hadn't changed, and it made me tremble and gulp at the possibilities I saw there. And then I looked over at my dad, and I couldn't swear that his expression was any different from Fields's.

When I went upstairs, I asked Robert again for the umpteenth time since we'd been together in the motel if we couldn't try to fuck—that I was all keyed up and about to explode.

He didn't laugh. He said he could see that and that he was sorry it was this way—that no one seemed to want to try to head it off. And he assured me once again that, no we wouldn't get the complete satisfaction I deserved if we tried, that I needed to realize that until I was eighteen I would be endangering not just myself but anyone who touched me, and that I needed to be strong—preferably strong enough to make that plane east before anything happened.

"I know it's going to happen, Clint. You're just too . . . too . . ." he couldn't find the words he wanted, which I found amazing for my tutor to fail at. "But Hollywood will eat you up and spit you out before you've learned to protect yourself. Better that it happen back East."

But Robert didn't leave me in frustration. With a sigh, he told me that he'd massage me until I'd gone to sleep. And I stripped and lay on my belly, while he poured oil on my back and legs and buttocks. He massaged me then, working my muscles well—and carefully not crossing any line on where he put his hands. But at the same time, he made no move, voiced no admonishment or objection, when my sighs turned to moans and I lifted my pelvis off the mattress and stroked my cock rhythmically into the bunched-up sheets as he massaged my back and thighs and buttocks. He got up and left me before I came, but I couldn't stop stroking, seeking some form of release. After I came, I collapsed onto the bed with a grunt and a groan and the sigh of half-satisfaction, looking around for someone to talk to of the pleasure that release gave me—but Robert was gone.

Chapter Four: Anticipation and Horror

"Does that sound like a good idea to you? Ready to do a little work?"

"Ummm, Excuse me? Sorry I wasn't listening." I turned and looked toward Theo Kline, shielding my eyes from the sunlight bounding off the tiles surrounding the pool at the ranch.

* * * *

I had been daydreaming, in anticipation of delights to come and in frustration at not having them there already. And my mind had been flooded with what I'd just seen and experienced—the enticement and frustration of it all.

I'd risen from the lounge at the pool, with the excuse of needing another drink from the pool house, but really to release the tension. Theo and Charles Tilton, sitting on each side of me, had been yammering about their coming production, the start of which now was only days away. The movie was tentatively titled *High Timber*, and it unabashedly was an adventure film ostensibly to provide a beefcake fix to sighing housewives but really, in the undercurrent of Hollywood fare, to provide beefcake for their wandering husbands enticed by other wandering husbands packaged in the eternal strong men fighting evil and promoting honest sweat and toil work choices.

My dad was starring in the film. Gordon Fields was the supporting actor. The women stars—intentionally—were of lesser box-office status—and mousey of looks beside my dad and Gordon. The film was to be of the changing of generations of lumberjack heroes in the forests of the northwest, played out as a struggle of the maturing hunk, my dad, and a newly arrived younger hunk, played by Fields, for the affections of the company owner's daughter, played by whoever. It was to be filmed, though, to signal to the subliminal, can-not-be-acknowledged actual targeted audience the struggle for sexual dominance between the two male actors. Of course the men would work shirtless and extensive shooting would be done of them flexing their muscles in logging the high timber.

"It's too high a risk," Kline was saying. I tuned into their conversation now, as they seemed to be talking about something deeper than the shooting of the feature film.

"We could make millions. And I mean double- and triple-digit millions," Tilton countered. "Much more from the second cut than the first. I have outlets. Abroad. They'd lap it up. And they are secretive. They would keep it for themselves."

"I told you about your kiddy porn films, Chuck. It will catch up with you one of these days. Doing this with this film could ruin Scott's career."

"How much career does he have left—at his age?" Tilton asked with a low laugh. His voice was husky, almost honey thick and sluggish. And that's when I was set on edge. He was so engrossed with his discussion with Kline that he didn't realize that he was hunched over me where I lay on the lounge, one hand very near my cheek and the other one laying next to my thigh—but a long, slender finger actually on the side of my bare thigh, gently stroking me.

We both heard Robert cough from a few yards away, and Tilton's finger pulled back, but he remained hunched over me.

"And it would be a nice final payoff for him too—and only a problem if the actual film leaked out to the open public. If it was only rumors of another cut leaking out, that would only add to the coffers of the public version. Come on, think about it, Theo. It's what we've always wanted to do. The Hollywood version and then a director's cut—a director's addition, actually—of Sloan and Fields giving our real target audience what they want. Sex scenes interposed where we only now have a tension that only the select few will see as sexual. Sloan trying to dominate Fields but being mastered by the younger man; Fields giving Sloan a good fucking. Taking advantage of what they're already doing without producing any profit from it. The passing of the baton, Fields's dick the baton. It would even give the film deeper meaning. It would make millions and be an underworld cult film."

"I don't know." It's what Theo said, but both Tilton and I could hear in the timbre of his voice that he was warming to the idea. "I'll run it by Sloan to see what he thinks. I know Fields would go for it. He's been after us to make straight-up homo films with grade A actors and believable, full-plot scripts anyway."

Crisis passed, Tilton looked down at me and I could feel the tip of his finger on the flesh of my thigh again.

"You'll roast, Clint, if you don't get some more lotion on," he said. "Want me to apply it?"

That's when I decided I needed another drink from the pool house. I did want him to apply the lotion. Right then I wanted even more from him. But Robert was there, his eyes boring into me in warning, and Theo was there, giving an admonishing look at Tilton. And I remembered what Theo had said about that edge that the dark, handsome, brooding director already was walking with the law. And it would be barely over a week now before I could freely give what I wanted to give. The question, though, was whether Tilton would want it then. Would I be too old for him then? I didn't know how men like him thought; I didn't know how any man thought—what about me aroused them like it seemed to do. And I wanted Charles Tilton—it was almost an animalistic need to experience him.

It didn't help going to the pool house. In one corner the TV game-show host, Andrew Dix, was sprawled in a

41

chair, pasty-white legs spread, with Emilio knelt between them, working Dix's cock with his mouth. Dix had Emilio's head trapped with two meaty paws, and Emilio was making gagging sounds as Dix brutally pulled the young Hispanic's head into his pelvis.

What really put me off balance was what I saw on a lounge in the back corner of the pool house as I opened the refrigerator and pulled out a Coke. The two were entwined like wrestlers, my dad on the bottom, and one of the younger hunks—someone my dad had called background eye candy for Grade B beach movies—was wrapped around him, dominating him, pistoning him hard and fast—and my dad's hips were rising off the lounge surface in rhythm to the plowing, jerking in an upward thrust with each of the hunk's grunting downward plunges, my dad taking in as much of the hunk as he could with each lunge.

They were locked in a lip kiss when I first noticed them, but the sound of the refrigerator door must have caught my dad's attention, because he looked around. And when he saw me, the only change I saw in him was that his eyes lit up and then smoldered. No sense of embarrassment at all—although that didn't occur to me until years later, when I became fixated on what my dad wanted to do—and had done—that summer. At the time I hadn't been indoctrinated in what embarrassment would look like in a sexually compromising position either.

Without a loss of a single beat, my dad's eyes latched onto mine, and we were instantly transported—each one of us seeing ourselves together but my dad in the role of the hunk and me as my dad. I could almost feel him filling my channel. I ached for knowing how that felt—why men moaned at it.

I snatched my hands away from the Coke bottle and it clattered against the other bottles on the refrigerator shelf. Turning then, I stumbled out of the pool house and around the path to the side and to the back of the pool house, where I leaned against the wall, panting. My hand diving under the waistband of my Speedo and encasing my engorged cock. There was no embarrassment involved, no sense of taboo.

Just the image of Robert in my head, telling me it was just too complicated and charged here—to wait until I got back East.

"Well, well, what has you all pent up?" The voice was hoarse, thick with want. I looked up to see Charles Tilton standing at the edge of the path.

"I . . . I just came for a drink," I stammered, snatching my hand from inside my Speedo and pulling my back off the rough, wooden wall.

"I saw that. I saw what you saw in the pool house. I'd decided I wanted a drink too." Then he laughed. "And I saw what you wanted. And it wasn't the drink."

He was there then, in my face. Not touching me, but close to me, his body just inches from mine in front of me, his arms spread around me, his palms flat against the wooden wall on either side of my head. His smile wicked, his eyes full of lust.

He sniffed the air. "You smell nice. The smell of musk. The smell of want. Ready for me, are you?"

I didn't answer. I was trembling with want. He had no idea how much I wanted him. Or any man at this point—but him especially.

His hands left the wall, but only briefly. They reached down and grabbed my Speedo at each side and—still without touching me with his fingers—jerked the suit down to my knees. He leaned back and looked down, and smiled. I couldn't hide it. I was hard for him. Then he was leaning back into me and his hands were back on the wall on either side of my head. He started to dip his face down into mine.

"Chuck!" The voice wasn't angry, but it was strong, demanding. I turned my head to see Theo Kline standing on the path.

A slightly pained expression flitted across Tilton's face, but then the sneery, possessive, entitled smile returned and he casually pulled away from me and backed up to the path.

To show he wasn't cowed, however, he remained standing for a long moment on the pathway. And he just didn't stand. He slipped his own bathing suit off and stood there, cupping his hardened cock in a hand. I gasped at the size of it, far bigger and thicker than anything I'd seen before. And his body took on the form of a satyr now. I'd already seen that he was hairy, with curly black hair running all along his body, but his hairiness was accentuated by the power of that cock and the confident, arrogant look on his face.

"I have a birthday present for you, Clint, right here. A supersized mansplitter worthy of plucking that sweet cherry of yours. You ready for it? You want it? I can tell you want it. You're hard for it. You're trembling for it. I like them younger, but you're worth the wait. You'll be here on your birthday to take all of this inside you? To open to the thrust and thrust and thrust and my fountaining off in your guts? Being as it will be your first time, we'll bareback. You'll love my cocking. You'll get the full service."

With each "thrust" I had emitted a low moan, and an even louder one voiced the "yes" I couldn't say. But as it turned out, I wasn't here on my eighteenth birthday—and it wasn't Charles Tilton who would be my first.

"Chuck. Not now. Not here," Theo said again, calmly. He laid a hand on Tilton's arm, and Tilton laughed and turned and strutted off, swinging his bathing suit saucily in an upraised hand.

Theo looked at me briefly and then also turned and walked away. If he'd stayed a minute longer, he'd have seen my spontaneous ejaculation. I pulled my Speedo up, and, being too agitated to go back to where Theo and Tilton were taking up a solitary station under the umbrellas between the house and the pool again, I turned and stumbled along the path, away from the pool. Robert hadn't been at the pool. Maybe he was in his cottage. I had to talk to someone. Maybe I could convince him to relieve me of this burden. I thought I'd die if I had to wait one more day. If Theo hadn't shown up, I'd joyously have let Tilton take me right there, up against the side wall of the pool house. Two weeks and legality meant nothing to me.

I heard the sounds as I approached Robert's cottage. Not for a moment did I believe it was him, though. I don't know why I didn't; I just didn't. But it *was* him. He was on his bed, kneeling, chest on the surface of the bed and his butt in the air. Naked. Gene, the blond hunk who I thought was buzzing around our group because of me, was crouched, also fully naked, on the bed, straddling Robert's hips, his beefy hands grabbing Robert by the waist, and fucking him like a dog. He was stroking hard and deep and Robert's body was bouncing around under him with each thrust. Robert's cheek was plastered to the bedspread and his face was turned toward me, unseeing though—because the expression on his face revealed that he was in heaven, walking on the clouds.

I couldn't watch, I retreated and turned, my back to the outside wall beside the door, listening, taking in every stroke and moan and groan and transporting myself to that place. I was jealous. It was both disturbing and intriguing to me that I was jealous. It was Robert I was jealous of. Receiving what I wanted. Being fucked hard and deep by the blond stud I'd envisioned taking me the last two nights as I tried to sleep. Robert getting what I believed I so badly needed.

When the moans had progressed through outcries and subsided into gurgles, I pushed off the wall and walked back to the pool. I dove in and swam across it before hauling myself out of the water and returning to my lounge chair. Theo and Andrew Dix were there. Charles Tilton wasn't. I saw him across the pool, accosting Emilio as Emilio emerged from the pool house, and with a look around to spy me and assure himself that I saw him, Tilton palmed the small of Emilio's back and guided him to the side of the pool house, clearly in my vision.

I watched him put Emilio in the same encasing stance against the wall that he had put me in and reach down and pull Emilio's Speedo down just as he had done with mine. But then he lifted Emilio's legs to hug his hips and, thrusting inside Emilio as the Hispanic youth arched his back and let out an audible groan, he fucked Emilio against the wall, raising and lowering the young Hispanic's back along the rough wood of the wall with the strength of his plowing cock. I could hear Emilio's groans and grunts from across the water. Emilio was looking up into the overhang of the trees, mouth gaping open, crying out his pleasure. But Tilton's eyes

45

were turned toward me. Even then it was me he was fucking in his mind—and not only in his mind; in mine as well.

* * * *

"Excuse me? What did you say, Theo?" I repeated, willing my attention away from the substitute fucking going on on the pool house wall.

"My assistant. I need an assistant for this film we're doing," Theo said. "*High Timber*. I talked to your father, and he thought it would be splendid short-term summer job for you. Give you a taste of the business. He's rather keen for you to go Hollywood too. What do you say, Clint?"

"Yes, sure, that would be nice," I answered, my thoughts if not my eyes still glued to what Tilton was doing to Emilio in my stead.

"Good, then. We leave day after tomorrow. Up to my mountain cabin. With your father and Gordon and a physical trainer. The two of them need some toning up before we can go north to Eureka. The Pacific Lumber Company's going to let us film up there where they are logging."

Shortly thereafter, Efenia came out of the house to inform Theo he had a long-distance call, and he left us, just Robert and me alone now by the pool, Robert now having returned to my side, glowing, but alone.

"You OK?" Robert asked.

"Yes, sure. Why not?"

"You seem flustered. I feel like I missed something when I went back to my room for a short nap. You want to tell me what happened?"

"Ummm, nothing. No."

But we were both watching Tilton and Emilio at the side of the pool house, where Tilton's upward strokes seemed to be going on forever and Emilio had collapsed now and was just bouncing up and down on the wall like a rag doll. A brief image of how this must be rubbing his back raw flitted across my mind, but even that I found arousing. Sweet and sour; pleasure and pain. I shuddered.

"He wanted to do that to you, didn't he?"

"Yes," I admitted in a small voice.

"And you wanted him to, didn't you?"

"Yes," in even a smaller voice.

"I want him to do it to me too," Robert whispered.

I looked around at him, surprised about where he had taken this—no admonition, no "You mustn't." Just the acknowledgment of how alike the two of us were. And the wide gulf that inevitably separated us because our wants were too much the same. I resented him a bit then. He'd already taken Gene. Now he wanted Tilton too.

"Robert?"

"Yes?"

"What is it I have that men want?"

"You mean besides being young and drop-dead gorgeous?" Robert said with a laugh. But when I didn't answer, he turned more serious. "They want your innocence, Clint. Did Tilton say what he wanted from you?"

I thought on that a moment, but then I remembered. "He wanted my cherry. He wanted to pop my cherry."

"Precisely. Tilton wants them young and innocent. He wants to take them far down the path. There are rumors about what he does—and that he films what he does and sells it. He will take a young man to the edge—and maybe beyond."

"And yet you want him—you want that?"

There was a moment of silence, and then Robert said, "Yes, I guess so. I want to know where the edge is. And a man like that . . . I want that too."

"Then we really are alike," I said. I shuddered at the thought—not so much at the thought of what Tilton did but at the thought that it blindly intrigued me. "But men. Regular men, not ones with the appetite of a Tilton. Is innocence what they want too?"

"That's what they all want, Clint. But in your case it won't stop there. You have so much more that they will want, even after you've lost your virginity. They'll be attracted to your own want and your own openness for it. That's what brings a man like Tilton buzzing around it. It's the peculiarity of your upbringing. I can tell. I saw it and feared for you in your vulnerability. But I also envy you. Because as you grow older, it will work well for you."

"What will?"

"Your openness and your want. You're so intense. I can see that you're just bursting with want. When men cock you in years to come, they will be aroused to new heights by the joy with which you receive and ride their cocks—and your insatiability in opening your legs for them. You will make men feel like supermen. There's no greater feeling you could give them. And you'll do it all without them losing their sense of your innocence. So each time, for them, it will be like the ultimate—taking your virginity. And the enjoyment they will receive will be multiplied by the enjoyment they sense that you get from it."

"But, it won't be real innocence, will it, Robert?"

"No, no, it won't. But it will be enough for them to feel it is. It will make them supermen and they won't be able to stop sniffing around you. And as long as you are enjoying it, it's all good."

"Then what will be the death of innocence for me? Have I already passed that?"

"No. The death of innocence for you will be when you go looking for it. When it stops being the man tracking and seducing and dominating you—but you going to him and begging for it—knowing that that particular fucking is bad for you, but begging for it nonetheless. But by then, there should be no tragedy in it. You will be ready and will have already experienced the thrill of being thoroughly, wondrously fucked."

"And you, Robert. Will you be—?"

"No, regrettably, I'm sure I will be gone by then." And then he stood, ready to go into the house, signaling that I was ready to go in as well, that we had studies to attend to in the safety of my room.

I looked over toward the pool house as I rose from the lounge. Robert was looking there too. Emilio was collapsed at the base the wall, in a tangle of arms and legs. Tilton was still there, close to him, facing the wall. The curve and length of his cock was still strongly evident. The perfect image of a satyr. He had his eyes on me, still, and he was panting hard.

"It was good that you accepted Mr. Kline's offer to be his assistant on the film between now and when you have to leave for Penn State."

"But you won't be going with us—up to Theo's cabin?"

"No. But it's time. I think it's almost past time for you to be away from your father's house."

* * * *

That evening I was sitting in the lounge, dimly lit except for the lamp on the table next to my chair, reading one of my school texts, reviewing for an at-home test that Robert was setting up for me upstairs. Emilio was in the kitchen with Efenia, helping her to clean up from the supper meal. The light from the kitchen door extended out into the dining area of the lounge, and whenever I looked up at the frame of light, I would see Efenia or Emilio drifting by from one end of the kitchen to another. From here, they looked like they were in a movie, a box of light framed by the dark surround of the dining room wall—a movie showing a calm, domestic setting I had never known, and probably never would know. They were having an animated conversation in Spanish that could have been either friendly or heated for all I knew. I just knew it was enthusiastic.

As I tried to concentrate on the textbook, I heard words unmistakably spoken in anger out in the front motor court of the ranch house beyond the open front door in the foyer. I heard the slam of a car door, the revving of an engine, and then the crush of gravel, as the car jumped away from the house. And then my dad was entering the front door and slammed it behind him.

He went straight to the drinks cabinet and poured himself a stiff glass of Scotch. He was muttering to himself. He turned then and saw me sitting there, and, as only an actor can, he changed his roles immediately and was all friendly and fatherly.

49

He came and sat down in the chair opposite mine. We were nearly knee to knee and he leaned forward and gave me a brilliant, all-white-teeth smile.

"Theo tells me you've accepted his invitation to be his assistant on *High Timber*."

"Yes, thanks, Dad. I'm sure it will be fun."

"And you can consider a career in movies while you're watching them being made."

"Yes, there's that."

"And we'll be going up to Theo's cabin on Wednesday. We can spend some time together—alone."

"That will be nice." I wondered where that was coming from. Spending time with me, alone, had never been part of my dad's vocabulary before that I could remember. And at night we were virtually alone right here.

"You know you'll be eighteen in another week."

"Yes."

"And you'll be going off to college soon too."

"Right. Robert's gotten the plane tickets for me, incidentally. I phoned your business agent, but he said no one had talked to him about that—but he and Robert worked it out. They should be ready to pick up any time now. I guess Robert will do that too."

"You're a handsome boy, you know," my dad then said, completely brushing aside the reference to his haphazard fathering—his relying so heavily on someone else to do everything for him. "And it's inevitable that people you come into contact with will know who your parents are. You'll have scads of friends. And many who will want to be with you."

"Yes, I suppose so."

"Be with you intimately, I mean."

I said nothing in response to this. He was leaning in very closely to me now and had his hands laying on the tops of my thighs.

"I suppose you know how it is with me—with men."

"Yes, that's been a bit difficult to avoid—especially since Mother flew off to Norway."

"We have an understanding, you need to know."

"I gathered that."

50

"But are you all right with that, Clint?"

I searched my mind, and from the depths of my preparation for life I wasn't able to come up with any reason why that wouldn't be OK with me—since I'd absorbed now that it clearly was OK with both of my parents.

"Yes, I don't see why not."

He seemed pleased—and relieved—at my response. And then he gave me a brilliant smile, a smile that made me shudder, but in a sense of anticipation rather than consternation. His suddenly relaxed stance and smile indicated that my response had changed our relationship somehow. I was afraid I knew how, and, interestingly enough, I didn't care. It didn't surprise or frighten me.

"I've watched you, Clint. I've watched you with other men. I do believe . . . you're an extraordinarily handsome and desirable young man, I must say. I—"

"I'm ready with your test." It was Robert calling me from the top of the staircase. I had no idea what he had seen or heard, if anything. But it had the effect of deflating my dad, who sat back gruffly in his chair, a sour look on his face now. His hand went out and gathered the Scotch glass and he took a big swig.

"Dad." I muttered. I didn't know really what I planned to say beyond that. But I knew that if he told me to go up the stairs with him at that moment, I would have done so. And I was on the brink of asking him if he wanted me to come to him in the night—to relieve an insistent itch we both had.

"Oh, go on up to Robert now. You mustn't miss your test." It was a dismissive, petulant command—spoken as if I had done something wrong, had rebuffed him. But I hadn't rebuffed him. And I don't think I would have.

At that moment, Emilio came out of the kitchen and headed toward the sliding glass doors out to the pool area. His quarters were over the garage beyond the pool house. But as he passed our chairs, my dad's hand snaked out and grabbed the Hispanic youth by the wrist.

"Come with me, Emilio. There's something I want to show you upstairs."

An hour later, after I'd taken my test and Robert had gone and I was stretched out on my bed, I could still hear the sounds of sex rolling out from my dad's room, and, if anything, the sounds seemed to be getting stronger. Emilio was becoming more and more vocal. I could tell that my dad was using a whip on him—and that Emilio was probably enjoying it—or at least acting like he did. I couldn't tell with Emilio. The only thing I was sure of was that he seemed ready to do anything to impress anyone who might be a stepping stone for him into the movies.

I'd found the small hand whip in his room days earlier and the restraints he used—and I could see the scratches on the headboard and the posts at the end of the bed where he must have bound men he was with—or been bound himself. And the thought of having sex this way—being bound and at the mercy of another who was being a bit cruel—aroused me. I hadn't mentioned this to Robert beyond our roundabout discussion about Tilton, because I sensed that, as similar as our wants seemed to be, that Robert's boundaries would be reached before mine would. That made me start to think I should have boundaries too—but I was at a loss what those would be. And I had never known how to define boundaries.

I writhed in my bed to the sounds of what was going on in my dad's room. I ached to know what it was, to be part of it—to at least have the chance to decide whether I wanted it too. I thought I heard the crunch of tires on the turning circle at the front of the house, but I couldn't imagine who would be arriving at this time of night—and it could have been just my imagination. My ears were tuned to the noises in my dad's room. The other sound had just been on the periphery. I mulled that for several minutes and finally decided to get up and go to one of the windows on the front of the house and see whether there really was a car there—and to try to determine whose it was.

But when I got to the hallway, I stopped, my attention arrested by the murky appearance of a figure—at least that's the form I had the impression was there. A man's figure. Down the hallway. By the half-open door into my dad's room. Emilio had been crying out in stifled cries that brought to mind the rubber ball gag I'd found with my dad's sex paraphernalia in his rooms. But the cries stopped, abruptly. And did so at the instant I saw the figure and involuntarily called out the name "Robert?" in a stage whisper.

But then the figure was gone—and the door into my dad's room was shut with a sound like a gunshot, pitching the hallway into utter darkness.

I returned to my bed and drifted off into a fitful sleep. I don't remember hearing any more sounds from my dad's room that night.

In the next few days I did try hard, however, to remember all of the events that night, although to anyone who asked I simply said I'd turned out my light after taking my test, plugged in the earphones to my radio, and went directly to sleep and heard nothing for the rest the night.

And my memory on these points was sorely taxed, because early the next morning, when I went out to the pool for my morning exercise before hitting the books again, I was the one who found him—Emilio, floating in the pool, face down, in a cloud of blood.

And then, later, when I was sent to fetch Robert when the police wanted everyone in the household to be gathered, I found his room empty and his suitcase and most of his clothes gone. His car wasn't in the garage either.

I was never to see him again. I was adrift now, on this ocean of new, frightening, and amazing experiences all alone.

Chapter Five: Finding the Rhythm

There was a flurry of activity at the ranch following the murder of Emilio and the disappearance of Robert—and then a few days when there was just me and my dad and Theo and Gordon, in addition to the remaining servants. There were no pool parties during this period, and Theo put off the plans to go up to his cabin.

Theo stuck close to me, showing great concern and what I would have recognized as mothering if I had much of a notion what that was. Even so, he behaved more toward me like Robert had done than my mother ever did, so I understood that he was trying to make sure I was all right. Both Charles Tilton and Andrew Dix came to the ranch a couple of times each—never in each other's company though. Theo shooed Dix away, and it was Tilton's fortune to come when police investigators were there taking their measurements and interviewing each of us yet again. And, upon seeing them, Tilton, who had quite enough problems with the police already, beat a hasty retreat. He did try to get me to take a drive with him once—and I would have been happy to do so—but Theo scotched the idea. I was Theo's assistant now on this movie they were making, and he actually gave me work to do. He told Tilton I was too busy.

My dad and Gordon Fields apparently had patched up whatever fight they had the night Emilio died, and they spent most of the time in my dad's bedroom or study, during which time I presumed they put at least a little effort into learning lines for the movie. And often they were both out by the pool with the physical trainer, who had shown up here rather than Theo's cabin to start getting their torsos in tip-top shape for *High Timber.*

I gathered it had been the physical trainer, Gustav, who had been at the crux of the disagreement between my dad and Gordon, because I overheard Gordon telling the police that he had been with Gustav the night Emilio died. Since then, though, Gustav had been staying in one of the cottages beyond the pool house until summoned to work with my dad and Gordon together, and then he went right back to the pool house. Gordon was spending the nights in my father's bed now.

I won't say my dad was cold to me during this period, but something seemed to have happened between us that I had completely missed. His moments with me were strained, and either Gordon or Theo were always there between us— almost physically, it seemed—and my dad talked in clipped tones and with an edge of irritation when addressing me— and he always seemed to be looking at his hands and trying to keep them in his pockets.

For a couple of days, it seemed like we were moving into a routine, albeit a highly tense one that included regular visitations by policemen, who were utterly polite and respectful, but who kept asking the same questions of all of us all over again. I continued to lie about what I had seen and heard. I convinced myself that it didn't have anything to do with what subsequently happened to Emilio. At the same time, I blotted out of my mind any suggestion that Robert was responsible for Emilio's death. That left me with a possibility I didn't like any better.

By the weekend, though, there was a flurry of activity that changed the routine entirely. My mother returned home in high dungeon from the filming of her art movie in Norway. She didn't return to a house of randy men, though. My dad got prior notice—but not much—of her arrival, and when her pink Mercedes convertible pulled up in front of the ranch house, there were just my dad and me and Efenia to greet her.

She spent her first half hour with Efenia and then the next hour ranting at my dad, ending in a series of instructions that were delivered like bursts from a machine gun and that left no room for discussion any more than bullets would. Theo and Gordon were to take me and the physical trainer, Gustav, on up to Theo's cabin; my dad could jolly well scare up another physical trainer and go to the Malibu house; and the family lawyer would be summoned to the ranch to deal with the lingering police contingent. And, as for my mother, she was going into L.A. to stay with Magda Nadar in her apartment. Now that her movie was in the can, she had obligations to promote it, and she needed to be near the movie studio. Magda conveniently lived near the studio lot.

It was thus that I celebrated my eighteenth birthday— without so much as a telephone call from either of my parents—at Theo's cabin in the San Rafael Mountains above Santa Barbara, where both he and Gordon Fields also had beach houses.

On the afternoon of my eighteenth birthday, Theo sent the personal trainer to Malibu, telling me he was going to take a couple of days to check out my dad's bulking-up progress. I had been training with Gordon for nearly a week myself, and I thought we both were muscling up and trimming down real well. Gustav was nicely built, although his face was ugly as sin—not, however, diminishing his sexual attraction. But as far as I could tell, he, like me—and Robert—was an exclusive bottom. I had plenty of opportunity to find that out while he was still with us, as he slept with Gordon and I'd seen them fucking.

My birthday dinner was just with Theo and Gordon, and they made much of my "being a man now." And they said being a man included being able to take a man's drink. So, along with the steaks and fries and a huge salad, followed by a birthday cake they'd somehow conjured up, they let me have a Scotch and water before dinner and wine with dinner. It wasn't enough to make me drunk, but I had a buzz on when I crawled into bed.

As gag gifts—along with the theme of me coming of age—they gave me a string of condom packets, a bottle of lube, and a pair of skimpy red silk sleeping briefs that they suggested I celebrate by wearing to bed that night.

"These gifts don't embarrass you?" Theo asked after I'd opened them, and laughed as easily as they did.

"Not at all," I answered. "I'm been waiting for this for some time. I've been busting to get to the experience."

"I've noticed that," Gordon said with a smile. "Anyone you got your eye on in particular?"

I did pause then, and blush.

"Not a girl, I don't think," Theo said. "I'd say Chuck Tilton, if my eyes don't deceive me. Seems to me you want to go to the extreme from the starting gate."

I didn't answer—couldn't find the words—but I didn't really need to answer. Theo had been right there when all of the men had been buzzing around me at the ranch like I was a honey pot. And he couldn't have avoided seeing that I had liked that—and had been frustrated about not being able to do anything about it.

"You'd do it right now if Tilton were here, wouldn't you?" Theo asked in a low voice. "You'd do it right here on the table and let Gordon and me watch." I didn't think the drool on his lips was from the steak.

After a paused I responded with a "Yes" in even a lower voice.

"Ahh, well," he said. "you go on into the cabin to go to bed now. I think we've allowed you almost too much liquor. But maybe it will help you to have super birthday dreams."

I left them then, thinking that the evening had ended in anticlimax. I had had fantasies about what my eighteenth birthday might be—the sexual liberation it might bring—and here I was, isolated at the end of the world again. I stripped down and pulled on the red sleeping briefs, put the condoms and lube on the nightstand next to my bed, and turned out the light and drifted into a sleep that—with the effect of the liquor buzz—had me riding the waves in an ocean.

All of the men at the rolling ranch pool party had gotten me in high heat for them just in conversations during the previous two weeks. And here at the cabin, Theo and Gordon had continued with the suggestive talk—they were both masters of this.

Once alone with me in the cabin in the dark later that night, after awakening me from sleep that Saturday night and to desire with the wandering of their hands and lips on my nubile body, Theo sat back in a lounge chair near the bed and worked his hard cock with his hand while he gave direction to Gordon, as the young actor slipped the silken sleeping briefs down over my hips and legs, worked his way down my body with his lips, and opened his mouth over my throbbing cock. Following this, his hand coaxed my thighs apart and cupped and gently squeezed my balls. I was whimpering and sighing and moaning and came rather quickly in the exotic and overpowering experience of my first masterful blow job, doubly impassioned by the deep, rich voice of the powerful movie producer voicing what the young actor would then be doing to my body.

I was well into the experience before I ever realized that this really was happening—that this wasn't the dream I wanted to have and had drifted into.

I arched my back and moaned when Theo told Gordon to spread my legs and go down between them and start tonguing my hole. I whimpered in fear and anticipation when he started talking of what he was going to be invading my channel with and how gloriously filling I would find it. I wondered briefly whether I was supposed to object, to break away and escape, but the pleasure was just too intense, and the young actor's body was just too beautiful.

I was on my back on the edge of the bed and Gordon was standing between my spread thighs, leaning over and sucking on my taut nipples. He raised his head and smiled at me—the smile that sent women all over the world into a swoon. And my dad as well. At the thought, I imagined this was my dad doing this to me—and I realized that the thought aroused me. But it wasn't my dad; it was his lover, Gordon. Gordon wanted me as much as he wanted my dad. That too was arousing. His fingers, which had been working inside my channel, were spreading my entrance, and I could feel his bulb at my hole. I was terrified, but I wanted him.

That was when I heard Theo's voice cutting through the darkness. Husky, thick as molasses. I could sense the lust in him.

"Move aside now, Gordon," he whispered in a hoarse, insistent voice. "I've waited for years for this moment."

Gordon's face withdrew, to be replaced with Theo's. And it was Theo's dick slowly entering me, plowing into virgin territory. And I cried out and moved my hips in rhythm with his as he moved deeper inside me. And I realized that I had been waiting for this for years too.

Theo leaned down over me and whispered in my ear, "Happy birthday, Clint. I hope you are happy with this."

"Oh, god, yes," I replied in a murmur punctuated with a groan. "Finally. Oh, god, yes. I . . . (gasp) . . . hoped it would be like this. Oh GAWD YES."

After Theo had filled and stretched and worked me in my first taking and ballooned out his condom deep inside me, he slowly withdrew from me while taking my lips in his. Then he stepped back away from me and pulled Gordon back into my line of vision.

"Now you," he said.

Gordon took my hips in his hands and turned me onto my belly, and I felt the insistent hardness of him thrusting strongly into me and swiftly and at length vigorously pumping as I groaned and begged him to slow down—but no, to do it just like that. Faster and harder and deeper. I know now—and appreciate—what a master cocksman Gordon was. He fully earned his reputation with theatergoers. His cock didn't just impale and pump; it made love to every square inch of my channel, sending my channel into waves and waves of undulating pleasure.

After he had ejaculated, he made to pull out of me, but I wrapped my legs around him and held his pelvis against mine, dug into his shoulders with my fingers, tightened my channel on his cock, holding him inside me.

He laughed and palmed and squeezed my buttocks. "Want it again, so soon?" he asked. Then he laughed. "Randy little trollop, aren't you. Like father like son, they say. Maybe later."

"No, now," I whimpered. "Again. And then again and again and again."

"Ah, Mr. Insatiable. I guess I could manage . . . such a sweet, sweet ass."

And manage he could, very nicely. And after him, Theo again. And then a recharged Gordon.

Later, after I had been fucked to exhaustion, Gordon pulled me up from the bed and settled me in the chair, and then he fucked Theo on the bed, while Theo watched me, giving me "that" look that told me we would be doing this at every opportunity. And I couldn't think of a single reason to object to that idea.

As I drifted off to sleep, I heard Gordon laugh and say, "Neat trick to get in there before Tilton and the lad's dad. I honestly didn't think he was going to make it to today. Can't get enough, can he? A real find."

And Theo's answer: "I've been working on this particular production for years."

When we left the cabin, there were no condemn packets left the string I'd been given for my birthday.

* * * *

Two days later, when the most physical training Gordon was getting or exercise that Theo was indulging in was between my legs, where they were both flabbergasted at my insatiable appetite for being fucked, Theo received a telephone call from my dad. The police investigation had been concluded. Robert had thrown himself down from the roof of a Las Vegas hotel and left a confession behind. He had killed Emilio in a fit of lover's jealousy because Emilio had been free and easy sexually with guests at our ranch and Robert had wanted him for himself. My mother—Magda Nadar in tow—had gone off to do the morning shows in New York. And my dad was bored and wanted to start up the pool party at the ranch again. The physical trainer my father had found had agreed to switch to pool boy, and my dad was finding him a quite satisfactory substitute for Emilio. Gustav had disappeared from the picture.

And my dad wanted us to return to the party.

Gordon didn't take the news of the new pool boy all that well, and so we hurriedly packed and were on our way back down from the mountains into Santa Barbara for a night at Gordon's beach house, where he regretted to inform us that he had only one bedroom and one bed. We made do with that without a problem, though, with me sleeping between the two and being fucked in alternating entanglements. Once again the two of them were amazed at how much and how often I wanted it. And, while I grieved for Robert, I saluted him for his foresight in knowing that once the dam was burst in my "getting it," I would never be able to get enough.

Robert had once put a phrase to it. He'd said it was mild satyriasis. I had to look that up. The thought that he'd said "mild" was comforting. And it sounded like a much nicer word for it than "slut," "male whore," or "promiscuous."

Neither Gordon nor Theo seemed to object.

In another three days, I was back at the ranch, and the party was in full swing. Within hours, I'd been fucked by all of the muscle hunks who had been the first to show up for the party at my dad's bidding—except for the personal trainer, turned new pool boy, whose name appeared to have been Joe, and Gordon Fields. Both of these guys were in a duel over dominance of my dad—which meant, of course, that he was still managing to dominate them. I was slightly disappointed to find Gene hadn't come back to the party, but I was so besieged with randy suitors that I didn't have much time to think about it.

I was beginning to thinking about this concept of domination, though. I knew now that I enjoyed being fucked. But the more I thought about it, it wasn't the simple act I craved. I also sought the domination. Theo had started this thinking in my brain. He'd picked out Charles Tilton as the one he thought I wanted the most of the men who were on my horizon. I'd thought it was Robert I wanted. But Robert had never shown an indication he would dominate me. And as I thought about it, from the moment I saw Charles Tilton in action, Robert had begun to recede from my sexual focus. Both Theo and Gordon dominated me in their own way— but I didn't shudder at the reality of what they did to me that I did at the mere thought of what Tilton would do.

The afternoon was wearing on. The hometown professional baseball teams were all playing at home, and the day men—I called them day men, because they were the ones who weren't living at the ranch, including my dad, the personal trainer, and me—were beginning to drift away.

My dad had been with Gordon, which means when he came out to the glass doors between the house and pool area and called out the name "Joe"—the personal trainer— Joe's very-well developed chest was pressing down on mine on a lounge, as he leveraged on his bare feet on tiles on either side of the lounge to work his cock ever deeper inside me. It was my first time with Joe, my dad having pretty much monopolized his services to this point, and I was moaning for him loudly as he reached a deeper depth and pistoned harder than most of the other guys could managed. It was a tribute to how hard he worked his body, how much stamina he could manage. He'd been pumping me nonstop for twenty minutes—and, although I'd come and likely would come again soon, it seemed like he never would. And I couldn't get enough of him, running my hands over his hard muscles, glistening with sweat. Listening to his snorts and groans—in full rut. Wanting me so badly that he was fucking me with wild abandon. Robert had told me it would be like this. I was in heaven.

I looked up and my dad was standing in the door, watching us, a murderous expression on his face turning to pique.

"Joe," he said more sternly—not louder, just more sternly. And Joe, knowing who paid the bills was out of me, murmuring "later," and had left me just building toward satisfaction number two.

I laid there after the two had gone inside, still breathing heavily. I thought there was no one else out at the pool, but as I gazed over at the pool house, I saw Andrew Dix, the TV game show host. He was sitting there, watching me, his dong out, cupped by his hand. I hadn't seen Dix fucking anyone the whole time he'd been coming to pool parties. He always seemed to be in it just for the blow job.

I considered him as he was considering me. I hadn't done much sucking. It had always been just a brief prelude to the fuck, and the guys who had taken me so far seemed anxious to get to the fuck. I didn't know if I wanted to spend a lot of time blowing a guy for him to just walk off and leave me when he was satisfied. But I didn't know I wouldn't like it unless I'd tried it a couple of times.

I was saved from whatever I was working up there by a movement I saw over at the corner of the house. Charles Tilton was walking around the house and into the pool area. He was dressed only in low-hung shorts and loafers without socks and a pair of sunglasses. He stopped when he saw me, still sprawled on my back on the lounge, naked, my cock erect and already craving more attention, slightly nodding at him.

He only paused for a moment before he walked over to the lounge, latched onto my wrist in a strong, painful snatch, and pulled me up on my feet. He pulled, almost dragging me, around the pool and to the pathway running down around the side of the pool house back toward the guest cottages.

Half way around the pool house, he slammed my back up against the wooden wall, where he had first cornered me and where he subsequently had fucked Emilio while watching me, and stood there very close to me, facing me. His breathing was heavy.

"Undo them?"

"What? I don't understand."

"Undo my shorts."

I reached down, hands trembling. I was scrabbling at the buttons at his waistband, and, impatient, he slapped my hands away and undid them himself. Then he moved his hands to my waist. He let me unzip him and push the shorts

64

down over his hips, whereupon they fell to the ground. He wasn't wearing anything under them. My hand brushed against his towering hard on, and I shuddered. He smiled an evil little smile at that.

"Kneel."

"Excuse—?"

The heel of one of his now-bare feet hit the back of my knee and I tumbled down, the head of his cock hitting my lips as I went down, and he thrust it inside my mouth, slicing between my lips like a knife through butter. I gasped and gagged as he roughly fucked my face, one hand brutally pressed into the side of my head, the other one fisted into my hair, and moving me in the rhythm he was dictating.

This only lasted a few moments, though. He pulled me up, slammed my back against the rough wood and had his hands under my thighs, lifting and spreading my legs. My ass had been working full time that afternoon, so I didn't pass out as his cock split me—thicker than anything I had had that day. One, two, three thrusts—deep each time. Each time almost exiting, but then thrusting deep inside me. I cried out at each thrust. Four, five, six, seven, eight. My mind counted them like bottles of beer on the wall. Nine, ten, eleven. And then I came up his belly in an ejaculation I'd been building with Joe.

He pulled out of me and I dropped in a pile to the ground, in the narrow space between his legs and the wall.

He was still breathing heavily. I could hear the air whistling through his nose.

"Come to the car. I'm taking you with me."

I raised my head to see him striding back to and beyond the pool, swinging his shorts at his side in his hand.

When he reached the other side of the pool, he turned and looked at me expectantly. I started to rise, my eyes glued to his figure. Desperately wanting more of that. But then, beyond him, standing just inside the house. My dad. Watching.

I did manage to stumble up then, but when I was on my feet, two guys, under my dad's direction, were carrying me down the path, away from the house and the pool—to the cottage where Robert had lived. I entered and collapsed on the bed Robert had recently occupied. And began to cry.

That night, exhausted—more mentally than physically—I was laying on the couch in the lounge. Only a few of the lamps around the tables were on and there was soothing music on the stereo. An opened bottle of Scotch and a half-filled glass were on the coffee table. It was my first—and, according to my plan, the only—glass I would have tonight. Still, I felt the buzz. I hadn't learned to hold liquor yet. I wasn't sure I ever would be able to. Robert had told me I didn't want to go down that route. He hadn't told me I didn't want to imbibe in male sex, though. Robert had his priorities.

My dad came into the room, his own glass of Scotch in his hand. His glass was much taller and had less Scotch left in it than mine did.

He was dressed only in his dressing gown, and the expression on his face told me that this would be "the night." Nothing in my makeup and my peculiar form of innocence saw anything wrong with that.

He said nothing. He just pulled up a footstool beside the couch and sat down on it. The dressing gown below the sash fell away as he did so and his erect cock was exposed. It was a very nice cock. And in recent days, I'd had a lot of opportunity to compare cocks.

He just said one word, in the form of a question. "Clint?"

And I only answered with one word, in the form of surrender. "Yes."

One of his hands went to the fly of my sleeping pajama bottoms, and he was holding my cock, which was rising for him, telling him in its own way it was OK. I heard and felt his intake of breath and looked steadily into his eyes, which were glittering with anticipation. He began to stroke me slowly, in long strokes. His thumb was on the head of my cock, which was producing precum for him. I moaned and my pelvis went into an involuntary anticipation.

"Slow, please," I murmured. "All the others can't wait. Inside me, please. But slow, deep."

"Oh, Clint," he murmured. His hand on my cock was trembling.

I was only wearing the bottoms, and his other hand began to glide around on my chest and then went up to the back of my neck, and he was lifting my face to his. We kissed.

While we kissed, I possessed his cock with one of my hands. When he pulled away from my lips, he leaned over and kissed down my sternum and belly, and his lips opened over the head of my cock and descended to the root. I moaned and moved my lips to the head of his cock.

And then the world was lit up. I heard the front door slam back hard against the wall, and my dad was jumping up and stepping away from me.

I raised my head and looked over the back of the couch. My mother, standing in the door, swathed in some sort of white, fluffy fur that set off her platinum hair and long white kidskin gloves nicely. Diamonds at wrist and neck and ears sparkling brightly. The premier Hollywood actress entering the scene, commanding the scene. Behind her, looking down, deceptively chastely at the marble floor tiles of the foyer, but with a satisfied little smile on her face—Magda Nadar.

My mother only had one, commanding, definitive word for my dad. "Upstairs."

And he turned and fled up the stairs.

To me she had only a few more words. "Pack. I'll have Grayson drive you to the Malibu house." Good old Grayson, Mother's long-suffering chauffeur and gofer—always at her beck and call, because my mother did not drive. She famously had told the world that it interfered with her drinking.

Rather anticlimactic words, but ones I'll never forget. Because they were the last words my mother ever spoke to me.

Chapter Six: Death of Innocence

I was alone, isolated from everyone, left to stew in my own juices far too long in the Malibu house. It was quite a shock treatment after the freeing debauchery I'd experienced the past week. Grayson stayed for two nights. But Grayson was no help to me. He was a fat, ugly, old man—completely sexless. If I were to cast a eunuch for one of my parents' foreign locale fantasy films, I could have done no better than Grayson. I'd been fucked almost nonstop since my eighteenth birthday. And I had loved it. And I had been made to go cold turkey. I could have come down from the high—if it was gradual. I'm sure I could. But cold turkey was making it worse, keying me up. I needed a man between my legs.

The day in between the two nights I had to lay in bed alone, listening to his hoarse snoring and knowing there wasn't anything he could do for what I needed—at least Robert would have held me in his arms and rocked me to sleep—Grayson went shopping for enough food for me to fix for myself for the next two weeks and to fetch my airplane ticket for Philadelphia and the instructions for the line of credit that had been set up for me to draw upon. My mother didn't call; my dad didn't call. I had no trouble understanding that they were separating from me. No one else knew I was here—no one with muscles and a smile and a hard cock.

I lay at night, continuing the scene with my dad that my mother had interrupted. Remembering what I had requested of him—being surprised that I had. I had thought I wanted from him what he gave Emilio that last night. But that wasn't the case, I realized. That's what I wanted from Charles Tilton. I wanted tenderness from my dad. I wanted him to pick me up from the couch and carry me up the stairs and to one of the guest rooms—not to his room, where he and Gordon slept, or to my mother's room, where she and Magda had made love. And not to my room either. But to one of the guest rooms, with no memories other than those that my dad and I would build. And then I wanted him to lay me on the bed on my back, take a pillow and put it under the small of my back, raising my channel to him—like I'd seen in a video of his, not like what the hunks had been doing to me for days, attacking me like animals in heat, not being able to fuck me hard and fast—and often—enough.

Then I wanted him to go down between my legs with his head and make love to my entrance with his lips and tongue until I moaned and begged for him. And then kneeling between my legs, never taking his eyes off mine, slowly, ever so slowly, entering me and entering and entering and entering, holding there, deep inside me, his eyes telling me of what a special experience it was for him, as it was for me. Holding—until I begged. And then starting a slow pump as I writhed under him and cried out for completion. Filling me with his love and his essence.

Sweating, having brought myself to a troubled, release, I flopped back on the bed and moaned. I thought it unfair. It wasn't my fault—well, not wholly. At least not completely.

There was no indication that my mother had split from my dad either. I had Grayson set up newspaper delivery for me—and I did so solely to peruse the entertainment section for any hint of a break between Scott Sloan and Laura Lake. All I found were reports of the crew for the movie-in-the-making *High Timber* departing for northern California, for Eureka. The actors and the producer, Theo Kline. No mention was made of Charles Tilton in the earlier reports.

And then, days later, I saw a brief mention of Rex Barnard as the director of the film. Just the one, though, and that always could have just been a one-off mistake in reporting, I thought. One of the reports said the Scott Sloan's wife, Laura Lake had gone up the coast as well.

Neither one of them contacted me about that; I had to read it in the newspaper.

I did receive another telephone call. It was from Theo Kline's office. On behalf of Kline, one of his secretaries thanked me for assisting him for a brief time on setting up the organization for the movie. He had a new assistant now, though, and he knew I would be entering a university back East for the fall session. A check for $5,000 would be in the mail. She didn't flinch at naming the amount. I'd put in less than a week of work on that job. No doubt, though, she was well versed in how Hollywood worked. I was the son of two major actors. Favors were done, palms were greased. She saw the $5,000 as a typical good-will gift signaled to my parents. I saw it as the cost of my virginity. I'd only been given the job so Kline could maneuver me into the mountains and be the first one to get his cock inside me. I was truly a whore now. I'd given it up for $5,000. I wondered what the going rate for it was in Hollywood.

I didn't resent that, though. It was probably a sign of the weird value system I'd been raised to, but I appreciated the work Kline had put into being the first one inside me. In some ways he'd been more of a dad to me than my dad was. He—along with Robert, of course—had been the only one who actually spent time trying to find out who I was, what I wanted to become.

It didn't bother me in the least that Theo had done this or claimed his "first" prize. If I didn't shrink from the thought of my dad fucking me, why would it bother me that Theo did? He had taken me out on the ocean several times on his yacht, the *Final Curtain*, as I was growing up. And although while we chatted during these outings he was quick to tell me that there was a place for me in motion pictures if I wanted it, he spent some time and effort asking me what I wanted to be.

I remember, no doubt being influenced by a movie my parents had just made, telling him once that I thought I'd like to be a police detective. Theo had a collection of *Ellery Queen* magazines on his yacht, and, impressionable lad that we all are at that age, I had been mesmerized about the prospect of being a detective. When I'd said that to my dad, he had laughed. Theo didn't laugh. He just told me that there were no bad jobs—just people who couldn't do jobs needing done very well. He looked hard—in a playful, grandfatherly way—at me then and told me he thought I'd make a splendid detective. And I never forgot that.

The shock of moving from an orgy to isolation had the unfortunate—or fortunate maybe, who can say for sure—effect of making me think over the events of the past couple of weeks.

Robert had been right about me—so right. All of the things he said would be set loose inside me when I turned eighteen and gave vent to my natural desires and frustrations had come to pass. He'd also told me not to fight it—to enjoy it to the extent I could—but to try to start learning to protect myself. I had to think about that. I didn't think I'd done too well about protecting myself yet. But it was so hard. Obviously my mother and even my dad had been pushed over the edge when my dad had finally come to me. I would have to think about that. Apparently there were some limits that I hadn't been taught—that I should think about and start developing.

But I was still the innocent. And I remembered what Robert said about that too. That I'd be the innocent until I begged for it. That not fighting what other men wanted, going ahead and letting them take it, wasn't marked against my innocence. It would be when I went to them—and begged them for it—begged them for what I knew would be degrading.

Thinking about such things was really too much for me at this age, and if I hadn't been left all alone, in a stark switch of activity, I wouldn't have thought even that deeply. And thinking that deeply started developing the doubt in my mind. The doubt was about Robert. It was Robert who had me thinking about the state of my innocence, and, at length, my thoughts turned to focusing on Robert.

How could he have murdered Emilio? Robert wasn't like that. My dad was the last one I knew to have been with Emilio, and he was beating Emilio. And there was the figure in the corridor that night. A man or a woman? I couldn't remember which—if I'd ever known. And there was something else, something that had prompted me to leave my bed in the first place. But what was it? I couldn't remember. I remembered calling out Robert's name, but that's only because the person could only logically have been Robert—or Efenia. Only Efenia had a room in the house, though. Robert's cottage was on the other side of the pool. But Efenia wasn't that tall—or slim. It was someone else, I was sure of that.

And jealousy. What jealousy? Emilio was a bottom—I never saw him topping anyone. He was always the one being fucked. And Robert. That had been our problem, the two of us—why we'd never made love. Robert said we were both exclusive bottoms. I just didn't know. I didn't know enough about these matters.

Wanting to clear my brain to take another cut at the logic of it all, I stood and went out to the balcony overlooking the ocean.

The kiters were out, flying their fancy-structured, many-colored kites along the beach, taking advantage of and using the breezes coming off the water to make their kites dance high in the air.

They looked so free and elegant. I loved watching them. I wanted to be free like that—to dance on the breeze like that.

One of the kites went off balance and careened down to the sand up the coast from the house. My eyes followed the line of descent.

I never saw the kite hit the ground, though, because I first saw him. Slouching against his car on the road above the sand dunes, dressed just in shorts, loafers, and sunglasses. Just standing there, looking at me. Bad boy incarnate. The forbidden enticement every parent warned their child to beware.

Charles Tilton.

He didn't gesture. He didn't have to now. The isolation had been too much for me. I descended the deck steps and started to walk toward him—and then to run, feet digging in, pounding on the sand, stumbling as I lost my footing, but rising right back up and recklessly running on.

He stopped the car ten miles up the coast toward Ventura on the Pacific Coast highway, turning away from the beach into an isolated picnic area, deserted on this weekday. He parked the car as far inland as possible, the trunk pointed away from the ocean. He roughly pulled me out of the front seat of the car and around to the trunk and slammed me down on my back on the trunk and jerked my shorts down.

He fucked me hard and long and deep there, each thrust moving my bare back on the sun-baked surface of the trunk. Seven, eight, nine. He didn't stop. He kept pumping. I had held my breath until he reached eleven strokes, afraid he'd tease me again and pull out. But he didn't. He kept on fucking. And my spirit flew up into the air and floated like a kite on the beach. He lowered his teeth to my nipples and punished me. I gasped and groaned and moaned and loved every deep stroke of it.

I came fairly quickly. He didn't.

After arousing me for a second time, he pulled out of me and I slid, exhausted, off the trunk and into a heap on the hot pavement. I begged him to continue fucking me. He laughed.

Tilton opened the trunk then and took out a car blanket. He walked away from me, into the verge of some spindly-trunked trees gasping for life in the salty ocean breezes, opened the blanket out on the ground, and laid down on his back, his erection still reaching ambitiously for the sun.

Then he just stared at me. After a moment, I walked over to the blanket, straddled his hips with my knees, positioned his cock head at my entrance—and fucked him to his completion. Doing it all myself. One more step away from innocence.

He said nothing as we drove up the coast toward Ventura.

I, though, couldn't get enough of him. I asked him to pull into another picnic area and fuck me again, but he just laughed. Then I begged him, reaching for his cock as he drove and trying to take it in my mouth, but he roughly pushed me away, into the corner of the seat and kept on driving.

When we reached his beach house, he dragged me up the steps and into the house and pushed me into the cushions of a couch. He went into the kitchen and took a beer from the fridge and popped the top. Turning, he leaned against the kitchen counter, took a deep swig, and then stared at me, holding the beer poised in his hand, half way between counter and his mouth. He was wearing a sneery smile. A victor's smile.

I stood up from the couch and started to roam around, checking out the layout of the beach house. The living room, dining room, and kitchen were on the upper level, where the best view of the ocean was, with two bedrooms and two baths below. Everything was tastefully and expensively furnished—at least until I got to the room on the road side of the downstairs, which must have been the second bedroom. The room was bare of recognizable furniture. The floors and walls and even the ceiling were covered in thick carpeting, in black. I don't know why I knew, but I did know that it was for sound proofing. The two windows were shuttered tight.

I stood in the doorway, trying to figure the furnishing of the room out. It was very much out of synch with the rest of the house. There was a sling of shiny black leather suspended from the ceiling by chains in one corner. And, in the center was a vinyl cube-like thing. Wide strips of heavy-duty webbed material were attached to the four corners at the bottom and straps hung down from the upper corners as well. There was a closet, with folding doors, which were half open. I walked over to the closet and folded the doors out.

75

The back wall of the closet was a Masonite board with attachments on it holding a panoply of sex gadgets and toys—whips and restraints and leg separators and dildoes and balls on strings—all things I'd seen in my dad's stash of magazines and had fantasized about. At the corners of the rooms were stands with video cameras on them, backed by other stands with studio lighting dishes on them. Wires ran from these back to the corner of the cube, wires with clickers on the end.

I felt him behind me, close behind me, chest touching my back, knees touching the back of my thighs, a powerful cock rubbing on my back. He was naked. His arms came around me and he was palming one nipple and my belly with his hands.

"Come into the other bedroom." He whispered to me.

"What do you do in here?" I asked.

"What do I do? I do my special guests in here. You aren't ready for this. Come into the other bedroom."

"Please, I want to know. I want to know it all," I said.

"You have no patience," he said. And then he laughed.

"Please, I beg you," I whimpered. And then I turned and went down on my knees and rubbed my cheek on his dick.

"Oh, very well . . . since you begged," he said.

And then he gathered me up in his arms and carried me over to the vinyl cube and pushed me down on it on my belly. My wrists and ankles were bound to the restraints at the bottom corners, and he was behind me, hunched over me.

"You want it, boy, you got it. We begin." I was blinded by the studio lights when they flashed on, and I heard the whirring of the video cameras start. I heard him laugh and then I felt the coldness of the beer bottle at my entrance. He worked the neck of it into my ass, tipping it over until beer flowed down inside me and around the neck of the bottle and down the insides of my thighs.

I cried out and then whimpered as he began to slow pump me with the neck of cold beer bottle.

"Had enough? Want to go home?" he asked in a gruff voice. And then that deep-throated laugh again when I whispered no, that I wanted to stay.

He pulled the beer bottle out of my channel and then he grabbed my hair in one fist and arched me back sharply while slamming his cock deeply into my ass and making me cry out in pain, surprise, and passion.

I didn't care. I begged him not to stop—ever. And he didn't for nearly a week.

* * * *

One Sunday morning, three weeks after I started at Penn State—having already declared that I wanted to study toward a criminal investigation degree—I heard a tentative knock at the door of my small, off-campus apartment.

I rose from the bed, trying not to disturb the football player deep in sleep from the exertions I'd put him through. He snorted, but didn't awake, just rolled over and embraced a pillow and moved his pelvis in a motion that had become a habit in the night. I quickly and silently pulled on jeans and T-shirt and padded out into the living room in my bare feet, closing the bedroom door gently behind me.

I opened the door to two serious-faced men in well-pressed black suits standing patiently in the outer hall, probably hoping that no one was home.

My dad's Bentley had careened off the Pacific Highway between Ventura and Malibu and down onto the rocks at the edge of the surf in the early hours of the morning. Indications were that my mother was driving and that the car had left the pavement at high speed. They had both died instantly. Magda Nadar was organizing the memorial service. It would be a major Hollywood event.

I knew my dad and mother would have liked that.

I was truly all alone in the world now—and now completely dead to innocence.

Numb after the two black suits left, I padded back into the bedroom and rolled the football player over onto his back. He was hard, in the throes of a wet dream, and

77

muttering dirty words to himself. I'd picked him because he was one big muscle of glistening dark chocolate, could go ten thick inches, and for the tattoos. I mounted him, easily slid down his pole, and began slowly to ride his cock. He didn't fully waken, but he responded naturally, encasing my waist with his big hands and helping to raise and lower me on his staff. I lowered my lips to his chest and traced the lines of the tattoo there with my tongue. Then, I moved my face to the hollow of his neck, the tears from my eyes rolling down his neck onto his tattoo, while I rode and rode and rode. The only way I could think of to combat this numbness I felt.

Death in Manhattan

Chapter One: The Gang Leader and the Professor

"Let me go in and check with the captain again."

"Thank you, that would be helpful."

The young woman had been giving me the once over, several more times than once, in the more than an hour that I'd been sitting outside the captain's office after the appointed hour that he'd summoned me for. And I think that if I had been sitting here more than fifteen minutes more, she'd have asked me if I was married and would pointedly have told me that she wasn't. But I already knew that she was and that her husband was a big bruiser and jealous as all get out. And he had every reason to be. I'd been clued in that she dropped her skirt for every good-looking young cop who came through this office. She was good looking enough; her problem with me was that I wasn't remotely interested in women.

I hoped this was about the detective's exam. It was the first time I'd taken it, and guys weren't supposed to pass it until something like the third time. But I'd felt pretty good about it. And I had more preparation than most cops on the beat. I had a masters in criminal justice from Penn State. And I'd been on the job here in Richmond, Virginia, for two years.

I could have stayed in Pennsylvania after Penn State. I'd been recruited hard by the Philadelphia force. But I wanted someplace not so cold—and someplace not so dangerous. Not dangerous in terms of life threatening—one shouldn't even think of being a cop if he was going to let that bother him. But dangerous in terms of what was just waiting to happen. I'd been ripe for the assistant football coach my first year at the university; it hadn't taken much for him to corner me in the locker room shower after everyone else was gone. After two years of that, though, he'd told me I was too old for him, and he'd left me alone—not that I wanted to be left alone. Since then he seemed to want them younger and younger every year. I didn't want to get embroiled in what I knew would come down about what he was getting away with. What I hadn't called him on. So as soon as I had my master's degree in hand, I skipped the state.

Thinking about that as I sat waiting to see the captain made me start thinking why this captain might have summoned me. He'd never done so before, and this wasn't my direct line of command. I was just a traffic cop in the 3rd precinct—the cushy West End of Virginia's capital. If it wasn't about the detective's exam, what was it about?

I hoped I'd been discrete enough about my personal vice. I knew it was enough to get me bounced off the force, but I had my needs. Maybe I was feeding my needs too close to home. I went to the clubs in Shockoe Bottom fairly frequently—well, increasingly frequently—but I tried to maintain a low profile. I'd only stay around long enough for the right guy to make the right proposition. I didn't exactly scream to the world why I went to those places. And if there was any hint of seeing another cop, I'd split.

But this led to me breaking out in a sweat. Alvaro Flores. Had Internal Affairs gotten wind of my linkup with Alvaro Flores? God, I hoped not. I hadn't known that Alvaro was head of the Latin Kings gang in the city until after we'd fucked a couple of times. And after I knew, I made sure not to hook up with him anywhere in public. I should have given him up, of course. But I couldn't do that. He could cock with the best. And I was so weak in that realm.

I first met him after I'd had a really rough day. Three teenagers had wrapped a car around a telephone pole near the campus of the University of Richmond, and I'd been the first one on the scene. Their bodies were in rough shape, and it had been overwhelming and disturbing. When I got off work, I wanted to blow off steam, to forget what I'd seen. And when I was in a mood like that, I wanted it rough. Alvaro and several other guys in leather had come off their bikes and into the Barcode club on East Grace.

He'd been what I wanted—a mean-looking tall Hispanic, all tattooed and muscled up and dripping with attitude. And I obviously was what he wanted too, as he gravitated right to me. He had me lapped at his table in quick time. I could feel his want for me, and it was making me pant for him. I think he would have taken me right there. I told him he could do what he wanted with me, but not there. So, he fucked me tied to his cycle in a shed where they probably were chopping cars. I didn't care what they were doing, as long as he didn't stop what he was doing.

That led to almost weekly encounters, during which I got my fix for the rougher side of sex. I was sure I'd been discrete about it. If the department had found out, though, that could very well be the reason I had been summoned to the captain's office. And if so, I could kiss the detectives' exam—

"Captain Stevens is ready to see you now, Sergeant Folsom." She was batting her eyes at me. I could almost feel her palpable need for me to show interest in her—to ask her out. That gave me a bit of strength as I moved to the door to Captain Stevens's office. She was his secretary. She did his typing and filing. If what Stevens had called me on the carpet for was about having sex with a Hispanic gang leader, she'd hardly be trying to get me to hook up with her. Besides, Captain Stevens was the deputy chief for operations. If they were on to me about hooking up with a gang leader, it should be the deputy chief for Internal Affairs' office I should be entering.

"Ah, Sergeant Folsom—may I call you Clint?—please shut the door and take a seat. I'm sorry I kept you waiting, but we're putting together a very important sting operation."

He hadn't given me time to say "yay" or "nay" to the informality, but I'm sure that was on purpose—to show his authority. I'm sure neither one of us believed for a minute that I'd call him Seymour.

I sat down and we eyed each other for a moment. I saw his initial smile turn into a more serious expression. "It has come to my attention that you are involved in a behavioral issue, Clint."

Here it comes, I thought. He couldn't even say gay activity, no less than fucking around with other men. My personal weakness was to be that I had a behavioral issue—not that I was a satyriasis and craved to have men's cocks inside me. Or that that had nothing to do with how good a cop I could be. I wondered if it made any difference that it was a gangster like Flores. Then I answered my own question—of course it made a difference. I was cruising where I knew I shouldn't be cruising. Good cops don't do that.

"I understand," I said. "You need go no further." I started to rise. I was already wondering what I could do with a masters degree in criminal justice if I couldn't be a cop. Maybe go for a law degree now? I didn't need a salary. I didn't even know how a cop could live on the salary they were paid. How much deeper did I need to bury my wants and desires in the next career?

"Please sit, Clint. The basic issue is something we can address later. For now, it seems that the position you've attained can be a great advantage to us in this sting operation I'm working on."

Oh, shit, I thought. He's going to put me undercover with Flores. I never told Flores I was a cop. He never asked; he was also too anxious to get inside my ass. I was never really a person for him. Just a depository for his lust. Not that I cared. But I'm going to go undercover inside Flores's gang and he's going to find out and I'm going to die. Then there will be no more personnel "situation" for the Richmond police department to be concerned about.

"Are you with me, Clint?" Stevens interjected into my racing thoughts. "As I said, we need not address your actions. I need you to help with our sting operation on Kwame Jackson."

"Kwame Jackson?" I was shocked. It was the same issue really, but I didn't think in a million years that it would be Professor Jackson who the department had connected me with rather than Flores.

"Yes, I've been informed he's quite attentive to you and that you have his trust—that you spend a couple of nights a week at his home."

"Kwame Jackson is a respected professor at the University of Richmond. Yes, I've been seeing him—and for the purposes you seem to have concluded. But what's the department's interest in Jackson?"

"He is one of the biggest drug dealers in the city and is a direct conduit to a major supplier of drugs in the United States."

"I don't believe it," I answered, sinking into my chair, the wind having been completely knocked out of my sails.

Kwame Jackson taught southern history at the University of Richmond. I had decided that if I was going to live in the South, I needed to get a better feel for its history and culture. I was basically a southern California boy, so neither history nor culture had meant much to me before. But as soon as I moved to Richmond, I realized that here it mattered very much. You couldn't get anything done in Richmond without an appreciation for how the South worked.

I had signed up to audit Jackson's class. Being a little older than most of his students and more assertive, I had gotten his notice in class. Well, as he told me later, it was my remarkable resemblance to my movie star father that had first got me noticed. He was a movie buff and knew my parents' work well—both of them were box-office stars in the era in which Jackson was following films closely. He was a contemporary of my parents.

Jackson had invited me to his home to look over the memorabilia of my parents' movies that he had collected. I went, but not because he wanted me to see his collection. I wasn't nearly as impressed with my now-deceased parents as he was; I had known them a lot better and more intimately than he did. I had gone more because he was one beautiful black man. Although in his late fifties, he was in superb condition and had the mulatto best-mix of Caucasian and black features that Jamaica, where he originated from, was famous for. From the first day I had attended his class, I had been mesmerized by his looks and the fluid way he moved around on the stage during his lectures. And I had quickly turned to imagine how he looked without the tailored suit and silk tie he always wore to class.

At his home I found out. He didn't really want to review his movie memorabilia collection either. He wanted to fuck me. And I let him. After I nearly hyperventilated at the beauty of his naked body and magnificent jet-black equipment, I stripped for him and turned my belly to his sofa, draped my arms and chest over the sofa's arms, raised my rump to him, and moaned and sighed as he covered me, slowly and completely possessed me, and fucked me to heaven.

Since that evening, as Captain Stevens had discovered, I had been in Kwame Jackson's bed overnight at least twice and sometime three times a week. And I'd yet to be bored by the working of that magnificent black cock inside me.

"We don't want you to stop seeing Jackson, Clint. We want you to cultivate his interest and trust. He somehow obtains large quantities of cocaine that enter from South America into Florida and is selling it on the University of Richmond campus—through students of his who he is controlling through sex. It's quite possible he is cultivating you to distribute for him too. He doesn't know you are a policeman, I surmise?"

"It's never come up. He went directly to my affiliation with Hollywood. I don't live the lifestyle of a policeman on

86

the university campus. He probably thinks I have no employment—and don't need any."

"Good. That will work to our advantage. If he's cultivating you, we wish for that to continue. The ideal will be if you can be with him when he gets the drugs from his supplier. You will, of course, work with us on this."

It hadn't been a question. And considering what Stevens knew—even if he didn't know about Alvaro Flores and the Latin Kings gang—the only other choice I had was to just get up and take a walk away from a career in law enforcement. I wasn't ready to do that. As nice as Jackson's cocking was, if he was a drug dealer to university students, he deserved to be put away. Besides, his wasn't the only cock in town. I was very good at proving that.

"Yes, certainly," I answered. "Just tell me what you want me to do."

* * * *

I didn't have to pretend that I was lost to him. I was laying, twisted, on Jackson's bed, my torso flat on its back on the surface of the bed with Jackson's torso hovering over me and his lips crushing mine. I was laying on one hip, with my buttocks cuddled into Jackson's groin. He had just ejaculated inside me, and he was slowly jacking me off with his hand. I came for him with a groan and a sigh.

We remained there for a few minutes, both lightly panting.

"I want you again," he whispered when his lips released mine. "I can't get enough of you."

"You don't have to ask," I murmured. And, indeed, he didn't. I'd help track him down if he was a drug dealer, but I'd let him fuck me any time he wanted to. I'd come to his jail cell for it, if it was permitted.

"Gotta make a stop," he said. "Gotta get hard for you again."

He pulled his softening cock out of me and turned and rolled out of the bed and onto his feet. This was becoming a ritual with him. He'd fuck me and, emotionally, he'd want to do it again right away. Physically, though, he needed time to recharge. He'd leave me and go into his bathroom, and shortly afterward, he'd reappear in full erection. And then his second cocking would be longer than the first, working me for longer before he ejaculated again. I, of course, had already shot off a couple of times.

I gave him a few minutes and then, suspecting what I'd find—and that it would be what I wanted to find—I left the bed, padded over to the bathroom door, and slowly pushed it open.

Jackson was huddled over the sink cabinet. He held a rolled-up banknote in his hand and was leaning over the surface of the cabinet. A piece of paper lay on the cabinet surface, with lines of a white powder on it. He was snorting a line into his nose.

"Can I have some of that too?" I asked. It quite obviously was cocaine.

"You snort?" Jackson said, turning his head toward me and showing surprise in his face.

"Sure. I move a little of it too. You should have seen some of the parties my parents' crowd had in Hollywood." This part was quite true. But neither I nor my parents had taken the drugs. At least I hadn't. Who could tell what my parents had been willing to do?

He stood up from the counter and handed me the rolled-up banknote.

"Enjoy," He said. "There's a lot more where this came from. You've been enjoying the longer fuckings from the effects of it. No reason why you can't dance on the clouds along with me when we fuck."

I leaned over the counter, turning myself so that he couldn't see that I was running the end of the rolled banknote alongside a line, rather than on it, and pushing the cocaine away with the other hand.

"Ah, sweet," I said. "I see you're hard again and I'm already dancing in heaven. Let's fuck."

I gave him the fuck of his life then—trying to show him that the cocaine had enhanced our lovemaking.

Afterward, as I lay in his embrace, I started pushing the nickel.

"Great stuff. Where do you get it from?"

"I've got a connection in Florida."

"Gotta get me some of that," I murmured. "Wasn't that sex incredible? Just think of what we could do, swingin' on the clouds together."

"Ever flown in a single-engine plane before?"

* * * *

"He says he has a Cessna Skylane he keeps at the Middle Peninsula Regional Airport near West Point, over toward Williamsburg. Says when he needs a new supply he flies down to near Miami. He seems to think he can fly under the radar."

"He and a bunch of other drug dealers," Captain Stevens said, with a snort. "And a lot of them seem to be right. If you can get on one of those flights with him and get a GPS aboard, we'll be able to follow him down. We can get his phones tapped and see who he's talking to on the other end. Then we can start putting together a bust."

"I can try to make the connection, yes," I answered.

"Scared?"

"Shit yes."

Jackson was on a high the day we flew down. He was so proud and taken with himself, showing me how smart he was that he said he couldn't wait for some sex. His plane, a single engine Cessna Skylane, was tied down between two other small aircraft behind a hangar. Before he had me release the tie downs, he pulled me into the backseat of the plane and I rode his cock. Seeing as how I assumed it would be our last time, one way or the other, I gave him a good ride, and after he was finished, I turned and slipped down on my knees between his legs and cleaned his fat, jet-black cock for him.

I told him I was as exhilarated by the adventure we were going on as he was, and he believed me. "Exhilarated" wasn't what I actually felt. "Scared spitless" was closer to the mark. I was more afraid of whoever he was dealing with on the Florida end than I was of him. But I was a cop. And I wanted to be a detective. If this was to be my one and only sting investigation—if I was going to be thrown out of the department as soon as this was over even if I survived it—I wanted to make this one a good bust—if this, indeed was the day.

Jackson hadn't told me before we took off that this was a drug run; he'd only told me that he was taking me for an airplane ride today. I thought I could tell by how keyed up he was, though, that this was the real deal. Chances were good that it was just a dry run, but he seemed too tense for that. And Stevens and his team were ready to suffer several false starts if that's what it took to reel Jackson and his supplier in.

I was glad Jackson wasn't telling me ahead of time when we were going for drugs—or even for sure that this is what he used the airplane for. If I wasn't given the details beforehand, there was no reason for him to believe that I had ratted on him.

"So, you asked about how I got the white stuff," he said after he'd gotten us up in the air. "Rather than tell you, I thought I'd show you. That's how much under my skin you are. I'm willing to cut you in on this cash cow."

"Yeah, you can count me in." I tried to sound excited about the prospect.

I wondered how many other students he'd fed this line to and suborned to push drugs for him on campus. Was this all an act with him—was he just using his gigantic dick and great body to recruit guys—and maybe girls too—to put their futures on the line for him? The possibility that this was what was happening—and that I wasn't as special for him as he was letting on—helped take the sting out of what I was about to do.

"Sound great to me," I repeated after a couple of moments of silence. "So, we're going for some stuff?"

"You could say so, yes."

"But I don't understand how this works."

"It's not hard. This is a big country and law enforcement is spread thin, thanks to the economy—and the immensity of the drug supply and demand. So are the aviation authorities—spread thin. I've got a system that keeps working."

"Great," I answered, holding my breath on whether he was going to explain it in detail for the commo link I'd stuck up under the instrument panel dashboard. And then he did.

"This Skylane has a souped-up engine and extra oil tanks. We can go faster and longer than the specs indicate. I file a flight plan for Tampa Bay. Then, as you can see I'm doing now, I swing out over the ocean and ride the waves low all the way down to southern Florida. My contact has a different camouflaged airstrip in the Everglades designated each time for a pickup. After we do a quick exchange, my cash for his crop, we're up in the air again, and curving out over the gulf, toward Tampa Bay. We arrive there ahead of time or right on time for the time and distance this baby is listed. It's so simple that it works every time. Used to be that airfields up and down the flight line checked in with pilots and spotted for planes. No one has the manpower to do that anymore, and there are a hell of a lot more small planes up here than there were a decade ago."

"Sweet," I said, with a whistle of appreciation—and a hope that Stevens's team got it all on tape.

Then I sat and prayed—prayed that the team wouldn't lose track of the plane and that this wouldn't be the day that Jackson's supplier decided to stop doing business with him and shot him—both of us—and took the cash without providing cocaine in return. That was the big unknown in all of this—Jackson's supplier in Florida.

But it was set to be just another simple deal completion.

The supplier, a mean-looking fat Colombian no doubt enjoying the delights of Miami Beach under a false political asylum privilege, was wary of me being there beside the plane while they made their exchange, but he carried through with the turnover. And he just sighed and motioned for the two goons with him to lower their machineguns when police roared in from all sides and pinned us all down between

Jackson's plane and the suppliers' Escalade. He was already on the phone to his lawyer before the cops got out of their cars.

I couldn't have been happier when I was roughly pushed down on my face on the tarmac along with Jackson and his friends and was manhandled as badly as they were. We were all bundled into separate vehicles for the trip out of the Everglades and back into Miami. The separate vehicles were employed so that Jackson wouldn't suspect that I wasn't going the same place as he and his friends were going. I didn't have a chance to check that out, because I never saw Jackson again. The Richmond police made sure that my testimony wasn't needed. They worked out a story that showed they'd busted the operation from the Florida end.

I was soon going back to Richmond, though, to face the music for an entirely different dance.

* * * *

"I have good news and bad news, Sergeant Folsom," the deputy chief for internal affairs said as I sat on the other side of his desk in Richmond police headquarters on Broad Street. The office of the deputy chief for operations, Seymour Stevens, was down the hall. It was significant that I was here in Internal Affairs now rather than in the Operations area— but I couldn't say I was surprised.

"What's the bad news?" I asked.

"Ah, I think you'd like to hear the good news first," the captain answered. He was being almost jolly. He was enjoying this. He was one of those florid-faced Irish types. He probably celebrated for three nights in a row when he was able to drum a gay guy off the force.

"OK, then, the good news first." I was being calm and droll. I wasn't going to give him extra enjoyment time.

"First, congratulations on your part in the bust of a major drug ring supplying Richmond. I'm sure there will be a commendation for that—although you won't be here for the ceremony."

Just as I figured.

"OK, the bad news."

"Wait. There's more good news."

Oh, goody.

"I'm happy to be able to tell you that you passed your detective exam."

I could have leaped for joy—if I didn't know that you couldn't be a police detective if you no longer were a policeman.

"But the bad news—for us, because your recent participation in the drug sting indicates that you would be a great asset to this department—is that you, of course, can no longer serve in this department. It isn't just because there is a rule against not declaring you are gay—and, yes, we know of your involvement with the Latin Kings gang leader, Flores, too—but it's also because those behind this major drug supplier you've just helped us catch might come looking for you here. So, if you want to stay a cop, we're going to have to move you."

"Want to stay a cop? If I want to stay a cop? I have that option?"

"Yes, of course. We're a small department here. But in some of the larger cities, men with your skills and . . . umm . . . your proclivities can serve effectively on special teams. The New York City police department is prepared to offer you a detective position on a special homicide squad. That is if—"

What could I say—and how fast could I say it? Not just staying a cop, but also making detective on a homicide squad so quickly.

"If . . . ? When do I need to show up to the assignment?"

Chapter Two: Keystone Cops

"Uh, oh. Hans has just walked into the bar. I think he's looking for me. We'd better split off. I should be working a mark."

I looked toward the door. Boxers NYC, a gay sports bar in Chelsea, was crowded, and the crowd that was there was teeming and boisterous, watching four different games on the overhead plasma screens and trying not to watch where the hands of the guys next to them were roaming. I thought it would take a few seconds for the mean-looking bruiser at the door to see us, and I needed to follow this lead further.

"Hans? Hans who?" I asked. "You in his stable? Maybe you can put me in contact with him."

I was talking to Marcus Dent, a young rent-boy who my new lieutenant, Burton Kahn, had put me onto in a case of two male prostitutes who had been brutally murdered in hotel rooms up near Madison Square Garden. There was some evidence the two had been brought up from the Chelsea gay bar district by the perpetrator. There were reports that the two of them worked this bar. Burton had given me a list of names of guys identified as friends of both of the victims. I was to try to fill in the dots.

"Hans Gelber. He's just the handler. It's all much bigger than that. He's gonna look this way. I gotta split and look like I'm working a mark. I can check if he's adding to the stable and let you know if I see you again."

"Did he pimp for Bernie and Tony too?"

Marcus gave me a look half way between suspicious and frightened. Bernie and Tony were his friends who had been offed. I hadn't told Marcus how they'd been killed; we were keeping that out of the paper. If I had told him, he'd be peeing his tight little pants now. They'd both been bound to beds and tortured and fucked with something larger than their channels could take. They'd also been sliced and diced. But I hadn't told Marcus this. I didn't want to panic him before I got all of the information out of him that I thought he had to give.

"I mean," I continued, "if they're gone maybe he has room in the stable for me."

"Yeah, maybe. But he won't like seeing me talk to anyone but a john—and you don't look like you need to pay for sex. So, please . . ."

I rose from the table as unobtrusively as I could and muscled my way through the crowd and over to the bar. The guys behind the bar were stripped down to their waists and wearing either silk boxers' shorts or tight football pants with big jock cups. I ordered a beer, turned half way around, leaned back on the bar, and surveyed the room. I wanted to get a good view of Hans Gelber, and I did spot him sinking down in the chair I'd vacated at Marcus's table. Marcus still looked frightened. Gelber was leaning in on him. He had Marcus's forearm in a strong grip and he was whispering something to Marcus that wasn't calming the young, spiked-hair rent-boy any. I managed to shoot off a couple of photos of Gelber on my cell phone without being too obvious what I was doing.

"You a friend—maybe a colleague—of Marcus's?"

I turned toward the voice and came up with a real hunk—muscular on top and trim at the waist; dark, sultry looks, with black curly hair; and dressed conservatively but expensively.

"Maybe both," I answered. I looked across the room to where the guy from the special homicide squad who had come out with me, Danny Thompson, was sitting at a table. He was being chatted up by two twinks, who, big, black bodybuilder bruiser that he was, he could have taken together. He looked like he was engrossed by what they were offering, but I could tell that he had one eye on me too.

"Anyone ever told you you looked like a young Scott Sloan? Scott Sloan, the actor."

"Yeah, I know who you mean. And, yes, I've heard that more than you can imagine." I'd heard it far more than he could imagine simply because Scott Sloan, the actor, had been my father.

"So, are you a friend of Marcus's too—or would like to be?" I was trying to make out the connections that had this guy talking to me. Was he part of the gang Hans Gelber was in?

"I've been a friend of his now and again, yes. But I'll have to say that you are more my type than Marcus is. Maybe we could be friends too."

"Maybe," I answered. The guy didn't look like he needed to pay for sex. I was trying to track down whoever had hooked up with both Bernie and Tony and then done them dirty. Maybe I'd taken a shortcut here. It was certainly worth a checkout.

I brought his face down close to my lips. And immediately after I'd touched him, I felt his hand go to my thigh. "You don't look like you need to pay. But I don't go for free," I whispered in his ear.

"Marcus doesn't go for free, either," He answered, with a smile. "I understand how it works. I've got a hotel room."

I had a bit of a panicked moment here. I couldn't be taking this across town. The only backup I had was Danny. This had just been meant as a feel-out of Marcus Dent for where he might fit in the gang. I was wired so that we were speaking in Danny's ear. But I couldn't maintain backup and be getting in any cross-town taxi.

"Umm, I don't know. I'm meeting someone here in an hour or so. I've got to stay close by."

"My hotel room is just up the block. You could be back here in an hour or so."

"OK, then, lead the way."

97

I signaled Danny to follow us as we headed for the door of the bar. The rest of the time we were walking down the block, toward the Gramercy Park Hotel, I spent trying to review the rules of engagement I'd had thrown at me right before we'd left the squad room. I knew I wasn't to proposition him and just was to allude to answers while he pitched me. And all the time I had to do it without revealing I was a cop.

We didn't make it to the Gramercy Park, though. He turned me into what was probably a fleabag version of that hotel a block before we got there. We were both looking around as we scooted up the steps and slipped into the entrance. He was probably looking to make sure we weren't seen by anyone; I was looking to make sure that Danny saw where we had gone.

We sort of beat around the bush in the hotel room, which wasn't half bad in furnishings, if not the cleanest place I'd ever been in, on who was going to do what to who for how much. I was sitting on the bed and we were talking about nothing in particular other than playing avoidance on how each of us knew Marcus and in what way. I was sitting on the bed and he was pacing around the room. When I thought I'd seen him tugging his shirt out of his waistband, I pulled my T-shirt over my head, being careful to take the hidden mike with it and keeping the shirt near my hip for acoustical purposes. The pace picked up from there. He came over and sat down on the bed beside me and pulled his shirt over his head as well.

The man was built, and he had half moons of black curly hair under his pecs and a line of that hair provocatively trailing down his sternum and down under the waistband of his trousers. I liked that.

I had heard him taking in his breath when I'd pulled off my T, so I could tell we were both impressed.

I probably went off the rulebook at that point, but I figured I could always write it up differently later if this was our guy. I moved my hand around to his waist on the other side of him. At this signal, he put his arm around my shoulder and pulled me into him. We kissed, and, I swear, if he wasn't someone I was trying to take down, I would have been all over him at that point. He was a real hunk.

"How much?" he asked, when we'd come up for air.

"Uh, fifty for oral; a hundred for, you know . . . OK?"

I needed him to say OK and then I'd have him for solicitation and we could take him down to the precinct house and grill him on the rest. Instead of answering, though, he snaked the hand of the arm around my shoulder under my armpit and grasped my pec, while his other hand went down to my belly and we were into another deep kiss.

I couldn't tell after that whether he was getting more intimate or had put me into an incapacitating hold. I sort of thought the latter, and my impression really was that he was the torture serial killer. I had a couple of seconds to consider what I was going to do to put him down.

But I only had a couple of seconds, because the common door between this room and the next was banging open and all hell was breaking out. All hell consisted of three cops from the Vice squad and one cop—a hot-under-the-color Danny Thompson—from Homicide.

There was a moment of panic and embarrassment and then we were all laughing our asses off. I had been measuring a Vice cop by the name of Brad Roberts for a serial murder charge while he was working on collaring me for male prostitution. The catalyst was Marcus Dent, the twink rent-boy we were both cultivating in the Boxers NYC bar. Roberts and his crew were trying to wrap up the sex stable Marcus was in, and Danny and I were trying to link the stable—and maybe the men behind it—to our serial murder case.

The other guys were joking around enough that Roberts was able to whisper something in my ear without them noticing it.

"I think you felt something too. After we clear this up, want to meet me someplace for a drink?"

One of rules of the special unit I'd joined in the NYPD was that I was in a unit that not only tolerated but used homosexual activity in its work The lieutenant who appeared on duty at the same time I did had repeated that over and over again. The kicker was that the one place I was not to practice it was in the workplace. "No fucking other cops," he had said. Of course, as time went on, he saw it happening and just looked the other way. I'd been in the unit for nearly a year and I'd already been involved with two other cops on the NYPD force, a guy I'd even lived with briefly, Pete, and now, in a more torrid arrangement, frequent encounters with Danny. And this didn't count some of the encounters I had with other cops while at conferences and doing liaison work with departments elsewhere up and down the eastern seaboard.

So, I should have told this Brad guy "no" right then and there, on the spot. But he was such a hunk and I was already being balled by the black bruiser on my own team, Danny Thompson, so, naturally I said OK.

We met at Splash, a discrete, dimly lit club on 17th Street. Brad showed me who was boss from the beginning, which was OK with me. I liked a man who took charge of me. He paid the cover, ordered our drinks, paid the tab, said we'd go back to his place, and he fucked me three ways from Sunday on his queen-sized bed, on the thirty-fourth floor in front of a full-wall glass window with a panoramic view of the city.

I got a good look at the city lights, because my head and arms were flopped over the side of the bed, while he held my legs spread out and up and pistoned me hard with his cock. So furious was his fucking that I kept sliding down toward the floor until my shoulders were on the carpet. He just swung his legs over the side and stood on the floor and kept jack hammering down into me until we both had come.

That left both of us breathless and panting hard until we'd cooled down. Then he reached down and pulled me up. He pivoted and slammed me down on the bed on my stomach. I felt his hands on my hips, pulling my knees up to support my weight, and then he was crouched over my hips and fucking me like a dog.

A good time was being had by all when our cell phones rang—both of them. He scrambled for his on the nightstand on one side of the bed and I for mine on the other side.

"Speak!" he said into his phone and "Yes?" I said into mine.

And then, almost in unison, we both said, "Oh, shit. I'll be right there."

* * * *

He was bound to the bed in the hotel room—this time it really was the Gramercy Park in Chelsea—at all four points. The bruising and torn skin at his ankles and wrists indicated that he had struggled hard—and fruitlessly—at the sexual torture. This was also shown in his bulging, lifeless eyes. His mouth had been stuffed with what would probably prove to be his own briefs. He had burn marks all over his body, and his ass channel had been stretched and torn by some not present—as far as they had discovered yet—object or objects. They would have to wait for the autopsy to see if he had also been fucked by a man.

It had only been a few hours since I had been talking with Marcus Dent in the Boxers NYC bar not more than five blocks from here. I had a fear at the pit of my stomach that he was dead because he had talked to me. I had a sudden urge to track down this Hans Gelber guy Marcus said was his protector and rattle him until his teeth fell out.

I had gone directly to the hotel, where I was met by my lieutenant, Burton Kahn, and Danny Thompson and others from the homicide squad. The forensic team was already on the scene and was antsy about getting into their work.

"This was one of the guys on the list I gave you," Burton said.

"Yeah, I know. I met with him last evening at the Boxers NYC bar. He did a little talking, but I sensed that there was more he was going to tell me. His pimp came into the bar, though, and I had to split off. I'll bet he was brought right here. I have a photo of the pimp on my phone. Here, this is him. Marcus gave his name as Hans Gelber."

"Yep, that's him," Burton said when I showed the photo to him. "He's pretty low in the pecking order, though. We're after Bruno Meister, who we think is at the top of this chain. A German crowd muscling in on all sorts of organized crime in this town, including prostitution—both male and female. I'll put out an APB on this Gelber guy, but I'll bet he's already home in Frankfurt and ready to live again on a new name. Ah, here are the other guys working this now— Vice."

I turned and my attention focused in on Brad Roberts, who was arriving with a gaggle of other detectives.

Introductions were made around the room and both Brad and I did what we could to act like we'd never seen each other before—even though half the guys in the room had seen us stripped down to our waists and in a lip lock the previous evening on the double sting screw-up we'd all been involved in. They hadn't seen us after that, though, when Brad was pounding my ass in his apartment.

I went off and talked with Danny, who was in a foul mood and kept eyeballing Brad, while he paired off with the Vice detectives. Our respective lieutenants talked the situation over and then Burton spoke to all gathered.

"It seems our investigations are merging at this point, so we're going to put our teams together. Folsom from Homicide and Roberts from Vice will team up as point men on this and both teams will work it. The sooner we can shut this German ring down the better. We'll give Roberts a desk at Homicide for the interim."

My heart skipped several beats. This was both wonderful and tragic at the same time. I had sensed a special connection with Brad Roberts in the night, but there was this rule about not fucking around with other cops. It was bad enough I was giving it to Danny Thompson. I didn't know how this was going to work out.

I could tell Danny wasn't sure, either, and was concerned about what was happening. He got all possessive on me. He didn't let me out of his sight all that day, and he insisted on coming back to my rooms in the near-tenement I lived in—by choice, as I didn't want to flaunt that I was sitting on a huge inheritance.

When we got there, he forced my back to the wall and frantically pawed and kissed me while he stripped me of my clothes. Then he brutally doggy fucked me on the carpet of the living room and dragged me into my bedroom. When we'd both recovered from the first fuck, he grabbed my ankles, jerked my legs wide, and jack-hammer fucked me.

It was just the way I liked it from him. But from his intensity, I sensed that he felt threatened and intended to fight for position and possession.

Chapter Three: Challenge for Commitment

I was at full stretch, on my side, along the body of the young Hispanic man, Trax, embracing him while he, laying on his back, his legs spread wide and heels dug into the cheap chenille coverlet of the hotel room, moaned in the taking he'd just endured from Danny Thompson. I didn't think he was faking his exhaustion from the cocking Danny had just given him. Danny had a monster cock, and he knew how to use it. And although Trax was a professional rent-boy, I didn't think he'd been at it long. He also was so small of stature that I'm sure he had a tight ass—or had had one before Danny just reamed it out for him.

Danny was working on me now, holding me from behind and sidesplitting me as I consoled and kissed and ran my hands over the limp body of the young Hispanic. It was all part of the "getting the lad's trust" scene we were working out with the young rent-boy we'd targeted in the Boxers NYC gay bar in our efforts to corner Bruno Meister and his German crime ring that was currently working New York City.

Brad Roberts was sitting in a straight chair across the hotel room, glowering at us, and slowly stripping down. I knew he wasn't happy at seeing Danny fuck me, but Danny hadn't been too happy either in the possessive attitude Brad had taken toward me since we'd been thrown together on the Meister case.

As for me, I enjoyed getting fucked by them both. They were both masters in their respective ways—and I couldn't get enough of good cock.

Trax had been on our list of young male prostitutes working the Chelsea district who we thought were linked to the German gang. We'd set him up at Boxers NYC, which seemed to be the center of the activity. And we set him up in such a way that we didn't think he—or his handlers—would figure out that we were trying to worm our way in the organization. We had been too forward with Marcus—in trying to get information out of him directly. He must have ratted out that someone was asking too many questions and had been silenced for reporting it. This time, we were going to try to get one of us—me—into their stable, where I could see what was what all by myself.

Neither Brad nor Danny had liked that idea, but I insisted that I be the one. They were both tops. Although the organization likely had tops, it was much easier to get inside as a bottom, I reasoned.

We had set it up with me being propositioned at a table at Boxers NYC by both Brad and Danny.

We had waited for Trax, a willowy and short, feminine type, to swish by the table, and Danny shot a hand out and pulled the little Hispanic onto his lap. Trax rewarded him with a squeal of surprise and a little giggle. I was sitting across the table. Brad was there too, draped all over me. Neither one of us minded that part.

"Whoa, there, little one," Danny said with a jovial tone in his voice. "I'm told you are for sale."

"Who told you that?" Trax squeaked. He made an unconvincing effort to get off Danny's lap, but Danny held him close and began moving Trax around on his lap so that the little Hispanic could feel what Danny was packing. Trax rewarded him with a shudder and a low moan and seemed to collapse in his laugh.

"We're trying to convince our new friend, Angel here"—Danny was motioning toward me—"to go to a hotel and do a little partying with us, but he's afraid to go alone with both of us. So, we thought we'd just add to the party. What'cha say? Up for a little party?"

"I don' know," Trax answered. "I'm not supposed to—"

"Two hundred and fifty for each of you."

"Two-fifty for each?" Trax and I said it almost simultaneously. Trax's eyes bugged out, and I tried my best to act surprised and awed as well.

"Yeah, but my friend and I here each get a go or two at each of you. Show them the money, friend."

Danny looked at Brad, and Brad put his hand down the front of his jeans and came up with a wad of money. I made to reach for it, but Brad palmed it and pulled me into him for a deep kiss.

"But not together—not both of you together?" Trax asked in a pleading voice.

"Not if you don't want it. If we want it, we'll sweeten the pot."

"Well, I don' know," Trax said again.

"Here. We'll give each of you your money, and you can give it to the barkeep of your choice to hold for you."

Trax looked dubious.

"Com'on, man," I said for the first time. "That's a big chunk of dough. I won't go alone, but both of us should be fine. Com'on, let's take the money to the bar."

My well-timed interjection won the day. Trax didn't act in the least like he suspected we were setting him up.

They took us to the same room in the same flea bag hotel up the street from the Gramercy Park where Brad had taken me on our abortive double sting. I'd since learned that the police permanently booked both this room and the room next to it, where their surveillance equipment was set up.

I went into a standing clinch with Brad inside the room, while he stripped off my T and jeans. Danny was doing the same to Trax—perhaps a bit more intimately than Brad was doing with me.

"Sit that one on the bed, friend," Danny commanded, and Brad sat me on the side of the bed.

"You, Cutie," Danny motioned to Trax, "Suck off Movie Star here." Danny was indicating me. Trax knelt between my spread thighs, took my cock in his mouth, and started to suck me off. Danny stripped and crowned his cock. Then he stood Trax up, so that he was leaning down into my lap, and began to play with Trax's hole with, first, his tongue and then a lubed finger.

Trax grunted and groaned—but he didn't lose purchase on my cock with his mouth—while Danny slowly entered him with his cock. But my dick did pop out of the little Hispanic's mouth and he embraced my waist with his arms and held on for dear life, cursing and crying in broken Spanish, as Danny picked up and wishboned his legs and began to wheel-barrow fuck him hard and fast.

Brad had pulled his shirt off his back, but then sat down in a chair and watched the performance, which went on for quite some time, before Danny grunted and pulled out of Trax's ass. He slipped the used condom off his dick and picked Trax up and threw him across me onto the surface of the bed, where Trax rolled over onto his back, legs spread, and moaned.

Recrowned, Danny pulled me off the bed and thrust inside me, which I rewarded with a cry that was in no way feigned. I could tell that Brad was about to jump off his chair, but I gave him an "it's all right look"—which it was—and Danny continued embracing me from behind and giving me a standing fuck, while Trax watched, entranced.

Danny didn't finish me that way, though. He picked me up and placed me on the bed, stretched full length along Trax's body, and then held my leg in the air and began to side split me. I tried to act like it was all new and overwhelming. Danny's fuckings were always naturally overwhelming, but I wouldn't say they were new.

That's when I embraced and used some time consoling with Trax and building up a rapport between the two of us.

When Brad thought there had been enough of that, he stood up, slipped off his briefs, came over to the bed, and took hold of Trax's ankles. Brad pulled the young Hispanic down to the foot of the bed, spread his legs, pushed a hard cock inside him, and began to slow fuck him. Trax arched his back and his hands went over his head. I grasped one of his hands in mine, and he looked up at me with a face of camaraderie and appreciation as we both were being fucked.

The expression in Trax's face had changed. Whereas he had reacted as if Danny was brutalizing him, he responded to Brad's fucking as if they were making love. A little shiver of regret went through me that I recognized as envy that Trax was getting something that I wanted. I enjoyed sex from both Danny and Brad, but this was telling me that maybe Brad was special. Trax seemed to realize and appreciate it. Perhaps I needed to put more thought into what I really wanted from a man—and what a guy like Brad had to offer.

When Brad and Danny had dressed and left—just to go into the next room, but Trax didn't know that—he and I lay on the bed in a full stretch embrace.

I started to shudder with almost suppressed sobs. I must have feigned that well, as the young Hispanic took me in his arms and began to rock me.

"There now, that was worth two-fifty, don't you think?" Trax murmured to me.

"Yeah, I guess. It's about ten times what I usually get."

"Ten times? You're shitting me. You must have one grabby pimp."

"I don't have one," I answered. "I just started doing this on my own. It's a hard way to make money."

"Yeah, sure, the way you're going about it—if you ever take only twenty-five for a fuck. You're a real hunk. That guy called you Movie Star. That's not an exaggeration. You could make a lot more."

"I don't know how I could."

"Hey, I know a guy. You could maybe join the stable I'm in. You could make a lot more than you are."

Trax took me to a seedy bar in a basement on 23rd Street. It was a dive that wasn't even on our radar for the Meister gang investigation. I knew that both Danny and Brad were out there somewhere, but they didn't follow us into the bar. We would have had to case the joint out and have dropped in a couple of times beforehand to be comfortable with one of us doing backup in the bar. I knew, though, that they were somewhere nearby. I had both a bug and a GPS device sewed into one of the calves of my jeans.

Trax took me to the back corner of the bar, where there were booths with high backs—dimly lit cubicles where pretty much anything could go on unnoticed, although as intimate as some of the guys were being out in the open, I didn't know what they expected they needed to hide in the booths.

"Dieter, this is the guy I called about," Trax said as we walked up to the booth.

I tried my best not to hyperventilate on the spot. The man who Trax had called Dieter was the man I knew as Hans Gelber. A presumed lieutenant in Bruno Meister's organization. The man who had been running the brutally murdered Marcus—and, before him, the equally dead Bernie and Tony. The man we all assumed had been pulled back to Germany following the murder of Marcus.

* * * *

"You may go now, Trax. I will speak with your friend here alone. Angel, you say his name was?"

"Yes, Dieter. He's my friend, Angel. Didn't I tell you he looked like one? He's good. I thought you might—"

"Yes, yes, quite a looker he is. Go to Wolfgang at the bar. He will take care of you. Here, Trax's friend, Angel, sit next to me."

Trax gave me a frightened look—and I wanted to give him a frightened look back, but I held onto my cool as best as I could and didn't reveal how nervous I was. Hans Gelber was already on his cell phone, and I heard the buzz from across the room. A mean-looking hulk of a man at the

110

bar put a cell phone to his ear. Hans turned to the wall and whispered into his phone. Trax walked off toward the man at the bar. I looked in desperation at the entrance, hoping to see Brad or Danny enter the bar. But they didn't. The man at the bar—presumably Wolfgang—was standing up from his stool. I pulled my cell phone out of my pocket, making sure Gelber couldn't see that I had it out, and fired off a couple of photo shots in the guy's direction from the hip. But I had no idea if I'd caught him on film.

I saw no more than that because Gelber was pulling me down into the booth, facing the back wall, and I barely had time to slip the phone back into a pocket of my jeans.

"Trax tells me you give good fuck," Gelber said. "You certainly look like you're worth top dollar. Let's see how you perform."

He had taken one of my hands and guided it to his crotch, while his other hand had unzipped his pants. I fished a good-sized cock out and started giving him a hand job. He pulled my T-shirt over my head, momentarily moving my hand away from his dick, but when he got it over my head, he grabbed my hand and returned it to his tool. While I stroked him, he tossed my T under the table and started prodding and exploring my torso with his hands, like I was some prized horse. He unbuckled my belt, opened the fly of my jeans, and pulled my cock out. He measured that with his hand, giving a grunt of approval, and was weighing my balls in his hand when I went under the table, kneeling on my T, and between his thighs and started giving him serious head with my mouth. He was lengthening out to a good eight inches with my attentions.

He didn't let me finish him, though. He hauled me out from underneath the table, brushed my jeans down and off my legs, and pulled my channel down on his cock, with me in his lap, facing the wall.

Clutching my waist with his strong hands, he growled, "Fuck yourself. Show me you're worth a hundred dollars."

I leaned over the table and gripped the opposite side of the countertop and began to raise and lower my channel on his deeply embedded staff and to rotate my channel back and forth, changing his gears and listening to him breath heavily and grunt and groan in the pleasure of what I was giving him.

Again he didn't come, though. He heaved me off his lap and pushed me out to a standing position beside the booth. I wildly looked around, but neither Trax nor the man presumably named Wolfgang were at the bar. There was no sign of either Brad or Danny either.

"Let's take this upstairs," Gelber said in a low, hoarse voice.

I stooped beside the table, searching under it for my clothes. I needed the jeans; they contained the GPS tracker and the bug—and my cell phone, with, hopefully, the photo of Gelber's confederate on it. But Gelber pulled me back up and turned me toward a doorway at the back of the room that was covered with a beaded curtain.

"Leave them. You won't need them."

I stumbled with Gelber not so gently pushing and maneuvering me through a dark corridor and then up a wooden-treaded staircase to the floor above. The corridor here had a window at the end of it, so it was somewhat lighter, but only somewhat. There were several doors leading off the corridor, and I could hear the sound of male sex coming from the other side of more than one of them.

Gelber pushed me to a door and banged it open. He propelled me across the threshold. I only had a moment to see that there was a double bed with some sort of framework over it in the center of the room and walls and ceiling lined with full-length mirrors before I arched my back with one arm being pulled painfully up to my shoulder blades from behind and Gelber's other strong arm whipping around my neck and pulling me into a sleeper hold.

Although I struggled against him, this was useless, and I quickly blacked out.

When I was conscious again—and only barely so—I found I was paralyzed to any hope of movement. My back was on the bed, my wrists were cuffed to the headboard, and my legs were stretched and raised, with my ankles cuffed to chains leading up to the frame above the bed. Gelber was between my legs, fucking me deeply. And I felt the sharp edge of a knife under my chin, pressed lightly against my windpipe.

"Back in the world of the living—if only briefly—Mr. Cop?" Gelber snarled. "You didn't think I saw you with Marcus in the Boxers bar the night we took care of him? He gave you up as a cop before he gurgled his last."

"Umm, ufff," was about all I could answer. I was still pretty much out of it, but in trying to speak, I realized there was a ball gag in my mouth. Gelber obviously wanted this to be a quiet session.

"Trax was right about one thing. You certainly are a movie star looker. So, I'm going to get to come with you and then we're gonna have a little slice and dice party. Ain't that nice? I'll start trimming you down as soon as I come, so you'll probably want to give me a good, long fuck."

Trax was the first word that got through to me. I worried about where he was; what had happened to him. Gelber would think that Trax knew he was leading the police to Gelber. But we didn't even know that we were being led to Gelber. And Trax didn't know we were police—and probably didn't know much about Gelber either.

My second concern was for myself. Surely Danny and Brad would show up eventually, if I wasn't coming out of the bar soon. So, I concentrated on letting Gelber come to the brink of an ejaculation, but then holding him off. If anything, he seemed to enjoy the prolonged fucking.

But there came the point when I knew that he couldn't be held off any longer. I felt him shudder and jerk and give out a deep grunt. There was a moment of suspended time when I knew he was savoring the ejaculation, and, despite my dilemma, I was on a high too, as he could reach deep inside me. And then I felt the knife moving from my throat and up to the side of my head. I realized that he was starting at an ear, and I felt the first prick of the knife and him holding my head down steady, my cheek buried in the surface of the bed. I prayed it would be a clean sweep of the knife.

But the cut of the knife never came. The room was bedlam, and Gelber was being pulled off me. I saw a flash of dark brown muscle and knew instantaneously that Danny was pulling Gelber off me and struggling for the knife. I had a flash of Brad's face in front of mine, showing a concern that seemed to go deeper than just one cop for another. He left me to help Danny subdue Gelber, and then he was back. That's when I heard the sirens. Brad later told me that they'd been going on longer—that he and Danny had been afraid they'd tip Gelber off before they could decide which room we were in and get to us.

I was still groggy as the medics carried me downstairs on a stretcher. I had insisted I was OK—that there was no real damage other than a sore neck from the sleeper hold and an arm with a dull ache, but they insisted on taking me to the hospital.

"If he checks out OK, they'll probably still keep him overnight," the head medic told Brad. "He'll be too spaced out to be walking around on his own."

"I'll take him to my place, if they'll release him to me," Brad said. "I'll make sure—"

He was interrupted by a shot. We were in the street by the ambulance and Danny was escorting a handcuffed Hans Gelber up the basement steps from the bar. Gelber went down in a splash of red and Danny was just standing there, looking down at Gelber's body in disbelief and shock.

Brad and I turned in time to see the assailant flee from across the street. Only later was I able to tell them that it was the guy I'd seen at the bar named Wolfgang. And it was only then that Brad told me that it wasn't the first time that night they'd seen the guy successfully flee the scene of a crime. He and Danny had come in from the back of the bar, figuring that I had been inside too long. If I was still dealing with something, they figured they could eyeball me from a door from the back.

They had encountered the conclusion of the Wolfgang guy slicing up Trax in a back corridor immediately upon entry, though, and they'd let him slip away in their haste to get into the bar and help me if that still was possible.

The only thing certain was that we'd finally caught up with Hans Gelber—for all the good a dead body would do us.

* * * *

"I thought for a few minutes—between the time we found Trax's body and when we were able to find what room you'd been taken to—that we'd—that we'd . . . that I'd . . . lost you."

"And that would not be a good thing?" I asked. I realized I hadn't slurred my words. I was getting better, coming out of the haze, although my neck still felt like hell.

"Decidedly not a good thing, yes," Brad whispered. He was cradling me in his arms on the big bed in his bedroom on a platform right beside a window wall looking out over the lights of Manhattan.

"Umm, it's nice up here," I murmured. "I could stay here forever."

"Yes, you could," Brad whispered. "Here in my arms forever. But," his voice changed, "I'll bet you're wondering how I can afford a place like this—whether I'm on the take."

"I hadn't thought about that, no," I answered. "But it's sure nicer than my place."

"I try not to let it get spread around in the precinct, but I'm a trust baby. I was left a pile. I'm a cop because I need something to do with my life—I do it because I like to."

"I do this because I like to too," I murmured. I'd taken his cock in my hand and started to stroke it and slap it against my belly.

"I'm serious, man. Some guys can't take that I can afford what I want. They resent being a kept man."

"Then we're twins," I said, with a laugh. I was holding our dicks together and slow pumping them. Brad was breathing heavily. "Because I'm a million-dollar baby too. I just don't have your good taste."

"Seriously?"

"Yep."

"So, it's true what the guys down at the precinct whisper—that you really are the son of those movie stars."

"Yes, I'm afraid so—but, like you, I try not to flaunt it. It's not money or fame that I earned."

"Then you think you maybe could live in a place like this?"

"Until we can find an even fancier place, yes," I answered.

"What are you telling me?"

"I'm not telling you—I'm going to show you."

"What? How?"

But I was already turning him on his back and straddling his hips. I moved his cock to my entrance.

"Hold it. Be careful."

"My neck can take it," I answered.

"No, not that. Over in that drawer," he murmured. "Condoms."

"No. This is what I'm going to show you. Skin on skin. Full commitment. I've been told by other guys that's what you want. Someone permanent, fully committed. Don't worry. I'm tested often."

"Oh, god. Oh shit," Brad moaned as I sank my channel on his bare cock. I grabbed his wrists in my fists and held his arms over his head and looked down into his face as I started to slow pump myself on his cock. The look he returned was equally intense. Surprise, pleasure, what I would come to understand was the look of love.

"If that's what you want too," I whispered.

"Oh, fuck, oh, shit. Yes, yes," he cried out.

"I'll quit the special homicide unit," I declared. "It'll just be you and me fucking. If that's what you want from me, that's what I'll try to give."

Brad had no idea what that meant I was giving up. I was a male-on-male satyriasis—someone who couldn't get enough of male sex. I loved cock. And I loved variety in men. I knew Brad could give me loving. But could he give me variety? Could I really do with just Brad? I'd have to try.

"It's what I want," he answered between groans as I pumped him. "But I know you want more than this."

116

Suddenly he was rolling me over and bringing me up on my knees and elbows. An arm wrapped around my belly from behind and he was straddling my hips. He began fucking me hard and deep in a jack-hammering pace, and my hips moved with him, meeting him thrust for thrust.

"Oh, god, yes," I cried out.

He came up with red silk cords from somewhere, and he was tying my wrists to the headboard.

"I know you want it like this sometimes, too," he murmured.

It was going to be quite a night. Just the sort of night I melted to.

Chapter Four: A Missed Assignation

The night of free-form debauchery didn't erase reality, and early the next morning Brad lowered the boom.

"That was very, very nice," I said over a cup of morning coffee while I perched in one of Brad's robes and nothing else on the bar stool at his kitchen counter. I made sure it was open so that Brad knew I wanted to exhibit myself to him.

"Yes, it was, as a one-time deal—for now."

"One time?" I was shocked. Was he cavalierly rejecting a commitment from me that had required far more than he could ever imagine?

"Of course you can't give up your special unit assignment yet," he went on. "We still have a gang to break up, and you know as well as I do that we'll do whatever we need to do to get to the heart of this case."

"Oh, yes, I see."

"Believe me, I'm not blowing off your offer, and I do want you to move in with me and for us to keep to just each other as much as possible. But I don't think it would be wise to go without protection until we can get this case solved and rearrange our lives. I'll make adjustments too. It doesn't all have to be you."

"OK," I said after a long pause. Then with a grin, "So, should we go back to bed and try it all again with condoms—just for comparison sake?"

"No. We're both late for work."

"Work? The doctor said—"

"If you can do what you did last night, there's nothing wrong with you. The sooner we track down and dispense with this Bruno Meister, the sooner we can get to reordering our lives."

I had to admit he had a point, but that didn't mean I didn't maneuver him back into the bed for another quick fuck.

Danny wasn't the least bit pleased to see Brad and me come in to the precinct together that morning. He saddled up to me as Brad was going to his own desk and started to say something. But I waved him off with a reassuring smile that I didn't feel on the inside of me. Danny's cocking would be the hardest thing for me to give up in this new life Brad and I were pledging each other to. And this was something I couldn't just blurt out to Danny. He deserved to have a private conversation about this.

"Clint, I have to—"

"Later. We'll talk later, Danny. We do need to talk, but we've got to get the case moving again this morning. That takes priority. Losing Hans Gelber means we have to regroup. But . . . thanks for saving me yesterday."

Without waiting to hear what he clearly still wanted to say, I turned to the room and chimed out, "Gather round the boards, boys and girls. We need to reweave the threads on the Meister case."

"No, unfortunately, we don't," a voice boomed out from the doorway to Lieutenant Kahn's office. The voice was Kahn's. We all turned toward him. He was looking grim. Standing beside him, was the chief of Vice, Brad's boss, Chuck Steele, who wasn't looking quite so unhappy.

"We're standing down on this case," Burton Kahn said. "Orders from on high. Word is that the Meister gang is pulling back to Germany and so are going out of our jurisdiction. With all the department has on its plate right now, as long as the gang is leaving town, that's good enough for them. Chuck here and I have been conferring, and we've agreed we might as well close down right away. Chuck wants his Vice guys back. They've got a full docket."

I could tell that Burton wasn't quite as pleased as Steele was over this turn of events, and looking around the room, it was obvious that no one else on the team—other than maybe Danny—liked to hear that our efforts were being shut down. I could already hear the wheels spinning in Brad's mind, and I realized that this meant we didn't have to wait to make good our commitment to each other.

I should have been euphoric. But the closing out of the Meister case came as a big blow—and the sudden realization of what total commitment to one guy, no matter how satisfying, really would mean was causing a lump to form in the pit of my stomach.

* * * *

Neither Brad nor I closed our own files on the Meister gang. Brad stayed with Vice, but I transferred over to the regular Homicide unit, although Burton Kahn stayed in touch with me and I did some incidental work with his unit with the only stipulation being that I wasn't on the hook to actually engage in sex during an investigation. There was also another limit that Burton and I agreed to. I stayed away from Danny Thompson in any of Kahn's cases I worked with. I figured that Danny was the greatest temptation facing me in trying to stay committed to Brad, and so I stayed away from him to the extent I could. Danny, of course, didn't like it. I never did have that conversation with him that I knew he deserved, either.

Danny's response was to try to make me jealous—even to the extent of dating women, especially women I knew. He eventually started seeing one of the intake clerks in Homicide, Sharenda, who I had become friendly with. She'd come in to work with a glow about her and would drop broad hints about someone keeping her real happy. Danny made sure that I knew that it was him. And he was right that it made me jealous. But every day I spent with Brad assured me that Brad was worth the sacrifice. Without letting her know why, I encouraged Sharenda to keep on monopolizing Danny's time.

Brad and I had been sticking with our effort of commitment for nearly two years before circumstances intervened. The Meister gang both helped us with that effort and was what eventually upset the balance. We both concentrated on doing our individual jobs well, but we also both kept our ears to the ground for any hint of the Meister gang renewing its activities in New York. We thought it was just a bit too convenient that the case had been immediately closed after Hans Gelber had been shot. Gangs like that don't disappear overnight. We both figured, though, that someone in the police hierarchy must be on the take and had protected the gang when it was most vulnerable. For that reason, whatever Brad and I found, we brought home to discuss and did our best to cover our hunt from others in our respective units.

Somewhere along the line, I got the idea that Brad was collecting more than he was sharing with me. Often when he didn't know I could see him, he was fiddling around with putting papers in a hiding place in the kitchen that I knew about but that he'd asked me not to get into—unless something happened to him. I scoffed at anything happening to him, but I respected his privacy and didn't snoop.

Having a close-held project to work on together like the Meister case helped hold Brad and me together. As for the rest of what kept us going for nearly two years as a committed couple, I lay most of the credit for that on Brad's efforts—and his forbearance for my weaknesses. I tried, but I was weak. I would be good for weeks at a time, and then I'd have a tough homicide to deal with or I'd just get the itch, and I'd go to a bikers' bar, get half blotto, and wind up in bed with a couple of guys for the nasty sex that Brad couldn't quite give me—but Danny could have if I gave in to him—and my resolve would be blown all over again. I'd go with strangers just to avoid going with Danny and making matters worse.

Brad took me back after each one of these falls from grace—and he wouldn't rag on me about commitment and my weakness. But in those nearly two years he also never got to the point again of letting us have unprotected sex. I kept striving for the day when he'd trust me enough for that to happen—which would signal our attainment of a committed couple. But I knew it was my fault that it hadn't happened. Still, I was trying my best, and Brad was being patient with me.

What changed everything after almost two years was when Sharenda appeared at my desk with a young, blond, twinky guy at her side.

"Clint, sorry to bother you, but this young man was sent over from Vice to talk directly to you. His name is Matt Dent. Mr. Dent, this is Detective Clint Folsom, the officer you were asking for."

"Thanks, Sharenda," I said as I watched her walk away. From the smile on her face and the way she almost strutted from the room, I was briefly pricked with the thought that she had gotten from Danny last night what would have been mine two years ago.

"Please have a seat. What can I do for you, Mr. . . . ?"

"Dent. Matt Dent." The young man had vice written all over him. In my time with the special homicide unit, I had become adept at identifying who was a rent-boy and who wasn't. And this Matt Dent most assuredly was. I'd seen it from the way he carried himself as soon as I'd seen him enter the squad room at Sharenda's side. He was young looking and relatively small and willowy—the preference of many habitual clients of his ilk. His hair was peroxided and spiked, he wore earrings, and his clothes were tailored to be close-fitting and a bit flamboyant. The colors of his wardrobe screamed "Look at me!" His manner, even in relating to me with the briefest of introductions, screamed, "Fuck me!"

The second time he said "Dent" the wheels in my mind started spinning. The name was familiar, and it—along with how he was showcasing his body—flipped the name "Meister" into my brain.

"Marcus Dent was my brother," the young man said right about at the same moment that his surname registered in my brain. "He was murdered, and I want to avenge that.

123

I've managed to infiltrate the gang responsible for his death, what we call the German gang in Chelsea. Every policeman I've talked to has said the gang no longer operates in New York City. But I know differently. A Lieutenant Steele in the office I was finally sent to says you were in charge of the investigation of my brother's death. I want to know what you are doing about the case—and how I can help."

And with that, one phase of my life ended and, after contacting Burton Kahn, the investigation of the Meister gang was reopened. This time, however, we didn't bother to report the reopening of the case up the chain of command.

* * * *

"I've agreed that you and I will meet him tonight at Barracuda—just the two of us—7:00 p.m."

"I don't like it, Brad. I don't like that this Dent guy has contacted us both--separately. That he hasn't told each other that he was talking to the other."

"He probably assumes there's someone rotten in the department just as we do," Brad answered. "He's just trying to be careful."

"Maybe," I said, "but I think we should wait to pursue this further with him until our researchers have fully checked him out."

We were laying with our arms and legs entangled in post-coital calm down on our bed overlooking the lights of Manhattan. As much as we both liked this apartment, I had never been able to feel more than a visitor here—so we were spending a good bit of our time looking for another one. I was used to living in a stripped-down fleabag, but Brad was having none of that. I gave in to his desires to live well. We could both afford it—separately as well as together—so it seemed petty for me to say I preferred the simple and the unassuming lifestyle. All I truly treasured was good cock— and Brad certainly gave that to me, no matter what housing arrangement we might have. So, I just let him do his apartment shopping. He seemed to be enjoying it.

I had just learned, though, that while Brad was supposedly looking at a couple of apartments with our Realtor this afternoon, he'd actually been meeting with Matt Dent—who had contacted him. I was more than slightly pissed that Dent was contacting each of us separately.

"There are things you don't know, Clint. I've been working another angle of this case."

This was the first time that Brad admitted to what I had been suspecting for a couple of weeks.

"It's not like you to keep secrets from me on this case, Brad. I don't like the smell of any of this. Until we have this guy checked out, we don't even know if he's talking about the Meister gang. We've been assured that they are operating only in Europe now."

"Dent dropped the name 'Wolfgang' when he talked to me—and he's not the only one who has come to me. A guy named Frenchie walked in yesterday saying he was being run by a Wolfgang too. And I gave him your name. He promised he'd come see you today."

"But what you're not telling me is something else?"

"If I'm right, it should blow this whole case open. If not, no one should even know that I considered it and was checking it out. Sorry, Clint, you'll just have to trust me. And now, you'd better get to work. This Frenchie guy could be at your desk already. We've got two angles on this thing now—both the Dent guy and Frenchie. We should be able to prove to the brass now that the Meister gang hasn't left New York."

We had breakfast together. I tried not to pout, but Brad could tell that I was ticked at him for not telling me everything. I had been put in charge of this investigation again—or at least the phantom of an investigation that Burton Kahn was enabling. I wasn't cutting Brad out, who had been kept at Vice, as Burton didn't want what we were doing known across departmental divides. But Brad was cutting me out. This wasn't the partnership we had been maintaining this past two years.

I let him kiss me when we both left for work, but I didn't put my whole heart into it. He could tell that I didn't, and his expression was one of hurt when we parted.

When I was going in to the special homicide squad room, the door was blocked by Lieutenant Kahn and Danny Thompson, both of whom were putting on their coats as they were coming out of the squad room.

"Good, Clint, you're here."

"What's going down?" I asked. "We've got a call?"

"I'm afraid so," Burton said. "A nasty homicide at the Chelsea Hotel over on 23rd. I have a bad feeling about this one."

When we got there, I saw immediately why Burton had gotten that feeling. The victim, a young black male, was staked out on a bed in the hotel room, cuffed on all four points. He'd been sliced up like the centerpiece at a luau. The first name that popped into my mind was Hans Gelber. This looked like work we had attributed to him two years earlier. But Gelber was dead.

"The Meister gang," I said dully.

"I'm afraid you're probably right," Kahn confirmed. "You were telling me they never left the city. I guess you knew what you were talking about. This looks like their work all right. After a lot of rattling, the hotel manager admitted that this guy worked businessmen at the hotel. The businessmen seemed to like it and kept rebooking, so the hotel management turned a blind eye to what he was doing. He worked mostly out of the bar downstairs. His name was Frenchie."

"Frenchie? Christ, almighty," I said. I flipped out my cell phone and tried to call Brad. But he wasn't picking up. I left a voice mail on what happened.

"You know this guy?" Burton asked, giving me an intense look. Danny also came in close.

"Maybe. I'll check a few things out and get back to you," I replied. My defenses had gone up. I could have kicked myself for not confiding in Kahn and Danny, but I suddenly was worried about what Brad meant about what he was working on and how it needed to be so close held that he couldn't even tell me about it. At this moment, I couldn't trust anyone—not even Kahn or Danny.

"Anything else to link this to the Meister gang?" I asked.

"Maybe," Kahn answered. "We showed some photos and drawings to the hotel manager. The only one that came up as a maybe was linked to the guy who often was with Frenchie down in the bar. The manager said that the drawing we had done years ago from your description of the Wolfgang character who shot Hans Gelber looked like that guy. So, what are you thinking?"

"I'm thinking the Meister gang is still operating here—and may never have left, Lieutenant. I'm thinking we'd better hurry and track them down before this goes up the chain of command and we're closed down again."

"That's what I'm thinking too. But I don't want you running off half cocked on this and playing superhero. You stay here until forensics is finished and the body taken away. The rest of us will go back to the squad room and brainstorm this. You can do so too, while you're here—and we'll compare approaches and notes when you get back."

"Lieutenant, I need to—"

"You need to get this cleaned up," he said gruffly. And the way he said it made me snap my jaw tight shut. Was he trying to keep me tampered down so I would keep my eye on the ball and not jump off side, or did I need to worry about what Kahn's role in all of this was? Whichever, this was not the time for me to be doing something stupid, like arguing with him or even letting him know Brad was working this case too.

For the next three hours, up to lunchtime, I was tied down at the Chelsea Hotel. I repeatedly tried calling Brad, but it was no go. I wasn't surprised. The Vice guys often were out doing their thing and had their personal cell phones turned off or left back at the squad room.

I didn't go back to the precinct after I was released at the Chelsea Hotel. I roamed around the district, hitting the gay bars, trying to track down any of the guys who had been on the watch list two years previously as being in the German gang's stable—and looking at every face I could, wanting to see that of Wolfgang, whose visage had been embedded into my mind two years previously. I hadn't managed to get a photo shot of him back then, when Gelber had tried to kill me while Wolfgang was slicing up Trax. But that didn't matter. I had been able to describe him enough for a dead-ringer drawing to be done, and I knew I'd recognize him if I ever saw him again.

But all of my scouting work was fruitless. And then it was nearly 5:00 p.m., and I decided I needed to get back to the squad room and catch the research staff and rattle their cages about the background check on Matt Dent before they could escape for the evening.

The only one present in the squad room when I returned was Danny, who was sitting at his desk and glowering at me when he saw me walk in. I said nothing to him. I felt wrung out and in need of a shower and a change of clothes before meeting Brad and Matt Dent at the Barracuda at 7:00. I stopped at my desk, though, and rang the research department and was assured that some information would be sent to my cell phone momentarily—that they were just about finished.

I looked at Danny and he looked at me.

"Clint," he said in a low, hoarse voice.

"Not now, Danny," I answered. "I've got to go out again and meet with Brad about something."

"Brad," he spat out.

I ignored him and trotted into the squad locker room, stripped, took up a towel, and went into the showers.

When I came out, Danny was standing there—naked, and with a magnificent erection. I had forgotten how melting his powerful and beautifully muscled-up body was. And the muscle standing out from his crotch was possibly his most magnificent one.

"Danny, no," I whispered.

"You can't avoid me forever," Danny growled. "I don't accept that you don't want it. I don't think that Brad can give it to you like I know you want it."

"Danny. We can't."

I tried to move past him, but he reached out and grabbed me and ripped the towel away from my waist.

"You can't fool me. You want it. You're hard for me."

Of course I wanted it. Every time I'd seen Danny in the past two years, I'd wanted it. I couldn't change in that way. I was addicted to cock—and his cock was one of the best I'd ever had. Of course, I wanted it. Like an alcoholic, the want would never leave me.

"Danny, no," I moaned.

He wasn't listening to me—or he didn't care how much I told him no. I wasn't struggling with him. He knew he was going to fuck me. He knew that I knew he was going to fuck me.

He pushed me down on my back on the narrow bench running down the space between the bank of lockers, squatted between my thighs, and, holding my legs spread with strong hands under my knees, attacked my cock and then my hole with his tongue and mouth.

"Danny, no," was all I could moan. But there was no pretense.

"Here. You crown it," he growled. He was standing over me with a condom in his hand.

Hating myself, and whimpering my unwillingness, I rolled the condom on his cock.

He straddled the bench and crouched between my thighs, lifting my legs up and out, and bringing my butt up off the bench. He was smiling cruelly, knowingly, down into my face as I took his proud, jet-black cock in both hands and guided him inside me. Then he was fucking me to beat the band, hard and deep and rapidly, as my "no's" turned to "yes's" and "oh, shit. Fuck me hard. I've missed you so much."

When I had come—and then Danny—we held there, both panting hard.

"When I want it, you'll give it to me." It was a statement, not a question.

"Yes," I answered weakly, my whole carefully constructed life crashing down around my shoulders. Ashamed but not able to say no, knowing that my weakness, my love of cock—and not just any big cock; Danny's cock—didn't permit me to avoid the truth.

"Good," he said. Then he turned me over, belly to the surface of the narrow bench, and crouched over my hips and fucked me hard again.

When I had showered a second time, not wanting Brad to smell the victory of Danny on my body, and dressed and come out into the squad room, he was gone. My computer monitor was flashing an incoming message, though. It was the report from the research department. Marcus Dent had had no brothers. And there was no record of a Matt Dent—at least not from the photo I had surreptitiously fired off of him with my cell phone.

"Oh, christ," I exclaimed. I looked up at the wall clock. 7:15 p.m. I tried, frantically, to call Brad on my cell phone. Again no answer. I ran for the door.

* * * *

I sat, numb, in my car outside the Barracuda bar. He hadn't been there when I showed up—a half hour late. They hadn't been there. Brad and whoever was pretending to be Marcus Dent's brother.

I had begged Brad to wait until we checked him out.

Oh, lord. Where do I start looking now?

My cell phone rang. I looked at the caller ID and almost didn't click into the call. My hands were shaking.

"Clint? Burton here. I'm so sorry. Bad news. The worst, I'm afraid."

Chapter Five: The Start of a Quest

"You don't want to go in there."

"I know I don't," I said. But I pushed on past Lieutenant Kahn and entered the hotel room.

I saw the young man who purported to be Matt Dent first. His body was huddled in the corner directly across the room from the entrance, crouched down and arms up as if he could protect himself from the vicious slashings of the knife. He, of course, could not.

I barely glanced at the bed, knowing what I'd find— Brad spread-eagled and cuffed at all four points. I turned away and moved back out of the door. Blood. So much blood. I was amazed that the human body could contain so much.

I was hyperventilating. Danny came out of the room and tried to fold me into his arms. I shrugged him off.

"We were supposed to meet at 7:00," I muttered. "I was with you at 7:00. If I'd been there—"

"Then it would have been both of you like that," Danny said. "It was a setup. You'd probably be dead now too if you'd made that meeting."

"Still," I said. I couldn't say anymore. I turned and fled to the elevators. I turned back around, waiting for the elevator, and saw Danny standing there, looking at me still. He had a pained look on his face. I couldn't blame him. None of this was his fault. If he'd gone too—along with me—as backup, we probably would have managed. But we didn't include him. We kept him in the dark—not fully trusting him.

Outside the entrance of the hotel, I stood leaning up against the wall and took several heavy breaths, trying to get control of myself. I was looking wildly around the street, trying to find something to focus on, something that would stop my world from spinning.

My eyes stopped on a figure standing across the street. My feet knew who it was before my brain did, and I started running toward him, dodging cars as I crossed the street. He turned to run, but stopped just long enough to not be able to melt away when I yelled the name "Wolfgang."

I cornered him in an alley. I saw the flash of light on metal as he drew a gun. But I was faster.

It was a kill shot to the gut—but not one with immediate effect.

"Who did it?" I demanded, as I crouched down over his body.

He grimaced and looked up at me with a questioning look.

"Yeah, you're going to die, and I'm sorry I can't make it more painful," I answered, brutally. "Tell me who killed those men up there."

"When I left, Bruno was there. I'd done Stan, but not the cop. I just made sure he was all ready for Bruno. I did nothing but get him strung up."

"Stan? The guy we knew as Matt Dent?"

He just groaned, but he didn't contradict me. So, I went on. "Bruno? Bruno Meister? He's here in New York?"

It was useless to wait for an answer on that, though. Wolfgang was dead. I took out my cell phone and made the necessary call, and then I was on the move again.

* * * *

It wasn't just Bruno I was after. There was something else. Brad had been working on something else. There had to be a reason why he and I had been targeted—why someone had gone to the effort to set us up with a fake brother of Marcus Dent and put us where we could be swept up and dealt with. There had to be someone in the department—someone who was threatened by our unauthorized investigation. It had to be someone who knew we were still snooping around a case that had been buried nearly two years ago. Someone who could get the case buried in the first place.

Brad had been working on this. He had to have notes hidden somewhere. And it couldn't be at his precinct office or even on his personal computers. It had to be somewhere well hidden. I knew where.

I raced back to our apartment. As soon as I opened the door, I knew that I'd been right. The place had been tossed. Everything we owned was out on the floor and had been ripped to shreds. I didn't care about that. That was good. They'd done me a favor. I could never live here again. I couldn't use anything we'd ever shared again.

I went into the kitchen, behind the island, and stooped down. The pots and pans had been pulled out of the cupboard under the island and were strewn around on the floor, but I felt around in back of that and was assured that the false backing was still there and in place. I grabbed a steak knife and started prying at the edges of the plank. I was sure Brad had had a more elegant way of getting his secret compartment open, but I didn't have the time or patience to figure it out. I had to know.

His notes were there. I quickly read through them and then picked up my cell phone and dialed a number.

"Where are you, Clint? We found a body in the alley, just as you reported. Wolfgang, did you say?"

"Yes, Lieutenant. He pulled a gun on me. I wanted him alive, but he didn't give me a choice."

"Where are you?"

"Brad's apartment. It's been ransacked, but I found what they were looking for. Lieutenant, the link. The missing link between the Meister gang and the police. It's what Brad was working on—why he got killed. It's Brad's lieutenant, Chuck Steele."

There was a pause, but when Kahn spoke, it was with strength and grit. "I'm not surprised. I've thought that for some time. You got evidence?"

"Brad almost had it all together. There's enough here to pin Steele down, I think."

"Stay right there. No going after him yourself. And, Clint, I know what Brad was to you. I'm putting you on leave. You've talked about going to Montana to fish. This is the time for that. Leave the cleanup to us here. You hear me?"

"Yes, Lieutenant, I hear you." Hearing him and following his instructions were two different things. I'm sure he knew that. I'm sure he realized that my mind was already locked on tracking Bruno Meister down.

He was right about this not being the time to go after anyone, though. I was exhausted and completely played out. I sank to the floor and waited there until Lieutenant Kahn and other team members showed up, took possession of the notes Brad had compiled, and made a cursory effort to put the apartment back in order.

"Don't bother," I said weakly. "I won't stay here any longer. Just leave it." Then I turned to the lieutenant and asked, "Where's Danny?"

"He's gone home. He said you wouldn't want to see him."

The lieutenant was diplomatic enough not to pursue that any further.

Two hours later I was standing in the street outside Danny's apartment. I had been standing there for more than an hour—fighting with myself. Not knowing what I wanted, and yet knowing.

He answered the door in just his sleeping shorts. Magnificent as always.

"You want to come in?"

"Just hold me," I murmured. "Yes, I want to come in, but just hold me."

"Whatever you want," he answered.

He knew, though, that I didn't just want to be held. And he gave me what I needed most just then. I was so weak in the world of men. There was no denying that anymore. But

I was a damn good detective. I couldn't remain faithful to Brad, but I sure as hell could track down his killer and make him pay.

Death on the Rhine

Chapter One: The Prey Is Sighted

The shadow by the stairway to the Helios deck of the MS *River God* drew back and sheathed the blade that had been held at the ready lest a moonbeam cast its damning light on dark intent.

Just moments to a death now.

The increased intensity of the groaning and moaning from the only occupied lounger on the rooftop deck of the Rhine River luxury cruiser told of the impending death. The small figure was splayed on its back on the lounger, trembling legs spread wide, arms flailing, torso writhing, as the larger figure hunched over it, stabbing, stabbing, cutting deeper with each thrust, each thrust met with a tortured yelp and a moan.

A final cry in duet, the thrust of death, and the small figure collapsed in upon itself with the hiss of a long, spent sigh. The hunching figure rose up on its feet, looming over its prey, gave a satisfied and wicked laugh, and wiped its dripping blade clean before sheathing it.

The epitome of one man dominating another man. Fucking. The act and second of ejaculation. That had been what Michel Foucault's *The Use of Pleasure*, the book NYPD detective Clint Folsom had read shortly after his partner—and lover—had died, equated to a type of death—orgasm as a point-of-death experience. And Folsom had become possessed by this concept and its association with Foucault's theory. He couldn't get the image out of his mind. The thought of that which followed the point of death possibly being one long, rolling orgasm initiated by a last-gasp ejaculation. Just as he couldn't get the vision of the hunched figure standing over his prey now in the moonlight on the top deck the *River God* as it sliced the waters between Mainz and the vineyard village of Rudesheim out of his mind. Bruno Meister. The man who had sado-fucked Folsom's partner and then killed him. And Folsom had traced the killer down on this Rhine River cruise and had followed him out on the open deck in the dark of night to take his revenge. But this obviously wasn't the opportunity he thought it would be. The men were just having sex.

Oh well, it was a six-day cruise to Amsterdam. There would be other opportunities.

* * * *

It was just the first day of the cruise, which had begun in Mainz. Folsom had run Meister to ground just an hour earlier at dinner in the Ambrosia restaurant on the Apollo deck for the first time since the master criminal had fled his crime in New York. The MS *River God* was a special ship, and this river cruise was even more special. It was a no-holds-barred gay-oriented cruise that would unleash ninety well-heeled and very horny men into the welcoming arms of the forgiving city of Amsterdam in just less than a week. This, of course, would be no big deal for Amsterdam. It was a sexual paradise and supermarket.

When the NYPD traced Meister down to this cruise, they developed plans to meet the ship in Amsterdam. But Folsom thought his partner and lover, Brad Roberts, deserved better than a chancy attempt at extradition from the very-forgiving Netherlands. And Folsom was one of the few detectives in the department who would fit in unobtrusively on such a cruise. The NYPD had given him a leave of absence to fish in Montana. But Folsom preferred to do his fishing here on the Rhine and to take care of business before the ship docked in Amsterdam.

Meister, a big bruiser of a German gangster who was on the far end of his fifties but who still held onto his commanding muscle and brooding good looks, was planted at the captain's table in the curve of the window at the bow of the boat. Folsom had found a seat for this first meal of the cruise on a nearby banquette, next to an Italian count who used his hands in conversation just as all Italians did and who wanted to have a conversation with Folsom's thighs and basket under the table. Wanting to fit in, Folsom was playing to the count's interest while he locked his attention on Meister, waiting for a chance to be alone with the monster he was pursuing.

Meister had many nefarious interests in New York, and Folsom and his partner, Roberts, had been zeroing in on an arrest, with Roberts near completion of the investigation of a police bigwig functioning as the inside man in Meister's operations. As far as Folsom knew, Meister had never laid eyes on Folsom—which made this close pursuit possible.

Roberts obviously had gotten just too close to Meister, if that was possible. When they found his body, he was naked and spread-eagled on his back on a luxury hotel room bed, his hands tied over his head to the headboard, his feet to the footboard, and a deep knife wound under his rib cage and traveling up into his heart. He'd been fucked, including with a monster-sized object that had torn him up pretty badly, and a thick sounding tube was still buried deep inside his cock. The autopsy determined the presence of the latex of a condom in his ass canal. The case had been broken open primarily because the condom had also broken open. The DNA led to Meister.

Folsom was numb from the death of his partner and lover, but he was seething with rage. The image of the connection of ejaculation and death had possessed his mind. He sought one sort of revenge death for Meister, but ever since that night Brad had died, Folsom had also gone on a frenzied search for the ejaculation form of death for himself. It had only been as he neared the point of orgasm that he'd been able to forget what he had lost and what had happened to his lover. And it was the image of the possibility of the sensation of perpetual orgasm in the embrace of his beyond-the-pale lover, Brad Roberts, rolling down through eternity that propelled him to discount the cost of killing Meister himself.

He was hoping, as he eyed Meister exchanging jovial, expressive conversation with the captain and the other honored guests at the captain's table and flirting with the small, but solid Croatian waiter, Tiho, that the Italian count had a cock as sensuous and searching as his hands. Because after he had dispatched Meister, Folsom very much wanted to be dispatched himself—to spend whatever time it took to uncover his crime of vengeance in the arms, and sheathing the possessing phallus, of a vigorous lover. The Italian count seemed more than interested in helping him with that problem.

Tiho was playing Meister for all he was worth, prancing around the table as he served the dinner, playing the coquet. And Meister was buying what Tiho had to sell. As the dessert course was served, Meister reached out while Tiho was placing a plate before him, wrapped a beefy hand around the young man's neck, and brought Tiho's ear down to his mouth. Tiho smiled at what was being whispered to him. Later, after coffee had made the rounds and been consumed and when the captain had stood, shaken hands all around with his guests, and left, Meister headed for the ship's foyer. Tiho was nowhere to be seen.

In the interim, the Italian count's hands had been having a conversation with Folsom's cock, which he had fished out of the detective's pants under the low-dipping cloth on the table, and Folsom was having a little trouble focusing on Meister's movements. This was his chance at getting Meister alone, however. The count would have to wait his turn at dispensing death.

Whispering a "Don't go away, I have to go to the WC," in the Italian's ear, Folsom disengaged the count's fingers, reholstered his piece, zipped up, and then rose and followed Meister down the corridor running between the suites from the dining room to the ship's foyer. He reached the top of the staircase leading half a deck down to the foyer just in time to see Meister go off to the left and through the sliding glass doors onto the open porch beyond where the gangway would start when the boat was docked and from whence the stairs led up to the open Helios deck.

Not wanting the desk manager to see that he was following Meister, Folsom walked on past the reception desk and into the Alexander Lounge. Passengers, having finished their dinner, were already gathering in there. The room had a Mediterranean motif, and three beef-cake, heavily muscled, blond-haired men were taking orders and tending bar. They wore only short, Roman soldier-type skirts, laced sandals, and gold arm bracelets. Gold-colored sequined masks hid the upper part of their faces and made one largely indistinguishable to another. Muscle perfected in triplicate.

Folsom just stood at the entryway, though, watching the reception desk with his peripheral vision. And when the desk manager turned away, he turned and slipped out the sliding glass doors.

He immediately, though, had to sink into the shadows of the porch, out of sight of both the foyer and of the upper part of the stairs leading to the Helios deck, because he wasn't alone. A now-naked Tiho, except for his rhinestone-encrusted short waiter's vest, was sitting on a step near the top of the stairs, and Meister was standing on a stair below him, with his back to Folsom. They both had their hands on the side rails, and Tiho was mouthing Meister's cock, as the German gangster slowly stroked his buttocks back and forth, clearly enjoying the sucking he was receiving.

One of Meister's hands came off the rail and disappeared in front of him, and from the groaning and grunting that Tiho had started to do and the fidgeting of his torso in the moonlight, it was evident that the German was opening the young Croatian's hole up with his fingers in preparation for a plowing. At length Meister gave a command, and they both disengaged and moved up the stairs and onto the lounger on the Helios deck.

Folsom followed them on up to the top, silently sticking to the shadows. He drew out his knife, anxious for Meister to finish with Tiho and for Tiho to leave. But Tiho didn't leave. After that first plowing, Meister gripped Tiho by the sides of his head and guided the young man's mouth to his cock again. Meister obviously wanted a second helping, and who knew how long it would take for him to reload and then finish with Tiho a second time—and perhaps a third—time?

With a sigh of resignation, Folsom turned and silently worked his way down the stairs again. It was a six-day cruise. There would be other opportunities. But soon, Folsom told himself. Very soon.

Chapter Two: Forced to Seek Another Form of Release

Clint Folsom was angry, tense, and horny as well now, having missed his first opportunity to dispatch the killer of his lover. He had sought one form of death—Bruno Meister's death. Having been denied that, he now had a gripping need for another form of death. It was time to see if the Italian count was able to live up to his potential.

Folsom crossed the foyer and mounted the half-story of stairs to the corridor leading through the suite section and back to the Ambrosia restaurant. But, as he approached the entrance into the corridor, he saw the Italian count at the door to one of the suites. And there beside him, being held with a firm grip on his butt by the count was one of the other passengers, a man in his thirties who Folsom had recognized from porn movies he had watched with Brad. The door opened, but they stood on the threshold, kissing deeply, and the count, having unbuttoned the porn star's shirt as they were kissing, moved his lips down the neck of the young, photogenic stud and through a thatch of curly hair toward a nipple, as the two disappeared into one of the suites. And, with that, disappeared that option for Folsom, unless he was up for a threesome. And of course he was—but he thought it might be presumptuous for him to join the party until and unless he was invited. These two also seemed a little more refined than the leatherman threesomes Folsom was accustomed to.

He turned and went back to the Alexander Lounge and bellied up to the bar. He ordered a scorpion from one of the three masked and minimally dressed bartender hunks, and the bartender laughed and flashed him a winsome smile when he did so. Folsom raised his eyebrow at that.

"Sorry, mate," the man said with a slight Australian brogue. "Just a private little joke. I'm sorry. But, say, you look a bit down. This isn't the sort of cruise for that."

"I was near death tonight," Folsom answered, as he received and swirled his drink. "But not nearly near enough."

The bartender said he didn't understand, and Folsom explained to him the equation he had recently read about death through ejaculation.

"I can help you with that, mate," the bartender answered. "I right fancy you. You look like you keep in tip top shape. And has anyone told you you favored that American movie star of the past, Scott Sloan."

"Frequently," Folsom said, although he didn't add that Scott Sloan had been his father. "I'm in such a state, I'd need it rough and hard," he continued, with a wistful tone. Now that he thought about it, maybe the Italian count wouldn't have worked well tonight. He seemed much too refined. Folsom wanted to sweat and squeal, to feel it deep and hard.

"Then I'm your death deliverer," the bartender said with a broad smile. "I can get away at any time. Or if you want to wait until after one, I can do you right here on the bar."

"Cabin 335," Folsom said in a hoarse voice. "Twenty minutes. The door will be unlocked." Then he tossed off his drink and quickly rose and walked out of the lounge, in a hurry lest the hunk behind the bar changed his mind.

He entered his cabin and tossed off his clothes and showered quickly in the small, but efficient bathroom. The cabin itself was bathed in soft light from recessed lighting around the edges of the ceiling. On each of the side walls of the cabin, with their blue-velvet upholstered headboards against the outside wall, were two blue-plush benches, either of which could be covered with a pull-down single bed. The walls and built-in drawers and bed frames were of a burled, blondish wood. The floor was carpeted in gold. The room attendant had pulled down just one of the beds and prepared it for the night. A sturdy table was set against the outer wall between the benches, and the entire width of the outer wall was a picture window, covered with gold pull curtains, now closed.

Folsom draped a silk robe over his shoulders but didn't bother to close it. He leaned over the table and opened the curtains. The ship was moving fast in the nighttime, its lights picking out a verge of grass and trees at the edge of the river in the near distance. Mist sprayed past the window, picked up as if of more substance than it really was in the reflection of lights from the ship.

Folsom turned at a sound, and the bartender had entered the cabin and was just shutting and locking the door behind him. He pulled at his legionnaire-style skirt and underbriefs and they dropped to the ground. Folsom swallowed hard and his eyes went wide. The masked hunk was horse hung. He let the robe slip off his shoulders, and the bartender gave a yelp of approval and desire and was at Folsom, pushing him roughly down on his back on the table top and coming up on the table on his knees, holding Folsom's torso firmly between strong thighs. He took Folsom's head and brought it up to his mouth and brutalized his lips with his own, forcing his tongue into Folsom's mouth, making feral animal noises of lust and possession.

At length, he rose up on his knees, grabbed Folsom's wrists in his strong hands, and forced them above his head and against the plate glass window. Then he force-fed his engorging cock into Folsom's mouth and face fucked him. Folsom gagged and fought for breath, loving every moment of the assault, seeking a rough release and death. As he fought hard to accommodate the huge tool, his eyes went to the bartender's shaved groin, and he almost laughed. There, in the soft crevice just above and to the left of the root of the

147

man's cock was a tattoo. It was of a scorpion. Thus the amused reaction from the bartender when Folsom had ordered a scorpion cocktail. Folsom reveled in the sting of a scorpion. He was going to be delivered by a scorpion. He was reveling in having ordered this volatile cocktail.

The hunk clambered off Folsom's chest and turned him onto his belly on the table. He could barely touch the floor with his toes as he opened his legs wide in response to the hunk's slapping of and pulling at his butt cheeks. The hunk was attacking Folsom's asshole with his mouth. He pulled Folsom's cock back through his legs and was alternating attention to his hole with attention to his cock and balls with tongue and fingers.

Folsom looked up into the night through the opaque window as he was being prepared for mounting and saw that the lights of buildings along the Rhine were becoming more frequent. They were approaching Rudesheim, where they would dock in a few hours and that had several wineries the passengers could explore on the morrow. His mind contrasted the peaceful scene beyond the window and the ravishing of his body here inside the cabin. He was panting and moaning under the assault of the tongue and probing fingers and was quickly moving to a death.

And just as he died and his seed spilled out onto the gold carpet below the table, he cried out in pain. At that very moment the masked hunk thrust his cock inside Folsom's ass, bumping his head up against the plate glass window and plastering his cheek against the pane, where his peripheral vision saw flashes of lights from the river bank against the spray of sea foam. Folsom grunted and writhed and begged for mercy and for slower and less forceful thrusts inside him, not really wanting it to stop or slow down, and not receiving any mercy. The bartender had his hips in a strong grip and was drawing him back into each deep thrust of his powerful phallus.

Folsom rose off the table in a involuntary movement to escape the onslaught or at least to keep the thrusts from going ever deeper, but the hunk just turned him and pushed him down onto the adjacent bed onto his back, spread his legs wide, dug his own knees under Folsom's buttocks, and started pumping him hard again. Folsom found straps at the side and the head of the bed to hang onto in seas that were only rough in his cabin. He arched his back as the hunk ravished his nipples with his teeth while he stroked his channel hard and pumped his cock with a strong fist.

Folsom died a second time, spouting semen up onto the hunk's belly before the bartender himself gave a cry of joyous release.

The bartender left him almost immediately then and without a word. He used the cabin's shower, and then was gone, leaving Folsom to whimper in his exhaustion. Just part of his job on this sort of cruise. The death and release had been a good one for Folsom, though. It had taken his mind from his loss of Brad and from his scheming for revenge—if at least for the hour that he was being plowed. He was drifting off, only half possessed now with his demons, well plowed. But the lurching of the side of the boat against wood as the ship docked in Rudesheim jolted him back into the real world, and he only slowly sank into sleep, planning how he was going to get Meister alone. Maybe in the streets of Rudesheim, far away from the ship. He must do it undiscovered, if he could. He wanted to be around for a long, long time to savor his revenge.

Chapter Three: Double Death in the Vineyard

At the buffet breakfast the next morning in the Ambrosia restaurant, Tiho was moving around a bit more gingerly and with a little less of the playful buoyancy and bounce than he had the night before, but he was still making an effort to play the role of everyone's favorite leprechaun. No doubt this was a studied role that won him extra tips at the end of the voyage; it certainly would make him a favorite of those seeking a young-looking, yet legally aged, partner to dominate on this cruise.

Bruno Meister wasn't in the restaurant, and Folsom had gone to great pains to determine that this was so. This wasn't really a surprise. The breakfast buffet was the one meal on the ship that was spread over several hours. And by the time Folsom had recovered from his own plowing the evening before and had come up for his meal, he could see that several of the other passengers had already eaten and had disembarked to explore the small wine village of Rudesheim. The MS *River God* had tied up very close to the town center.

The Italian count strutted in, master of the room, his blond porn star in tow, as Folsom was drinking his last cup of coffee. They were seated before the count saw Folsom, but he did see him as Folsom got up to leave and motioned the

American detective to join the blond and him at their table. Folsom didn't have time for this, though; he was hell bent on finding Meister and dispatching him as soon as possible. He didn't want to offend the Italian, however, so he went over to their table, told them that he had something he had to do but maybe he'd see them later, and bent down and gave the count a nice kiss on the lips—just to register that his retreat wasn't a matter of disinterest.

Then he went looking for Meister. He found him, decked out in gym shorts and a T, sitting at the bar in the Alexander Lounge, deep in conversation with one of the masked bartenders. Folsom couldn't tell if it was the same one who had so roughly and effectively fucked him the previous evening, but he was the only one of the three in the lounge at the time. Folsom walked on by, not wanting to show that he had any interest in what Meister was doing or to connect himself in any way to Meister. He stood at the window for a bit, feigning interest in what was going on out on the riverside market street beyond the boat dock. But all the time he was fingering the blade in his pocket, pumping himself up for the justice he was about to dispense.

When Folsom turned, he saw that the bartender was gone. And then Meister got off the stool as well and headed toward the foyer. Folsom waited until the German gangster was out of the lounge door and then quickly moved there himself to see where the German was headed. He took the stairs down to the B deck below and then turned right to descend to the C deck that ran part of the way under the Alexander Lounge. Folsom followed Meister at a discrete distance.

Having reached the C deck corridor of cabins, Meister moved to the very end of the corridor. The door at the end entered one of the crew areas, but Meister didn't go there; he turned and entered the last door on the right at the end of the corridor. Folsom knew this to be the ship's small exercise room, an exercise room for brochure purposes only, as there was only room for a couple of tread mills, a rack of weights, and a bench that could have been used for bench pressing if there had been room to move the weights around in—which there wasn't. Folsom doubted that Meister could make any use of the room for exercise, but then he wasn't thinking clearly on the type of exercise Meister liked to do.

Folsom waited for a few minutes to enable Meister to get into an exercise routine and to be less likely to be prepared to react quickly. The detective reasoned he could be in and out in less than a minute, doing what he needed to do and being long gone before Meister's body was found.

As he drew nearer to the door into the exercise room, though, Folsom could hear low moaning. The door was slightly ajar and Folsom only needed to nudge it a bit to be able to see the weight bench. All Folsom could see initially, however, was the back of one of the bartenders, sans his Roman soldier-style skirt. Folsom's eyes went to the carpet next to the machine and he saw the rectangular wooden box and the surgical items inside. Sounding wands. The bartender then moved to the side enough that Folsom could see the naked body of Bruno Meister reclining on the bench, with his wrists tied off on the handle bars of the treadmill machines on either side of the bench. His eyes were closed, and his head was lolling back in his own world of ecstasy.

Meister was a large, barrel-chested man, but he was more a mass of compact muscle than fat. He was quite hairy all over and his cock was plump—very thick in erection, although not particularly long. Now it had the end of a tube protruding out of its piss slit, a tube that was being twirled gently and inserted slowly by the bartender.

Having heard a slight sound or sensing, perhaps, that they were being watched, the blond hunk turned toward the door. He didn't see Folsom, but Folsom couldn't quite see what he needed to see—he couldn't tell if there was a scorpion tattooed on the man's groin close to the root of his cock. Unless all three of the bartenders were similarly tattooed, if the scorpion was there Folsom would know that this was the guy who had put it in him the previous night. If he was into this sort of kinky sex, Folsom might need to avoid a rematch with him.

Folsom pulled away from the door and quietly moved down the corridor. He didn't want to hurt anyone else; he only wanted to make Meister pay for his crime. He'd have to wait for another opportunity to do so.

Folsom retreated to the Alexander Lounge with a paperback novel and staked out an observation post for the return of the bartender and/or Meister. The other two bartenders were in service in the lounge when Folsom returned to it, but for the rest of the morning there was no sign of either Meister or the third bartender.

Folsom had barely begun to eat his lunch in the restaurant, only half full now, presumably because many of the passengers were exploring Rudesheim, when he saw Meister disembark and walk off into the town on a steep hillside cobblestoned street. The detective rushed to follow him, but when he reached the street running across the edge of the river, he couldn't even be sure which of three streets whose mouths came down to the river in close proximity was the one Meister had taken. Taking a stab at a choice, Folsom started up a street that the village map he'd taken from a stack on the reception desk told him led up to one of the wineries the ship's passengers had been told would be open for their inspection and tasting.

Near the top of the street, just opposite the entrance into the winery, Folsom caught sight of Meister sitting in an open-air street café. Another man was sitting with them, and they were having an extremely animated conversation; it almost looked like they were arguing. Folsom retreated to the shadows near the entrance to the winery and observed the two men. With a creepy sense of confusion and surprise, Folsom came to realize that he knew the other man. It was a German senior police detective by the name of Sigmund Frist. Folsom had met him at an international police convention after Brad Roberts had died and Folsom had sunk into total debauchery. Folsom and Frist had even had a short fling in bed during that convention, with Folsom trying out a new man each night. Folsom remembered that Frist was very good in bed.

But what was he doing in Rudesheim, and more important, what was he doing talking with Meister? Could it be that Meister was going to be arrested before Folsom could get to him? This wouldn't be fair.

Meister flounced up from the table, as did Frist, and Meister started walking briskly down the street, with Frist closely following him and throwing angry words at his back. To escape notice, Folsom entered the winery, only to find himself face to face with the Italian count and his porn star tagalong.

"Oh, there you are, you lovely boy," the Italian count said with a big grin on his face. "We have just received permission to take some wine, cheese, and bread out into the vineyard. Would you care to join Lance and me for a lovely afternoon among the vines?"

Folsom saw no reason to refuse—certainly not as long as Frist was anywhere near Meister.

The count and the porn star gleefully danced out into the vineyard, the luxuriant vines heavy with grapes, and found a good vantage point to plop down where they could see the river and village below but could not easily be seen from those two perspectives. By the time Folsom caught up with them, they essentially were naked and were devouring cheese and wine like there was no tomorrow.

The two pulled Folsom down onto the spread blanket between them and undressed him while plying him with wine. The three were drinking out of shared bottles, and it didn't take Folsom long to suspend his concern about Meister and surrender to their sensuous attention.

In a purely wanton act, the Italian poured wine down the front of Folsom's naked torso, and the blond porn star licked it off with his tongue. The count was kissing Folsom deeply on the lips when the porn star started giving attention to Folsom's cock, balls, and asshole. Soon all three were writhing around on the ground, making three-way love. The Italian was lithe and willowy, and his patrician nature showed through. He wasn't young, but he'd taken extremely good care of himself, and the attention he showed to Folsom proved that he was highly trained and skilled in the art of making love. His cock was long but slender. The porn star was perfectly muscled, in keeping with his trade, but his cock, although of respectable length, was more slender than Folsom would have guessed would be ideal for movies.

It was while contemplating this and being maneuvered into a sandwiched position between the other two, who had gone into a yoga-style seated position with their legs folded over each other's and sitting closely together, that it hit Folsom that he remembered what the porn star's movie specialty was. He was known for those rare depictions of double penetration. That's why his slender cock wasn't considered a debit.

But by the time the American detective realized what he was being maneuvered into, the two had a half-drunk Folsom between them, facing the Italian, and the Italian had a hand wrapped around his own cock docked with that of the porn star, and the porn star was pulling Folsom's hips down between them and spreading his butt cheeks with strong hands. Before it happened, Folsom realized that he was going to be double penetrated by those docked cocks, but he so sought the death of orgasm that double death seemed worth the try. Thus, with much groaning and moaning and crying out of being filled to the limit, he just descended on the doubled poles and lost himself in the counterthrusting and four-handed body massaging of his exuberant companions.

It was a whole new and incredible sensation for Folsom, and his companions were also quickly lost in the feel of cock rubbing on cock and counterpistoning inside the undulating walls of an ass channel. They were all moaning and groaning and crying out in wine-enabled ecstasy, lost in the most intimate of threesomes, each straining to hold his ejaculation in check for as long as possible and reveling in a three-way fuck that they wanted to go on forever. The Italian and porn star came almost simultaneously inside Folsom, and then the porn star inclined his shoulders back to the ground and pulled Folsom's torso with him while the Italian slid his prick out of Folsom and expertly sucked him off, giving him the coup de grace in a trio of sighs and moans. It was a good death for Folsom and a pleasant afternoon in a sea of frustration and anger.

Chapter Four: Solace Found in a Willing Waiter

"Well, look who we have here."

Clint Folsom knew without even looking up that Inspector Sigmund Frist had recognized him.

"Hello, Sig," he answered, gesturing for his old acquaintance to take a seat in one of the velvet-upholstered barrel chairs in the Alexander Lounge. It was after dinner on the MS *River God*. The ship was still tied to the dock at Rudesheim, preparing for the run through the most scenic, castle-crowned section of the Rhine late the next morning and into the afternoon.

Folsom had returned from the afternoon romp in the vineyard a little bowlegged but still horny. He had been ridden doubly and well, but he was in the mood to fuck something himself now. In the months following Brad's death, Folsom had expanded his sexual activity to include topping. It wasn't to be a long-lasting period, but, for now it was just part of his reaction to having lost his lover. The cute little waiter, Tiho, was the first to cross Folsom's path when he returned to the ship, and he didn't seem to mind in the least when Folsom drew him into his cabin and began to kiss him passionately.

Tiho himself made the first serious move when he opened his shirt and bared his breast and offered Folsom two pert little nipples with silver rings through them. Folsom ravaged them with his lips and teeth as he hunched over the waiter who had been backed up to the table between the benches. Tiho was making little yipping sounds and murmuring in some sort of East European language. Folsom certainly hoped the young man was voicing his pleasure, but he didn't much care. He wanted to get sucked and then to fuck something.

Folsom stripped Tiho's pants off and then his own, sat the waiter up on the table, reversed him, and forced him down on his back, his head at the end of the table facing Folsom. Then he braced his thighs against the table edge, took Tiho's head between his hands, and fucked down into the waiter's mouth until his cock was throbbing, full, and dripping.

Folsom then turned, unclipped one of the raised beds at the side and brought it down over the bench. He gathered Tiho up in his arms and turned him and put him down on the bed, sideways on his butt, spreading his legs wide. Tiho watched him in awe as Folsom struggled to roll a condom on his horse-hung cock and then pushed his legs out as wide as he could and arched his back as Folsom thrust inside his puckered hole.

Tiho screamed in surprise at the invasion, but his hole was slack and well used, and he immediately mustered his English capability to let Folsom know that his efforts were appreciated. Folsom rode Tiho hard and long, trying to dispel all of the frustrations of his loss of his lover and his pursuit of Meister across Europe. And Tiho rode with him, expertly meeting his thrusts with counterthrusts of his own, well versed in the type of servicing required of the crew on such a voyage as this.

Spent and exhausted after a prodigious release of semen in an orgasmic death, Folsom turned Tiho in the bed when he had finished him and stretched out beside him. The American hugged the East European morsel to his breast, as the well-fucked and even-tempered lad hummed lullabies to the troubled passenger. When Folsom's eyes closed and his breathing became regular, Tiho unentangled himself and tiptoed out of the cabin. He had enjoyed this fuck. It wasn't like what that bull of a German did to him. That one made him want to kill.

Folsom had slept in his cabin until dinner, moving from there straight to the lounge for drinks. He would have offered to buy the German policeman a drink, but Frist was already hefting an industrial-sized scotch and water. "I haven't seen you before on the ship," Folsom said, trying to sound as casual as possible.

Folsom warily neglected to say that he'd already seen Frist earlier off the ship and up the hill in Rudesheim, having an argument with Bruno Meister. He was very afraid that Frist was going to be taking Meister out of circulation for some other crime before Folsom himself could bring Meister to justice for the murder of his partner.

"No, I just joined the cruise here in Rudesheim," Frist answered. "There are too many inquisitive eyes in Mainz. It would have been unseemly for me to join the cruise there. This cruise has quite a reputation."

"So, you aren't here on business?" Folsom queried.

"No, pleasure," Frist responded. "And you? Are you here to track some dastardly criminal to ground? Or are you here to get fucked?"

The questions lay there in bold outline. Not even Folsom's own police department in New York knew he was here to track Bruno Meister down and kill him. How likely would it be that his intent would be negated if he told a senior German police official what he was doing here? And, indeed, could Frist already know and just wanted confirmation before he stepped in to prevent Folsom from taking his revenge?

"Pleasure, just like you," Folsom said after a pause, trying to muster up a broad smile for Frist. His smile wasn't as broad as Frist's was, though.

"And could perhaps your pleasure be my pleasure too?" Frist asked.

"Perhaps," Folsom responded. He answered thusly only partially to put Frist off the track of why he really was here. He also well remembered what a skillful lover the German policeman had been.

Frist sat there for a few minutes, swirling his scotch in front of his face, drinking in Folsom over the rim of the glass. "You look better than ever, Clint," he said at length. "You have yet to reach your prime, I think. Have you been well fucked since we last were together? Someone special in your life? Someone here on the cruise with you?"

"Not here on the cruise. But, yes, yes, there was someone in my life. But now that's over. And it happened before you and I met." Frist was either being very coy, or he really hadn't either heard about the murder of Brad Roberts or was unaware of any connection between both Folsom and Bruno Meister. There was no question that he knew Meister, however. Their argument at the café in the town that afternoon had made that clear.

"And it ended sadly?" Frist asked in a low voice.

"I think you could safely say that," Folsom said and took a deep pull on his drink.

"I would very much like to fuck you again," Frist pressed in a low, hoarse voice. "Would that be possible—for old time's sake? I think I was able to give you pleasure."

"Yes, yes, you did. Perhaps. That's what this cruise is all about." Folsom decided he needed to fully maintain the cover of having taken this cruise for the hookups.

"Have you been in the club downstairs? In Hephaestion?" Frist asked.

"Club? There's a club downstairs?"

"Yes. The stairs are just over there beyond the bar. I think it might put you in the proper mood. It's the very heart of this cruise. Come down there with me now—and then later we can go to my cabin."

Frist tossed off his scotch, stood, and held out his hand to Folsom, who also stood and meekly followed his German counterpart down into the club named for Alexander the Great's male lover. On the way to the stairs, they passed the bar, and the masked blond bartender on duty

160

there gave Folsom a smile that seemed to claim intimacy. Folsom wondered if this was his lover of the previous night, and he smiled back in encouragement. He would like to have more of what that guy had given him.

Frist drew close to Folsom as they descended the stairs. Half way down he stopped and pulled the younger detective to him and kissed him deeply as he inserted one hand inside his shirt and tweaked a nipple and cupped his butt with the other one. Folsom's cock gave a lurch in memory of how Frist had seduced him at that police convention earlier and had, first, made gentle love to him and then had ridden him hard and long in a second wild fuck. Folsom knew that this would be one night of many orgasmic deaths in which he could become lost to the pain of this world.

He had no idea how orgasmic his night would be.

Chapter Five: The Inspector Comes

The blue and gold of the Alexander lounge turned into the scarlet and gold of the Hephaestion club as the American detective, Clint Folsom, and the German police inspector, Sigmund Frist, descended into an area that took perhaps a third of the room of the lounge above it but that held quite a few banquette-style seating areas on three tiers going down to a small, round center stage. The decor here was as reminiscent of the Greco-Roman era of the Mediterranean as was the Alexander lounge. On the top tier to the right of where the staircase descended ran a red-padded bar in a semicircle around the room, and Frist perched on a bar stool here and spread his legs and brought Folsom's butt into his crouch.

As far as Folsom could determine, this space was tucked into the bow area under the lounge and he could make out a doorway under the stairs they had descended that probably went back toward the corridor that ended at the turn into the exercise room.

Frist had wrapped an arm possessively around Folsom's belly and had his chin on the younger detective's shoulder. Folsom could already feel Frist's groin come alive and he sighed at the thought of what was to come. He had remembered Frist has being a superb cocksman, with power hammer drive.

"Want something to drink?" Frist murmured in his ear. "Just tell the bartender; he's come over for our order."

At the same time Folsom was ordering a Scorpion, he turned toward the bar and did a double take. Yet another one of masked blond hunks was there to take his order and was giving him the same "I know you; I've had you" smile. This set Folsom into some confusion; there could only be one of these studs who knew him so fully that he could share such a smile with him—and yet they had just left another such one up in the Alexander lounge. Folsom decided that they all probably were just very well schooled and that fucking the passengers or not fucking them was all the same thing and came with the territory; they were just taught to treat them all intimately, as required, and let the generous tips drop where they may.

Folsom and Frist were not alone at the bar. Seated next to them on a barstool, showing close interest in them from the moment they entered the room was a massive jet-black man, who Folsom had already been told was some vacationing potentate of a central African nation, traveling secretly outside of his region, spending his country's treasury, and indulging in his taste for other men who didn't succumb to his charms simply to keep their heads on their shoulders.

As Folsom took his Scorpion from the bartender, whose hand lingered on his in the exchange a tad more than necessary, the lights on the walls around the chamber started to dim, and spots opened up on the stage area below. A large number of the ship's passengers were in attendance, and many of them were already well into pleasing each other intimately. In keeping with the spirit of this, Frist's free hand had already unzipped Folsom and was cupping his package directly, skin on skin. No one around them seemed to mind or to pay them much attention; they all were paired off and doing much the same themselves.

The ebony giant moved his barstool a little closer to Folsom and Frist, and his eyes were glued to Folsom's crotch, even though nearly everyone else was checking out the lit stage area.

As Frist nibbled and kissed the hollow of his neck, Folsom tried to focus on what was happening on the small stage below. An opaque, Plexiglas cross-beamed X rose out of the center of the stage. The stage was empty, but not for long. To the sound of a slow drum beat, the door under the stairs opened and two figures emerged and slowly made their way down to the stage. The one who seemed to be in command was a somewhat older rendition of the masked blond bartender trio. He was a good twenty years older than the bartenders—perhaps in his mid forties—and was rangier than they were, but he still had good, ropy muscle tone, his muscles so hard that the veins stood out on his arms, torso, and legs for lack of interior room to run. Like the bartenders, he was dressed only in a short Roman-soldier skirt, which in his case was gold lamé in contrast to their shiny white; gold sandals, with gold laces rising to his knees, gold bracelets snaking around his upper arms, and a gold-sequined mask. He was carrying a gold box under his arm and was swishing a gold multistranded whip in his other hand. The other figure was that of a short, lithe young man of olive complexion and of a sloe-eyed, dark, curly haired beauty that was almost feminine in its delicacy. He was dressed in a loose shocking-white tunic and was wearing sandals similar to his companion's, except in simple brown leather. And he had a gold collar around his neck that sparkled under the spotlights. The tunic hid his torso, but his lightly muscled arms and legs indicated a well-formed, if willowy frame.

The drums stopped their beat as the two reached the stage, and a disembodied voice asked those assembled to give a welcome to Roman the Magnificent and his assistant, Dieter. There was a smattering of applause that didn't really mean any disrespect; it meant more that many hands among the audience were so buried in their own devices that they couldn't readily disengage and welcome the evening's entertainment appropriately.

Frist and Folsom did clap, though, and Frist took advantage of having his hands now free to pull Folsom's head around and give him a deep kiss. He then pushed Folsom's pants down on his thighs, unzipped and freed himself, and

165

brought Folsom's butt back into his crotch, with Folsom's balls and cock lying on top of Frist's sturdy piece as it thrust its way between Folsom's thighs. Frist held his hand there, letting the two pricks become better acquainted. Folsom took a big swig of his drink and tried to keep his rising desire in check as Frist slightly rolled his hips, rubbing the root of his tool back and forth on Folsom's exposed channel entrance.

Another hand had come into play now. The African leader, his heaving chest about to burst through the white linen tunic-style shirt he wore over equally white linen pants, was running a beefy hand up and down on Folsom's inner thighs, coming ever closer to the engaged cocks.

The drink was strong and put Folsom a little out of kilter. But he took another big drag on it and then tried to focus his attention to the center of the state. What he really wanted to do was push Frist to the floor, sit on his cock, and ride him until all thoughts of Brad Roberts and how he died and who had killed him were fucked out of his mind. But then Frist might become suspicious and start unraveling Folsom's true intent for coming on this cruise.

Down on the stage, the older man, obviously Roman the Magnificent, was tying the diminutive Dieter in spread-eagled fashion to the Plexiglas crossbar, his back against the crossbar, so that his arms and legs were spread and he was firmly fastened to the crossbar at his wrists and ankles. Then Roman opened the gold box he had brought onstage with him and took out a nasty-looking pearl-handled hunting knife and, as the drums took up a gentle beating again, this time accompanied by the sound of flutes, he began shredding Dieter's tunic. During this process, which had caught the audience's attention and fancy, the young man swayed about and made a mock attempt to pull away from his bonds.

Roman stepped up to the young man, wrapped his fists in the shredded material covering his chest and ripped it away, revealing a slender, but well-muscled and perfectly proportioned torso. He then went behind the youth and ripped away the material behind as the whole center stage began to revolve. As the crossbar turned, Folsom and Frist could now see Dieter's slender, deeply dimpled hips and firm, rounded butt cheeks.

Roman the Magnificent stood back and started swishing the young man's torso with the multistranded whip, not doing any damage, really. But Dieter writhed around as if it were otherwise, and lips of lust and anticipation were being licked all around the banquettes.

Frist had two of his fingers in Folsom's mouth now, and the younger detective was giving them suck, his eyes slitted with wanton pleasure at this and what was happening between his legs as he watched the playacted debauchery begin on stage. The ebony potentate was drawing ever closer to Folsom and Frist and he now was fisting and stroking Folsom's piece.

Roman went to his box of tricks again and came out with a handful of small golden clamps, which, to the tune of much groaning and moaning and feigned begging from Dieter and an increase in the rhythm and volume of the drums and flutes, he began clamping onto the youth's body, concentrating first on the nipples and then in a V from there up to Dieter's shoulders and then on his inner thighs, rising toward the groin.

As Dieter writhed on stage under this onslaught, Frist withdrew his saliva-moistened fingers from Folsom's mouth and moved his hand down between his thigh and that of Folsom. Folsom began to writhe just as Dieter was doing as Frist's fingers rimmed his ass and then entered him. The African was stroking Folsom hard now and had his head nearly in Folsom's lap. His other hand had gone under the stool, and now fat African fingers had joined slender German ones inside Folsom's ass.

"Uhh. Oh God," Folsom exclaimed to Frist with a release of breath. "What are you two doing? You said we'd go back to your room. It was to be just the two of us."

"Haven't you remembered, Clint?" Frist whispered into his ear. "Remember? I can do you here and there and in the corridor in between too and alone or with others. You liked that before. The danger of that. And then I can turn you to the African, and he can use my cream as a lube." Both

Frist and the African were breathing hard now and working their fingers together.

"Oh God, Oh shit!"

"And do you like this?" Frist asked in a husky voice.

"Oh, oh, y-e-s."

"And this?"

"Oh shit. Oh fuck y-e-S-S!"

The African had his lips on Folsom's cock now, but this was just too much, too fast for Folsom.

"Please not this, not here, not now," Folsom exclaimed. He pushed the African's head away. The African sat up, looking very disappointed.

"Later," Folsom managed to say through gasps of what he and Frist were doing with their fingers. "Later would be fine," he said to the African. "When I can concentrate just on you."

This seemed to placate the ebony giant, who could naturally see that there was no reason for him to be sharing such a luscious tidbit with anyone else, and he sat back on his barstool and turned his attention for the first time to the entertainment on the stage.

Roman had been flicking the clamps on Dieter with his golden whip, and Dieter was tossing his body back and forth on his restraints and moaning loudly. Roman went back to his golden box and extracted a mammoth-sized dildo. Dieter looked at it and his eyes went wide in well-schooled fear and trepidation. As Roman played the dildo up and down between Dieter's butt cheeks, Frist rubbed his cock against Folsom's hole, holding his hips to him with a strong hand on Folsom's belly.

Roman poised the dildo at Dieter's asshole for a full revolution for all in the audience to see, as Frist took a silver packet from his pocket, tore it open, and rolled a condom on his erect cock.

Roman slowly pushed the dildo into Dieter's hole as Frist lifted Folsom's hips and pulled him back on his skewering cock. Dieter cried out and arched his back. Folsom gave a little cry, arched his back up to where his shoulders dug into Frist's chest, and threw his arms up and around

Frist's neck. The two moved into a deep kiss as Frist's tool worked its way ever deeper into Folsom's channel.

They were lost in lust—but only for a second. They both heard the cry from the stage and focused their attention there. Roman and Dieter no longer were alone on the stage. A naked hairy figure as outsized as a bull—not fat exactly but stocky and with a thick ram between his legs—had jumped up on stage. He was quickly followed by another figure, who Folsom quickly identified as one of the masked blond bartenders, now without his skirt on. The bull, who Folsom realized with much shock was Bruno Meister, grabbed the whip from Roman and was lashing Dieter hard with it. The young man was writhing and crying out for real now, it appeared.

Both Roman and the bartender, who evidently had been with Meister before he had become crazed and stormed the stage in a lust called forth by what was being acted out there, stood aside and let Meister have his way, although both had expressed of deep hatred on their faces. As the bartender turned, Folsom zeroed in on the groin. There was, indeed, a tattoo there just above a lovely sized prick. Folsom couldn't tell at this distance whether or not it was a scorpion, but he thought it highly likely that this was his special bartender.

With much vocalization of his burning lust, Meister stripped Dieter's bonds, picked up the dildo from the ground and herded the young man off the stage and through the door below the stairs. When they were gone, Roman and the masked bartender exchanged dark looks and followed on behind.

"It looks like the show is over," Frist said as he pulled out of a now distracted Folsom.

"Who the fuck does he think he is?" Folsom asked in indignation, trying his best not to reveal that he'd ever even seen Meister before.

"That's easy," Frist said with a bitter laugh. "He's the big cheese here. That's Bruno Meister; he owns this tub and everyone working on it. He can do what he wants with them."

The magic between Frist and Folsom was lost now, if only temporarily. "Perhaps we should use this opportunity to adjourn to my cabin," Frist said with a touch of regret in his voice.

The two adjusted their clothing, and Frist lifted Folsom's unfinished drink from the bar and watched him chug it before they left.

Frist supported Folsom as they mounted the stairs, walked through the Alexander lounge and foyer, and descended the stairs to the B corridor cabins. Folsom was feeling a little woozy now, an apparent combination of the invigorating and draining day he had already had the effects of the strong drink. Frist's cabin was on the same corridor as Folsom's but on the other side of the ship.

As had been the case in Folsom's cabin the previous evening, the steward had lowered only one of the beds and, after helping Folsom shed his clothes, Frist sat him on the edge of this bed, disrobed himself, and then knelt between Folsom's thighs and gently sucked Folsom to a orgasmic death.

Folsom was having trouble focusing. The cabin walls seemed to be moving, although he knew the ship was still docked at Rudesheim.

After Folsom had ejaculated, Frist rose and sat beside him and made slow and gentle love to him with his hands and lips and tongue, while Folsom sighed and moaned and tried to focus on Frist's expert lovemaking.

At length, Folsom fell over onto the bed sideways, and Frist stretched him out on his belly on the bed, his legs together. Folsom was aware of Frist stretching out on top of him—but just barely. However, he was very much aware when Frist straddled his exposed butt cheeks with his thighs. Folsom jolted awake and nearly lifted off the bed at Frist's first thrust inside him, but he got the old lover's measure as he entered his channel strongly and deeply and began to stroke his hips up and back on Folsom's thighs, in a wavelike fashion, his thighs encasing Folsom's and his chest propped up from Folsom's shoulders with arms locked and hands buried in the mattress. As Frist's cock dug deeper and stroked harder, Folsom gathered up a wad of sheeting in his mouth to keep himself from screaming in tones that could be heard beyond the cabin's walls and grabbed for those storm straps at the head of the bed.

Folsom was still conscious when Frist came in a first ejaculation of ecstasy, and he was barely conscious while Frist nibbled at his ear and rolled on a fresh condom, and then renewed his stroking down into him. But then Folsom slept. The sleep of the dead. The welcome release from the cares of this world, while Frist continued thrusting, thrusting, thrusting.

Chapter Six: Rhine on the Rocks

Folsom was set adrift on the Rhine, but it was a gelatinous Rhine, which supported his body as he lay on his back and which swayed him back and forth with the current. But the current wasn't being provided by the flow of the father of all German rivers; the motion was being provided by a multitude of men between his legs, moving him back and forth on their hard cocks. He was being taken to multiple deaths by ejaculation by a procession of men, some nearly identifiable as his lost lover, Brad Roberts, and to a long line of other men who had known him. He sighed and moaned for them with sounds that seemed to be echoing back at him in loud mutterings that blended with the sounds of the water rushing past him. He momentarily tried to reason how the water could be gelatinous and rushing at the same time, but he felt weak and groggy and just laid back and enjoyed the fucking.

The grinning face of a man in a mask rose up between his legs and he was being entered again. And this time he was being invaded with a member that was impossibly thick. He grunted and groaned as it just kept feeding into him at a depth he'd never experienced before. He tried to raise his head to seek assurances that his masked assaulter was bottoming out, but the figure rolled his torso up onto Folsom's belly so that his view was blocked. However,

173

after Folsom had taken several more inches inside him, the masked figure took Folsom's hands and brought them between his legs and wrapped them around a smooth plastic grip. He placed his own hands over Folsom's and guided him in stroking himself with the oversized dildo that was mining his ass passage.

The sound of the rushing water grew louder, overpowering Folsom's groans and moans so that he couldn't even hear himself. He felt like he was in a drunken stupor, but he felt himself bucking hard against the mammoth dildo churning around inside him. It slowly retreated and he turned his head to the side, pulled a string of the gelatinous material into his mouth, and bit down on it to keep himself from screaming out. Even this confused him, as he was both terrified of what was happening to him and in a deep state of ecstasy at what was turning and stroking inside him.

The clouds of confusion began to dissipate around him, and he no longer was floating in the river. He was in one of the cabins on the MS *River God*—not his own cabin, but one quite similar to it. He was stretched out on the bed, his face only a few inches from the edge of the table. One thing remained the same, however: something was stroking back and forth deep inside his ass channel.

As he became more conscious, Folsom realized he was in the embrace of another man, who was stretched behind him, both of them on their sides. The other man was holding him firmly encased in his arms, with a hand on Folsom's belly that pushed in so that Folsom's hips met the thrust of the man's cock. The man was murmuring in Folsom's ear in words that were becoming increasingly clear.

"You're so nice. Such a sweet, warm ass."

Folsom recognized the voice and turned his head to receive a deep kiss on the lips from Sigmund Frist, whose body suddenly became quite taut. Frist gave a little cry, thrust his hips against Folsom's butt three times in short, insistent strokes of spurting release, and then fully relaxed against Folsom with a satisfied sigh.

"That was so nice. As good as all the rest," he whispered. "You're amazing."

"All the rest?" Folsom asked in a hoarse voice, a voice he had been searching to exercise for some time but only now seemed to be able to command.

"Yes. We've been fucking all night. Look it's day already. And look at those." He laughed as he pointed to a pile of spent condoms on the floor beside the bed and under the table. "This is why I come on these cruises. For the release, pent up from months of hard work." Folsom saw that, indeed, they had been very busy. He remembered little of it, having slept so deeply after the exhausting previous day. But he didn't even consider telling Frist that he'd been more than half out of consciousness most of the night. He also had a splitting headache and his mouth felt like it was full of cotton.

Folsom looked up at the window wall running around the head of the bed and the inner edge of the table and saw that Frist had spoken the truth. Daylight was streaming through the window. He could also feel that the ship was under way, plowing down the Rhine toward Koblenz. They had left Rudesheim behind.

Disengaging himself from Frist, Folsom asked if he could shower and then declined the offer that they shower together. If they'd done it as many times as Frist indicated they had, he thought they both had had enough. All he could think of was getting rid of this headache and going back to tracking Bruno Meister down and killing him.

After he emerged from the shower and as he was drying himself off, Frist, still stretched out, naked in the bed, was looking very pleased with himself and looked very pleasing to Folsom still.

"We're underway," Folsom said, noting the obvious just to fill the air with something more than the smell of sweat and sex.

"Yes. This is our Romantic Rhine day," Frist answered. "The entire day until late this afternoon flowing down the most scenic stretch of the Rhine—lots of castle ruins perched on high hills with vineyards running down to medieval villages at the river's edge. It's a day just for sitting and gawking at the landscape, although I would be content to just sit and gawk at you."

Folsom managed to retreat from Frist's cabin without so much as another kiss or embrace—he knew that if he let Frist touch him again, it was likely they'd be in bed for the rest of the morning.

His cabin was being attended to by the steward when he reached it, and after an awkward greeting without explanation on why the room had obviously been unused since it was set up for night the previous evening, Folsom went on to the restaurant for a buffet breakfast.

He ate quickly, not bothering even to check on whether Meister was about and then returned to his cabin, stripped, and pulled on a Speedo. He'd go topside and try to shake this headache and take in the sights as well.

About half of the passengers had chosen to oo and ah over the Romantic Rhine cruise, complete with commentary from the bridge, from the comfort of the Alexander lounge. But many others, like Folsom, chose to watch the scenery slide by while getting a tan, and were topside, on the Helios deck. A few of these men were paying some attention to the landscape; several more were more interested in the sights of other men stripped down for tanning; and a large group was already fucking on the lounge chairs and completely oblivious of the centerpiece of their sightseeing cruise.

Folsom didn't make it very far down the line of loungers before a black, beefy hand reached out, took his wrist, and brought him to a seated position on a lounger. It was the African potentate, wearing only a thong, and looking like a massive black statue, with more well-defined gleaming muscle than Folsom had ever seen on a man before.

"Remember me?" the African said, showing a full set of pearly whites that contrasted with the blackness of his handsome face.

"Of course," Folsom responded. "How could I forget?"

Another big grin from the African.

"You said maybe later."

"Yes, yes I did."

"Can this be maybe later?" the African asked, although his hands were well ahead of his mouth. He already had a beefy paw between Folsom's prick and the inner lining of the Speedo.

"Yes, why not?" Folsom said and then the need for discussion had ended. In short order Folsom was stretched out, reversed, on top of the African, Folsom's mouth working the African's gigantic tool and the African's thick tongue working Folsom's asshole.

When he was ready, the ebony giant lifted Folsom's body by his waist as if it was a paper doll, and with much huffing and puffing from them both, brought Folsom's ass down into his lap, slowly skewering Folsom's channel on his massive pole. Then he pulled Folsom's shoulder blades back onto his chest, moved his legs to the side of the lounger, dug his heels into the deck of the ship and began a long, rhythmic stroking up into Folsom to the tune of much gasping, panting, and impassioned cries—from both of them.

When they both were spent, they just lay there, Folsom stretched on top of the African, and watched the ship's passage through the rocks of the Lorelei, with their legend of siren songs luring seafarers to their death on the tricky shoals of the passage of the Rhine between two rocky crags.

As they passed this formation, a shadow fell on Folsom and he looked up to see Frist staring down at them. He didn't look the least bit pleased. In fact, he looked rather upset.

"Look, Sig, just because we . . . ," Folsom started to say, but Frist motioned him to stop with a cutting gesture of his hand.

"I don't give a crap who you fuck or how often you fuck them, Folsom. I just came to get you because there's something you need to see . . . in your professional capacity. Could you come with me below, please?" It didn't really sound to Folsom like either a request or a question. Frist obviously was quite upset about something.

Folsom had the sinking feeling of having been dashed on the rocks by the siren song of the Lorelei, but he had no idea why he felt this way.

Chapter Seven: A Stolen Death

Sigmund Frist, who had been plowing his American counterpart, Clint Folsom, the previous night couldn't have picked a worse time to want further attention from Folsom. Folsom had been waylaid this morning on the Helios deck by a heavenly endowed African potentate who had him stretched out on a lounger and was mining his ass with his very royal manhood.

Folsom's first thought when Frist interrupted this little orgiastic death out of Africa scene was that Frist was jealous and territorial. But then he discerned that there was something much more serious behind the German's gruffness and insistence that Folsom go below with him.

With apologies to the good-natured African, who was easily placated with the promise of a rematch, Folsom rose and pulled on his Speedo and slipped a T-shirt over his head. Seconds later, he was padding along behind Frist down to the Apollo deck, where the major suites were sandwiched between the Ambrosia restaurant and the reception foyer and the Alexander lounge.

Frist responded to none of Folsom's questions as they descended from the sun deck. He just went to the door of the Zeus suite, looked around to ensure that they were not being spied on, indicated that Folsom should open the door, pushed him inside, and then shouldered the door closed behind them.

Folsom gasped, hardly believing what he saw. He had seen this tableau before—and it was one that he'd never forget and that marked the turning point in his life. He was forced to look away in horror. He turned to Frist, who was looking very serious and was pulling surgical gloves on his hands. He didn't, however, offer Folsom a pair.

Bruno was stretched out, on his back and naked, on a king-sized bed. He was spread-eagled with his appendages bound to posts at the four corners of the bed. He was quite dead, and the grotesque grimace set on his face indicated that he hadn't died easily. A thick sounding wand was buried deep in the piss slit of his cock and he had bled from both his ass channel and from a knife wound below his rib cage on the right side of his torso.

This scene was all too familiar to Folsom. This was exactly the scene of his lover and partner's death, a death that Folsom had been tracking Bruno Meister down for having committed. This was such a fitting death for Meister, but a gorge of rage rose from Folsom's belly that Meister had escaped him—that someone else had gotten there first.

"Who. What . . . ?" Folsom stammered out.

"The knife wound was enough to kill him," Frist said. "But the anal bleeding indicates he was probably fucked by an oversized object as well. Probably just a kinky sex party gone bad, but this is quite an inconvenient mess."

"Yes, probably just a party gone bad," Folsom repeated in a shocked monotone. But his mind was crying out that no, the similarities between this scene and that of Brad Robert's death were just too coincidental. No, something else was afoot here. He was sure of it. But who else on this ship other than he himself could make this connection. He had to think. And he had to hide these thoughts from Frist. Frist, first of all, was a policemen. And this was his territory.

"I don't understand. Why are you showing this to me? Are you taking on this investigation? Who else knows of this."

"That isn't all," Frist responded, clearly indicating that show and tell wasn't over and the answering of questions hadn't begun. He motioned for Folsom to open the door and follow him back down the corridor. They went down the stairs in the foyer to the deck below and walked into the short corridor of passenger cabins under the midship portion of the Alexander lounge. Folsom heard the sound of sobbing, which increased as they walked toward the end of the corridor, toward where the door to the exercise room was on the right and the door into a crew area. Eventually, Folsom assumed, leading to the door under the stairs in the Hephaestion Club room. Frist turned to the right into the small exercise room, which seemed overflowing with men and equipment.

The first man encountered was the ship's captain, who was standing stiffly just inside the doorway with a deep-creased frown on his face. Looking past him, Folsom saw the source of the weeping. Roman the Magnificent, the tormentor of the previous evening in Hephaestion, was hunched over the weight bench and wailing to beat the band. He seemed to be playing the tormented rather than the tormentor today.

And then Folsom saw the reason for Roman's lamenting. He was shielding and hugging the naked body of his erstwhile assistant, Dieter, which was propped on the bench, wrists tied to the handlebars of the treadmills on either side of the bench and ankles to the feet of the opposite ends of the treadmills. There was a sounding wand buried in his piss slit, and a knife wound under his rib cage, and, if he could have seen past Roman's protecting body, Folsom was sure that there would be bleeding from his rectum too. There was entirely too much of this going around.

Folsom stood, dazed, watching the touching farewell love scene between Roman and Dieter, a near twin of the one he himself had had with Brad Roberts when he had come upon that murder scene. No, there was no coincidences in these two deaths on the Rhine, Folsom told himself. And he was sure there was a link to Roberts's death as well.

While Roman was grieving and the wheels were spinning in Folsom's mind, Frist and the captain were speaking in low tones at the door. But when Folsom turned toward the door, Frist was gone and the captain was taking command.

"The German authorities will, of course, come on board as soon as we reach Koblenz late this afternoon," the captain said. "I'll send someone down to tend to Roman and to seal this door. But in the meantime, Mr. Folsom, I would appreciate it if you went to your cabin and stayed there and didn't speak of this to anyone."

"Yes, yes, of course, Captain," Folsom responded and turned immediately and walked back up the corridor. He had been in such a daze upon the discovery in succession of two identical deaths that, as he walked slowly back to his cabin, he couldn't remember whether any mention of Bruno Meister's death had been made to the captain at all.

Folsom was surprised to find Frist waiting for him in his cabin. He tried to discuss what had happened with Frist, but his mind was working too slowly in gauging what to say that didn't bring in the connections to Robert's death or reveal that Folsom himself had planned to kill Meister. Before he could form what to say or ask, Frist was shushing him and had pulled off his T and had his torso arched back as Frist attacked his nipples with his lips and teeth. Folsom was pushed down on the bed that had been lowered before he entered the room, and Frist slid his Speedo off his hips and down his legs. He spread the younger American's legs wide, thrust inside him, and fucked away all of Folsom's questions. Exhausted once more by overwhelming sex, Folsom was nodding off as Frist left him and exited the cabin. It was only right before sleep claimed him that Folsom remembered the most pressing question that he had. How had Frist gotten into his locked cabin?

The captain had Folsom's dinner delivered to his cabin that evening. A trembling and obviously troubled Tiho brought the tray in. He was on the verge of saying something to Folsom, but then he clamped his jaw shut and scurried out of the room, the very personification of a scared rabbit.

About an hour after the boat arrived in Koblenz, Folsom got the call that a German inspector wanted to talk with him in the library. Folsom had watched the boat round the bend at the gigantic bronze statue of Kaiser Wilhelm the First, and move up into the Moselle River. Then he had seen from his cabin window the police launch come out to the boat, which had anchored about a hundred feet from the dock. He had no idea what the other passengers were thinking about the failure of the ship to dock and to open its doors for access to the city's waterfront. Folsom told the captain that he'd be in the library in a half hour.

But before that, Folsom knew he needed a drink. He left his cabin, bypassed the library, and went up into the Alexander lounge. He ordered a stiff scotch on the rocks from one of masked blond bartenders, having no idea if it was his masked bartender, and moved to a table near the stairs down to Hephaestion. He could hear music coming up from the sex club down there, and he wondered momentarily whether the evening show down there would go on in spite of Dieter's death and Roman's reaction to that.

"There you are, Mr. Folsom. I suppose we can talk here as well as in the library."

Folsom looked up to find he was being addressed by a pudgy middle-aged man with a very stern expression on his face.

"I am Inspector Fritz Manfeld of the Koblenz office of the Bundespolizei. I would like to ask you a few questions about this suspicious death. Und so, shall we get right down to it?"

Folsom took a deep swallow on his scotch and motioned for Manfeld to sit down at the table.

"I'm Detective Clint Folsom of the New York Police Department."

Manfeld raised his eyebrows. "And you are on this cruise for . . . ?"

"Pleasure," Folsom responded.

"I see," Manfeld answered after a brief pause in a flat tone. It was only then that Folsom realized what a bad choice of words he had made. But being on the cruise to do gay cruising had been his cover. He couldn't very well change his tune on that now.

"And did you know the deceased?"

"No, not either one," Folsom answered. This was quite a stretch, but technically correct. He'd known every nook and cranny of Dieter's body following last evening's performance and he knew much more than that about Bruno Meister, but he hadn't personally met either one of them. So his response wasn't really a lie.

"Either one?" Manfeld said with a set expression on his face. "Can you tell me how you know there was more than one, please? The captain indicated you entered the exercise room to see the body of the young man, Dieter Krungsheft, but we only discovered the other body after we boarded the ship."

"Excuse me?" Folsom asked with surprise and confusion. "Sigmund Frist and I saw Bruno Meister's body shortly after noon. Hasn't he reported that to you?"

"Sigmund Frist? Do you mean Inspector Sigmund Frist from Frankfurt?"

"Yes, he's the one who showed me the bodies."

"I know nothing about Sigmund Frist being involved in this. We're a long way from Frankfurt." Manfeld was forming a little set frown on his brow.

"He's a passenger on the cruise," Folsom pressed. "He called me in to view the crime scenes."

"I hardly think that's possible," Manfeld retorted, his voice taking on an indignant tone. "I hardly think Sigmund Frist would be on a cruise of this sort. And why would he show you the crime scene? And if he were here, why wouldn't he have reported to the authorities that he'd found Bruno Meister dead?"

"But he was there in Meister's cabin—and so was I."

"I've closely examined the passenger list, Mr. Folsom, and there is no Sigmund Frist on that list. Believe me, I would have recognized that name if I had seen it."

There was a slight pause then, and with a very cold and deliberate voice, Manfeld said, "And so, you would not be surprised, Mr. Folsom if, when we research the fingerprints in Meister's cabin and on the sexual device we found there, we find that you had been in the cabin?"

"No, of course not. As I said, Frist took me in there and . . . what sexual device?"

"We found a thick rubberized male phallus of nearly half a meter in length on the floor at the foot of the bed in Meister's cabin. It was bloodied, and we suspect it was used on both victims. You claim you didn't see that or handle it, Mr. Folsom? It was a little hard to miss."

Folsom's mind was racing. In the horror of what he saw and the short time that he was in the room, could he possibly have overlooked seeing a thick and bloody dildo of some sixteen inches in length on the floor by the body? No, he couldn't imagine that being possible. He was a trained cop. No matter how shocking the scene, his instincts would have made him memorize the most significant objects on site. He couldn't believe that the dildo could have been there when he was in the cabin.

While his mind was racing, a uniformed policeman had come into the lounge, whispered something in Manfeld's ear, and then withdrew again.

Manfeld gave Folsom a hard look. "According to the cabin attendants, you didn't occupy your cabin last night, Mr. Folsom. And an attendant was there this morning when you returned to your cabin."

Folsom started to form a response. Obviously he was going to get nowhere, if he told the inspector he was being fucked by Frist all night in the latter's cabin. And what was the number of that cabin?

Manfeld didn't really wait for an answer, though. He forged ahead with another question. "Do you have a pearl-handled hunting knife in your possession, Mr. Folsom? If we were to search your cabin, would we find such a weapon?"

Folsom was thrown off kilter. Certainly not, he was thinking. But he had seen such a knife. Where, he wondered.

Just then, the masked bartender came over and got down low between Manfeld and Folsom and started pestering Manfeld on having something to drink—on the house, captain's orders. At the same time, he was gesturing behind his back at Folsom, pointing toward the stairs down to Hephaestion.

Taking the hint, and not caring at all for the direction this police questioning was going, Folsom slipped out of his chair and down the stairs, while the bartender was occupying the attention of a flustered police detective.

As Folsom hit the bottom of the stairs, the spotlights were gleaming on the stage below, and Roman and Magnificent was strutting around in his almost-nothing costume just as he had the night before. He was apologizing that his assistant was indisposed, but that the show had to go on. Surely there was someone from the audience interested in a little bondage and S&M, he was saying.

"Ah, yes, up there, on the stairs. The perfect man," he was saying. "Shine the lights up there."

Folsom was blinded by the strobing lights. Roman couldn't mean him. But, incredibly, he seemed to mean him. And there was no better way, he thought, to escape the confusing and damning questions of the German policeman, if only for a few moments, than to hide in plain sight.

Thus, he gave no resistance when the voices from the audience surged around him, urging him to take the challenge.

He found himself down on the stage, being strapped, wrists and ankles, spread-eagle style to the Plexiglas crossbeam.

Roman came up close behind him and whispered in his ear, "Help me and I'll help you. Play to the audience." He then started ripping a perfectly good shirt and pants to shreds on Folsom's body with a box cutter, accompanied by wild cheering and enthusiastic applause. It hit Folsom then. Roman was not using the weapon he had used before. The previous evening he'd used a pearl-handled hunting knife. This must be the same knife Manfeld was accusing Folsom of having in his cabin. There was little Folsom could do about the implications of this now, however. He was trussed up to the crossbeam like a deer on a spit. The stage began to revolve.

He glanced up into the crowd and saw that Manfred and the uniformed policeman had come down the stairs and were frantically searching the banks of patrons with their eyes. But Folsom had guessed well. They did not expect to see Folsom on the stage as part of the act and so they didn't see him there. In short order they had left, seeking their escaped suspect somewhere else on the ship.

Roman flicked Folsom with the whip, and he writhed in exaggerated response, playing for the audience as Roman had requested. He writhed for real, however, while Roman was applying and tweaking the clamps on his nipples and other sensitive areas of his skin. He was moaning and groaning. But his cock was filling out too. This rough treatment was getting him excited.

Roman was lathering up his asshole, and Folsom tensed his body against the crossbeam and howled to the ceiling as Roman thrust his gold-condom sheathed cock into him from behind, on the other side of the crossbar, and rode him hard to loud chants of "houza" from the appreciative audience.

This was a departure from the previous evening's act as well, Folsom realized. Last evening, Roman had used a mammoth dildo on Dieter. A mammoth dildo. Now missing from the act. Folsom shivered at the thought. Meister had been fucked with a mammoth dildo.

At length Roman whispered in Folsom's ear, "Now, I'm going to release you and you are going to take your bows with a grin on your face. And I'm going to help spirit you away and try to keep you out of the hands of the German police. I want you to find Dieter's killer—and you have to be free to do that. Agreed?"

Folsom nodded his head in agreement—not being sure he wasn't now responding to Dieter's killer—and Roman ballooned out the head of the condom with his semen deep inside Folsom, and the evening's entertainment was over. Roman ceremoniously released his captive, and the audience cheered its pleasure and appreciation. Roman and Folsom then took their bows and disappeared with a flourish through the door below the stairs and into the area that contained two crew cabins before reaching the door into the passenger corridor where the exercise room was located. Roman quickly told Folsom that one of the crew cabins was occupied by the three masked blond bartenders and the one across from it had once been occupied by Roman and Dieter. But Folsom was now replacing Dieter in Roman's bed, if not in his heart—but safe nonetheless in at least the short term from the police search of the passenger areas of the ship for the vanished American.

Chapter Eight: The Choice of Suspicion or Trust

After his narrow escape from the pounding questions of the German police about Bruno Meister's death, by way of accepting a pounding of his ass by Roman the Magnificent on stage at Hephaestion, Folsom meekly followed Roman into his cabin through the door under the stairs in the sex club. The cabin was the same size as Folsom's was and had the same two pull-down beds over benches with a table in between. But it wasn't nearly as well-appointed as Folsom's was. It also had the prolonged lived-in look and the jumbling of costumes and makeup boxes that nearly all entertainers' dressing rooms had.

As they propelled themselves into the room and Roman clicked and locked the door behind them, Folsom scurried to the corner of one of the pulled-down beds and made involuntary gestures of pulling the shreds of his clothes together to protect himself. It was rather an idiotic move of modesty in view of the fact that Roman had just finished fucking him from the rear and could arguably be said to know Folsom fully now. But it wasn't his honor or reputation Folsom was protecting. There was every reason to believe that Roman had killed Meister after Meister had killed Roman's assistant and lover, Dieter. Roman had followed

Meister and Dieter out of the club the previous night, and it was highly likely the dildo Roman used his act and the knife found in Folsom's room, both of which had apparently disappeared from the stage props for Roman's act, were the murder weapons in one or both killings.

Roman was standing there, his fists tight and his muscles taut. He had a look of rage and hurt about him, and with his gold outfittings and mane of white-gold hair, he looked like a lion about to pounce. Folsom shrank back into the corner of the bed, ready for the onslaught, taking a defensive position.

"What?" Roman roared. "Why are you looking at me like that? Surely you don't think—"

"I don't know what to think," Folsom stammered. "This is all happening too—"

"Do you think I'd have saved you back there, if I thought you'd—?"

And then Roman stopped and gave Folsom a look of horror. "You don't think I—?"

"What am I to think?" Folsom spat back. "You have a motive for Meister's killing. He attacked and brutalized your assistant even before they'd left the stage last night. And there's the knife and the dildo. Where are the ones you used in the act last night?"

"I don't know," Roman said, his voice having turned to a frustrated wail. He sat down heavily in the opposite bed and lowered his head to his hands, defeated for the moment. "I have no idea where the props are."

Then he looked up, with a defiant look on his face. "But I didn't kill Meister. I wanted to. I've wanted to for a very long time. But I didn't do it. And I'd never have killed Dieter. Dieter was my life."

Roman was on the edge. His voice had a sobbing quality to it now. Folsom sat up on the bed, using a cajoling voice now.

"Tell me. Tell me why Meister was able just to walk away with Dieter last night like that. Surely you knew what Meister had in mind to do with Dieter. To do to Dieter."

Another sob. "Yes, of course I knew. But Meister owned Dieter. He owned us all. He took Dieter and Tiho and many of the rest from an orphanage in Croatia. Whatever they have faced and suffered here, it's better than they could have expected where they came from."

"Then you had no real grudge against Meister?" Folsom asked quietly, soothingly.

"Unfortunately, not true," Roman said with an air or resignation. "Meister was about to send Dieter and some of the others back to Croatia and break in a whole new set of crew for this boat." Roman laughed bitterly. "He said they were getting too old and that he fancied more variety. I tried to keep Dieter; I even offered to buy him. But Meister had just laughed at me."

"And Tiho?" Folsom asked. "Was he to be sent back too?"

"Yes, and others as well."

"And the bartenders in the Alexander lounge? Them too."

"Just Ralf. He wasn't like the others, though."

Folsom didn't directly ask which one Ralf was. Instead he asked, "And was it Ralf who Meister was with before he took Dieter off last night? The one who followed them out with you?"

"Yes, that was Ralf."

"And why was Meister sending Ralf away?"

"He had gotten too cocky. He'd become Meister's favorite in his little sex games. But he was taking control too often. Meister didn't trust him anymore."

"And Ralf didn't want to leave?"

"No, certainly not. . . . Wait, you don't think Ralf . . .?"

"Someone did it. I have no idea who killed your Dieter, if Meister didn't do it himself. But there were several who had motive for Meister's death. And Ralf—"

"But Ralf saved you. I sent him up to the lounge to help you escape. Surely you can't think—"

"Someone killed Meister," Folsom repeated. He had taken Roman's hand and was willing the older man to look

191

into his eyes, trying to gauge what was surprise from foreknowledge and guilt from innocence. "Ralf had motive and means as much as any of the rest of us. If you didn't kill Meister and I didn't, Ralf might—"

"You didn't kill Meister?" Roman blurted out.

"No, no, of course not," Folsom said. And then he stopped and really looked into Roman's eyes. "Did you save me back there because you thought . . .? Did you believe that I had caught Meister with Dieter's body and then had done the same to him in revenge? Is that why you saved me?"

Roman didn't answer. He just lowered his eyes, shuddered, and let out a big sob. Tears were flowing now and he lifted his head and let out a primeval yell. Folsom moved to the bed beside him and took Roman in his arms and rocked him back and forth.

"There, there, shush," Folsom murmured as he rocked Roman's torso. "You are so tense. You have every right to be angry. I didn't kill either one of them, but you can take your rage out on me, if you like. For whatever reason, you saved me back there."

They went into a 69 position on the bed and endured both Roman's vigorous face fucking of Folsom's cock and his almost brutal attack on Folsom's own prick with his teeth and mouth. When Roman was filled out, Folsom stripped his Roman skirt off of him and looked around for a condom packet. But Roman was too worked up for that nicety. He pushed Folsom down onto the bed on his back, spread his legs, and thrust into him, diving again and again, coming nearly all of the way out and then plunging in again. He was marshaling all of his anger and frustration and grief over the death of his lover, offering a different kind of release and death to Folsom. Folsom writhed under him, experiencing his own frustration and grief at the loss of his own lover, welcoming the death by ejaculation that Roman was offering. Sighing for it; moaning for it; begging for it. Naked cock skin reaming the naked skin of an undulating ass passage. Thrusting, thrusting, thrusting. And then exploding, with a shared vision of releasing death. Folsom's insides flooded with a warm cascade of fluid. And collapse.

Once more Roman was crying, and once more Folsom embraced and consoled him, nestling the grieving man's butt into his groin. And now it was Folsom fucking Roman. But this time it was a more loving, languid, giving taking and receiving—a sharing of grief and consolation.

In time the grieving of both was relieved by the cover of sleep, their arms entwined, Folsom's cock still deep inside Roman's ass. Roman slept quietly, exhausted by the exertion of gripping and dealing with his frustration and anger.

Folsom's dreams were more troubled, however. He was being pursued through the ship by Inspector Manfeld and a bevy of uniformed policeman, who seemed to be Tiho, the bartender now identified as Ralf, Sigmund, Roman, and even the dead Dieter. He was turning away here and there from slashings of a pearl-handled knife and was been clubbed by a mammoth dildo. He was searching for some place to hide, but there wasn't anywhere where the uniformed figures didn't find him. And then he found himself in a helicopter of a sort, but more primitive than a helicopter—some sort of straw contraption. And beside him, taking up most of the space, was the grinning African potentate. And the ebony giant was whisking him away from danger on the ship. But then Folsom found himself on a bed covered with the hides of exotic creatures. And his arms and legs were spread-eagled and tied to the corners of the bed. And the naked African king, his body glistening with sweat and radiating power and force, was dancing around below him, a large dildo in one hand and a pearl-handled hunting knife in the other, both of which were covered in blood. Native African boys were standing beside the bed and shooing flies away and moving the air with large palm fronds. And the ebony giant was chanting and laughing. Folsom's ass was being massively entered, and a thick tube, whether the dildo or the African's cock, Folsom knew not, was invading him ever deeper. And he was screaming and gasping and bucking against and with the invader. The African was huddled over him, leering down at him, the knife was poised over Folsom's breast . . .

"Wake up," Roman was saying in a loud, hoarse whisper. "You're moaning and crying out to beat the band. You'll have the police down here in no time."

"What's the use?" Folsom was saying bitterly as he came out of his nightmare. "They'll find me sooner or later anyway. They'll search the whole ship. And they've surely already started doing that methodically."

"But that doesn't mean they'll find you here," Roman said. "We can always try our best to prevent that." Then he stood and opened a drawer in a built-in bureau at the foot of the bed and took out a small key. He walked over to the closet, opened it, and stepped in. Almost immediately, he told Folsom to come over and take a look inside. And when he did, he discovered that the panel at the back of the closet was open and there was a small locker about four feet high and six feet wide and deep through the opening.

"What . . .?"

"This is an unused storage locker built into dead space between here and the wall of the club room," Roman explained. "No one's come to use it the entire time I've been on this ship. There's a good chance it isn't even on any plans the captain may have given the police. It's a better hope than none. When and if the police come, you can stow away in here."

"But will I be given enough notice?"

"Both doors into this corridor have buzzers on them. We want to know if any of the passengers are straying where they aren't wanted. If someone's coming, the buzzer will . . ."

And just then a buzzer did sound. Roman pushed Folsom into the storage bin and shut the door firmly behind him. It was pitch black, and it was with great dread that Folsom heard the turning of the key.

He was locked in. He didn't even know if he could really trust Roman and now he was Roman's prisoner. In the dark. All alone, with his ragged, heaving breath to remind him how terrified he was.

Chapter Nine: Thinking Inside the Box

Folsom heard some muffled discussion from the other side of the door between his cramped, dark prison and the back panel on the closet in Roman's cabin and then some rustling around in the cabin followed by the slamming of the cabin door and then . . . silence . . . for the longest time.

A good thing he wasn't claustrophobic, Folsom was thinking. And then thinking about that, he started to become claustrophobic. Was he getting enough air? Why couldn't his eyes adjust to the dark? Would Roman ever return to set him free, or would he die in here? Or was Roman really the killer and when he opened the door, Folsom would be met with the sweep of a pearl-handled knife? No, it couldn't be that. The police seemed already to have found that knife. But they found it in his own cabin—or so they wanted him to think. What was it that Manfeld said? Did he actually say they'd found the knife in his cabin? And, if so, how could that be? Was he hyperventilating? Was it hotter in here now than when he'd been shut up?

Folsom pinched himself hard on the arm and willed himself to slow down his breathing and the racing of his mind. Breathe in and let it out slowly. Again. Must become calm.

And when he had become calm, he started to work the problem out. Roman had thought that he, Folsom, had killed Meister—or at least purported to think that—and was willing to help him for that very reason. And he would have killed Meister if someone hadn't beaten him to that. That's what he had come here to do in the first place. Had he let Roman know that? No, maybe not. If he did, and if Roman killed Meister, there would be no real reason Roman would kill him too. They still could cooperate. It wasn't Folsom's place to bring Meister's killer to the bar. He was an American cop off duty, not a German cop. It was Sigmund Frist's responsibility. No, not that either; that Manfeld guy was investigating the death. Frist made clear he wasn't on the cruise in his official capacity. But why then was he seeming to take charge? And then he disappeared. But of course if the German police didn't know of his preferences and that he'd be on a cruise like this, of course he'd have disappeared as soon as the police showed up. And Frist had made quite clear that he had joined the cruise at Rudesheim so he wouldn't be noticed joining the cruise in Mainz, which was in his jurisdiction. And why had he been arguing with Meister in that café in Rudesheim? The thoughts and fears were pressing—were becoming oppressive.

Folsom was hyperventilating again—both his mind and pulse racing at an increasing rate. Calm down. Breath slower. Purge your mind. Let your mind work on this subconsciously. Think of something else. Roman's cock stroking in and out of your ass, filling it, rotating in it, mining your insides as only a mature, experienced top can do. And the maddening variety of it. At first forceful and vigorous from anger and frustration and then turned to a tender, languid fucking. The way he played your nipples and stroked the curves and crevices of your body. The sensuous sucking on your toes as his cock pulled out and then stroked back into you to the hilt. . . . Your sighing and moaning. This is how you liked taking it—rough and forceful and then slow and totally possessing you. It was the way Brad had given it to you. The best of orgiastic deaths.

There was a rumbling from below in the ship, and Folsom felt the pull. The ship was underway. It hadn't docked in Koblenz at all. It was supposed to be docked here for a full day. But it was on the move through the water and picking up speed. Where was that detective from Koblenz then? Was he still on board? And where was Roman? Was he ever going to get out of this dark box? Who else could possibly know he was in here?

Ralf, one of the masked bartender triplets? Ralf had helped save Folsom from the police. And Ralf had fucked him hard and had obviously enjoyed doing so. They had some connection; they both loved what they got from each other. Could Roman have had time to let Ralf know Folsom was locked in this storage box? But was Ralf the one who had killed Meister? And would he feel threatened by an American detective? Did Ralf know he was a police detective?

Dieter. Who killed Dieter? The rational explanation was that Meister killed Dieter in a similar way that he had killed Folsom's lover and partner, Brad Roberts, and that Meister had subsequently been killed in the same way because he had killed Dieter. That was the only rational explanation for these deaths. That worked out if Dieter died before Meister did. The police would know that eventually, but how could Folsom find out? God, why was he being the cop on this? He didn't give a fuck who killed Meister. But should he care who killed Dieter? Wasn't that the key? And who would be motivated to torture and kill Meister if Meister had killed Dieter? It all came back to Roman.

Think, think. No, calm down. Conserve your energy and your breath. Is the air getting stale in here? Did I hear a buzzer? Was that a sound in the cabin? Somebody entering the cabin?

Folsom put his ear to the door of his prison. There indeed were men's voices, muffled but distinct. One angry; the other placating.

"Swear you had nothing to do with this, and that you don't know where the American is, Roman."

"Yes, I swear, I swear."

The sound of a slap and a yelp.

"Maybe I can fuck the truth out of you."

"No, no, Sten. I swear. I could never had killed Dieter and I didn't kill Meister. Oh, God no, you're hurting my arm, Sten."

"Spread 'em. Feet apart. I don't give a fuck about Dieter. But it's all ruined now. If you killed Meister, you ruined everything."

"Ohhhh. Not so fast not so deep! Your fingers. You're killing me. Give me time. Gr-o-a-n. I didn't kill Meister."

"But you wanted to. You wanted to kill Meister for what he was doing to Dieter, didn't you? Get your hands away from there. Take it like a man—like you gave it to that prick Dieter each night on stage. Not so easy to take what you give, is it? But what I have is longer and thicker than what you've been sticking Dieter with, isn't it? Ughhh."

"Ahhhhhh, nooooo. Oh, God. You're too big. It's too . . . ahhhhhh!"

"And you don't know where the American is?"

Moan, grunt, groan.

"Tell me."

Muffled pleading and groaning from Roman.

"Tell me."

"No, no, I don't know. I swear. Oh God, stop. You're splitting me."

"Jesus, you're tight. So prissy and chummy only with that Dieter. Well, Dieter's gone now. There are other cocks in play. I'll stop when you're begging for it. You'll tell me if you see the American, won't you?"

"Y-e-s-s. Ohhhhh."

"And you love me inside you, don't you? You can't get enough of what Sten has got, can you?"

"Yes. I mean no. Ohhhhhh, I don't . . ."

A sharp cry from whoever was assaulting Roman. And then, "There, that does you. I've marked you now. Now you're my bitch. I plan to pick up the pieces from Meister. Are you with me on that?"

A muffled "Yes."

"Remember what I said. We can tag the American with this. The scuttlebutt is that the knife was found in his cabin and his fingerprints are on the door of Meister's cabin and on the dildo. It's a slam dunk if they can find a motive. I'll get you a replacement for Dieter in the act. But your ass is mine now. Don't you forget it."

The sound of a slamming door and of subsiding moaning and sobbing from inside the cabin. But Folsom, still locked in his dark prison, hardly heard these sounds at all.

The dildo, he was thinking, a shiver running down his spine. The guy who had brutalized Roman said Folsom's fingerprints were found on the dildo. There wasn't a dildo there when he saw the murder scene in Meister's cabin, Folsom reasoned. Maybe one was there and he just overlooked it in the short time he had been in the cabin? No, he was a trained police detective, and an extra-size dildo is a little hard to ignore. The prints on the door, sure, Folsom could remember having opened and closed the cabin door. But on the dildo? How had his prints gotten on the dildo? Or was the scuttlebutt around the ship off the mark? Just false gossip, as most gossip was? Yeah, that must be it. But he could feel the noose tightening around his neck—and they hadn't even gotten around to discovering the strength of the motive he had to kill Meister. He couldn't feel indignant about that at all; he'd meant to kill Meister all along. The irony was that he didn't get the satisfaction but might swing for the crime anyway. Talk about divine justice.

Chapter Ten: Escape and Its Cost

"You heard?" Roman asked Folsom when he'd unlocked the storage bin behind his closet and stood back as Folsom stumbled out into the light.

Squinting his eyes, Folsom said. "Everything."

"Oh," was as much as Roman said as he stumbled back and collapsed on the bed. He was holding a tissue to a bleeding nose, and bruises were already beginning to form on his cheek and torso. What looked that finger prints were materializing in blue on either side of his rib cage.

"Thanks, man," Folsom said as he sat down beside Roman and put his arm around his shoulders protectively. "Thanks for not giving me up. Who was that, anyway?"

"That was Sten. You'll want to stay away from him."

"And who is Sten?"

"He's one of the three bartenders. You probably heard that he's making a bid to take over Meister's operations. He's just nasty enough to succeed in that."

"So let's see. You say I should trust Ralf and can't trust Sten, and they are virtual twins."

"Well, they're not really twins. When the masks come off you can tell them apart. But I guess that won't help you if you haven't seen them unmasked."

"Does Sten have a scorpion tattooed on his groin?" Folsom asked.

"No, that would be Ralf." Then Roman looked up and he smiled. He winced from the pain, but he couldn't help but smile. "So, you really do know Ralf, don't you?"

"That's right. We've managed to meet."

"He does get around and I'm not surprised that he zeroed in on you. You're quite a catch." Then he winced again.

"Come on, you need to get cleaned up," Folsom said. "And you'll need to get those bruises attended to."

"You need a shower too," Roman said. "I can tell it was really hot in that storage room. Now, your manly smell turns me on. But if they search the room again, I'd hate to see you give yourself away. Come we'll shower together—then we'll find some clothes for you to wear. We've got to get you out of here sooner or later, and you'll start a riot going through the ship wearing those shredded clothes."

When they got into the bathroom, Roman rummaged around in the compartment under the sink and came up with a new toothbrush. "Here, you can brush your teeth. I'll meet you in the shower."

And meet him in the shower he did. When Folsom pulled aside the shower curtain, there Roman was, under a stream of water, his shoulders and heels plastered to the tiles, but his hips arched out and his cock curved up, hard, ready, and inviting. With a laugh, Folsom turned and backed into the tight shower and settled on Roman's cock and was mined deeply as Roman soaped his conquest up and they rinsed off together.

As soon as they were out of the shower and toweling off, Folsom returned to the crisis at hand.

"So, where do we go from here, and why is the ship underway? Why didn't it dock in Koblenz? Is Manfeld still aboard?"

Roman responded in reverse order. "Yes, Manfeld's aboard, but the scuttlebutt around the crew is that he got dressed down for having let you slip away and not finding you. The Bundespolizei have directed the ship to go directly on to Cologne, where there's a regional police headquarters. I assume the ship will be swarming with police as soon as we dock there, and they'll take the *River God* apart board by board if they have to to find you."

"And the up side of that is?" Folsom asked, as he picked through the clothes Roman had on offer for him to wear.

"We do have a plan."

"We," Folsom asked. "How many 'we' are we talking about here?"

"Ralf, Tiho, and I," Roman answered. "We've put our heads together, and we'll have you off the ship almost as fast as the police in Cologne are coming on board."

"I'm not sure what good that will be," Folsom responded. Roman and his friends were amateurs at this. They had no idea the vice the police would have Folsom in. "All of the passengers' passports are being held at the reception desk. And I'll be completely lost in Cologne. They'll pick me up there almost as fast as they'd find me on this ship."

Roman laughed. "Ralf, Tiho, and I are survivors. You have no idea what Tiho and I had to do to get out of Eastern Europe to the West. Not all of the passports are at the reception desk. Tiho managed to get yours pulled even while the police detective was interviewing you—and he took another one for good measure. They realize yours is gone—and that was another thing Manfeld was dressed down for. But they're not likely to notice that the other passport is missing until the *River God* docks for the last time in Amsterdam and the passengers are picking up their passports to leave the ship."

"I don't understand," Folsom said. "What good is having the other passport?"

"Tiho was clever. He took one of a man who looks a bit like you but has noticeably different colored hair and a distinctive tattoo on his neck. He's got an ear stud too."

"And so?" Folsom asked.

"And so, look around you. This is a dressing room for a stage show. By the time we dock in Cologne, you're going to have that hair color and an inked tattoo. I'm sorry to say that the ear piercing isn't going to be temporary, except

203

that the hole should close up again fairly quickly if you don't want to keep it. Personally, I think you'll look stunning with a diamond in your ear. The important thing is that you'll have a relatively clean passport to use in Cologne and you'll still have your own to help you get out of the European Union area at some port the police won't be watching."

"I've never been to Cologne; it's unlikely I'll be able to maneuver there," Folsom said, "and I can't just walk away from this case. I don't care who killed Meister, other than resenting that they got there before me, but Dieter deserves having his murder solved."

"If you didn't kill Dieter, the German police will find out who did. They are very good at their jobs," Roman responded. "But why do you say you resent someone else getting to Meister before you did?"

Then Folsom told Roman everything—about the murder of his partner and lover, Brad Roberts, and about his decision to track Meister down and personally making him pay for that crime.

"Yes, I can understand that kind of anger and wish for revenge," Roman said with a quiet sense of determination in his voice. "I feel the same way about Dieter. But don't worry, we'll get you out of here, and I've already been in contact with someone in Cologne who will take care of you if you give him what he wants?"

"Give him what he wants?" Folsom asked.

"Yes. He's partial to handsome American tail. He'll let you stay in his flat. But he says if he's to take the risk of harboring a fugitive, his price is that you share his bed as well. Do you think you can handle that?"

"No problem, I'm sure," Folsom answered.

"You sure? He's a big bruiser of a guy—and can be pretty rough."

"Even better," Folsom answered with a grin.

"OK, so let's see how you do as a silver blond. I guess we'd better make you a total silver blond. You never know when . . ."

The sound of a buzzer cut through the walls of the cabin, and Folsom was bundled back into the storage bin behind the closet and he was locked into the darkness while yet another search was conducted by the policeman who had accompanied Detective Manfeld on board in Koblenz.

This time, Folsom was able to keep his calm even though he didn't like being shut up in this coffin the second time any better than the first. But this time, he could begin to see a way out of this predicament. He realized, though, that the case would have to be solved, and someone other than he had to be fingered for the murders on the ship before he would have a prayer of returning to the States, not to mention to his NYPD duties. So, it was up to him to help solve these crimes. And the longer he thought and calmly weighed the evidence and the possibilities, the more a nagging question needled at him. As soon as he could, if he was successful in disappearing into the streets of Cologne, he'd have to get to a phone with an international connection and check this nagging question out.

When Roman opened the door again, they barely had time for Folsom's cosmetic transformation before Tiho was knocking at the door and saying it was time for them to try to move forward.

Folsom did ask Roman to check out one thing for him, though, and pass the answer on through the big bruiser friend, if possible. "Could you find a subtle way to ask the captain if he will confirm that Sigmund Frist was on board? I'm worried about what has happened to Frist, and I saw he and the captain together; I know the captain knows he was here when the bodies were found. Oh, and do you have a roster of the ship's crew I could have?"

Roman rummaged around in a drawer and came up with a roster and handed it to Folsom. Then he said he would query the captain about Frist but that Folsom needed to worry about Folsom. He and Tiho needed to try to get to the other part of the ship while coffee and desserts were still being served in the Ambrosia restaurant and everyone was watching their approach to Cologne.

This was the most dangerous part of Roman's plan. Getting to the other side of the ship and to the other store room that Tiho had picked out to hide Folsom in until they could execute their escape plan. The timing on that would have to be precise.

They had no trouble getting through the public areas of the ship. They encountered no one but passengers, who were more interested in each other than in a waiter and a bottle blond, no matter how cute they both were. It was only as they were approaching an alcove off to the left of the main corridor of the stern crew area that they encountered a threat. And it was a threat in big time. Manfeld was bearing down on them. He was holding a cell phone to his ear and was having an animated conversation.

Tiho pushed Folsom off into the alcove, backed himself against the door into the laundry room, and pulled Folsom to him. He took Folsom's hand, planted it on his basket, brought Folsom's lips down to his, and went into a firm lip lock, accompanied by deep-throated moaning. Manfeld passed them right by, carefully not even looking at them, up to his chin now with disgust about what was going on on this ship.

"OK, it's safe to go on now," Tiho said, moving to push Folsom away. "It's just a bit farther now. You can wait in a storage closet for a half an hour or so while we dock in Cologne."

"No," Folsom said in a husky voice. "You shouldn't start something you don't want to see finished. And I've had enough of storage closets. This laundry room suits me just fine."

For nearly the next half hour, several of the crew members passed the laundry room, and they even looked in to check out the moaning and groaning, but none of them were surprised. It was just Tiho and one of the passengers again. Tiho was bare-assed on the top of a washing machine, and a studly silver-blond passenger with a flashy diamond ear stud had Tiho's legs spread wide and was fucking him hard and chewing on his tits.

Before they departed, Tiho was looking quite worried and concerned, and it seemed like he wanted to tell Folsom something but couldn't.

"What is it? What's wrong, Tiho?"

"I can't say. Not here, not now. But if you are able to meet me in the cathedral tomorrow afternoon at four, I do have something you need to know. But I'm afraid of telling you now; afraid of what you'll do."

There was no time to pin Tiho down on this. Folsom almost tried to make time, but suddenly Tiho was gone and Folsom was standing in a corner of the kitchen, ready for the plan to unfold, a plan that did not allow him to linger beyond the assigned time.

Even Folsom had to admit with appreciation that the escape plan was quite slick. The ship docked on the Rhine right next to the train station and the famous Cologne cathedral. The main gangplank came down and the waiting legion of police officials bustled on board. As the last of them entered the ship's foyer, the service gangplank at the stern of the ship, where the kitchen was, came down for fewer than ten seconds, a figure scurried off and moved quickly into the shadows of the trees on the river promenade, and the gangplank was pulled right back in, as if it had never been extended in the first place.

The directions on the slip of paper in Folsom's hand were quite clear in coordination with the tourist map of Cologne he had been given. As directed, he went through the bustling train station, where it would have been nearly impossible to follow him from any distance if someone was tracking him from the ship, and then up into the Dom Platz, the cathedral square. Three streets past cathedral square, down the Hohe Strasse shopping street with its teaming masses of people aching to drop their euros, Folsom turned on Brückenstrasse, which melded into Glockengasse. One more turn into Krebsgasse, and he found the innocuous section of flats he was seeking. He pressed the button above the name he had been given and he was buzzed in immediately. The connection had been made. The man named Fritz was waiting for him on the third landing.

Roman had been spot on. He was a big bruiser of a brute—well over six feet tall, bald, and heavily tattooed and muscled. Folsom had been told he was a bouncer in a popular nightclub in Cologne, and Folsom could well believe he'd be really good at that job.

There was no language barrier. His English was excellent—and explicit and to the point.

"Roman said I could try you out before I committed. You have a problem with that?"

"No," Folsom answered. What would it have mattered even if he did, Folsom wondered.

"Well, come on in then and strip."

* * * *

"Oh God, oh God, Oh Jesus. Yesssss!"

Folsom was headed toward a good death.

Fritz had shown him a thick strip of black leather with thinner belt-like extensions at either end and asked if Folsom knew what it was for. Folsom had seen a plow belt before and didn't register consternation that Fritz had one. He was amazed and fully appreciative, though, that Fritz could support his full weight with it from behind him, with the belt stretched around Folsom's belly and holding him suspended in air in front of Fritz, as the burly German bouncer fucked him hard and deep from the rear. And fucked him and fucked him and fucked him.

When Folsom was allowed to fall, exhausted, on the three-quarter bed in Fritz's one-room flat, he had only two questions. "Did I pass? Can I stay?"

"Oh, yes, you passed," Fritz answered with a big grin on his face. "Sehr Gut!"

It was good that Folsom had gotten a good nap the second time he'd been locked in the storage bin behind Roman's closet, because Fritz was so pleased with his new toy that he woke Folsom repeatedly through the night with panzer assaults on his ass canal.

Chapter Eleven: Early Morning Delight

"There, do you like it like that?"

"Oh, god, yes. Like that. And deeper, deeper." Folsom was groaning at the fucking he was receiving from the bruiser.

"Then open wider so I can get down there. Ja, like that. Ja, that's good. Sehr gut."

"Ohhh, ahhhh. M-o-a-nnnn."

Folsom was on his knees on the mattress, his chest flat on the bed, hanging onto the brass rods in the headboard of Fritz, the bruiser's, bed for all he was worth. The bruiser was on his knees behind Folsom. He held Folsom's hips steady with his beefy hands, and he'd been working at getting his cock deep inside Folsom for a couple of minutes now. The morning light, such as it was, was streaming in the window above the bed, across naked, heaving, sweating bodies. It had been a wild, semen-flooded night, but it was going to be a rather gloomy day in Cologne. Already the street noise of a busy commerce day intruded into the room, mixing with German exclamations of passion and approval and Folsom's gruntings and groanings and cries and sighs.

Plumbing deeper and deeper. One of the bruiser's fists went to between Folsom's shoulder blades, pushing him into the mattress, urging Folsom to raise his butt even farther to his invading sledgehammer. Pump. Push. Pump. Dive. Moooaaannn.

"Oh, Christ. Oh, god. I . . . can't . . . take . . . any . . . ohhhhhhhhhh."

Folsom's fists were flexing and gripping on the brass rods to the rhythm of the German's intense stroking and digging. He wanted to scream. To cry out in ecstasy and release and throbbing fulfillment. But the bruiser had warned him the night before of how thin the walls were in these blocks of flats. So, he bunched up sheeting into his mouth from the pillow his face was being smashed into and bit down on the wadding hard.

Retreat. Slide. Relief. Plunge. "Arghhhhhhh. Yes, yes, oh y-e-s-s!"

"Gute, gute. I'm in."

"Ooffff." The bruiser was pushing Folsom's hips to the mattress and coming down with him, remaining dug in to his root. His chest was pushing into Folsom's shoulders, and his strong legs were encasing Folsom's thighs and pulling them together.

"Oh, oh." Stretched and filled like never before that night. Throbbing cock, buried deep. Ass wall, undulating, caressing engorged cock. The German grunting and groaning now as well. Hand working its way between Folsom's chest and the mattress, finding and tweaking a nipple. The thumb of the other hand wrapping around and finding Folsom's mouth. Folsom pulling it in with his lips and giving suck. Folsom's fists on the brass rods. Opening and closing. Tightening and flexing—to the rhythm of the fuck.

Fritz began swiveling his midsection around on Folsom's butt now. Grinding into his ass at all angles and Folsom was panting and groaning, loving every second of it. Whimpering to be taken deep and hard.

The bruiser losing control now, going wild. Rotating his cock around inside Folsom with undulating movements of his hips. Withdrawing and slamming back in and rotating his pelvis. Both crying out in harmony for the intensity of it, urging more intensity. Folsom moving his hips in a countermotion against Fritz. Both trying to move as one sychronized perfect fucking machine.

Folsom cried out in death, the death of ejaculation. Warm, sticky fluid spreading between his belly and the mattress.

The bruiser came back up on his knees behind Folsom and pulled his cock out. He jerked the condom off and flipped it onto the floor, on top of the others lying there. Throbbing tool in hand, he stroked three times, gave a cry and spouted white, cloudy semen across the small of Folsom's back. The two sighed and murmured, as the bruiser spread the fluid around on Folsom's back with his still-hard cock, working the salve into Folsom's skin. Folsom came up on his knees, turned his face to the German's, and the two kissed deeply, the bruiser holding Folsom to him with a hand on his belly.

When they disengaged, the bruiser pushed Folsom's chest back to the mattress with a firm hand between his shoulder blades and reached over to the nightstand and fished out another packet. He opened that with his teeth, and extracted the disk. He rolled the condom out on his still-engorged cock and then entered Folsom once again with a forceful thrust and a slap on his butt cheek.

Folsom moaned deeply. His fists opened and closed on the brass rods. Flexing and releasing—to the rhythm of the fuck.

Later, the room now as bathed as it was going to be in the light of day, the German was cuddling Folsom, both stretched out on the bed, Folsom's back encased by the German's strong torso, humming with great satisfaction to themselves in the afterglow of night-long sex.

"That was incredible," the bruiser whispered. "You can stay here forever. I don't care what you did. I'll protect you."

"That sounds nice," Folsom said. "But I think it's afternoon already. I have to be somewhere at four this afternoon and I want a couple of hours free to do something first—and all of this lovin' has made me hungry. Do you think I have enough tail on credit here for some food."

"Naturlich," the German responded with a hoarse laugh. "Here, you can eat this again." And then he took his cock in his hand and slapped it against Folsom's thigh.

"Later. Gladly later," Folsom said, joining in the bruiser's joke. "But how about some real food now? And then I'd best be on about my business."

As they were finishing up their meal, the German covered Folsom's hand with his and looked deeply into his eyes with some concern.

"I'm worried about you out there on the street alone. If you have to go out, why don't you let me go with you—to protect your back?"

Folsom tried to keep the conversation light. "I think you're the one I need to protect my back from. How many times have you attacked me from the rear already last night and today?"

"Maybe once or twice," the bruiser answered with a straight face. And then he broke into a broad grin. "OK, OK, maybe five or six or nine times. But you seemed to be enjoying my visits. Viellicht we have time for another visit before you have to go, nein?" His eyes were twinkling and the hand he wasn't covering Folsom's with had found Folsom's basket.

"No, nein," Folsom said with a laugh as he slapped at the German's intrusive hand. "But seriously, don't you have to work today? Roman said something about you being security for a club."

"Ja, it's a very nice club," the German answered. "It's called Chains. You'd fit in there very well. I'll have to take you there. But, no I don't have to work today. Yesterday and today are my days off. I'll have to work tomorrow night. There's a lot of time for us between now and then."

"Well, I'm sure I can handle this little outing on my own. I think I can find the cathedral again without any trouble, and I found my way here, so I know I can get back. You'd better sleep today. You'll need your rest and strength for tonight. I'll be back."

Both gave a hearty laugh and moved into a "good-bye for now" kiss.

At fifteen after three, Folsom was back on the street and headed in the direction of the Rhine and the cathedral, whose towers he could see in the distance as he reached each intersection. He also was looking for the Internet café he'd seen on his way to the bruiser's last night.

Ah, yes, there it was—on Brückenstrasse. A café downstairs and a bank of computers along a counter with stools on the second floor. He paid for the first hour of use and went up the stairs. The clerk had told him which computer had an English-language keyboard. He wouldn't have known that the Europeans had a slightly different keyboard than Americans did. If he hadn't been given the right keyboard, all of his y's would have come out as z's, and vice versa. Probably no problem, really. Trudi probably could have figured it out. Trudi, the squad's researcher back in New York was brilliant—and fast.

Folsom was praying Trudi would be fast today—and not prone to asking too many questions. Actually, it would be morning where she was.

Trudi was great, though. After he had keyed in that he couldn't answer questions and needed this information asap, she settled right down to business. He tapped out the eight names he needed a specific question answered for and then sat, agonizing, at the machine, nursing the cup of strong coffee he'd brought up from the café downstairs. He had finished that one and was pining for another before Trudi got back to him. But he stuck with the computer. He couldn't risk missing Trudi's answer.

When the answer appeared on the screen, he almost couldn't believe it—but then, it did make sense. Those four. Not the others, just those four. He'd rather hoped it would only be two, then he'd have known what to do. But there were four of them. He'd have to give this some more thought.

He looked up at the clock. It already has hard on four o'clock, and he had a good three blocks to go before he reached the cathedral. And then there was the problem of finding Tiho. The cathedral was huge, as was the plaza in front of it. And it always was swarming with visitors. One of

213

the largest in the world, it had escaped bombing in World War II for its value as a beacon for Allied bombers, and so it was one of the most important surviving religious buildings on the European continent.

Folsom reached the cathedral plaza. He scanned the crowds, but there was no Tiho there as far as he could tell. So, he went inside and moved around the periphery of the main chamber.

There, there, over in the corner. He could see him now. Tiho was there. And he looked scared and lost and very, very nervous. Tiho had seen Folsom now and gestured for Folsom to follow him. Tiho moved off toward a small side chapel, where few were praying and wandering about. When Folsom entered the chapel he looked about in panic. Tiho was nowhere to be found. But then Folsom saw that a door to a confessional cubicle was open and he could barely see that Tiho was inside, beckoning to him.

Folsom entered the confessional and hugged the small waiter, trying to assure him and let him know he was safe. They turned in the cubicle until Folsom's back was to the back wall. Tiho was in a state, and Folsom endeavored to calm him—with kisses and fumblings and strategic uncoverings and Tiho sinking his ass on Folsom's cock as the latter half crouched in the confining cubicle and ran the slight, burbling waiter up and down on his pole. The young man was arched back against the confessional door, his legs spread as wide as he could get them around Folsom's hips, his feet pressed into the back corners of the confessional, his fingers laced behind his head in the grill of the window in the confessional door.

"Oh, oh, you fill me so. You're so good in me. I think I'm going to . . ." And he did cum, and the ejaculation caused him to calm down enough that, while still gently pumping Tiho's ass up and down on his hard cock, Folsom could coax him to talk. , Folsom asked Tiho what he had to pass on and why he couldn't have told him on the ship.

"If I'd . . ." m-o-a-n "told you I'd seen Frist in the captain's cabin back there on the ship last night, you wouldn't have left when you did," Tiho said. And then, "Oh, yes, oh, yes. Just like that . . ."

"You're probably right," Folsom said, his hands relentlessly pumping the hips of the young man up and down on his tool. "Go on, I'm glad to know Frist is still alive and with the captain, but there's more to it than that, isn't there?"

"Yes . . Ahhhhhh, yes. . . I was serving a dinner to them both in the captain's cabin, and I . . . oh God, yes . . . I heard snatches of them talking about the murders. And then he came in and . . . Ugh." Tiho lurched again, and Folsom assumed he'd had a second orgiastic death. But it wasn't that kind of death.

"He? He who, Tiho?"

But Tiho couldn't answer. He was just hunched there, his back against the cubicle door and his legs now dangling on the outside of Folsom's thighs, his feet on the confessional bench. He had a surprised, dazed, lost look in his eyes. An intense look. A look edged with pain and an unanswered question of "why."

"Tiho, Tiho," Folsom put his arms around the young waiter as he slumped against Folsom's chest. And Folsom felt his hands get wet. He pulled them away. Blood. His hands were covered with blood.

Chapter Twelve: Running for Safety

Folsom was stunned and immobilized. He shook Tiho and looked into his eyes, willing him to be alive. But Tiho was already gone. His eyes, full of amazement and hurt, just stared back at Folsom in glassy emptiness.

There was no room to maneuver out from under what was now dead weight in the confessional booth. Folsom twisted around and eased Tiho's body down on bench built into the back wall. He could see now that there was blood on the lattice of window in the confessional booth door. Tiho had been stabbed through the latticework. Someone had followed Tiho here and killed him to prevent him from passing information to Folsom.

But that wasn't necessarily so, Folsom reasoned. His mind was racing. He was wiping his hands on Tiho's pants, trying to get rid of the blood on his hands. And his mind was racing on what had happened and what was happening and where he should go from here. He wanted this all just not to be happening.

Whoever killed Tiho could just as easily have been following Folsom himself. Who was to say that Tiho was the intended victim? Tiho had been in the confessional first and Folsom had followed him in. Anyone on the outside who had seen them go in could easily have assumed that it was Folsom who had his back to the door. The killer would have struck blind. He had no idea who he was stabbing in that confessional. Chances were good that either or both Tiho and Folsom were intended targets.

He had to get out of here. He had to make his way back to the Krebsgasse flat. His hands were as clean as they could get now. He had to leave the confessional and look in all directions for the assailant while still not sending up the alarm. He had to do something for Tiho, though. He couldn't just leave him here. Of course he couldn't do anything for Tiho. He was a fugitive. If he did anything for Tiho, he'd just be blamed for killing him and that wouldn't get anyone anywhere.

Folsom slowly opened the confessional door and looked from one side to the other. Good. No one was looking at him, or at least it appeared that this was so. He slipped out and walked in a curved approach to the chapel door, trying not to seem either to be in an unusual hurry or to be too direct in his exit. He made it to the chapel door and was in the south aisle, scrutinizing the many people swirling around in the naive. There were several groups listening to tour guides through earphones. He was right next to one, a group of Americans that meandered around him, the bulk of the group between him and the main, west entrance. This gave him the ability to look through the group in that direction without really being seen well from there himself.

When his eyes became focused, he discerned that Fritz the bruiser was standing there, very near to the main entrance. It was obvious that the bruiser was looking for him. He must have followed Folsom. He must have decided that Folsom needed someone watching his back after all. In this he had been prescient.

Folsom waved his hand and started to move toward the front of the nave, seeking the safety of his new buddy.

"Sssstt. No, you don't want to go over there," an insistent voice intruded from behind Folsom's left ear. And Folsom felt a strong hand on his arm, an arm that was pulling him back, toward the front of the nave to the left of the chancel, the sanctuary. Maybe toward sanctuary. Most likely not.

Folsom turned in surprise and fear, taking a defensive stance. The man who had hold of him was a solid, handsome young blond. A regular hunk.

"Who? What?" Folsom was confused, still in a daze over what was happening and how fast it was happening.

"It's me, Ralf. You have to leave here. No, no, you mustn't go to that man. You were being betrayed. Roman was betraying you. That man wants to kill you. Here, come with me. Now. Hurry."

Folsom turned toward Ralf, but as he did so, he thought that the bruiser had caught sight of them and was headed in their direction.

"Come, come. There's another way out. I'll take you to safety. Then I'll explain it all."

Ralf was safety. He hadn't been one of the four. Roman hadn't been either, but maybe Folsom just had been misled by Roman's attention to him on the ship. There was no time to think. Folsom knew nothing about the bruiser. Not really—other than he was an amazing fuck, of course. And if Roman was evil, surely the bruiser was too. Ralf was safe.

Folsom stopped holding back and went with Ralf as they attached themselves to a tour group that was moving to a chapel at the side of the chancel for a short lecture on the oldest known wooden crucifixion still in existence.

"Here, over here," hissed Ralf. "The gift shop. It has an exit to the plaza."

They passed a sign for a WC that pointed down some stone stairs in the south transept. Folsom made an involuntary move in that direction, the washing of his hands of the remnants of Tiho's blood flooding his mind.

"No, no, there's no time for that," Ralf said insistently. "We'll stop somewhere where it's safe and you can wash yourself and I'll tell you of Roman's treachery. Then I'll take you to safety until the police can come."

"The police?" Folsom said with alarm.

"Yes. You're in the clear now. It's all known. But you are in grave danger still. Come, we must hurry."

Out the gift shop door they went and into the milling crowd in the Dom Platz between the cathedral and the main train station. Ralf hustled Folsom through the teeming station and out onto Sachsenhausen Strasse, and they headed away from the Rhine. After they had been briskly walking for several minutes, Ralf pulled Folsom into the door of a store at the corner of Tunis Strasse and then, just as quickly, through another door onto Tunis, and they were walking briskly parallel to the Rhine, back beyond the cathedral. Within another fifteen-minute walk they were in the Neuemarket Platz, and Ralf at last slowed down and took Folsom into a biergarten that had entrances on three separate blocks and allowed him to go to the men's room and clean himself up as best he could.

When Folsom returned to their table, he saw that Ralf had ordered two large steins of beer, which were just arriving. He also realized for the first time that Ralf was carrying a briefcase with him.

"Here, this will refresh you and calm your nerves," Ralf said, pointing to the glasses of pale ale. "This is Kölsch. It's the best beer Germany has to offer and is, of course, brewed right here in Cologne."

"Tell me what is happening. Why is someone trying to kill me and why aren't the police still looking for me?" Folsom wanted direct answers to direct questions now.

"It's quite straightforward, really," Ralf said. "Roman hated Meister for what he was doing to Dieter and then he was enraged when Meister went too far in sex and accidentally killed Dieter in the ship's exercise room. Roman went to Meister's cabin and took out his revenge in the same manner Meister had killed Dieter. Then Roman decided to make a power grab for Meister's sex enterprises."

"That can't be," Folsom said. "Sten assaulted Roman in his cabin and said he was making such a move for control."

"Sten?" Ralf said and laughed. "Sten, like me, is just a bartender, a lowly employee. Roman confessed that he and Sten staged that to throw you off the track and to win your confidence in him. Roman knew you were an American

220

detective and were stalking Meister. He didn't know for sure what you were up to, but he wanted you neutralized."

"But Sten . . ."

"Sten works for Roman. And they're lovers. Sten is the one you have to look out for. Roman has been arrested and has confessed all. But Sten is on the loose now. I don't know who attacked you back there in the cathedral. It must have been either Sten or Fritz, that club bouncer friend of Roman's we sent you to. Roman had me fooled as well. Tiho and I thought he was sending you to safety. I knew nothing until Roman confessed. But, you must be wounded. The blood. Is it bad? Do we need to go to a hospital?"

"Me? Wounded?" Folsom stammered. "No. That was Tiho. Dead. He asked me to meet him in the cathedral. So he could tell me something?"

"Tiho? Dead?" Ralf seemed stunned. "Ah, but that makes sense. Roman had said something about Sten looking for Tiho. They were afraid Tiho was on to them. That must be why he was killed. That detective, Sigmund Frist, said—"

"Yes. What about Frist? That's what Tiho was trying to tell me. Something about the captain and Frist and another—"

"Ah, so Tiho did manage to tell you something. So, you aren't safe now. If they killed Tiho, they surely will want to kill you too. Come, we'd better go—"

"Frist," Folsom said, showing determination not to leave the biergarten until he had some more answers. "Has he been in the captain's cabin all of this time?"

"Apparently yes," Ralf answered. "He was in a difficult spot. He was a detective who had stumbled on to two murders in a place he should not have been. He has a reputation to preserve. Under those circumstances it would make sense that he retreated to the captain's cabin and was doing what he could to help in the investigation, through the captain."

"Oh," Folsom said. "But, then, what was so important about Tiho telling me—?"

"Come, we've stayed in one place—out in the open—for far too long. I know of a friendly hotel near here. We'll go there and I'll contact the police, and we'll get you to safety."

Folsom wasn't finished with questions he wanted to ask, but Ralf was obviously finished with answers he wanted to provide out here in the open on Neuemarket Platz. He threw down some euros on the table and pulled Folsom out through an entrance that was on a different street than the one they had entered from.

A short walk of a couple of blocks and they were in another small square, and Ralf guided Folsom into a hotel entrance with the name Marsil over the door. Ralf offered another wad of euro notes to a man at the reception desk, evidently enough to keep the man from asking for the requisite passports to be registered. The man handed Ralf and key and they were on their way up the elevator.

In the elevator, Ralf put an arm around Folsom and drew him close and kissed him on the ear. "I've been wanting to get close to this for some time, I'll have to admit," he said in a hoarse whisper. "I think I can find something for us to do while we're waiting for the police escort."

As soon as they entered the room, Ralf pushed Folsom up against the wall next to the door and covered his face and neck with kisses while he unbuttoned his shirt and fanned his palms on Folsom's heaving pecs. He moved his lips down to Folsom's nipples and his hands down Folsom's belly and onto his basket. He was stroking Folsom's prick to life through the material of his pants.

Folsom gasped and pushed Ralf away.

"You want it, I know you do. I can feel it in your body," Ralf was saying in a soft, yet hard-edged voice. "You want me to do you as much as I want to do you."

"Let me shower first," Folsom pleaded. "Let me wash this death off of me first. Then we'll fuck."

"Fine. I'll call the police while you're showering," Ralf said. "But I'll tell them we won't be here for another hour and a half. They should give us time to become well acquainted."

Folsom moved into the bathroom and turned the shower on full blast and as hot as he could take it. He stripped and stood under the pulsating water for a long time, trying to wash the death of Tiho off him and to come to terms with what was happening in his life. He didn't feel horny, which was a first for him—although he knew he would have no trouble accommodating Ralf and giving Ralf a good time. He just felt empty and dead. Is that what this came down to? He'd come to Germany to kill Meister for murdering his partner and lover, and Meister was dead. Big deal he hadn't been the one to kill him. Meister had gotten what he deserved. And Folsom bore no grudges against Roman for having killed Meister. Roman was under no threat from Folsom, and he damn well should know that. All of this manhunting business was unnecessary nonsense—just a meaningless misunderstanding. Life itself was meaningless. It had been meaningless since he had lost Brad Roberts.

At last Folsom left the shower and toweled off and padded out to the bedroom in the nude. Ralf had also stripped down to his shorts and both of them sucked in their breath, thrilled at the sight of the other. Folsom did feel a little horny now. Ralf was a real hunk. He's been very satisfying the first time he had taken Folsom hard and rough, and he was just as desirable now.

"Called the police?" Folsom asked.

"Yes. They should be here in a bit over an hour now. You took your time in the shower."

"But I'm here now."

"Yes, you're here now. And it was worth the wait. Come here. Come to me."

Folsom did as Ralf directed. He liked to be dominated. He was ready to slip into that role. He wanted Ralf to take care of him. To take him hard. To make him forget—if at least only for a few moments of orgiastic death—if that was possible.

Ralf wrapped his arms around Folsom and rubbed skin against skin from pecs to thighs. He kissed Folsom deeply on the lips and then sat him down on the end of the bed, sank to his knees, and began giving Folsom head.

Folsom sighed and moaned and ran his hands through Ralf's blond hair for a short while. After a bit, he lay back and spread his legs and tilted his pelvis up to give Ralf ready access to his asshole with his fingers and mouth.

Ralf took advantage of Folsom's gesture, but after giving him some intense attention, alternating between Folsom's tool and his asshole, Ralf stood and pushed Folsom up on the bed. Folsom got the message and moved up until he was stretched full length on the bedspread. Ralf slipped off his briefs and came up onto the bed on his knees, straddling, Folsom's calves. He bent down and took Folsom's prick in his mouth again and sucked and pumped him there, taking time out to lick and pull at Folsom's balls with his teeth.

Folsom was moaning and moving under Ralf, gently stroking up into his soft mouth, reaching release, exploding in a death by ejaculation. How often he had done this with Brad. Folsom was thinking of Brad as his hips jerked for a second time and he released a second spouting of cum. Ralf's finger pushed into Folsom's ass, finding the prostate, and Folsom died again. Never-ending ejaculation. Getting closer to death, closer to Brad. Heaven.

Maybe closer than he thought.

Chapter Thirteen: A Half-Sought Ending

Ralf took in Folsom's ejaculate in his mouth and, briefly, rose up Folsom's body and merged their lips, sharing the saltiness of Folsom's prodigious manhood. He then moved back down Folsom's torso with his moist lips, kissing his way back to the very center of Folsom, and licked his cock clean.

The two were panting, both keyed up, both wanting more. Ralf moved his encasing knees farther up Folsom's body now, wrapping their cocks together with an encasing fist and stroking them together as he worked Folsom's nipples with his lips and teeth. Folsom murmured his approval and flung his arms around Ralf's head and held him close.

This wasn't the same Ralf who had ravished him earlier, the one who had bulled his way into Folsom's cabin and thrust inside him and pumped him hard with no preparation. Folsom liked both versions of Ralf. This is what Brad had done for him too—gauged his mood and been either lover or rapist as Folsom signaled he'd wanted at the moment.

Ralf was sitting saddled on Folsom's chest now, handling his rising cock with his hand. Stroking Folsom's neck and chin and cheeks and lips with his cock. And then laying his mushroom cap on Folsom's closed lips. Folsom opened his mouth to Ralf's nicely hung manhood, and Ralf slowly entered him and tested all angles of the warm cavern being offered to him. Folsom's eyes were closed. He was savoring the gentle, yet insistence approach. Ralf rotated his hips, hitting all of the inner walls with his mushroom cap and then slowly, slowly, yet relentlessly, he started to pump Folsom's inner spaces with his engorging cock. Stronger and deeper and ever more rapidly he pumped. Folsom had no trouble accommodating him and matching his rhythm, at least at the beginning. But then Ralf had Folsom's head in his hand and he was face fucking him with more intensity. Folsom started to gag, but he was loving this. He loved being dominated and forced to the edges of endurance.

He opened his eyes. And then the shock set in. Sudden realization. Anger and terror hitting him at the same instant. He bit down hard and the blond hunk yelped and jerked his cock out of Folsom's mouth. Folsom bucked his body up, lurching away from the other man, trying to escape him. But his assailant was quick to recover. He kneed Folsom in the lower belly, knocking the wind out of him and socked him hard in the jaw, stunning and immobilizing the American long enough for him to reach his briefcase and take out leather thongs and tie Folsom's wrists off at the headboard.

When he had opened his eyes, Folsom had seen that there was no scorpion tattoo on the man's groin. This wasn't Ralf. This was Sten.

Sten gave him a wicked smile as he extracted a mouth plug and popped it into Folsom's mouth, the American still stunned by the body and cheek blows. He then tied the plug off. Folsom wouldn't be doing any talking or yelling.

After that, he took a condom out of his briefcase and rolled it on his engorged cock. He moved to between Folsom's legs, spread them wide, thrust inside the American detective's ass, and fucked him hard to a finish.

The fucking went on endlessly, and Folsom began to take hope that the police would show up before Sten could do him any real harm. But then he realized. Sten hadn't called the police at all. And Roman probably hadn't confessed to anything. And the police were probably still searching for Folsom as a suspect in the murders of Meister and Dieter— and now probably Tiho as well.

Sten arched his back and his muscles tensed and he gave a little cry as he unloaded inside the condom inside Folsom. Folsom gave a little prayer that this condom was as weak as the one Meister had used on Brad and that this at least would leave DNA that could be traced back to Sten.

Sten was off the bed now and fumbling around in his briefcase. He came up with a rectangular box, from which he extracted several sounding wands.

Folsom strained at the bonds on his arms and flailed his legs.

But Sten just laughed. "You know what will happen if you don't hold perfectly still for this, don't you? These tubes will tear your cock apart from the inside. If that's what you want, keep throwing those legs around. If not, you'll want to hold very, very still."

Folsom went very still, and Sten sat down on the end of the bed, Folsom's left leg stretching behind his buttocks and his right leg spread wide.

Folsom tensed and began to sweat as the first, small wand was poised at his piss slit and then slowly, ever so slowly, worked in and up his urethra channel. Folsom gurgled in surprise at the invasion. It didn't feel half bad, although it made him want to piss. Sten swirled the wand slowly inside the passage and Folsom arched his back. He wanted to move his body, to writhe away from the wand, but he had to be careful to keep his pelvis perfectly still.

Sten slowly pulled the wand out and Folsom sighed in relief. But only momentarily, because Sten had a larger wand in his hand and was pushing it into Folsom's piss slit. Folsom growled his indignation, wanting to scream instead. Sten laughed and started to move the wand in and out, fucking Folsom's cock.

This was too much for Folsom. When Sten pulled the wand out of Folsom's cock, Folsom shot his seed strongly and profusely.

This turned Sten on and he was pulling on his cock. He stood and sheathed his cock with another condom and then pulled Folsom's butt to the edge of the bed and thrust inside him again. Folsom grunted. Then he began to whimper as Sten pulled a thick wand out of the rectangular box and, after burying his cock to the root inside Folsom, began to run the tube deep into Folsom's cock. Folsom realized that this, exactly, was how Brad, Meister, and Dieter had been found, and he had no illusions about what Sten had planned for him.

When Sten had finished fucking Folsom a second time, he withdrew, leaving the thick sounding wand buried and reached into his bag of tricks again. This time he came out with more leather thongs and tied Folsom's ankles off to the corners of the bed at the footboard. Another dive into the bag and out came an incredible thick and long dildo.

He was feeding this slowly into Folsom's ass, and Folsom couldn't help himself this time; he was writhing and bucking his body against the mammoth object moving up inside him. He knew he was just moments from being torn apart.

Sten stopped with this torture, however, and went back to his briefcase. This time he took out a nasty-looking hunting knife. There was blood on the blade. No doubt Tiho's blood.

Sten laid the knife on the bed between Folsom's legs and went back to rotating and pushing on the giant dildo.

Folsom felt himself slipping away. The fuck was extraordinary, and, except for the probability that Sten would get away scot-free, Folsom felt he was ready to go. He was going delirious, seeing and feeling himself floating on a wave of never-ending ejaculation. So this was what death was about. In the distance between the clouds, he thought he could see figures. He willed them to come closer. He willed for one of them to be Brad, for Brad to be beckoning to him, to be inviting him to cross over. The figures held off, though, hovering at the near distance. Folsom was moaning deeply, his own moaning coming back at him as if in an echo chamber. The dildo was pushing, rotating relentlessly, filling, stretching, to and beyond his limits. . . . Sunlight flashing on the blade of a knife, now held over Folsom's quivering belly, moving to the point of release. . . .

Chapter Fourteen: A Beginning
Disguised as an Ending

Folsom gave a muffled scream of terror and pain as the knife struck him. It, surprisingly, was only a glancing slice across his naked thigh. But trussed up as he was, spread-eagled naked and bound on the bed with sexual devices possessing every orifice, he was completely at the mercy of whatever game Sten was playing. He steeled himself for the next slice of the knife, dreading where that might be, keeping his eyes tightly shut as the last defense available to him.

But the final blow did not come, and he heard a yelp and a gurgling noise and opened his eyes as Sten fell on top of him, their eyes now glued on each other's, and Sten's registering as much surprise and pain as Folsom felt.

And then the leather thongs binding Folsom's wrists and ankles to the bed were being sliced away and Fritz, the bruiser, was helping to push Sten's gasping body off of Folsom and also, as delicately as possible, relieving Folsom of the beleaguering sounding wand and oversized dildo.

"What? How?" Folsom sputtered as the plug gag came out of his mouth.

"I saw Sten entice you out of the cathedral," the German club bouncer said.

"So you followed me even when I told you not to," Folsom said, still in shock and not thinking on all cylinders. If the German hadn't followed him, the German couldn't have saved him from a painful death.

"Roman told me to take care of you, and I know Sten well. I knew you were in serious trouble and didn't seem to know it. I lost you in the Dom Platz, but we have a network here, men like you and me, and I eventually connected with the desk clerk at this hotel, who identified you both from the description I gave him. Sorry it took so long—almost too long."

"Yes, yes, Thanks for coming to the rescue."

Sten was gurgling ominously on the bed beside Folsom. It was clear he didn't have long to live. His death stab at Folsom had been deflected when the bruiser broke in and hurled himself at the bed. But then the knife had done its work on Sten.

Folsom turned to him and brought his head very close to Sten's. The misguided bartender's eyes were beginning to glaze over, and he was grimacing and panting from the pain in his gut. Folsom started to talk to him in soothing tones, not really to comfort him all that much but to both make sure he wasn't a threat anymore and to squeeze whatever information he could get out of the man. Folsom's instincts as a police detective were winning through his own pain, pain that had been inflicted by this man he was now cajoling.

"Who did them, Sten? Who killed Meister and Dieter?" Folsom hadn't forgotten Tiho, of course, but it was almost self-evident now that Sten himself had killed Tiho.

Sten was trying to say something. Folsom put his ear close to Sten's mouth and was able to hear the name he needed. And then Sten was gone.

"You should go clean yourself up," the bruiser was saying. "I'll call the cops, but it's up to you whether we stay here and wait for them."

"Roman." It suddenly hit Folsom. If Tiho had been killed for what he knew, Roman was either equally a target or was already dead. Where was Ralf now, Folsom wondered.

Regardless, he had to make an attempt to help Roman if he could. He knew he could count on the bruiser to back him up on this and get him back to the ship the fastest way possible.

Miracles of miracles. The bruiser had somehow come up with a motorcycle to aid his search for Folsom and it was sitting right outside the hotel door on Marsil Platz. A quick zip down Muhlenbach to the road paralleling the Rhine and they were at the ship within eight minutes. The guards the police had stationed on the dock and at the entrance to the ship just stood and gawked with dropped jaws as the man they were searching for on the ship was storming the ship from the dock with a gigantic bodyguard of his own in his wake.

Folsom asked the guy on duty at reception where the captain's cabin was, and then the bruiser asked him more pointedly and far more effectively, and the conga line was off to the races—Folsom followed closely by the bouncer, who was bouncing off the walls of the narrow corridor and keeping the tagline of policemen from reaching Folsom. The desk clerk was far in the rear but making every effort to get there in time to enjoy the fireworks.

Folsom and the bruiser burst into the captain's cabin just in time to save Roman. He was trussed up on the bed in what had now become a familiar sacrifice stance just as his assailant was about to deliver the coup de grace.

The bruiser hit the ship's captain in the midsection and sent him careening to one wall, while Folsom bounced Roman's attacker against another wall. They went down in a heap, and it was touch and go for a moment or two. But Folsom's determination and thirst for vengeance was ascendant and, when the knife had struck home, and Folsom's opponent had gone quiet and gurgled his last breath, all of the pain and frustration Folsom had gone through since Brad Roberts had died was also laid to rest.

A wheezing Inspector Manfeld, accompanied by an even more official-looking police detective, arrived at the cabin door at that precise moment. Their eyes swept in tandem from Roman's naked, spread-eagled, and tortured body on the bed to the captain hunched in one corner, nursing a bleeding nose and being watch like a hawk by a monster of man and then to where Folsom was sitting next to the body of Roman's assailant. Their mouths were working but no sound was coming out. Until this very moment, they did not know and would not have believed that Sigmund Frist had been here, under their noses, hiding out in the captain's cabin all of this time.

Frist was beyond interrogation now, but it didn't take the ship's captain long to cut the best deal he could by telling the police—who now accepted Folsom as one of their own—all that he knew.

Folsom already knew some of what the captain was going to say. His checking of the names he'd gotten off the crew list against U.S. immigration records, with the help of the NYPD researcher, Trudi, had revealed that the ship's captain and Sten had accompanied Meister to the United States, arriving in New York, and were in the States when Brad Roberts was murdered. The e-mail exchange with Trudi had also revealed, however, that Sigmund Frist was in New York at the same time. Folsom would not have been satisfied about who had actually killed his partner and lover, Brad, if the captain had not spun out the story. Although even then he'd never be positive.

The captain and Sten had arrived at the scene of Roberts's murder after he had died—or so the captain claimed. It was the captain's understanding that Meister had fucked Brad—and that much had already been verified by the DNA—but that Frist had done the knifing that had killed him. Frist and Meister had been equal partners in Meister's sex enterprise schemes; Frist had ensured that Meister could conduct his activities in Germany through his influence in the police department.

But Meister had gotten greedy and was blackmailing Frist, whose activities and proclivities were being kept a secret from his police system. That's why Meister had to die as well. Dieter had been killed first; Frist had come upon Meister fucking Dieter in his favorite way in the ship's exercise room. Frist had joined in the fun and had killed Dieter as part of

234

that fun. Then, an unknowing Meister had been taken to his own death in his cabin by Frist.

After that, Frist had tried to implicate Folsom in the murders, knowing that Folsom had come to revenge his partner's death and thus was highly vulnerable to being fingered for Meister's death. Folsom himself was able to figure out that Frist had drugged him before bedding him and going off to murder Meister while Folsom would think they were still together and were engaging in all-night sex. Folsom's dream of handling a dildo during their sex was a half-conscious awareness that Frist was getting his fingerprints on one of the weapons. And Frist had access to all of the cabin keys on the ship and had planted the knife in Folsom's cabin when Folsom had encountered him there the day following the murder.

The captain claimed, of course, that both he and Sten were just unwilling and forced employees caught up in a web of threats and bullying to do what Meister and Frist wanted them to do—and there was no one else alive now to totally belie his claim.

The next day, the police gave clearances for the ship to sail again to meet its schedule for arrival in Amsterdam, albeit with a skeleton crew made up of the lucky survivors of the recent days' mayhem. The police offered Folsom a hotel stay in Cologne until all of the paperwork was finished—and the bruiser begged him to stay with him instead.

But Folsom wanted to recover in his own way. He asked permission to sail on to Amsterdam and to return to Cologne—and, yes, to the bruiser's bed and shower and sofa—it was melting just to think of the good times he'd be having with the bruiser—a few days later by air.

As the ship pulled away from the dock and Folsom waved to Manfeld and company and the somewhat disappointed Fritz, he turned and headed for the Alexander lounge. Half way there, though, he was accosted by the African potentate, wanting to claim his rain check on their romp on the Helios deck lounger, and Folsom thought, what the hell, and permitted himself to be carried off to the king's cabin.

The African took him in the tiny shower from the rear against the tiles, lifting Folsom's body up from the floor with the thrusts of his insistent cock, and then again in the middle of the cabin, with the ebony giant standing on his feet, in a semicrouch, and Folsom suspended in air, legs jutting out on either side of the African's hips and the king pumping Folsom's pelvis up and down on his glistening sledgehammer. And finally, with the African flat on his back on the bed and grinning up at Folsom as the American straddled his pelvis and did a long, vigorous pole dance on his engorged cock.

Later that night, as the ship was nudging into the suburbs of Amsterdam on the Amstel canal, Folsom and Ralf finally met up and went back to Folsom's cabin, where Ralf fucked him three ways from Sunday in relentless, deep-assed thrustings on the table, the floor, and the bed, tossing used condoms left and right all night.

It was at the height of this debauchery that Folsom realized that it wasn't the orgiastic death that he sought and now was receiving in perpetual ejaculations. It wasn't an ending of anything; it was a beginning. Ejaculation gave life, not death. He would never forget Brad Roberts and what they had together, but Folsom no longer sought to mourn by seeking death through sex; he could now fully rejoice in life through sex.

He wondered how hard it would be for Ralf to get a Green Card for U.S. residency. Maybe with his help, if Ralf was interested.

Chapter Fifteen: It Ain't Over Until It's Over

Folsom awoke to Ralf's sex-satiated, very satisfied snoring. They were both on their sides in one of the beds in Folsom's cabin on the MS *River God*, the American's well-worked butt nestled into the Australian's well-exercised groin and his strong arms encircling Folsom. The palm of one of Ralf's hands was spread on Folsom's lower belly, and the American detective had not been this content and well-fucked since he was living with Brad Roberts, his partner at the NYPD—and his lover—whose murder had propelled Folsom to Europe in search of revenge over his killer.

Folsom felt at peace this morning. Both the murderer he had pursued and the murderer he had found were dead now. And his own outlook on the relationship between death and life had changed in the brief time since Ralf had taken him to bed last night and fucked him endlessly, at first wildly on every surface in the cabin and then tenderly, but never as roughly as he had the first time he had taken Folsom. Before they slept, Ralf said he would show Folsom some rough fucking this morning, some variation of it that they hadn't done before. And now Folsom was looking forward to it— because now he didn't think of being fucked to ejaculation as a form of death; he thought of it as a form of rebirth into life. He wanted Ralf to fuck him fully back into life.

Both of the young hunks were startled very much awake by the ringing of the telephone. Folsom answered it, and as he did so, he disentangled from Ralf and sat up on the edge of the bed. Folsom opened the curtain and saw that the ship was docked in Amsterdam, very near to the main railroad station. The two lovers had missed the dawn, but not by much. It had been raining, and a sea of bicycles, workers on their way to their offices, was sweeping by gracefully on the main road that circled in front of the station.

Folsom was groggy, but the voice on the other end of the line brought him completely awake.

"Have you seen him? Has he returned?" Inspector Manfeld sounded quite concerned.

"He, who?" Folsom answered dumbly.

"The ship's captain. He escaped us in Cologne. We didn't put enough of a guard on him at the police station before he was booked. He just vanished. We're afraid he's headed back to where you are. To Amsterdam. To the ship."

"No," the American continued with his not-quite-awake dumb act. "I haven't left my cabin yet this morning. But I'll go see . . ."

Ralf was sitting up behind the American now, his thighs encasing Folsom's, his hands all over Folsom's body, pinching and squeezing him here and there. Folsom felt that promised rougher fuck coming. He tried to pry Ralf's hand from its squeezing hold on his nuts, but he wouldn't let go. He had his teeth in the hollow of his prey's neck.

"We'll be there as soon as we can get the helicopter up," Manfeld was saying. "Just hold on until we get there."

That was going to be hard to do, Folsom thought, as he dropped the telephone receiver back into its cradle and sent his now-free hand into battle with Ralf hands. But it was a losing battle. Ralf was much stronger and more determined than his prey was.

"No, Ralf. The ship's captain has escaped in Cologne and may be on his way back here. We must—"

"We must finish what we were doing first," Ralf said with a throaty voice. And he wrapped an arm around his victim's midsection and raised him up and set him back down on his now-hard tool, working his way deeply into Folsom's channel, as the American thrashed about and groaned and grunted and moaned. Ralf pulled the joined couple back over onto their sides and thrust hard and rapidly in and out in Folsom's ass with his cock as he clawed the American's chest and belly with his fingernails and thrust Folsom's leg up in the air with his strong calf.

He was gnawing quite vigorously on Folsom's neck with his teeth and the American arched his back, pushing his shoulders into Ralf's bulging pecs in an attempt to writhe away from him. This was a mistake, however. One of Ralf's hands went up so that the heel of the hand was blocking Folsom's mouth and he was pinching the American's nose closed with a finger and thumb.

Folsom was thrashing about, but Ralf was just too strong. The American was gasping for air, as Ralf put his mouth very close to Folsom's ear.

"This is the special fuck I promised you last night," he whispered. Folsom could hear the lust dripping in Ralf's voice. "This is very popular here in Amsterdam. Did you know that the sweetest enjoyment of ejaculation is a sort of a death, when you are at the point of dying? Like when you can't live without the next breath but you can't breathe?"

Yes I knew that, Folsom wanted to scream. But he also wanted to yell that he was past that. He didn't want to die in ejaculation anymore; He wanted to live in ejaculation. But, of course Ralf couldn't hear his victim, because Folsom couldn't really scream anything. It was all he could do to try to search for air.

Ralf's pounding cock was hitting Folsom's prostate hard, and just as the Australian stud flooded the American hunk's insides with his cum, he squeezed Folsom's balls hard and the American shot off as well. This also was the moment Folsom blacked out from the lack of oxygen.

When Folsom awoke, he was alone. The droning of the police sirens no doubt were what had brought him around. He painfully sat up in the bed and pushed the curtains back. There were several police cars parked at the ramp up to the ship's entrance. He had no idea whether Manfeld and his people had arrived or whether he had called in an advance contingent from the Amsterdam police. The cars were empty, but their sirens were still blaring.

Folsom heard pandemonium in the corridor outside, and, as soon as he could get his shit together and throw on a pair of trousers and a T-shirt, he joined the chaos.

All of the attention was on the lower level, with all feet headed for the captain's cabin.

He was already dead when Folsom got there, lying in front of an open wall safe, a knife dug in up to its hilt in his back.

The policemen now on the scene were Dutch. Manfeld and his crew were nowhere in sight. He must have prepared the Dutch police though, because they quickly accepted who Folsom was and that he was to be privy to the investigation.

Seeing the captain lying there in his own blood, not just stabbed, but his body sliced here and there with the knife blade, brought the scene of Brad Roberts's murder back to Folsom full blown. It surfaced details of that scene he had pushed back into the interior of his mind that he hadn't allowed myself to think about. Brad's body had been sliced as well. Not deeply, just shallow cuts. Almost ritualistically, primitively. And what was that Brad had told his partner about the case the night before he had died? What had Brad told Folsom that the two of them should do?

On impulse, Folsom bent down to the body. Something was clutched in the captain's dead fist. With the permission of the Dutch detective, the American pried the fist open. Just a scrap a paper, a torn edge of a document of some kind, something to do with the ship.

Not much to go on, but the captain had returned for whatever this scrap was attached to, and he had died because he had returned for it.

Folsom stood up and told the detective he had to go see about something immediately, that he had to call his researcher at the NYPD, Trudi, and pursue the question that Brad Roberts had wanted him to check out. Suddenly the answer to that question was very important. And Folsom told the Dutch detective what he needed to check out.

Folsom was heading down the corridor toward the reception desk and the only computer on the ship linked to the Internet, when he was accosted in the corridor by a hulking figure.

"I would very much like to resume that fucking we were so nicely doing yesterday afternoon," the African potentate was saying in a clipped, very British voice.

"I just have to check on something first," Folsom said, a little irritated that the African stud was after him before Folsom was ready for him. But he just stood there, filling the corridor between Folsom and the reception room with his black beefcake figure.

"I think now is fine," he said with a big grin. And he had his arms around Folsom and he was squeezing him, and, in particular his fat fingers were squeezing vital arteries in Folsom's neck, and the American blacked out for the second time that morning.

Folsom found himself on a bed covered with the hides of exotic creatures. And his arms and legs were spread-eagled and tied to the corners of the bed. And the naked African king, his body glistening with sweat and radiating power and force, was dancing around below him, a large dildo in one hand and a pearl-handled hunting knife in the other, both of which were covered in blood. Young men, a couple of the waiters from the boat, Folsom realized, were standing beside the bed and moving the air with large palm fronds. And the ebony giant was chanting and laughing. Folsom's ass was being massively entered, and a thick tube, whether the dildo or the African's cock, Folsom knew not, was invading him ever deeper. And he was screaming and gasping and bucking against and with the invader. The African was huddled over him, leering down at him, the knife was poised over Folsom's breast.

Folsom realized, with horror that he had been here before, in a dream. But this was no dream. He also thought, rather idiotically, that he should be paying more attention to his dreams.

But then Folsom realized it wasn't large palm fronds the two members of the ship's crew were holding onto; it was two ends of ropes in some sort of pulley system. And Folsom's wrists were somehow attached to this system, and the two young crew members pulled on the ropes at the mad African's gesture, and Folsom's torso was being raised, his arms being raised up in a wide stance. He was hanging from a bar overhead.

The African was chanting something almost ritualistic as he danced around the bed on which the animal pelts were spread. With two swishes of the nasty-looking knife he had in his hand, he cut the bonds that had Folsom's ankles attached to the corner posts, and Folsom's leg's were free.

But only for a moment. The African potentate bounded up on the bed, danced around Folsom momentarily, and then was behind him, thrusting his huge cock inside Folsom's ass. The two crew members came in close beside the bed on each side and each grabbed one of Folsom's ankles and wishboned them to the side.

The African was crouched between Folsom's raised legs and was fucking strongly up into his ass. His was swishing the knife around in front of Folsom, and Folsom gave a surprised scream and then a gasp as, in two swishing strokes, the knife had sliced very shallow cuts across his chest and on one of his thighs.

The African savagely pulled Folsom's head back with his free fist in the American's hair and whispered in his ear, "Not quite the way I did your lover, Brad Roberts, but maybe I'll finish you the way I intended to finish him—and the way I would have if he hadn't lurched unfortunately and run into the knife."

Folsom was terrified, but he didn't respond to the African hulk's admission. However, Folsom now knew who had murdered Brad.

The blade of the knife gleamed in front of Folsom's eyes, catching the light of the overhead fixture.

"Ever fantasized about being fucked to death with the blade of a sharp hunting knife?" the African hissed into Folsom's ear. "We do that back in Tuliewanna. That's a very special execution we have for worthy opponents. Are you feeling worthy, Mr. Folsom?"

A swish across a bicep, and Folsom cried out in pain.

"The captain? Why the captain?" Folsom managed, trying to get the African concentrating on something else other than carving him up.

"You needn't ask that," The African whispered menacingly in his ear. "You figured that out. I heard what you said to the Dutch policeman in the captain's cabin. You asked him to check out what country this ship was registered in. Tuliewanna, of course. Landlocked Tuliewanna. Flag of convenience and all that."

Swish across a buttock and Folsom stifled another scream. The African pulled his cock completely out and then slammed it home again, and for that Folsom did groan loudly.

"Just one step from there and you'd have figured out that I own this operation, that all of the rest fronted for me. Frist, Meister, the captain, the whole lot of them. The captain came back for insurance, for the ship's registration papers, so he could hold that over my head. He had covered for me in his testimony that Frist killed your Brad Roberts. But he thought he could have something to hold over my head so that I didn't just kill him then. He was wrong, naturally."

The African had the blade under Folsom's chin now, and Folsom could feel the dribbling of blood more than any pain from the slight cut there.

And then he caught something out of the corner of his eye. Some movement over by the cabin's door. And then Ralf was bounding in the room and moving quickly toward the bed.

Folsom's immediate thought was that he was afraid that if Ralf attacked the African directly, the blade of the knife might slip—with very unfortunate consequences for Folsom. But his next thoughts were very confused. Ralf bounded onto the bed, but he wasn't attacking the African, he was grinning from ear to ear. And he and the African were kissing deeply over Folsom's shoulder. And then Ralf was holding Folsom's thighs in his strong hands and he was crouching in front of and below Folsom, sandwiching the American between him and the African.

And Folsom felt a second cock at his asshole. Pushing in beside that of the African. An impossible feat, but one that he somehow was accomplishing. Folsom was howling in pain and surprise, but he was being deeply skewered by two fat cocks despite his objections. And they started fucking him vigorously in unison, as he arched his back and turned his head to the ceiling, looking for relief from any quarter that would offer it. And he was moaning and groaning. And panting and pleading. But he was taking it, and it was sending him to the moon. Right up until he blacked out for the third time that day.

This time Folsom awoke in the arms of Fritz the bruiser, his favorite fuck friend from Cologne, well after the good guys had arrived and broken up the fun of the African and Ralf. Fritz had helicoptered in with Manfeld. Fritz had saved Folsom at the last minute so many times now that Folsom decided to go back to Cologne under his protection and in his embrace until the German and Dutch police could sort out just how many layers of control and intrigue were involved in this MS *River God* operation.

As far as Folsom cared, knowing how well the bruiser had topped him, they could take their jolly sweet time in sorting it out.

Chapter Sixteen: The Fat Lady Sings

Fritz and Clint Folsom were sitting on a banquette, teasing each other through the folds and openings of their clothes in the dimly lit club and listening to the fat lady sing. This wasn't the Cologne leather club, Chains, where Fritz was the bouncer, though. As a reward for saving him twice from being fucked to death during that Rhine River cruise, Folsom had brought Fritz home with him for a week on the town in the Big Apple. The German had been like a little puppy dog—well, a St. Bernard, really—a St. Bernard in heat. He'd polished Folsom's apples repeatedly since they'd returned to Clint's New York apartment. And he practically had Folsom undressed and swinging on his prodigious dong right here in Francine's, where the American had brought him to try to get some relief from nonstop screwing in the sack.

Francine was the fat lady singing on stage. Francine and Folsom went way back to her early days, when she had to keep this club a secret. Now she was the toast of the Village. No one messed with Francine anymore.

One of Clint's favorite waiters wafted by in a tight little cocktail dress, blew the police detective a kiss on his way to another table and gave him that "just a minute, I'll be right back, Hon," wave that he did. Folsom liked Reggie. He had a dick long enough to reach your tonsils, and the two sometimes went off into one of the club's back rooms on nights he wasn't too busy and the detective was bummed out from a particularly nasty homicide, and the sassy waiter would swab Folsom's tonsils for him from the inside and make him forget about the job entirely.

"So, who's the hunk, sweetie?" he rasped at Folsom in his Bette Davis voice when he came back by the table.

Clint introduced him to Fritz, relieved at the release of pressure on his package, as Fritz offered a hand to Reggie and Reggie took her sweet time returning it.

"Francine's in rare form tonight," Folsom said to Reggie, as Reggie stared into Fritz's blue eyes and did very suggestive things with the German's beefy thumb. While Fritz and Reggie were exchanging meaningful looks, the detective took a look down on the stage. He'd seen this act of Francine's before. She did it frequently. She came out decked out in bolts of shiny satin material and big pearls and sang her best Aretha Franklin impersonation, while two comely young men slowly unwound the material until she was down to just the pearls around her neck, two gigantic pearls hanging between her thighs and big black dick to take your breath away—and her act ended with "her" doing both of the young men right there on stage at great length and with astonishing variety. All the time flashing the face of a beautiful woman and the cock of a horse. She was only half unraveled and two thirds of the way through "Respect" when Folsom gave her his attention this evening.

"You've been gone, Clint, my pet," Reggie murmured through pouty lips, "Or you would have known that Francine's retired from the stage part. She's only performing tonight because that bitch, Clarice, didn't show up for her two spots. Francine's doing this one and will repeat it later."

"Why's she stopped performing?" Clint asked. "She's still in magnificent shape."

"She's in mourning. Eddie and she have split. She says she can barely get it up anymore, let alone trot it out." Reggie leaned down into Fritz's face with her own and gave him a big, sloppy kiss while Folsom absorbed this information of the breakup. She moved the German's hand to the mound of her cocktail dress, letting Fritz know what was on offer.

Folsom had always thought that Francine and Eddie were a mismatched pair—but he'd also always thought they'd be together until one or both of them got killed from indulging in their nefarious activities. Francine was a gigantic black queen given to opulence and sweeping gestures, and Eddie was an undersized—but well-decked out—blond street punk who would forever look like a twink and would steal your balls and have them pawned in ten minutes flat if you didn't hang onto them when he was in the room. Together, they both had barely stayed on the unjailed edge of the law and just a few steps ahead of the competing neighborhood gangs for years. But as badly matched as they looked, Folsom always thought they were devoted to each other, that they'd kill for each other if they had to.

Fritz brought Folsom back out of his thoughts by pawing him roughly and intimately and trying to pull the American up on his lap between the banquette and the table. Reggie was gone now, but the waiter had revved up Fritz's engine and Clint was the one who was at hand—and well covered with hands.

Folsom liked being pawed by Fritz, though, The German had those bouncer hands all over Clint while he inhaled the American's lips with his. He had Folsom's pants down close to his knees, and a big palm under his butt with a forefinger buried someplace Clint found real interesting. And he was lifting Folsom up and over toward his lap when the couple felt the presence of someone else standing by the table.

"So, you decided to start without me?"

Fritz and Clint both looked up, and both smiled sheepishly. The missing corner of the trio that had arrived here this evening had returned to the table. Ralf. Folsom's beautiful blond Australian hunk from the Rhine River cruise.

"Yah, yah," Fritz responded good-naturedly. "You vere gone so lange, ve had given up on you."

"It's a long way to the men's room," Ralf replied with a laugh. "Past some very interesting rooms and some pretty inviting tail."

"So, I guess you're just too tired now and ready to go back to your hotel," Folsom said, teasing him.

"Not a chance, Clint," he shot back. "You promised me a good time when my cruise ship returned to port, and I'm calling you on it. Besides, you still owe me for the mistaken identity."

Folsom conceded that Ralf was right. Clint had completely misjudged—actually, misidentified Ralf—back on the MS *River God* when that African potentate had almost finished the American detective off. Of course it was Ralf's own fault. He hadn't bothered to tell Folsom that the third of the trio of bartenders on that cruise, Pieter, was a spitting image of Ralf himself, down to similar tattoos high on their thighs. Ralf's was a scorpion and Pieter's a crab. It hadn't been a coincidence that they were almost identical and were both bartenders on the *River God* cruises. They had originally joined the cruise company as a "twin" sex act, but they hadn't seen eye to eye on how slavishly to follow the lead of the men controlling the operation and had parted ways as an act. Ralf had kept some control over what he would do for the operation, while Pieter, along with the other bartender, Sven, had sold out entirely to the company. It had been Pieter, not Ralf, who had attacked and doubled Folsom with the African chief—and who had no problem seeing the nosy American detective killed in the effort.

Folsom had done what he could for Ralf when he discovered Ralf hadn't turned on him. Ralf, of course, couldn't work on the MS *River God* anymore. So, Folsom helped get him a bartender position on the Talbot cruise lines, headquartered here in New York and cruising mainly in the South Seas. But Ralf was in port now, and for this reason, as much as any other, the three friends, made that way from shared danger, were out on the town.

With a sigh, Fritz suspended his efforts to get Clint onto his lap, and the American sank down into the banquette beside the German. Ralf slid in behind the table and very close beside Clint on the other side. They both had arms around Clint's neck and hands working in tandem in his lap, and Folsom turned from one to the other to receive kisses from two very aggressive, insistent lovers. Their breath was hot on his neck, their hands were everywhere—he had no idea that four hands could be in some many places at one time—and they were hot and heating up.

"What?" Folsom asked. Ralf was whispering something in his ear, but he was speaking in such low tones and the music was so loud down on stage, marking the arrival of Francine's special delight weapon, that Clint hadn't heard what he'd said.

"Fritz and I have been talking," he repeated. "We want to do you."

"No secret there—or problem," Clint said with a laugh. "You and Fritz have been doing me for weeks."

"I mean together. Both of us, together."

"You're both doing me together right now," Clint said. What was it that Ralf meant, what he was trying to say without directly saying it, he wondered.

"No, I mean do you, both of us. Together. You know, together. We saw you being done that way and we know you can take it. You were hot doing it. Together."

Oh.

Folsom looked down on the stage. Francine already had one of the young guys mounted on her tool and she was just spinning him around and he was flopping back and forth, giving the bug-eyed audience a good show of being split in two. It was very convincing. It was very hot. Folsom was being aroused. Folsom was just about up for what Ralf and Fritz were asking.

"Well, maybe later," he said. "We can go back to my apartment. And then we'll see . . ."

"Here," Fritz wheezed into one ear.

"Now," Ralf breathed into the other ear.

"Right here and now?" Folsom asked, his jaw going slack. "Won't Francine be pissed? The floor show is supposed to be down there, not up here."

"I talked to her backstage, before she came on," Ralf said. "She said we could use her dressing room. She'll be a while. She hasn't exhausted the first guy yet, and the second one looks like he has more stamina. And she says she won't be back in the dressing room until after her second performance. We have a couple of hours."

Fritz was already fingering inside Folsom's ass with a big fat finger and Ralf was fisting his cock, so he wasn't being given a whole lot of decision room here.

But at that moment, when Folsom was about to accede, he froze in place.

Flash had just entered the club. The 220-pound, 6 foot 4, hunk of sultry Latin manhood going by the name of Hernando Ramierez, Flash to his friends, was here in the club. The new guy in Folsom's NYPD division who hadn't been assigned to a specialty yet, but who wanted to be assigned to homicide, where Folsom worked, just as Folsom wanted him to be assigned to homicide. Folsom had had his suspicions about how Ramierez hung, and here he was in a transvestite club. Folsom didn't know whether to hide under the table and let Fritz and Ralf make love to each other above him, hiding him from view, or to invite Flash to come over and lay on the table and let all three of them feast on him.

Flash solved the dilemma himself by spying Folsom out and coming directly over and giving him a big, unconcerned smile and greeting him. So, Folsom guessed there was no question in Ramierez's mind which way Folsom swung—and it didn't seem to bother him. Good signs both. Very good signs.

"Hi, Clint," he chirped and just stood there between the action on the stage and the suspended action in the trio's banquette. "Hi, guys," he directed at Fritz and Ralf as well. They both perked up, instantly recognizing that another member of the all-stud team was in attendance. Four really hot studs, for there was no doubt at all that Clint Folsom and friends were real hot studs.

"Uh, hi, Hernan— Flash," Clint said. "What brings you here?" How lame was that to ask, he immediately recognized. "Uh, what . . ."

"I'm here on business," Flash said. "But relax. I have no problem being here. And I certainly have no problem with you being here. The club owner, Frank somebody, has been receiving death threats, and I've been sent over to check it out. Still don't have my NYPD specialty assignment, so I'm getting all of the calls they can't pigeonhole easily. I'll have to find this Frank and—"

"That's Frank down there on stage," Folsom said, not entirely successfully covering a smile. "Here she's know as Francine, though." At that moment Francine was playing gardener. She had her young man, still the first one, splayed out in front of her, holding his weight on his hands, palms down on the floor, and his legs spread up, back, and out, Francine holding him like a wheelbarrow and planting seed in his ass with her trowel.

"Oh," Flash said and sat down on the banquette beside Ralf, a little confused still.

All Folsom could think of at the moment was Eddie. He was such a hothead, Clint was thinking. He'd gotten himself in a heap of trouble now, though. He must have mouthed around, in his tiff with Francine, that he was going to do Francine in, which was just like the flamboyant little bugger. And now that had gotten back to the police, who had been expecting the gangs to put out a contract on Francine for years. They didn't care what happened to Francine all that much, but everything was in a tenuous balance down here in the Village. Something like Francine getting rubbed out could light the whole neighborhood like a bonfire.

"We were just going to take Clint back to Francine's dressing room and fuck the stuffing out of him," Ralf said sweetly to Flash. "Would you like to come with us and wait for Francine there?"

"Ummm. OK, sure," Flash said, not wavering a moment from Ralf's Australian directness.

Fifteen minutes later Folsom was stretched out on his belly on a makeup table stool in the middle of Francine's dressing room. Ralf held the American's arms in his hands and had his mouth going up and down on Clint's cock as he crouched his hips under Folsom's face. Fritz was standing between Folsom's thighs, holding the American's knees in his hands and stroking his cock in and out of Clint's ass. Flash sat almost nervously on the edge of the divan nearby, but then he got comfortable enough to pull a very nice brown cock out of his pants and play with himself as he watched his fellow detective being plowed. The longer Folsom got plowed, the more comfortable and naked Flash got. Clint kept his eyes on the other detective as much as he could. Folsom wanted the hot Latino. And Folsom wanted the hot Latino to want him, so Folsom gave him a good performance with Ralf and Fritz.

After a while Ralf motioned to Flash, and he stood and came over and stood at Clint's head with the Australian, and South American and Australian cock met in all-American mouth while Folsom moaned for the German mining operation going on at the other pole.

Then Fritz was pulling Clint away from his international conference and carrying him on his embedded cock over to the divan. Fritz laid down on his back, bringing Clint down with him. Fritz folded Clint's legs up into his chest as he lay atop the German, Fritz's cock still deep inside the American. Clint looked straight ahead, and a grinning Ralf was approaching him, stroking what he was about to feed into his American prey. Ralf liked to be a little rough and cruel, and Clint liked him to be that way. Ralf had the cap of his dick pressed at the rim of Clint's hole above Fritz's buried piece. And then Clint was gasping, and gulping, and panting as Ralf started working himself inside the American, gliding in his cock on top of Fritz's. He grabbed Clint's ankles and wishboned his legs widely, opening him as much as possible for the double penetration. Clint dug his fists into Ralf's shoulders and kneaded them as Clint shuddered and lurched with each inch of depth the thick Australian achieved. Clint's head lolled back and Flash was there in a . . . well, yes, in a flash . . . taking his fellow detective's lips in his firm, hot Latin mouth. Clint had no idea the Latino would taste this sweet.

Hernando kissed Clint deeply, lovingly, giving him comfort and assurance as Ralf's cock relentlessly moved up into Folsom's passage on top of Fritz's dormant, but very hard cock. Flash pulled his mouth off Folsom's and kissed down his chest and belly and into his pubes. The Latino gave Folsom sweet and gentle head, as Ralf and Fritz huffed and puffed, doing all they could to bottom out inside their shared lover together. Then Flash was throwing his leg over Folsom as the American detective lay on top of Fritz on the divan and kissing Ralf now and presenting his cock for Clint's attention, which he happily gave it.

Flash and Clint were 69ing when Ralf and Fritz bottomed and started to counter stroke inside Folsom. All four hot and bothered and intense in their intimately shared fuck.

It was all too exciting for Ralf and Fritz. They both came quickly, crying out and twitching and then sighing almost in unison as their cum mingled inside Clint. They pulled out of Folsom and kissed each other in their new-found intimacy. Flash and his detective counterpart weren't done yet, though. They had barely started. All the time they were 69ing, Folsom was having flashbacks of Brad, Brad Roberts, his murdered lover and partner. Clint had been helping Ralf get settled in the States in the hope he could be a replacement for Brad for the American detective, knowing there could be no such replacement. But this Hernando was something else entirely. Not Brad, of course, but in his own way maybe every bit as good as Brad.

Clint needed to know. Clint wanted to know if there was a possibility. He told Ralf and Fritz to go back to the club showroom. They'd had their fun for now. Clint wanted to be with Hernando. The two friends from Europe left in good spirits and without a bit of resentment, great and generous sports both. Just the thing for a perfect group party. But Clint wanted to try Hernando out alone. Clint wanted to know if Hernando could be the perfect lover.

And he was. He stretched out beside Clint on the divan and made slow, sensuous love to his new friend with his hands and his lips and his tongue—and with his sultry Latin voice. He took Clint slowly and completely. He turned Clint this way and that way, running his hands over his curves and gently, sensuously into his crevices, rubbing his thighs and calves against Clint's, his long, curved toes—just like his impossibly long, curved-up cock—along Clint's legs, as he turned his new-found lover here and there. His belly and nipples rubbing against Clint's, and then against his butt cheeks and shoulder blades. His lips buried in the hollow of Clint's neck, tracing Clint's throbbing veins, throbbing for him. Wanting him inside. Begging the hot, hard Latino to fuck him.

But still Hernando made love to Clint's body. His cock rubbing across Clint's belly as he took his lover's mouth gently but relentlessly in his again. Hernando's fists trapping Clint's. Not letting his captive touch him. Him doing all of the touching.

Him stretched out along Clint's back, imprisoning Clint's arms with his, not letting Clint touch him, while his hips moved, up and down, back and forth, around and around, his long, sensuous cock rubbing around on the small of Clint's back, and on Clint's butt cheeks, and along his thighs and then between his thighs, making love to the sensitive skin of his inner thighs.

Clint moaning and writhing. Feeling the fuck even though Hernando hadn't even entered him yet with that long, long, slender, throbbing tool. His cock stroking up and down in Clint's crack, with Clint stretching as wide as he could, wanting the hot Latino inside him. The underside of hard cock stroking up and down on Clint's hole, causing it to pucker out in invitation. Clint sighing and groaning and begging for it. "Fuck me, fuck me, oh, fuck me now." Clint was exhausted, just from the anticipation of it and from begging for it. Hernando was holding him still, making him whimper for that long, long cock.

And then the peace of the entry. Just gliding in, lubricated by the healthy, virile profusion of cum of Ralf and Fritz and the stretching their double monster cocks had done.

Hernandez floating above Clint, the only contact for those moments his long, curved cock, as it glided into his new lover, deeper, deeper, its mushroom cap caressing Clint's undulating passage walls as it moved into him. Deeper than Ralf and Fritz had managed together. Deeper than Brad had ever gone. In, in, in. And then out most of the way. And back in, deeper still. Clint moaned deeply and licked his lips. And the contact began, slowly, tentatively, lovingly. Hernandez kissed his lover deeply on the lips and then pushed a long, thumb into his mouth. And Clint sucked deeply on it, as Hernandez's cock glided back in. The Latino lover shuddered and came in a quiet flow. And Clint almost sobbed in relief and acceptance. Both at the beauty of it and regret that it was over.

But it wasn't over. Flash was still as hard as ever. He turned Clint on his back and knelt below him on the divan and pulled Clint's pelvis into his hips. This time he fucked Clint in vigorous strokes. Joyfully. His eyes locked on Clint's. Full of pleasure, laughter, and lust. He played with Clint's nipples and then he held Clint by his hips and smoothly, athletically rose up into a crouch and then a stand, on top of the divan, Clint stretched below him, the two of them attached at the pelvis. Hernandez stroked hard down into Clint's channel until he came a second time, in a strong gush this time. He laughed and lowered Clint onto the bed, and brought his mouth down onto Clint's dick and quickly and expertly sucked him off, while Clint writhed under him and bucked against him and arched his back in pleasure. Fully taken.

But not fully. Hernando sidesplit Clint then, pumping slowly and deeply and strongly into him. Kissing Clint on the neck, murmuring words of love into his ear. Making love to him, not just fucking him. Clint sighed in satisfaction, wanting it to go on and on and on, sheathing that wondrous long, long, hot Latino dick.

But their lovemaking was arrested by a commotion out in the hallway beyond the door, and Ralf and Fritz reappeared.

"The fat lady," Fritz only managed to get out in an excited voice.

"Don't tell me. She's finished her second song set and wants her dressing room back." Folsom said in a tired, but satisfied voice. He was reluctant to give up this glorious coupling, but at least he'd always know that it wasn't from a lack of stamina or enthusiasm and interest on Flash's part that it had come to an end.

"Afraid that bird isn't going to be singing again, mate," Ralf interjected.

"What . . .?"

"She's dead. Someone did her right there in front of our eyes on stage as she was finishing her last lad of the night."

"Oh, shit," Hernando exclaimed and jumped off the divan. He headed for the door to the dressing room's bathroom. "Here while I was enjoying myself, I wasn't doing what I was sent here for. I was supposed to keep her . . . him . . . whatever alive, not fuck around while he was being done in."

Clint turned to Ralf and Fritz. "Go out there and see that no one touches anything. Tell them there's a couple of policeman on the site and we'll be out in a couple of minutes. And I assume someone's called 911. And for God's sake don't tell them the policemen are back here doing each other."

They turned to go, but Clint held them for one more instruction. "And start asking if anyone knows where Eddie, Francine's ex, is. He'll be everyone's prime suspect even if he didn't do it."

"That won't be necessary," Clint heard Hernando say in a quiet, flat voice behind him.

All three looked over. Ramierez had opened the door to the bathroom to reveal a young blond man, obviously well past any help, lying in a pool of blood on the bathroom floor.

"Eddie, I presume?" Ramierez asked.

"Good guess," Folsom answered.

As the two detectives pulled on their clothes, preparing to go out and receive the arriving police squad, Clint leaned over and gave Hernando a tender kiss on the lips. "Welcome to homicide," he said. Flash smiled broadly. Another kiss, and then Clint said, "And welcome to my bed, if you'll have me." This time Flash's smile stretched his cheeks to the limit.

Death in Eden

Chapter One: Last Flight to D.C.

I knew who he was the minute he entered the plane. The acclaimed fullback for the Washington Redskins, Jentel "Boom Boom" Huff more than filled the aisle of the 737 I was taking out of JFK for National Airport. They've changed the name to Reagan airport now, but for those of us who have been around for a while, the small airport near the Pentagon and across the river from Washington, D.C., which was originally built for shuttling congressmen, will always be National.

This was a last, midnight-special commuter plane from New York to Washington, and it was a Tuesday, so the plane was nearly empty. Despite that, we'd gotten assigned seats, and fickle fate being what it was, Huff's assigned seat was at the window in the same row near the back where I had the aisle. I got a close-up of his well-rounded muscular glutes as, not waiting for me to stand and get out of the way, he struggled across me and overflowed more than settled in the seat between me and the window. The man wasn't fat; he was one huge muscle, which he earned honestly from the work he did very well on the football field.

He was outfitted in expensive, well-cut duds, tailored khaki trousers and a form-fitting emerald-green polo shirt that followed every contour on his barrel chest and strained over his bulging biceps. I felt grungy and wrinkled in contrast in my jeans and second-day white shirt, having come straight to the airport after a grueling day on the streets and following the call that had summoned me urgently to Washington's Virginia suburbs.

As the doors were closing, the stewardess came on the intercom and, before starting her set spiel about what to do if the plane came down over water, told us the obvious—that the plane wasn't full on this flight—and that we were free to find an empty seat more to our liking once we were airborne. I was happy to hear the part about the seat changes, but her spiel about water safety sent me off into a flight of cynicism. When had a plane ever crashed into the ocean and any of the passengers survived, I wondered. And what ocean would we be crossing on our short hop down the East Coast from New York to Washington?

We were up and the bell dinged quietly and the flashing seat belt sign went off within minutes of our scheduled departure. That's why I preferred traveling either very late or very early—there was more of a chance of being somewhere close on time and of having your baggage arrive at the same time as you did. Although I was just traveling with a carry-on this time. The Loudon County police chief, an old very special friend of mine, hadn't given me enough notice to more than throw a couple of day's worth of work clothes in my duffel.

"Umm, the stewardess told us we could spread out after we were airborne. So, if you—"

"Oh, I don't mind, if you don't," Huff responded, and he flashed me a big, white-toothed smile that shone particularly bright in his chocolate-brown face. "I kinda like to talk to someone on short flights like this. I'm a little shaky about flying."

"Umm, OK," I answered. I didn't want to be impolite. And it would be a short flight; I could take being crowded out into the aisle with the feeling of a massive closeness for a flight this short. Huff was so broad in the chest and shoulders that his biceps were quite an imposing and mind-possessing presence.

"I'm Jentel Huff," he said, flashing that big smile and turning as well as he could in his seat and presenting a giant right-hand mitt for me to shake. He had a strong grip, naturally, and didn't let go immediately. And when he did, he stayed turned to me and his hand went down to lay lightly on my knee. "And you?"

"Yes, I knew who you were as soon as you entered the plane," I said. "Oh, and I'm Clint. Clint Folsom."

The mitt raised and fisted and he punched me lightly in the chest. It was obvious that he was a hands-on player. "Shit," he said good-naturedly. "It's hard going anywhere without being known now, especially since the season's about to start up again. You won't tell anyone about me being scared to fly, will you?"

"No, of course not," I answered with a laugh. "What happens on the plane stays on the plane." His good humor and overwhelming presence were infectious.

"Good to hear," he answered, also with a low laugh, and that mitt dropped to my knee again.

"Going home or do you live in New York?" he asked.

"Live there; going down to Washington on business," I answered. He probably was fishing for what I did for a living, but I didn't volunteer it. People sort of clammed up and got uncomfortable when they knew what that was. And, of course, I didn't have to ask Boom Boom Huff what he did for a living.

The stewardess came by and offered us a drink, and we both bought a beer.

"And this is Devin, my kid brother," Huff was saying thirty minutes later as the conversation was getting rolling along real well. "We've got him down at a private prep school in central Virginia. He wants to follow me into professional football, and he's probably got more talent than I ever did. He's a little slow on the books, nineteen already and not yet ready for college, but he won't have any trouble getting an athletic scholarship once we decide on the best college for him."

Huff had already shown me pictures of his wife and his two little girls. He'd had quite a reputation as a womanizer in his first couple of years in the NFL, following a few sex scandals at Florida State, but the pictures indicated he'd really turned himself around.

"So, will they be at the airport to meet you?" I asked.

"No, they don't think I'm coming home until tomorrow," Huff said. "I got finished shooting a commercial in New York a day early. I'll be surprising them when they wake up in the morning and I'm there."

Huff went quiet then, and he was eyeing me rather funnily. I had seen this look before, and I suddenly was uncomfortable and felt the row wasn't really big enough for both of us. The hand on my knee wasn't laying lightly any more. He was gripping me pretty hard.

The lights in the cabin had been out for a while, giving the late-night passengers some tease of an opportunity to get a few minutes of shut-eye before we arrived.

Huff was breathing heavily. I looked down, not wanting to see that look in his eye. But what I saw when I looked down, was the big, dominating, black hand on my knee. I felt myself stirring. Huff didn't know a thing about me. But I knew everything about me. And I knew what turned me on. I was sweating slightly and I could feel myself rising inside my jeans and I could hear the raggedness of my own breath.

"Clint," he whispered.

And I turned to him and our lips met, and I felt his mitt move up my thigh and settle on my basket, his fingers tracing the rise of me through my worn jeans.

The seat belt light flickered on and the warning tone dinged and the lights in the cabin flashed up. We both were clumsily pulling apart as best we could and turning from each other, and Jentel Huff melted as best he could into the window frame. I didn't give him another look until we landed, and then I fairly shot out of my seat, grabbed my duffel from the overhead bin, and raced for the exit.

I was getting into a cab out on the curb at the airport, when I heard a voice from behind.

"Mind if we share the cab?"

I knew who it was. "OK. OK, I guess," I said. My eye was on the cabbie, whose eyes were all wide and full of worship as he took the bulking form of the Redskins' fullback in. There weren't enough cabs to go around out here at this time of night, and I knew if anyone was going to get this one, it would be Jentel Huff.

"Where are you going?" Jentel asked when we were both stuffed, bicep to bicep, into the backseat.

"The Marriott Key Bridge in Rosslyn," I answered. "It's just on the other side of the Pentagon from here, across the river from Georgetown. And you?"

"The Marriott will be fine with me," Jentel said in a low, husky voice.

* * * *

I was on my back on the edge of the king-sized bed, arching up on my shoulders in pain and pleasure, trying to open as wide as possible for the big black cock Jentel was stuffing into my channel. I had one fist in my mouth, trying to stifle my cries, and the other one was bunching up a large handful of silken bedspread. The room was dim, lit only by a bedside lamp and the lights of Washington across the Potomac that shone through the eighth-floor window of the Marriott.

Jentel had been too anxious, too driven by lust to get inside me, for me to be completely ready for him. He was gigantic, but I liked them this way. I didn't have a problem with that. But he could hardly wait for us to get into the room. I had wanted to shower first—I'd had a rough day on the streets of New York—and I wanted to be clean for him. But he couldn't wait. He was naked within seconds, and then he had pushed me down on my back on the bed and stripped me, and he was covering me close.

We kissed passionately and then his lips and tongue were all over my torso. He spent a good deal of time snuffling up in my pits with his nose, and he was sighing and making guttural sounds of pleasure as he licked and nibbled there—more than nibbled; he was biting me, deep in passion. I worried briefly about bruising, but in my pits, who would notice? And, besides, this unexpected pit play was turning me on too. The locker room turn on, I supposed. In turn, I was letting my hands wander on the bulging curves of him. I

263

loved hulking muscle, and he had it to spare. I raised and spread my legs to him, asking him to fuck me, letting him know it was what I wanted.

I had produced lube and a condom from my duffel before he pushed me onto the bed, and he was working my ass with his meaty, lubed fingers. He was just moving too fast, too anxious, and he was just so big. Big black cock; blacker than the chocolate-brown of his beautiful, well-developed body. I wanted to suck it and stroke it, but he wasn't giving me time for that. He wanted inside me, and I was all right with that too.

When I felt his bulb at my rim, I arched my back up off the bed and reached down with both hands and held the root of his cock steady. I opened my mouth wide in a cry of taking as the bulb plopped past my sphincter, and then I let go of his cock and fisted one hand and grabbed for the silken bed spread with the other as he pushed his way in, downfield, toward the goalpost. He had found his seam and was galloping downfield. And then he was thrusting and thrusting and thrusting. Touchdown!

Jentel went rigid, only his hips grinding in short, out-of-rhythm jabs, and then I could feel the head of the condom balloon out deep inside me as Jentel gasped and took in breath in a long, noisy, ragged drag. I let out a little yelp of my own and also went rigid as I shot my load up onto Huff's heaving belly.

He was grinning that big white-toothed grin down at me. "Man you are good for a white bitch," he muttered, still breathing heavily. His hands were all over my sweat-slicked body, worked hard by a hard black body pounding between my open legs.

"You're a pretty good baller yourself," I answered in a weak voice. And he was. All those sex scandals he'd been in with those white girls. He was making it pretty evident there had been some white boys too.

He stood away from me just a bit and rolled the spent condom off his still-engorged tool. I sat up on the edge of the bed and reached out and took his cock in both of my hands and brought my mouth down on it, opening wide around his knob and sucking with pressure. It was fascinating how much blacker the appendage and his lemon-sized balls were than the rest of him. He stood there, trembling slightly and sighing for several minutes, as I worked to take as much of the deep blackness into my mouth and throat as I could. Soon, though, he had taken my head into his now tender hands, lovingly holding me like a trophy football, and moved my head on his cock in counter rhythm to his slightly swaying hips.

"You got another condom in that duffel bag?" he asked in a low, husky voice.

"Several," I said after pulling my mouth off him and looking up with a sly grin. "But I'd like to get a shower first, I think."

"I think not," he answered in a low growl. "I like you just as you are."

And he liked me repeatedly, marching through three or four more condoms, into the night, over the back of a straight chair and him sitting in the chair and me pumping myself in his lap, and at last, Jentel side-splitting me in the king-sized bed, both of us on our sides and me nuzzled rear to pelvis against him, me being held closely and still, encased in those big strong arms of his and him stroking inside me in long, deep slides that were still energetic and long flowing hours into this workout.

I was exhausted, however, and was asleep before he had filled the head of the last condom.

Chapter Two: Scent of a Man

I woke up, thinking at first that it had all been one long wet dream. But when I opened my eyes, there he was, over at the full-length window, leaning his shoulders back against the side frame of the window and looking out over the morning traffic inching back and forth over the Key Bridge linking Georgetown to the Virginia suburbs. He was magnificent in nakedness and repose in a way that made the football posters and commercial shots of him that woman flowed over pale in contrast. His knees were slightly bent, and the leg toward the window was lifted, with the pad of his foot resting on the window frame. His dong was jutting out and hanging down. A good eight or nine thick inches of it as I gauged it from where I lay tangled in the mussed sheets of the bed. He was smoking a cigarette and looking out on the city with unseeing eyes. He seemed to be looking at something inside him. I suspected I knew what.

"Regrets?" I asked in a low voice. "Because . . . I mean . . ."

He turned that radiant smile on me and snuffed out his cigarette in an ashtray on a small table in front of the window.

"Come here for a few minutes and then ask that question if you still want to," he said. That voice was husky again. And his cock was beginning to jut out.

"I think we used all the condoms I brought," I answered, almost apologetically, even though it had been Jentel who raced through the condoms.

"No problem. I brought my own." And he had. He pointed to the top of the table in front of the window, and there was a small pile of condom packets there.

"I think I should shower first," I then said. "I haven't washed for over a day now. I must stink like a pig."

"I think not," he said. Still smiling, but voice like steel now. Knowing what he wanted; not to be denied. "Come here. Now."

I disentangled myself from the sheets and moved toward the window.

"I don't think this will work. I'm a big man." I was panting, worked up by his kisses and his tonguing on my torso and snuffling up into my pits. But I was skeptical about what he was trying to position my body to do. He was still standing, leaning against the frame of the window, crouched a bit farther down, trying to lap me on this thighs, facing him.

"No problem," he muttered, his voice full of lust. Knowing what he wanted and determined to get it. "I'm bigger—in every way," and then he laughed and I smiled too, as he most certainly was. "And stronger," he continued. "I lift heavier weights than you every day. Hook those knees on my hips. Now!"

And it was obvious that he did lift those weights and was quite strong enough, because he grabbed me with his hands around the small of my waist and lifted me and settled his cock head on my hole. I reached down and held his cock until he had broached my channel by a good couple of inches. And then I cried out as he slowly forced my pelvis down on his ass splitter and, when he had bottomed, began pumping me up and down on his tool, handling me like I was a writhing, groaning rag doll.

"Oh, god, Yessss! Oh, no, no . . . no . . .slowly . . . yessss! Oh, shit, Jentel. Oh, Shittt! Faster, harder, deeper!"

Afterward, still skewered on him as he crouched against the window frame, still panting slightly, both of us looking down into the rush-hour traffic on the busy Rosslyn streets below: "Why me? In the plane. How did you know?"

"I didn't know, not for sure," Jentel whispered. "And I wasn't thinking of you. I was thinking of me. I just knew I had to have you."

"But how? Why did you . . . ? What did I do . . . or say . . . that . . . got to you?"

"Your scent," he answered in a low voice. "The scent of a man. Your scent put me in heat. And then I had to have you. I don't know how to explain it."

But he didn't have to explain it. I had heard it before. I had something that got to men who were even slightly inclined. And I hadn't showered before going to the airport.

A long pause.

"Can we shower now?" I asked.

"Will you see me again?" he responded.

A slight pause.

"Yes, I don't see why not."

"Then we can shower now. I won't use this last condom."

But he did use the last condom, in the shower, taking me from the rear, under the streaming water, pushing my belly up and down on the slick, soapy tiles of the shower with the strength of his cock jack-hammering up into me.

At the door, as he, dressed in what he'd worn the previous day, was about to leave ahead of me: "How long will you be here?"

"As long as it takes," I answered. "As long as my business here takes. And I'm not sure now how long that will be."

"And when I want to fuck you again—"

"Then you will fuck me again," I responded.

That big white-toothed smile reappeared.

And as he opened the door to leave: "And, oh, Jentel," I said, "What happens in the Marriott stays in the Marriott."

A repeated grin and a "thanks," and he was gone.

* * * *

269

I got the call on where I was to go soon after Jentel left. A car had already been rented for me and was waiting down on Nash Street. In little time at all I was cruising out on the George Washington Parkway and taking the Route 193 back road through the very wealthy, deceptively rural residential area around Great Falls on the Potomac, and then on out the quickly developing Route 7 corridor to just beyond Leesburg, the center of the Northern Virginia hunt country. I'd picked the Rosslyn area for my hotel not only because it was just across the Potomac from the nation's capital, but also because it gave me ready access to a relatively pleasant, counter commuter traffic, scenic drive out to Loudon County, where I'd been summoned by the chief of police of one of the richest counties in the nation.

As I drove, I wracked my brain how Johnny "The Club" Wallace, at one time the scourge of New York City's underbelly, had managed a connection with the rolling hunt country of Virginia's Loudon County.

"It was the witness protection program," Peter Blair, the aforementioned chief of police, told me when I was standing on the front porch of a modestly sized, but obviously high-priced southern colonial house not more than ten miles beyond the moneyed "countrified" town Leesburg had become.

"I knew he'd gone into the program," I said. "But he would have really been out of his element here, I'd think. I mean one of the Mafia's chief hit men?"

"Yeah," Blair said. And then he laughed. "But I guess they were using psychology. This would probably be the last place the Mafia would look to find him. We call this area of the country Eden, you know. With some folks thinking Washington, D.C., is the center of the world, all of the rich and famous who gather here need someplace close by where they can canter their horses and enjoy their entitlements."

Pete Blair was still looking good. He was older than I was by about ten years, but he'd always been the Marine model type. Big and bulky with muscle that cried out of long hours in the gym. A crew cut and rugged blond good looks.

He could be taken for an FBI agent, which probably didn't hurt him in finding a high-paying job out here in the manicured countryside when he had so abruptly left New York. All because of me.

Not wanting to dwell on that, I snapped my attention back to the work at hand. "Well, it looks like the Mafia wasn't fooled. Is he in the house still?"

"No, they carted him away during the night. Didn't want the area Moguls to be disturbed. Not in the house. Out in the barn. Let's walk and talk."

We started off for a barn a couple of hundred feet back from the house that looked quite a bit better painted and maintained than most of the houses in my Brooklyn neighborhood.

"And it isn't so simple as fingering a Mafia hit, either. Sal M. has been dead a while himself, and the leadership of that family has passed on to the point where it's kind of late to come after The Club for yakking to the DA. And there are other possibilities."

"Other possibilities?" I asked. "Oh, is that where, over at that saw horse in the center there?" We had arrived at the barn. The yellow tape was discretely just inside the structure, and I could see where the pool of blood was. Right there at the chunky wooden saw horse.

"Yes, that's where. He was found hog tied to the saw horse. His own M.O. Clubbed to death."

"That all?" I asked. I knew there was probably more, and I was right.

"No, not all, of course. He'd been worked on in the ass with the club before he was beaten with it. His own method."

"And raped too?" I asked in a small, thin voice. I had to know, but I was having a hard time talking about it and breathing steady too.

"We won't know until the autopsy is finished, Clint." And then Blair lowered his voice to a level that none of the techs working the scene could hear. "I'm sorry, it may have been a little insensitive of me, calling you down from New York and all . . . but . . ."

271

"Yeah, I am sort of curious why you brought NYPD Homicide into this, Pete—and, especially, why me?"

"A couple of reasons, Clint. The first one being that no matter what happened, you are the one who knows Wallace's cases the best. And it's sort of delicate here for another reason."

"Oh, what's that, Pete?"

"You asked why we couldn't just assume the Mafia had caught up with Wallace. It's because there is other 'stuff' in play here. You know Wallace. Even though he was in the program, he was close to being taken in for another crime here."

I didn't say anything. I just stood and stared him down until he went on.

"We're not far from a Loudon athletic prep school here, Clint. You know, promising athletes who aren't academically ready to go on to college yet, but so much in demand for college athletic programs that they are given extra schooling to make the grade."

"And so," I said.

"As I said, you know Wallace. We had him pretty much dead to rights on a molestation of one of the nineteen-year-old boys in that program. So there was bad blood focusing on him hereabouts that had nothing to do with his previous life up in New York."

"I'm not surprised, of course," I said. "But that's even more reason why you should be able to handle that down here. You were one of New York's finest detective supervisors, Pete. Why do you need me for a simple murder investigation down here that, as you say, may have no connection to New York at all?"

"Well, here's the thing, Clint. The boy's father is the Commonwealth's Attorney in this county and I myself am on tape telling Wallace I would personally tear him limb from limb. So, you see, we do need some outside help, and under the circumstance, with your history with Wallace—"

"Oh. OK, I get it. So, can I see the body."

Chapter Three: Back in the Saddle Again

Johnny Wallace's body was beat up pretty badly. It definitely looked like a hate crime to me. But that didn't take much imagination to suppose. The man had been strung up naked on a saw horse and fucked with a club nearly the size of a baseball bat before being bludgeoned with it. Divine retribution, I thought.

I didn't spend all that much time with the body, but I did find a surprise or two that set me thinking for a couple of days.

They'd finished the autopsy and could only say a "maybe" on the question of sexual rape going beyond the foreign-object penetration—mainly because of the size of the foreign object used. But I couldn't have mustered up regrets if there had been some positive results for body fluids or something. Which brought us back to my earlier question when we were done and Pete had settled us in a faux British pub at the edge of Leesburg that was so clean and dolled up that it wouldn't have been out of place in Disneyworld.

"Those aren't all of the reasons I'm down here on this case, are they?" I asked Pete when we were settled with our Belgium beers and a bowl of gourmet nuts.

"I was real sorry to hear about Brad Roberts." was his response. "Real sorry. My condolences on that. Really."

Good old Pete. Never approach directly when you can beat around the bush.

"Yeah, well, I haven't gotten over that," I answered. "But I did get even." It hadn't been more than six months since I'd pursued the killers of my NYPD Homicide squad partner—and lover—across Europe and closed out on them. That hadn't closed out on my feeling for Brad Roberts any, though.

"But I've missed you, Clint. Missed you real bad. So, yes, there's another reason I got you liaised down here for the Wallace case. I could do that because of your earlier connection with Wallace. But I wanted to do it because of us. I need to know where we stand now. What the possibilities might be."

There, it was out. Pete Blair had been one of my "significant others" in New York before another cop, Danny Thompson, and then Brad Roberts had come onto the scene. Pete had been the older man who took me under his wing and shared all of his professional experience with me and had wound up sharing his bed with me too. And then Brad had come along, and I drifted into being a Pete for Brad. And then one day it was Brad in my bed and Pete had withdrawn from the NYPD and headed south.

"Pete. The past, you know—"

"I know I took it hard," Pete said in a low, insistent voice, after taking a big swig of his beer. "I know I wasn't paying enough attention to you. It was the job. You know the job. It can just swallow you up. I can see where Danny and Brad were attractive to you. So much younger, and obviously wanting you so bad."

"Pete—"

"And now that you are here. I just need you so bad, Clint. Just the scent of you across the table from me. I think that's what I miss the most. Just having you here, close to me. I'm genuinely sorry about Roberts, but . . . ."

* * * *

I had forgotten those moves of Pete's that had me melting to him. He was a consummate lover, closely attentive to his partner and with the small, unexpected moves that could put a man needing attention over the edge. But, if anything, perhaps too sensitive and gentle and attentive for some men. And I probably was one of those men. With me, it was variety that floated my boat. I loved what Pete did to me. But maybe not a steady diet of it. I liked to be ridden and taken hard now and again too. That was probably what had killed our relationship. Probably if it hadn't been Danny Thompson and then Brad Roberts, it was destined to having been someone else.

Pete's small, centuries-old townhouse was just a short ride away from the faux British pub. He still lived alone. If he had replaced me, he'd had him cleared out entirely before I got there.

Pete liked to enfold—and I liked to be covered and completely controlled. So, it didn't take us long to find our old, comfortable position. I was flat on my belly on his queen-sized bed, only my hips slightly elevated by a pillow, stroking the sheets with my cock to the rhythm of his fuck. He was on top of me, covering me closely, nipples pressed into my shoulder blades, thighs encasing mine, using his knees for leverage in the stroking of his cock deep inside me, my hips raised slightly to meet his crotch. He had his head close to mine, kissing my neck, teasing my earlobe with his teeth, whispering to me of remembrances of my smell and how it drove him crazy, and enticing me to turn my lips to his frequently for long kisses.

But what I found most melting, most intimate for some inexplicable reason, was that he ran his arms along mine and held both of my hands in his, our fingers entwined, him holding me gently in thrall to him there, a symbol of how closely we were joined as he fucked me.

And he fucked me as no other man did, in long, deep, slow, gliding strokes to the very depth of me. Former lovers, we fucked naturally, and my channel muscles were so familiar with every vein and bump in his cock that they expanded and contracted to meet his slides and made undulating love to his tool. Thus perfectly set, his cock moved in and out in long strokings for time unending, culminating in mewings of taking from me and sighs and moans of a prolonged, prodigious flow from him that backed up between throbbing cock and channel and burbled out onto the sheets.

We lay there afterward, each thinking thoughts of "how it once was," fully satisfied once more, sweating slightly from the last few minutes of writhing that preceded our almost simultaneous ejaculations. I was laying on my back, arms over my head, and Pete was stretched beside and hovering over me, one hand gently teasing my cock and balls, his nose and tongue buried in one of my pits, drinking me in.

"You know you are hopelessly promiscuous, don't you?" he murmured to me. But it wasn't an accusation. He was smiling down at me. Perhaps feeling a little smug that it had been so easy.

But I remembered his fucking. I knew before I got on that night shuttle from New York that he would fuck me—if he still wanted to. Being promiscuous didn't bother me if I could be fucked as expertly as he did it. If he hadn't left New York, I would have let him continue fucking me even while I was fucking Danny and then Brad. Brad had said he didn't knew I could only slowly more solely to him. He'd said he'd take me any way he could get me. It had been Pete who pulled out of me and left. It was Pete who was looking for the one and only.

"You know I don't let any man put his stamp on me, if that's what you mean," I answered.

"No, it's not. Not really. It's just that you're so natural about it. And you draw men so naturally. I guess it would be inevitable that you fucked a lot."

"Umm, umm," I answered lazily. "And if you keep doing that to me, you can fuck me again." His hand was doing wonders for the erection angle of my tool. I reached down and started bringing him back up to erection too, and his intake of breath told me we wouldn't be talking for very long.

"Oh, I intend to. It's been too long," Pete responded in a low, husky voice. "What is it, though? What is it that you seek in fucking, Clint?"

"Oh, I guess the death wish," I answered. I'd been asked this before.

"The death wish?" Pete's forehead was wrinkled, and I knew I needed to disabuse him of where my answer had spun his thoughts off too.

"I don't mean actual death. But, you know, there are philosophers who have written about ejaculation as a brief death, as being as near to death as you can get and live. And I live for being on that edge—for the moment of ejaculation. And not just mine, but the second when I have brought a man to his ejaculation, to the elation of his brief brush with death. Sort of a life in death connection. Does any of that make sense?"

A short pause, and then, "Yes, I guess I can see that. For a moment I was afraid—"

"—that coming down here on a case about Johnny Wallace would make me remember and think sobering thoughts?" I filled in the sentence for him, and he didn't answer so I knew I'd filled it in correctly.

"There were moments, yes, when Johnny Wallace was fucking me that I thought I was going to die—even, perhaps, that I wanted to die and get it over with. But, no, I don't have nightmares about that. And that's not what I meant."

"So," Pete said, with what might have been a forced smile and jocularity. "Shall we see how many times we can kill each other again before we have to trot off and get you introduced to the Commonwealth Attorney?"

"Sure," I tossed out. "You keep a vocal count of yours, and I'll sing out mine."

Then Pete rolled me back on my stomach, simultaneously pushed a pillow under my belly again to raise my hips to him, as I sighed and moaned as he entwined my hands in his, covered me closely, and slid down, down, down inside me.

It was good to be home—if only for a brief visit.

Chapter Four: Clubbing Memories

Pete need not have brought up my knowledge of Johnny The Club Wallace. I had that particular fucker ingrained deep inside me.

A couple of months before Pete transferred to the NYPD from San Francisco, I'd been working the gangster beat from the angle of how some of them liked their sex with another man. I'd gotten a bit too close to Wallace's employers in the Mafia, and that's when I'd met Johnny—and his club.

His club of choice at the time was a flexible rubber policeman's billy club. And his M.O. was to tie up his victims in some fleabag hotel or other at the fringes of Manhattan and to torture them for whatever information the Mafia wanted by raping them with the club first and then clubbing them to death with the same billy club. I was probably the first one to find out that he fucked the ones he was attracted to between the two acts with the club—and I only found that out because I probably was the first one who ever survived his assault. He got an erection off doing his victim with the club when he found the victim attractive, and I suppose he didn't think there was any reason not to put a well-worked hole to use while it was there.

I guess you could also say that it was because of me that Wallace had found his way into witness protection and had ended up here, finished off by a much thicker club than he once was prone to use.

I remember the hotel well because of its name. It was the Jefferson Davis in a particularly depressed section of the city, and despite my plight, I found that a bit amusing, because if there ever was a loser of a hotel it had been this one.

The hotel was a gay dive that rented by the hour, which was Wallace's ultimate undoing, because he'd plunked down the money for three nights, which became somewhat of a flag-waving memory jog for the night clerk there when my buddies on the force turned out to scour the city for one of their own.

Wallace had tracked me down in the Club Europa one night when I was crying in my beer over being overworked and having found someone I hoped to settle down with fucking my upstairs neighbor in our bathtub one night. I was out cruising for a quick "oh woe is me" fuck that night, and Wallace came on to me. He looked good and promised a rough fuck from how he approached me, which was exactly what I was looking for that night. He somehow slipped me a Mickey in a bar drink, however, and I was well short of sharp when he took me into the Jefferson Davis. A quick fuck was what I was after, so I might have gone with him without the senses deadening, but now we'll never know about that. I certainly had my guard down. I'd been warned a hit had been taken out on me, but, like all young and stupid men, I felt I was invincible.

What brought me out of my stupor was Wallace starting his routine by working the lubed billy club inside my ass. I was naked, with my wrists tied above my head to the brass poles in the headboard, and my T-shirt stuffed in my mouth to keep me quiet while he worked me. He told me exactly who he was, why I was where I was, and what he planned to do with me.

While he worked, Wallace was getting aroused, however. He stripped down, and I saw that he wasn't called The Club just because he carried one that he beat people up with.

280

Fucking me with the billy club was turning him on, not the least, I suppose, because I could take it. Pete, who first met me as part of the rescue party, would be interested to know that I was even more promiscuous then than I am now, and my ass was open enough in those days to take a Mac truck careening up it.

Soon Wallace was breathing real hard, and his tool was even harder. I was sweating at the strain of taking the billy club inside me, and Wallace bent down over me and was giving me the sniff test and licking me from head to toe. He came up on the bed, kneeling his butt cheeks back on his heels and working his thighs under mine as he spread my legs out and exchanged his billy club for The Club. He grabbed my hips with his hands and pulled me back and forth on a tool that rivaled the billy club in thickness and depths reached.

Playing for time, I acted like I was really enjoying his work inside me—which, in fact, I was. It was just the rough fuck I'd ventured out for that evening, although I wasn't wild about the notion that he planned to finish it off by beating my skull in with that billy club of his.

I must have done well, because he didn't kill me that night—or the next night, either. He kept me there and fucked me whenever he'd gotten up the steam to have another go at me.

And he was still fucking me when my cop buddies kicked in the door and saved my sore ass, not having been ID'd by the hotel's night clerk but having been the "drunken friend" part of his unusual story of a prepaid long weekend starting the night I'd disappeared.

Caught in the unfinished business with club showing, Wallace had been quick to turn state's evidence on his employers, and that's what had gotten him into the witness protection program and down here in an Eden that was totally off his regular beat.

This didn't tell me what had gotten him murdered, however. I didn't give a shit for him, and Pete knew that—he'd been pretty straight that he'd used my connection with Wallace to get me down here and back into his own bed. I

281

did, however, find any unsolved murder case absolutely fascinating, and it was something that wore at me until it was straightened out. And I was known to have an intuition about these cases. My intuition about this killing told me that it hadn't been the Mafia that had caught up with Johnny; my intuition was that it more likely was his inability to keep his own club in his pants. Besides, if it was just a belated Mafia hit, that was no fun.

I decided the next move was to track down this prep school youth Wallace was said to have raped. And I knew that the only way I could get to him would be through his father, the local Commonwealth Attorney. So, as Pete and I were having a sandwich in his kitchen after our nooner in his bed, I asked him how soon we could get into to see the number one lawyer here.

"You have an appointment at two," he answered. "And if that goes well, you can drive to the school later in the afternoon so that you can meet Wallace's victim—his name is Jason. Then we can come back here and—"

"Let's take that part a bit more slowly, Pete," I interrupted. I was fine with Pete fucking me, but not exclusively. If I slept with anyone tonight, it would be with that Redskins' fullback, Jentel. If, of course, he was hooked enough to want another go at me this soon. His dick wasn't any bigger than Pete's, but it was jet black and more vigorous than Pete's—and it fascinated me.

"A guy's gotta have his sleep, Pete. I'm going to be bushed, and it would be good to start off tomorrow fresh and giving this all of my brainpower."

Pete never had known when I was lying to him; it had taken him forever to discover that I was two-timing him with Danny.

Chapter Five: Not Quite as Advertised

After we'd cleaned up from our little roll in the hay at his place, Peter Blair took me over to the Loudon County Court offices, which proved to be not more than three blocks from his old townhouse, near the major intersection where Route 7 coming out of Washington, and Route 15 coming down from Maryland at Point of Rocks converged—both old stage coach roads going back to pre-Revolutionary War days.

We had a timed appointment with the Commonwealth Attorney, Warren Dabney Jr., who kept us waiting for well over a half an hour beyond that just because he could and to show me, I'm sure, how important he was. The bastard left the door between his office and the reception room ajar enough so that we were able to see that he was reading the newspaper and eating a sandwich his secretary took in to just after we arrived.

I got the message without Peter having to say anything. This was going to be a pro forma meeting, just to establish that we had met. And that the only interest the Commonwealth Attorney had in having me investigate this murder was to keep him—and his son—out of it.

I might not have bothered him at all, except that I was sort of curious who he wanted saved the worse, his son or himself.

"I think there's something we all can agree on from the start, Detective Folsom," Dabney said after we'd finally been given audience. "This Wallace was a scumbag of the lowest degree. If my office had been fully informed that such as he was in our midst, we would have moved him along, federal government or no federal government." And with this, he glowered at Peter Blair, who shrank down in his seat a bit. The relationship between them was obvious, and equally obvious was where Blair sat in all of this, having known who Wallace was and why he had been salted away under Dabney's nose.

I certainly didn't respond negatively to Dabney's statement myself. No one in the room knew as well as I did what a scumbag Wallace had been—although perhaps I shouldn't jump to those conclusions too soon, I corrected myself.

"And we can certainly take care of ourselves here in Loudon County," Dabney continued. "But, under the circumstances, Police Chief Blair thought it best to bring in an outside investigator. And he thought you would be the best one to help us close this case down quickly."

And there, in a nutshell, it was. And I wasn't a bit surprised. They wanted me to investigate as little as possible, conclude that Wallace had been killed by someone outside Loudon County, wrap that up in a nice little report, and, as an entirely independent investigator, let the feds know that Wallace had probably been knocked off by the Mafia, which, by the way, was no real big problem because the case that had gotten him into the witness protection program was dead now anyway. And they thought I was the best one to slap this coat of paint over it all because I had a history with Wallace myself.

Well, they might be right. I didn't begrudge whoever had offed Wallace. But to be able to write a convincing report, I'd have to go through at least a few formalities.

"Yes, well, for the purpose of the report, of course, there will be a few bases I'll have to be able to say I covered," I said.

"Such as?" Dabney asked. He had been leaning back in his swivel chair, his feet on the waxed paper in the center of his desk that his sandwich had come in. He was on full alert now.

"Peter has already told me that there are some possibly embarrassing angles to this case—leading to needing someone from the outside to come into the investigation."

"Oh?" The eyebrows went up even more.

"Well, I think, certainly, that any report I could run through the feds on this would have to pin down good alibis for your son, you, and Peter, here. I understand Wallace had been brought up on rape charges for molesting your son and that Peter was heard publicly to threaten his life on that."

"His murder doesn't have anything to do with that," Dabney said with a snort. "The man was killed by his Mafia buddies. They killed him the same way they had paid him to kill others. It's an obvious message."

"Yes, pretty convincing," I said. "But the feds—"

"My son is away at school," Dabney said in a somewhat strained voice. "And as for Peter and me, when was it that they've placed the time of death, Peter?" Dabney had swiveled around to glare directly at Blair, who had been quite silent the whole time. He certainly wasn't giving me any help.

"Between 10:00 p.m. and midnight, night before last," Peter said in a small voice that I would have had no idea he could ever be cowed to when he was so forcefully fucking me just an hour earlier.

"There you go, then," Dabney said. And he gave me a broad, victory-laden smile. "Peter and I were at his place playing poker during those hours. So, we couldn't have done it, neither of us."

"Just the two of you playing poker?" I asked. It was instinctive; it had just slipped out without much thought to it.

"Yes, just the two of us. Is there a problem with that?" Dabney's voice had gone hard.

"No, I'm sure there's not," I said. "That's certainly what we can put in the report." I left that lying there in a pregnant pause. Dabney was no dummy, I'm sure, on how good an alibi would have to be to keep the feds from taking a closer look. I had no question that by this time the next day, there would be more fine upstanding citizens of Eden willing to say they were in that poker game.

But I also was impressed to have caught that Dabney had thought to protect his son first. Unfortunately, that led me to assume that he was afraid for his son for some reason.

"And your son?" I said. "How far away is this school?"

"It's down in Syria, almost up into the Blue Ridge Mountains. The Spring Hill Academy. A fine post-high school prep school for gifted athletes to help them succeed at the university while carrying a full athletic load. My son is a star football player." The pride shown through the man's gruffness, and I accepted his genuine interest in and concern for his boy.

"And that's how far from here?" I asked.

Dabney didn't respond immediately, so I turned to Peter.

"Peter? How far is it from here?"

"An hour's drive," Peter squeaked in an uncomfortable voice. Dabney glowered at him again.

"And your son has a car at school?" I asked Dabney when I turned back to him.

"Of course. But—"

It was my turn to show some steel and to assert myself. "I'll, of course, need to go talk to him. I can go straight from here. Would you please call the school and tell them to expect me?"

Dabney was turning red now and starting to bluster. "That's absolutely not necessary. He was at school. There is no need—"

"Let's not start by making a serious blunder, Mr. Dabney," I said, now taking control. "The feds most certainly will want to have your son discounted as a suspect in this. The best thing we can do is show that I talked to him early and that my report clearly rules him out."

Dabney looked at me for the longest moment. He was a lawyer, though, and I'm sure he was a damn fine lawyer.

He didn't hold out for the bluff more than a second or two. I had already discerned that his concern for his son was genuine.

"I'll have my secretary call down there as soon as you leave, Detective. Just know that you need to be as sensitive and discrete as possible. My son has been through a trauma. I know there is no way he could be involved in Wallace's murder, but we're doing everything we can now to help him forget what Wallace did to him and to allow him to return to a normal life. Something like this could easily obscure the path he's on to a professional football career."

"I will, of course, handle the interview with discretion," I assured Dabney. "But perhaps you can tell me how Wallace had access to him to begin with."

"John Wallace was a volunteer assistant football coach at the school," Dabney said. And now I could see the anger returning to his face. "Those witness protection bastards let an animal like that work with young men at a residential school."

* * * *

I wasted a good forty-five minutes while I drove along a babbling stream into the foothills of northern Virginia to the town of Syria, trying to devise the best way to approach Dabney's son, Jason, in a way that would not add to his scarring from having been molested by his football coach.

I thought of those nine thick inches Wallace was carrying and the cruel way in which he could use them, and I just wasn't sure what the best approach to the questions I'd have to ask would be.

As I drove into the gates of the isolated prep school campus, I was passed by a yellow big-daddy Hummer going in the other direction. I might have missed who was driving, but I had focused on the vanity plate, which read "Jentel," and the huge Redskins professional football team sticker in the back window was unmistakable. I was certain that my Rosslyn hotel lover, Jentel "Boom Boom" Huff, was at the wheel. Then it dawned on me. He had told me he had a

287

younger brother enrolled at an athletic prep school. What he had said led me to believe that it was farther south, down in central Virginia, but it made sense that it would be this one. The Redskins' training camp was between here and Washington, D.C.

At the school's administrative office building, which evidently Dabney's secretary had called as promised and greased the skids well, and I was told that Jason Dabney would be over at the field house at this time of day, either at football practice or cleaning up from football practice. The paths were well marked, so they let me find my own way.

I heard them before I saw them, and there was no mistaking what they were up to. Peter had given me an excellent description of the Dabney youth, so even at the angle I first spied him, I instantly knew it was him. What I hadn't even considered, though, was how much he looked like my lost lover, Brad. That completely knocked me off balance—or at least it was my initial shock.

They were in the shadows, off in a corner of the field house, but near the front door. A blue wrestling mat was down on the floor, and the young man—Jason—was upside down, his shoulders bearing his weight, his arms spread out wide and his fists clutching at the plastic surface of the mat. His butt was in the air and his legs open wide. Standing over him, holding his thighs, and fucking down into his ass was an older, naked man, maybe of thirty or thirty-five. Muscular, well cut, athletic. Jason's body was lithe and subtle, a blond beauty, almost Apollo like in his attractiveness, his wavy hair spread out around an angelic face, which at the moment was intensively lost in the sex act. The man fucking him was at least partially black—dark haired, with a thatch of curly hair that spread down from his heaving pecs and surrounded a penis darker than the rest of his skin, encased in a jet-black condom, which appeared and disappeared inside the young man's channel at a highly athletic, vigorous speed. He wasn't just fucking at the surface, either, he was jack-hammering down deep into the channel.

While I watched, the older, dark guy pulled out of the younger one and reached down and took a bludgeon of a

288

black dildo off the floor and began to fuck the younger guy, which led to a lot of moaning and groaning from the bottom. After a bit of this, though, the older guy tossed the dildo off to the side and returned to cocking the younger one.

Nothing was happening to Jason that he didn't want happening to him. He was moaning and groaning and crying out for more, deeper, and more rapidly.

I slipped inside but drew into the shadows at the other side of the door. I watched, not unaffected, as they fucked on for several more minutes. I could tell by the way the older man cried out and jerked that he ejaculated first, and then Jason gave him a big smile and shot several spurts of his own cream up onto the older man's belly.

I stayed and waited for several minutes as they disengaged, kissed, and headed toward the rear of the field house.

Then I went back there myself, easily finding the darker man in a windowed office half way down the gymnasium floor. He was covered by a T and shorts now, with a whistle on a string around his neck, and took a look at the note I'd brought from the administrative office and motioned me to a door in the wall that was posted to lead to the shower rooms.

"Jason's back there, in the showers. He stayed later than the others for some extra practice. He's probably the only one back there. You can't miss him. Tall, with a mop of blond hair."

Yeah, I'd seen the sort of practice he'd stayed late for.

* * * *

"Hey, a detective, cool," Jason Dabney was saying when he came out of the showers and found me sitting on the bench in front of his locker, waiting for him. "Sent to talk to me about Mr. Wallace being killed. Guess my dad blew a gasket over that, didn't he?"

Jason had been swinging a towel when he came out of the showers. He didn't bother to put it around him now, either. He was naked and moist, with his mop of hair flat now and hanging down around his face in strings. And he was looking mighty fine. And he reminded me of my Brad, which made me ache in the crotch. His cock started moving to attention as soon as he saw me sitting there, but he didn't bother to try to cover that up. He just sat down, straddling the bench between his legs, his balls and cock pointed at me, and gave me a big, welcoming smile.

"Yes, he did," I answered. "I'm helping with the investigation on that, and I really must pin down where some people were the evening before last . . . including you, I'm afraid. An investigation report is going to have to go to authorities beyond the county, and your dad wants to make sure that it is as airtight as possible."

Jason stood then and opened his locker wide. He was only about a foot from me now—or at least his erect cock was. And it was still pointed at me. He was playing a game with me. And I was having trouble not showing him I was interested. But there was a problem with that—well, several. The last thing I wanted to do in this investigation was to get involved with a suspect, especially the son of the Commonwealth Attorney. And the other problem was that he had shown quite graphically that he was a bottom—and so was I, although, for someone as luscious as him, I'd been known to swing the other way and to have enjoyed it immensely. I'd certainly done that with Brad without a problem.

"OK, that's easy," he answered. "I was at home, in Leesburg. An evening with the family."

That was a surprise. "So, you weren't here at school?"

"No, I was at home."

He hadn't been prepped by his dad, and he didn't go for the safest of answers.

"With your family?"

"Yes. Well, with my dad. He's the only family I've got. Mom's dead. Cancer. A couple of years ago. We were watching TV. A world soccer game. Manchester United won. You can check out the schedule and score. The coverage didn't end until almost 1:00 a.m."

That sounded honest enough. So, I wondered now why Dabney had given an alibi to Blair—and why Peter had let him do so.

"Well, you know, with the case and all . . . Wallace and . . . you."

"That we were fucking?" Jason said. Then he snorted and laughed. "God, Dad just won't get it on that. Wallace didn't molest me. I went after him. He was an assistant coach here. He showered with the team. I mean, if you'd seen the dong on that dude. I couldn't get enough of it. My dad's living a fantasy. That rape case wasn't going anywhere. I wasn't going to lie and get a hung horse like that in trouble."

I was stunned. And I knew that Jason wanted me to be stunned. He stood there, waving his meat in my face. God, he was trying to make *me*.

"Of course there wasn't anything serious between us," Jason continued. "I like my meat dark, if you know what I mean."

Well, yes, I'd gotten a little inkling of that just now out in the shadows of the gymnasium.

Jason reached into his locker and took out a photograph and showed it to me. "Here's my lover, if you'd like to know. Almost as good at football as I am. But in all of this Wallace stuff, his family moved him to another school. If you want to know the truth about the other night, I was home because I had threatened to follow him down south that night, and my dad had taken my car keys so I couldn't leave the house and do that. Dad had caught the two of us together that evening at the house and there was a big fight, and my dad sent him away and made me stay and watch the game on TV with him."

I was sitting there, studying the photo he showed me.

"This young guy was at your house in Leesburg early in the evening the night of the murder?" I asked.

"Yeah, he had to drive all the way back to near Charlottesville, to his new school. I don't know what curfew they have; I sure hope he made it."

"Thanks," I said, standing and handing the photo back to him. And trying not to lean into him and let myself

291

get lost into what he was showing and obviously offering. "I may have to come back and ask you a few more questions."

"Hey, do you really have to go so soon?" he asked. He was smiling and holding his engorged cock in one hand. "You're a real hunk, Detective. Sure you don't see anything you'd like? Wanna suck me? Or fuck me?"

"Umm, no thanks," I said, not really knowing what else to say in circumstances that were equally embarrassing and enticing. "I don't think anything like that would be wise. It certainly would make things more difficult for everyone in this case."

I could have bluffed it out, I suppose, tried to act indignant or get cop tough and tried to scare him. But I was wearing pretty tight trousers, and he'd been eyeing my crotch. He could tell how interested I was. I wasn't fooling anyone.

"Maybe later, then," he said. And that big smile. "Maybe after the case is over. I said I liked dark meat, but I didn't mean to suggest I was exclusive. You're even better looking than Wallace was, and it looks like you're packing almost as much as he did. Sort of sorry he's gone. That was one club of a cock he had."

Yes it was, indeed, was what I thought, but what I said, not having anything but a weak response was, "Yeah, maybe afterward. If we're both still here."

Once I'd gotten back to the car, I didn't start up right away. I had to think for a moment. I'd recognized the black kid in the photograph, the guy Jason said was his main fuck. That was Devin Huff, Jentel Boom Boom Huff's younger brother. And Jason had revealed that Devin was in Leesburg the evening of the murder. That was only about a fifteen-minute drive from the murder scene. I wondered whether there was any angle that placed Wallace and Devin together in such a way that would make Devin a murder suspect.

I guessed I had to add an interview stop to my report list. And I wasn't really comfortable with the circular motion this case was suddenly taking.

Chapter Six: Time Out

Returning to Leesburg from the prep school in Syria shortly before 5:00 p.m., I went to the county office building and to find Peter Blair in his police department office. I decided not to tell him that his "rape" victim in the Wallace case lacked just a tad bit of credibility as a victim of molestation—and probably wouldn't half try to lie about it on the stand. First, that case was just about as dead as Wallace was, and, more important, Jason Dabney's testimony to me, which I tended to believe, erased Peter's own alibi for the time of the murder. I was still bothered that Peter had let Warren Dabney spin that lie for me, so I decided to keep whatever cards I could get close to my chest for a while.

After I'd checked in at the reception desk in the county office and before Peter sent down for me, I decided to check another thing that had bothered me one more time and, showing my credentials and the letter that assigned me to the Wallace case, asked to be admitted to the basement morgue again to take another look at Wallace's body.

Peter found me there in the morgue and gave me a funny look when he walked in. That I was standing next to the gurney with Wallace's body on it and putting my shirt back on probably had something to do with that. What had bothered me earlier hadn't been dispelled upon a second look.

"Don't worry, Peter," I said to his questioning look. "Wallace and I haven't been having the sex of the dead. I just wanted to recheck something."

Blair didn't pursue the point, and I didn't fill him in on anything either.

"Glad you're back," he said. "Just in time to stop for a drink and then to my place for dinner and a little—"

"No thanks, I'll pass for tonight, I'm afraid," I cut him off, knowing what he was going to suggest for later. "I'm bushed and it's a long drive back to Rosslyn."

"You know you can stay at my—"

"Thanks," I cut him off again. "But I need some separation while I process, and for the very reason you brought me down here, appearances require that we not be in bed together—in either the literal or literary sense. Not the least is because you're still a suspect."

"Still a suspect?" Peter blustered. "This afternoon, we—"

"Yes, well that was this afternoon, Peter. The Dabney kid tossed out your alibi. He said he was with his father on the evening of the murder and that you weren't. What's the truth of that, Peter?"

He stood there, dumbfounded. I'd surprised him with the question, which was exactly what I had intended to do. He didn't think fast enough on his feet. He just stood there, his jaw working, but no sound coming out.

"That's what I thought, Peter. The kid sounded like he was giving an honest answer. So, do you want to tell me why you let Dabney give you a false alibi here, sort of informal, or should we go back to your office for a more formal deposition?"

"Dabney calls the shots around here," Peter finally said. "He said he wanted to keep it all simple—and he didn't want to own up to his son being anywhere near this part of the state that evening. So, I just went with it. He calls the shots."

"Yes, I got that impression—about him calling the shots," I said. "You weren't such a pushover in New York, Peter. You had more balls there. But it's pretty cushy here in

294

the rich Eden for Washington, D.C., isn't it? It's so easy to sell out down here, isn't it?"

"Fuck you," Blair said with some heat, his fists balled up and his face getting a little red.

"Not tonight, thanks," I answered. "So, do you want to tell me where you were between 10:00 p.m. and midnight the night before last, Peter? I can't write a half-assed report, or the feds will be all over this case. You're the one who brought me down here to do this."

"I was home, alone, in bed. Where I am almost every night. That's been my late evening ever since you left me, Clint. Nice alibi, right?"

"It will have to do for now," I answered. "If you come up with anything that will strengthen that claim, I'm sure you'll tell me. In the meantime, I guess you know we'd better cool it and not be seen as too chummy—for your own good."

"Yeah, I guess so," Peter said. And the regret in his voice was palpable.

"That doesn't mean you can't visit me one of these evenings at the Marriott in Rosslyn, of course," I then said, softening up a bit. "Just to compare notes or something."

"Yes, I'd like that," Blair said in a quiet voice.

"But not tonight, OK?" I said. "I really do need to do some thinking and sleeping tonight. Whatever comes out of this investigation, I'll only have a couple of days to do what it is I've got to do."

And that was that for Peter and me for that evening.

* * * *

I was beat when I opened the door of my room at the Marriott. It was pitch black in there. When the room attendant had turned down the bed, she'd closed the curtains. That was a little irritating. I checked in here to get the panorama of the Mall from the Washington Monument to the Capitol building, which was as impressive at night as it was during the day, and, besides, it made me grope for the light switch. I had no idea which side of the door it was on.

295

It wasn't to the right. When I turned to run my hands on the wall to the left, I gasped as a fist of steel wrapped itself around my wrist. This was followed by a pull on my arm that turned me and slammed me down into an armed desk chair, taking me completely by surprise and knocking the wind out of me.

I had little time to react. My assailant was far stronger than I was. He also was stark naked, and soon I was as good as naked too. Holding me in a choke hold with one massive hand gripping my neck in a way that had me concentrating foremost in getting the next breath, he was ripping my shirt open and pulling my trousers off.

Letting go of the chokehold, he spread and lifted my thighs over the arms of the chair, and his mouth possessed my mouth in yet another breath-taking maneuver. He had thick, lubricated fingers at my ass while he gripped the hair at the back of my head with the other hand and arched me back in the chair.

And then he was coming down onto the seat of the chair on his knees between my spread legs and was forcing a plump bulb of a thick cock at my hole—and thrusting inside me, spreading my channel walls wide, and heading his staff far up into me.

By the time his lips and teeth and gone down my neck and he was snuffling up into one of my pits and I felt him licking and nipping me hard there, I realized that I was being fucked by Jentel Huff, the starting fullback. After that I just relaxed and went with the fuck. When he got tired of taking me from the front, spread over the arms of the desk chair, he turned me, with my knees pushing into the back of the chair seat and him covering me from behind, my legs close together now, and his cock churning ever deeper inside my tightened hole. His fingernails were digging into the aureoles of my nipples and his face was buried in my other pit, biting and sucking me there in my tender underarm when I ejaculated and felt him jerk and fill the bulb of his condom as well.

Later, while he was side-splitting me languidly on the bed, taking his time now after his initial full-field assault, he started quizzing me on my day. He told me about his—a day of hard hitting and pattern running at the Redskins' practice field in the Virginia suburbs of Washington, D.C., and then he wanted an equally detailed description of my day.

I gave him a general gist of it, but I didn't tell him that Peter Blair had fucked me or that a prep school youth had wanted me to fuck him. I gave him enough detail to let him know I'd been busy, but I didn't tell him everything by any means. But there were other things I wanted to know myself.

"How'd you get in here, Jentel? And should I expect a reception like this every night?" I barely managed to get that out, though, because he was stroking me deep and strong now. "Oh, god, oh, god," I murmured with a gasp. "Oh, yes, there. Just like that. Oh, GOD!"

"I can get . . . uh, uh . . . that's soooo sweet . . . into just about anywhere I want. As long as I'm recognized. And it's hard not being recognized in this town. Oh, no you don't . . ."

I had rolled away from him, wanting to turn on the light on the nightstand, but he gathered me back in his strong arms and sent his cock deep up my channel.

"I just wanted to turn on the light," I said. "I want to see you stroking inside me. God, it's beautiful."

That had impressed him. He let me reach over and turn on the light and then he raised my leg so I could get a good view of his long, thick cock moving in and out of my hole.

"Oh, God, Oh GOD!" I cried out and shuddered. As I watched, he fisted my cock, and I spouted off for him within a matter of a few seconds.

We lay there, spent, and then I asked the zinger. "Didn't I see you in a Hummer leaving the Spring Hill Prep School grounds down in Syria this afternoon?"

I heard him suck in air and his grip on me tighten, from behind, his body stretched along my back. Then he relaxed, and I knew he had decided what he wanted to say.

"Yeah, I was there. My brother, Devin, recently transferred from there down to another school further south.

I still had some financial business to clear up with them at Spring Hill. Why do you ask?"

"Oh, no particular reason," I answered as nonchalantly as I could. "I just thought I saw you and wondered why."

At least he hadn't made up an elaborate lie, I thought. Awfully peculiar that coincidence of meeting up with him and winding up in bed with him when his younger brother had some connection to the case I'm working on. Just a little worrying.

Jentel let me take a shower then. Or at least he let me get into the shower and turn the water on. As I was soaping up, the shower curtain was being jerked aside and he had my belly to the slick, wet wall tiles and my feet off the ground, as he got his thighs between and under mine and was pushing my belly and chest up and down on the tiles with the strength of the plowing of his cock, while he got his face into one of my pits, raising my arm over my head, and attacked my tender flesh with his teeth.

Chapter Seven: Digging into Devin

The very first thing I did when I was able to struggle, bowlegged and fully satisfied, out of the bed in the morning was to thumb through the Wallace case folder until I found the number I wanted and called the Loudon County medical examiner. He gave me an appointment for 10:00 that morning and told me the procedure would take an hour or so. He assured me that the tests I'd suggested be taken on the body of Wallace could be completed by then and that everything would be expedited. Then, although I needed a shower badly, I struggled into my clothes and went looking for some breakfast before braving the morning commute on the George Washington Parkway, which would be brutal even though I'd be heading out of the city rather than into it. Jentel Huff had left me at first light after a night to remember of sexual calisthenics.

I'd checked the position of that Wallace case folder on the desk before I'd opened it, and, as I suspected would be the case, the files had been rearranged. Very interesting. Well, I'd be driving down to just outside Charlottesville that afternoon to interview Jentel's brother, Devin, and then we'd see what there was to be seen.

After getting clear of the medical examiner's office in the basement of the Loudon County office building, I went looking for Peter Blair in his police chief's office on the third floor of the same building.

"Gettin' in kinda late, aren't you, Clint?" he said when I entered his office, cleared files off his guest chair, and plopped down with a sigh.

"Not really. I've been around and about out here since a couple of hours ago. Following up on a lead. Is the offer still open for a meal and a shower at your place?"

"The shower being . . . ?" He left the question hanging in the air, his expression quizzical, with a touch of nervousness and hopefulness at the edges.

"After a roll in the hay . . . yes, if that's still what you want. but, actually, a shower, then lunch, then you can have your way with me, followed by another shower, if your water pressure can take it. And then I have to drive down to Charlottesville. So, I'll need to be off by 2:00."

"I'll bet I can get you off by 12:30," Peter said, a wide grin of relief stretched across his face. "Does this mean you've made some decisions on me as a suspect? You'd been pretty definite about staying our distance until that was resolved. And my alibi ain't any better today than it was yesterday."

"Yep, I think I've narrowed it down considerably, and you are fading fast as a suspect—although I still don't know either why you threatened Wallace or permitted Dabney to cover you with that weak alibi. You must have known I would blow holes through that."

"Loudon County isn't anything like New York City, Clint," Peter responded. "We have only a few big daddies down here, and, on the whole, they are bigger daddies than you'll find in the overhead of the NYPD. This is a very cushy job I've landed in. When Dabney says jump, I jump. And when Dabney has gone over the moon because his precious kid has been fucked by a hoodlum stashed away in the country here, it isn't Dabney who's has to pay the hoodlum a visit—it's me. I wouldn't have killed him, of course, but I was doing everything else I could to bring him down."

"And as for my fake alibi," Blair continued. "That wasn't really for me. That was more for Dabney's son. Dad
300

didn't want there to be any hint that his son was anywhere near where Wallace was when he bought it. Dear little Jason just didn't go along with the script. We needed someone to help us push this off to the side quick. With your history with Wallace, I guess I thought . . . well, I guess I thought wrong. I should have remembered how straight an arrow you were."

"Speaking of Jason Dabney," I said. "Who reported that he'd been molested by Johnny Wallace?"

"He did that himself," Blair answered. "He came straight to me. He was afraid, at first, to go to his father. He told me that Wallace had offered to bring him home from football practice at Spring Hill one afternoon and instead of bringing him home, had taken him to his farm and tied him up and fucked him in the barn where we found Wallace's body."

"Reported it himself." It wasn't so much a request to repeat the information as it was an effort to fully absorb what Blair was saying. "And did he say whether Wallace used a club on him? That was Wallace's M.O.—using a billy club to work himself up."

"No, no, he didn't."

"And you didn't think that was strange?" I asked.

"No, not really. It was hard enough for the kid to tell anyone what had happened to him. I can see him leaving out the part of the billy club."

"I suppose so," I said—but more to put Peter at ease than because it satisfied me. The kid certainly hadn't been shy about taking a billy club-sized dildo from his coach the previous day. "And speaking of clubs, want to put yours to a good use?"

"If you're comfortable fraternizing with me now, of course." Peter said. And the hopeful grin was back.

"Probably now more than a few minutes ago," I answered.

We stopped at the fanciest KFC I'd ever seen and got chicken boxes to go for lunch and, when we'd come back to Peter's townhouse, I showered while Peter got the table set on his back patio. Then I padded out in just a towel, and we barely had the chicken taken care of before Peter had me bent over the table and was fucking me doggy style for all he was worth—as if there had been too few yesterdays and scant prospects for tomorrow.

After we'd cleared away the lunch mess and both reloaded our cannons, Peter took me to bed and fucked me the way I'd grown to love from him. I was full stretched on my chest with only my pelvis raised by pillows, and Peter was fully covering my back with his stretched body, touching me in as many places as he could, his arms overlaying mine and his fingers entwined with mine; his heart beating against me under my shoulder blades; his lips in the hollow of my neck; his thighs encasing mine, and his hips swaying slightly, rhythmically, as he fucked me deep with his peace-conquering cock.

I would have liked to have gone to sleep like that following our mutual ejaculation. But I had things to do and a case to wrap up, so shortly after 2:00 p.m., I rolled Peter off to the side of me and headed for the shower one more time.

Right before I left, I told him that I was expecting a report to be delivered to him from the medical examiner's office before the close of business and I wanted him to open and study it and be prepared to let me know what he thought—that if he wasn't in his office when I came back through Leesburg from Devin's prep school, I'd come by his house.

"No, I can't spend the night. And I'm hoping that report will tell you why," was the last thing I said to Peter before I left.

He stood at the door to see me off, looking both wistful and well fucked. I could tell that he was already thinking about the possibility of us returning to old times. And, at that moment, I had no idea what I thought about that. I was concentrating on the case; I always was like this when I sniffed the beginning of the home stretch.

* * * *

There were no surprises for me at Devin Huff's prep school, the cushy Fork Union Academy, far enough out of

302

Charlottesville so the young men would have to work hard to get into trouble, but close enough into the lush territory that could be considered Eden in the northern-to-central Virginia corridor to feel at home among the highly privileged. Like Spring Hill, Fork Union specialized in bringing the grades of promising athletes up to justify entry into the richer collegiate environments along the Atlantic Coast.

Devin was sent out to me at a bench on the oak-shaded lawn that spread in front of the antebellum administration building. He was a hulking, but strapping black hunk of a young man. His musculature bore out his reputed football prowess, and his shyness and politeness reflected his close family upbringing and the benefit of good, expensive schools. I remembered the pride with which the Redskins' star player, Jentel Huff, had talked about his younger brother back on the plane as I was flying into Washington. And the Devin Huff who presented to me was just as I expected him to be.

I was sorry I had to do what I had to do now. But life isn't fair.

"You know why I'm here, don't you, Devin?" I asked gently after we'd gotten through the preliminary introductions. I quite purposely didn't tell him that the big brother he worshipped had been fucking me earlier that morning.

"Yeah, it's about what happened to Mr. Wallace the other day. I figured it wouldn't be long until you were down here to talk to me."

"Oh, and why is that Devin?"

"'Cause I knew you'd find out that I was nearby, at Jason's house that night."

"That's right," I said. And I breathed a sigh of relief. I could sense the honesty in the boy. Fear, yes, and confusion—and a large dollop of unearned self-loathing. I could see that too. But, although I'd have to draw some things out of him, I knew it wouldn't be because he would lie to me about them.

"I need to talk to you about what happened before that, Devin," I continued. "I know it's painful, but it needs to get out. It's important. And that part isn't your fault. I know that too."

Devin was looking down at the ground. He couldn't look at me now. And I saw his shoulders waver, and I could feel the sob that wanted to escape his body but that he was too scared and proud to let free.

"You only transferred down to Fork Union a couple of weeks ago. Isn't that right, Devin?"

A pause and then an almost whispered. "Yes, that's right."

"And who was it who got you transferred down here?"

Another pause. "My big brother. He plays for the Redskins. Jentel Huff. He's helping to train me. I want to follow him into the pros. He's always helped me. He's good to me."

"And I'm sure he wants to protect you too, doesn't he, Devin?"

A quiet "Yes. Always."

"It was Spring Hill where your transferred from, wasn't it, Devin?"

"Yes."

"And Mr. Wallace coached you there, didn't he?"

"Yes. Well, he helped. Mr. Dobbs, he's the coach there. And he was always good to me too. He and Jentel had played ball together. Mr. Dobbs was like a brother to me too."

"And it was you who Mr. Wallace molested, wasn't it? Not Jason Dabney."

Silence. Devin's head was down, and he was quaking a bit.

"I'm sorry, Devin. But this has to come out. I'm sure you know that. I'll bet you understand that you'll feel a whole lot better when it comes out. I'll need a few details, just to be sure. But I'll keep it out of the public as much as I can—if you are open and honest with me now. Jason's taking all of the heat for this, Devin. That's not really right, is it?"

"No. I didn't want him to, but he said that would be better. He's done it before; he said it wouldn't mean as much if he said it was him."

"Was this incident at school or somewhere else, Devin?"

"At his place. In his barn. He said he'd take me into town to get some things I needed at the drug store. But, instead, he took me to his place . . . and he wouldn't let me leave. I tried, but he tied me up . . . and he . . ." Devin couldn't go on.

"Did he just do it then, Devin? Or was there something he did first? I wouldn't ask, if it wasn't important. Just this and we don't have to go into details."

"He . . . he had this black club . . . and he . . ."

"That's enough, Devin," I said. "That's all I need to know . . . except . . . had you been with a man before . . . with Jason, maybe?"

"No . . . never . . . I mean Jason kept talking about it and wanting me to get it on with him . . . but I hadn't done it with him yet . . . until, until . . ."

"The night Wallace was killed? At Jason's house. And Jason's dad found you two together."

"Yes. But even then we were only beginning to . . . when Jason's dad came home, and I had to leave. But then later, when Jason came up with his plan, he wanted me to fuck him so bad . . . and so I did him the next day—and I liked it. And now I'm so confused by it all. But that wasn't anything like what Mr. Wallace did to me . . . that hurt so bad."

"That's OK, Devin. We're almost done, and we're over the worst part. And then when you left Jason's house that night, you . . . ?" I needed him to say this.

"I drove straight back to school—here at Fork Union."

"Straight down here?"

"Yes."

"But nobody can vouch for that?"

"No, nobody. I wasn't expected back and I didn't get back until after lights out. I just let myself in and went

305

straight to bed. So, no one can vouch for me." Devin sounded defeated.

"You didn't go to Mr. Wallace's farm and murder him?"

"No. No, of course not." Devin's head had shot up, and he gave me and angry, belligerent stare. "I wanted to kill him. Yes, of course. But if I was going to kill him, I'd have done it right after . . . right after . . . what he did to me. Not weeks later."

"OK, last question, Devin. You're doing great. Just one more question. Who besides Jason did you tell about what Mr. Wallace did to you? Anybody?"

"Well, yes . . . after a few days trying to hold it in, both my brother and coach. Mr. Dobbs, got it out of me; he could see I wasn't actin' right. But they both said they'd keep it quiet. That they'd get me transferred to a prep school just as good with the football as Spring Hill and they'd see that something was done about Mr. Wallace so that there would be no scandal."

"And has either one of them said anything to you about your being involved in Wallace's death since he was murdered?"

"No. No. I've talked with both of them. And Mr. Dobbs would like to get me back to Spring Hill. But we haven't discussed the murder."

I stood up. "Thanks for being straight with me, Devin. There's not much I can say about what Mr. Wallace did to you—except sympathize and try to let you know that you're not the only one—you're not alone in that. And he won't ever do that to anyone else again. But I guess I don't have to tell you that I need you to stay in the state and available for the remainder of this investigation."

"Yes, yes, I understand," he whispered and his head went back down, his drooping shoulders screaming his shame and fear.

"I'll have to tell my brother about this—and I'm sure he'll tell Coach Dobbs," Devin said as I was gathering up my briefcase and preparing to leave. "I don't keep any secrets from my brother."

"I understand that; I'm counting on that, actually. He'll be able to get a really good lawyer, I'm sure."

Chapter Eight: The Big Bite

I was exhausted that night. There was nothing I wanted to do more than sleep, but I lay there, naked, in the bed in my hotel room, my adrenaline flowing and my mind working lickety-split. At nearly 3:00 in the morning, in the darkest and most silent hour of the Washington, D.C., night, I heard the click of the hotel room door lock in answer to a master card.

He was quiet, moving so cat-like for a man of his bulk. I tensed as soon as he entered the room, but I forced myself to relax, even to snore quietly. He needed to know that I was asleep, vulnerable, open to him. He stripped by my bed, right where his magnificent cock would be at my eye level, if I wasn't turned away from him, not wanting him to know my eyes were open. I heard the sound of the ripped tin foil, as he worked with the condom. And, more ominously, I heard him struggle to pull on the latex gloves. That was the point at which I knew I was right—that I had solved the Wallace murder case. That I could go back to New York on the morrow—if there was to be a new day for me. This was highly risky.

He came down on the bed behind me and covered my body close from behind. He was kissing me on the back of my neck and he laced his strong arms below me and over me and took both of my hands in his and entwined our fingers. The material of the gloves was so thin that I would never have known he was wearing them if I hadn't suspected—and hadn't been awake and waiting for him.

He roused me sexually, as he had always done before. He knew how to work me, and I acted as if I was coming slowly awake. That I was glad that he was there and was open to him and would, as always before, open to him and receive his masterful fucking.

I felt the wetness at my channel opening, where he was fingering me and working lube into my crack. The knob of his cock found purchase in my hole, and his hand came around me again, and his fingers interlaced with mine.

He was so much stronger than I was. There was no question that I was under his control, his strong arms wrapped around my torso and his hands possessing mine. And his cock began its stretching journey up toward the center of me as he started to side split me.

I sighed in acceptance and in recognition of how much I enjoyed him. If he discerned in any way that the sigh was primarily a sigh of regret that this was our last fuck—one way or the other—his body did not betray him.

"Did Wallace take you willingly for the initial fuck, or did you force him from the very beginning the night you murdered him?" I had just murmured it—the first indication I had given him that I was fully awake. And I could feel his body tense up and his shudder went through both of us. We were so united as one, his arms encasing me and his cock deep inside me, that I could feel every change in him. His arm hold on me became steel like. I was completely at his mercy physically.

"What? What did you ask me?" he muttered. He'd heard me clearly. I could tell by the shocked reaction of his body that he had. But his mind wasn't as quick as his body. That was a quirk of his profession. The body reacted out of trained habit first; the mind was slower when there were complex factors—or wishful thinking—to slow it down.

"Did you plan to murder Wallace all along and build up to it, or was it a sudden, unplanned outburst of anger? It will make a difference at the trial, you know."

"What trial?" he muttered. And then there was a low laugh. He obviously didn't know that I knew that he was wearing gloves—and knew what that signified—knew what he meant to do from the moment he'd entered my hotel room.

"You know I could snap your neck right here and now and be done with it?"

"Yes, if I was the only one who knew," I whispered back to him. That would set him back a bit, I thought—no, I more hoped than thought. All the precautions in the world couldn't keep him from killing me now if that's what he took a notion to do.

"OK, I'll play," he said. "But only because you are such a good fuck. I'd been doing him for a week before, so he didn't know that it was coming. He was one sick bastard; he needed to be put down."

"You can escape the worst, Jentel," I said. "What he did to Devin—there will be extenuating circumstances. You could just turn yourself in now."

"Or I could do some cleanup and take my chances," the star Redskins' player said. "Why'd you have to go down to Fork Union and weasel it all out of Devin? Why couldn't you have just let it be? Dabney brought you here to paint it over. Wallace was scum. Why couldn't you just let it be? He deserved what he got. The Dabney kid was willing to substitute and is brazen about what he is. Nothing good could come out of Devin being brought into this. He doesn't have the backing that the Dabney kid has. This would have ruined his chances for a life."

"And do Devin and the Dabney kid deserve to have this hanging over them forever?" I asked. "They would always know even if most everyone else could be kept in the dark." I had to admit that I'd struggled with this same question myself. I knew why Dabney and Blair had latched on to me to bring into the investigation. No one had more reason to believe that Wallace got what he deserved than I did. But Jentel had taken this into his own hands. And no one deserved to die that way—even if their own bread and butter had dictated that that was what they themselves did to people.

But I had more questions to ask before this was finished—one way or the other.

"It wasn't chance that we met on the flight from New York, was it, Jentel? You were playing me from the beginning, weren't you?"

"Yep," Jentel said. And then he laughed again. "I told you a star Redskins' player can get pretty much what he wants in this part of the country. I knew you'd been sent for—and why—almost before you did. Some new buddies in the Loudon police department were eager to tell me whatever I wanted to know. I flew up to New York just so that I could get hooked up with you. I needed to keep track of what you knew and what you planned to do about it. It was all cool until you went down and talked to Devin today. He told me everything. I knew, even if Devin didn't, that you had all you needed to figure it out. That monster fucked my Devin. I couldn't let him get away with that."

"And so, wouldn't it be a good idea if you just turned yourself in and made the best of it?" I asked. Jentel was gripping me so hard that I was beginning to have trouble breathing. He had brought up one of his strong hand and had the heel of it lodged under my jaw bone. I knew that one powerful thrust of that, and he could snap my neck.

"I don't think so, Clint," he whispered. And there was resolve behind the tone of his voice. I knew he was trying to work up to finishing with me. His cock was still moving inside me, though, and I hoped that this was conflicting his actions—that he at least wanted to reach a climax before he broke my neck.

"I was very careful," he was saying. "Just like I'm being careful now. I'll make sure there is no connection between you and me for them to find. Just like I was careful with Wallace."

"Not careful enough, Jentel," I said. I needed to inject doubt into this. And I could tell I had. The pressure of the heel of his hand had lessened.

"You didn't take your fetish into account," I whispered.

"What do you mean?"

"You know, how you like to play in a man's pits—how you like to drink in the scent of a man there and nibble and bite and bruise."

He was quiet now, and he had loosened his grip on me enough for me to breathe a little easier.

"Medical forensics are really great now, Jentel. I noticed the same bruising in Wallace's pits that you've been causing in my pits in our fuck sessions—you know, the bite marks. And not just the bite marks. The saliva left as well. You should have more carefully cleaned Wallace's body—and made me thoroughly shower after we had sex, Jentel. And even then, though, there were the teeth marks. Maybe most of all, you should have not given in to your fetish when you planned to kill one of your fuck partners. We have lab results on both the marks on Wallace and on me, Jentel. You're the one who is fucked."

Jentel didn't have a chance to tell me what he thought about that, because I said that last bit loud enough for those hidden in the various spots of my hotel room to hear. The lights went on and Jentel went limp.

Afterward Warren Dabney told me how much he didn't appreciate me having set up the bust as I did—that he didn't really like the thought of the media circus that would descend on his precious little Eden of Loudon County to replay the juicy bits of this trial—juicy bits that would include his own son unless he could do a fancy two-step to keep that out of the press. Which undoubtedly he could.

Throughout Dabney's diatribe, Peter Blair stood silent, sucking up to Dabney when push came to shove. Well, fuck 'em, I was thinking as Dabney was foaming at the mouth and the police officers were hauling a suddenly defeated Jentel Huff away in handcuffs—and a hotel robe. Fuck 'em both. I'd half thought of doing what Peter told me he wanted. Taking a cushy job down here in Eden and returning to his home and bed every night. Giving up my risky promiscuous ways. But I couldn't live this way—under the thumb of someone like Dabney—no matter how much they paid me. And a couple of fuck visits a year was going to have to do with Peter. If he wanted me more full time than that, he jolly well could come back to New York.

* * * *

It might have been Dabney's attitude or it might have been that I'd kept Jason Dabney's invitation to return to him in the back of my mind all along—because he reminded me so much of Brad. But on the afternoon of the day after the case was broken, I was making my last rental car trip down into the rolling hills countryside of Virginia's Eden.

I had called ahead, so both Jason and his dark-skinned football coach, the very solicitous Mr. Dobbs, were ready for me.

They took me into the gym where the wrestlers practiced and locked the doors behind us. Then, as Jason lay back on a weight bench and spread his legs so I could easily get my tongue to his hole, the coach had his lips to mine. And when I insinuated my pelvis in close between Jason's thighs and buried myself inside him and started to pump him hard, the coach was behind me and doing the same thing to me, his arms wrapped around me and his strong fingers working my nipples. A very satisfying sandwich lunch before I boarded my plane to return to New York after a relatively quick and satisfying case closing.

~

Clint Folsom's adventures will continue in the **Clint Folsom Mysteries Compendium: Volume 2**

About the Author

Habu is one of the pen names of a former supersonic spy jet pilot, intelligence agent, male model, movie actor, and diplomat. A wild youth in South East Asia was spent enjoying whatever sexual opportunities came his way, and much of his gay male writing is about recalling incidents from those days and inventing ones he'd perhaps have liked to experience. He now leads a very quiet and ordinary happily married family life.

An American, he is a published mainstream novelist and short story writer under another name and in another dimension of his life, but he has written or cowritten (with Sabb) over 500 published short stories and nearly 100 published erotica e-books, primarily of gay fiction but also memoir, straight fiction and ménage fiction. His hand and creative writing can be seen in stories and books by habu, sr71plt, Dirk Hessian, Shabbu, and Stephen Kessel—among unrevealed others that might surprise readers. The fictionalized GM memoir *Flying High* is loosely based on his life experiences. He can be found at the adults only gay male site http://www.barbarianspy.com/, which he shares with Sabb.

BarbarianSpy

FOR LITERARY HEAT

Not all books listed below may currently be on release.

BOOKS BY DIRK HESSIAN

Xtreme Erotica

The King's Men

Shores of Tripoli

Prophecy of Noto

General Erotica

Constantinople

The Beautiful Way

Blue and Gray

Colonel's Treasure

Beginning of Time

Labyrinth

Pretender's Fate

BOOKS BY HABU

Gay Erotica

Memoir Faction

Flying High, Diving Deep

Xtreme Erotica

Second Coming

Vortex: Sacrificed by Curiosity

Dark Angel Sounding

General Erotica

Death to Blonds

Gotta Keep Trying

Finding Amnad

Habu's Christmas Balls

My Neighbour's Spa

Beyond the Beaded Curtain

Hard Knocks U

Man's Man

Trip Money

Clint Folsom Mysteries Compendium Volume 1
Clint Folsom Mysteries Compendium Volume 2
Grab Bag 1
Grab Bag 2
Grab Bag 3
The Indian Doctor
Sailorboy
Home to Fire Island
The Sporting Life
Platres Conclave
Fetish Galore!
Choke Hold
Literary Gay Erotica
Cairo Surrender
The Handyman
Homeward Bound
Journey to Mirage
Menage Erotica
13 Ways for Halloween
Luther
The Indian Prince
BOOKS BY SHABBU
Finding Jason
Dirty Pool
Operation Black Jade
Cigars!
Angel in the Barn
Gayly Complicated
Despoiling David
The Tree of Idleness
I Met a Man
The Interview
Rough Road to Happiness
BOOKS BY SABB
The Legend of Holleystone Grange
Surprise Encounters
She is He
Wrong Man

Loyal to his King
Barbarian Tales - Book One - Traveler's Tales
Barbarian Tales - Book Two - Journeys Begin
Barbarian Tales - Book Three - The Inheritance
Barbarian Tales - Book Four - Road to Persepolis
~

www.ingramcontent.com/pod-product-compliance
Lightning Source LLC
Chambersburg PA
CBHW030932260626
47169CB00002B/447